blue
rider
press

I MET SOMEONE

I MET SOMEONE

BRUCE WAGNER

BLUE RIDER PRESS

New York

blue
rider
press

An imprint of Penguin Random House LLC
375 Hudson Street
New York, New York 10014

Copyright © 2016 by Bruce Wagner

Library of Congress Cataloging-in-Publication Data

Wagner, Bruce, date.
I met someone / Bruce Wagner.
p.   cm.
ISBN 978-0-399-15936-7
1. Celebrities—Fiction.   2. Lesbian couples—Fiction.   3. Mothers and daughters—Fiction.
4. Psychological fiction.   I. Title.
PS3573.A369I25   2016   2015033107
813'.54—dc23

Printed in the United States of America
1   3   5   7   9   10   8   6   4   2

Book design by Lauren Kolm

for David Cronenberg

NOW

Nor hath Love's mind of any judgment taste:

Wings, and no eyes, figure unheedy haste.

And therefore is Love said to be a child,

Because in choice he is so oft beguiled.

A Midsummer Night's Dream

They sat in cushioned chairs at a burnished roundtable. The lighting was reverential, *spiritual*, evoking the mahogany jewel box temple of an Emirates airport lounge. Chet Stoddard wore his trademark silver-hinged Persols, discreetly absurd seersucker suit, and dumbass bowtie.

His head subtly lowered as he spoke in hushed, trademark reverence, a P. T. Barnum reciting showbiz psalms.

"It's 1995. You're a household word. Beloved by the filmgoing public, deeply respected by your peers. You have an Academy Award on the mantel and in the years that follow will acquire two more: one for Best Actress—your second—and a third for Best Supporting.

But in 1995, Dusty Wilding makes a decision—a *choice*—that will cause a seismic shift, a challenge to the paradigm, virtually altering the landscape of popular and *political* culture. She comes out as a gay woman. Why?"

She paused. Mystery-smiled. Slowly, softly blinked. Looked downward, while forming a humble response. Everything about her was warm and direct, elegant, uncompromising.

"I just think it was a way of taking control of my life. You know, Chet, my role model was always Elizabeth Taylor. Still is! She was *so brave*. And when she knew something was right, Liz didn't give a hoot *what* the world thought. I think—I think I wanted to have that kind of courage. And I knew in my heart what I was doing was right."

She never gave interviews while making a movie, but Chet was an old friend who'd always given her the same respect accorded to more typical guests, movers and shakers on the world stage of politics, science, human rights. Writers and mavericks, Nobelists even. He was in L.A. for a month doing Hollywood-centric shows, and she was happy to do him the favor, even in the middle of a shoot.

"You're one of the rare actresses who does it all"—he went on, a trademark steamroller of quantifying slavishness—"from screwball comedy to tent-pole blockbusters like *Bloodthrone* to edgy, independent film. Tell us a little about what you're working on now."

It was cold in the studio. Her arms were studded by gooseflesh, like the pointillist clouds of a mackerel sky.

"Well, it's called *Sylvia & Marilyn*—"

"About the poet Sylvia Plath."

Chet got his serious, I've-done-my-homework groove on.

"Yes. It's an amazing, alternate history that takes place in 1985."

"Directed by Bennett Miller."

"The amazing Bennett Miller."

"*Capote. Moneyball. Foxcatcher.* Had you worked with him before?"

"No! But whenever I ran into him, I was *shameless*. You know—I'd just kind of corner him and say, 'We better work together . . . *or else.*'"

The host's dead whore smile hung by the fire while the eyes decamped to consult his notes. "The film takes place in 1985 but Plath died in '63, by suicide."

"Yes. And the film explores—Dan Futterman wrote the script and it's brilliant—what might have happened if she had lived."

"Her husband was Ted Hughes—"

"Also an amazing poet," said the actress.

She was so watchable: the cascades of red hair, the vintage YSL suit, the legendary porcelain skin.

"His book *Crow* was a college favorite of mine," said Chet, flaunting his trademark brains. "Did you do much research?"

"A fair amount. And she—she's so amazing. I was really interested in—fascinated by the time *before* she became 'Sylvia Plath.' The years in New York when she worked for *Mademoiselle.*"

"When she was trying to make her name. Now, *Hughes* was a notorious womanizer. Many say that Sylvia killed herself over one of his affairs."

"With Assia Wevill," said Dusty, with a nod. "Assia killed herself too! *And* she killed the child they had together—"

"Wow."

"—a little girl that he never acknowledged as being his own."

"What was it about Hughes?"

"He was *very* handsome. And a poet. A *great* poet . . ."

"The women were *not* happy campers. Was he an *homme fatale*?"

"Well, I don't sit in judgment, Chet," laughed Dusty. "But in *our* movie—spoiler alert!—Sylvia leaves *him*."

"For Marilyn Monroe," he said, with winking comeuppance.

"And Ted *Hughes* takes his own life! Marilyn is her true love."

"In the film."

"In the film. Oh my God, Bennett is going to kill me! I'm going to blame it on you, Chet! You always get me talking, you're a very bad man." He took the compliment with a trademark grin of smarm and humblebrag. "But you know, actually they were born around the same time. I think Marilyn was a bit older than Sylvia."

"Did the two ever meet?"

"*That* I don't know. I'm sure *Bennett* does."

"So something *could* have happened."

"I think it's kind of amazing to think so. That's the brilliance of Dan's script—its plausibility. You start to think, *Did this really happen?* It's brilliant and thought-provoking, but great fun."

"Can you tell us about the work you do for Hyacinth House?"

(Coyly prefaced by the wince of a smile, to punctuate the segue.)

"I've been working with the foundation for almost twenty-five years." She was glad to suddenly be talking about something real. "They're an amazing organization that's literally changed thousands of people's lives. And mine as well. I think of them as family."

The married couple slept in separate rooms. Not just to sustain eroticism but because it felt civilized and right—though when Allegra began to show, she had a craving to share a bed with her wife. One of the things that turned her on, Dusty too, was pregnancy porn. They streamed it on the BeoVision, watching two women making love and suckling each other's milk, sometimes both in the third trimester. When Allegra wanted to branch out and watch a man join the fun, Dusty would huff and leave the room in faux disgust while

Allegra giggled like a scamp. After the miscarriage, they didn't watch those videos anymore.

Five a.m. . . .

She heard the gate open as Marta let the driver in. She spooned her lover, reaching around to caress the gravid belly with her fingers. Allegra acknowledged the touch with a small, narcotic exhalation, and the actress disengaged, bending to softly kiss the baby bump good-bye.

She showered, threw on her favorite decade-old Lululemons, and went to the kitchen. The dutiful majordomo had a mini-croissant and cappuccino waiting (in the vintage *Tonight Show* cup Allegra bought Dusty online) and was sweetly chastised by her employer for such unsolicited devotions. What would she do without Marta? She left the fattening croissant.

She paused before the mirror in the entrance hall, taking her first real look of the day: a fifty-three-year-old makeup-free movie morningstar, beatific and unadorned, half astonished she'd survived, fragile and unbreakable, childlike, ancient, with lustrous, hardcore, wide-open heart—redoubtable warrior-queen and doubting heroine, her own personal favorite in a suite of silver gelatin images from an illuminated manuscript bound in vellum and for glory, consecrated to the coffee tables of an Annie Leibovitz Elysium. She was her mother's daughter, burdened by the miseries of that provenance, and the mother of all daughters too, exuberantly dunked in public ownership, holy terror, and joyful noise.

An abashed assassin sent by Botticelli . . .

"Morning, Jeffrey!"

He held open the door of the SUV.

"Good morning, Dusty. How was your weekend?"

"Awesome. *Mellow.* You do anything?"

"Took the family for a hike in Eaton Canyon."

"Where's that?"

"Altadena?" he said. The interrogatory lilt signified a respectful smudging/diminution of the possession of knowledge that might lie outside his illustrious passenger's realm—third-generation Teamster politesse.

"That's awesome! *Love* Altadena. Smoggy, though."

"A little bit, but it really wasn't too bad. Pasadena can actually be worse. We usually do Griffith Park but I like to switch it up."

"*Love* Griffith Park."

A P.A. adorned in mountaineer-lite—her airbrushed, kewpie-doll features gave her the look of an American *anime*—stood obediently by the trailer as Dusty alit from the Lexus.

"Hi, Samantha!"

"Hi, Dusty! How was your weekend?"

"*So* good. And you? Get in any trouble?"

"We had a production meeting yesterday," said the tomboy soldier, playfully wrinkling her grindstone nose.

"Well, *that's* no fun."

"Then we went out *drinking*—" she added, tossing off the hard-working, high-spirited crew's go-to corollary with rote aplomb.

The P.A.'s walkie crackled. Came a voice from the battlefield:

"*We need Dusty in thirty, for blocking.*"

"In her trailer now," replied the grunt to her headset.

While Dusty got situated, a replacement P.A. rapped on the door and entered, bearing aluminum foil-covered plates.

"One egg-white omelet with Worcestershire on the side," he said. "And onion rings from In-N-Out."

Dusty peeked from the bathroom, rhapsodic. "Rory, you are *amazing*. Can you just put it on the table?"

"Absolutely."

The replica of *The Tonight Show* set circa 1985 was dead-on. By coincidence that was the year of her first appearance.

The party line had it that Carson was a cold, misanthropic prick, but she never saw that side. He'd been faultlessly kind and hugely supportive of her career. He retired a few years before Dusty came out, but when she did, he sent flowers and a beautiful letter ruefully signed "the man that got away." (They were both Gershwin fans and did a duet of the song in the last week of his show.) She always had the feeling he was "interested" but for whatever reason held back; he was a wolf and a player for real, but when they were together he was never anything less than the urbane, dapper, acerbic gent in Johnny Carson Apparel. She probably would have balled him if he'd pressed the point—she wasn't too proud to say she had a Daddy thing (like Sylvia!). Probably she just wasn't his type. He seemed to go for those brittle, hair-shellacked, Stepford-wife gals.

The lookalike host was already behind his desk, his jovial sidekick on the couch beside him, warming up his Ed-laugh like a singer doing arpeggios. They were straight-up clones—insane and hilarious. She fucking *loved* this script.

"People, we are getting very close!" announced the First A.D.

The hubbub fell to a murmur. There was always reverence in the decibel drop that presaged a shot, and rank fear too.

Bennett, the director, sat in front of the monitor, in headphones. The agitated D.P., scowling in a private world of permanent aesthetic dissatisfaction, looked over his shoulder to check the director's screen before skittering away. The script supervisor sat beside Bennett in front of his own monitor, watching YouTube on an iPad.

"All right," said the First loudly. "Last looks!"

Patrice, Dusty's hairdresser (they'd been together twenty-three years), did his nominal thing while a wardrobe person picked microscopic lint off her pantsuit. The makeup gal powdered the nonexistent shine on her forehead.

Ready for picture.

Bennett called "Action."

The Johnny pursed and twitched his lips. "Our next guest is a Pulitzer Prize winner and one of America's most beloved poets . . ." She flushed with off-camera butterflies, just like before real talk-show appearances. The Johnny gave her total déjà vu. "Author of *The Bell Jar* and many others, her new book is a delightful children's story written with Shel Silverstein—*Gobbledygoo!* debuted this week at number one on the *New York Times* bestseller list. Ladies and gentlemen, please welcome the very gifted, very lovely . . . Sylvia Plath."

When lunch was called, Dusty lingered a moment while a few Polaroids were taken, for continuity. With a coterie of attendants surrounding her, she reminisced about her first appearance on *The Tonight Show*. All hung on her words—one of those countless unspecial-special below-the-line moments with a star during production. Bennett came over with a young woman in tow.

"'Sylvia,'" he said. "Meet your daughter, 'Ariel.'"

"Oh my God," said Dusty, genuinely enthused. "It's *you*. *Hi!*"

"Hi, Mom!" said the Ariel.

The Australian actress wasn't yet in wardrobe; she had finished a film in Europe only the day before. Dusty was completely disarmed—she reminded her of Miranda, a first love. They embraced.

"I am *such* a fan," gushed Bonita. "I'm practically a stalker."

"I can't believe we never met!" said Dusty.

"We actually *did*, a *long* time ago. But you wouldn't remember."

"I *totally* would, why can't I?"

"I was, like, ten," she said, a little coy. Bonita knew the story would be a perfect icebreaker. "I was a camera double for the girl who played your daughter on *Lone Wolf*."

"Are you *serious*?" said Dusty, delighted. "That is *so funny. Now* look at you, with your Golden Globe! And I *loved* you in *Odious*, you were *so amazing*."

"Oh my God, I can't believe you saw that!—"

"Of *course* I saw it."

"She sees *everything*," said Bennett.

"I was *so impressed*," said Dusty. "I don't think there's anyone your age doing what you do. Anyone *anyone's* age."

"Oh my God! I mean, coming from *you* . . .'"

"Don't you so love *Bill Nighy*? I saw *The Mercy Seat* on the plane and cried—I just totally blubbered! I lost it!"

Bonita turned to Bennett, blushing. "She's really seen my movies! Dusty Wilding's seen my movies!"

"Told ya," said Bennett. "She's the maven."

He suddenly got called away and vanished.

"Isn't Bill dreamy?" said Dusty.

"Oh my God, *yes*. I want him! Not as a *boyfriend*, but as a dad!"

"He could be both!" said Dusty, and Bonita laughed. "He could be your father, your grandfather, *and* your boyfriend."

"You're *wicked*," she said, with a gleam in her eye.

"Bill and I just worked together with Michael Winterbottom."

"Yes!" said Bonita, remembering. "He *told* me he was going to be working with you—we haven't spoken in probably . . . six months? But he was *so* looking forward to that. He *loves* you."

"Isn't this script so much fun?"

"*Crazy* fun."

"It's amazing. Were you a Plath fan? I mean, before?"

"Not *majorly*—I was more a Katherine Mansfield kinda gal. But I am one now."

"Katherine Mansfield! Look at *you*, you're *smart*."

A Second A.D. approached Bonita, with that blissed-out, in-production, Pixar zombie smile. "The EPK folks are here—do you want to head over to makeup?"

"Perfect."

Dusty said, *"Go,"* and they hugged again. "I am *so thrilled* we're working together."

"Oh my God, seriously, *I'm* the one who's thrilled! I cannot *tell* you what I think of you as an actress. And a *woman*. How much you have *totally* influenced me."

"Aw! You're so sweet."

Bonita kissed her cheek and went off.

The camera crew hadn't broken for lunch—the D.P. was on the bedroom set, lighting a shot—and as Dusty walked past the director's monitor, an image caught her eye. Her double, around the same age, bore a striking resemblance, not just in skin tone and hair color but in the gaze itself. It wasn't unusual for the expressions of stand-ins to evince a *de rigueur* Zen-like blankness; the meditative patience and willful suppression of personal identity required for the job often bubbled up in a Mona Lisa smile lending itself to all manner of inter-pretation. Their countenances became looking glasses. To Dusty, dou-bles brought with them an inadvertent whiff of the sacred that both charmed and mesmerized. Like denuded dream statuary, they came to represent Woman, bountiful and bottomless and eternal. Staring at the loop of herself-as-the-other-as-herself, the actress zoned out and sunk deep, in full fathom of the immanent familiar: that inscrutable, almost sardonically knowing face that represented her own.

It was empty and serene, riveting as an ancient bulletin or the light from dead stars.

"That's amazing! What kind of feedback did you get?"

They were having dinner at Mr. Chow.

"We read scenes in class and the response has been really good," said Allegra. "The teacher said it was the best script he's read all year."

"Oh my God, Leggy! Isn't that so amazing?"

"I didn't know if he meant the best script in *class* or . . ."

"Oh fuck it, it's *awesome*. Aren't you so happy?"

"I *guess*," she said, reticently. "It's just hard to—sometimes—I mean, of course everyone keeps asking me if *you're* going to be in it. Like, when's it going to be a *movie*. The *teacher* doesn't say that, but—you know, everyone's all, *'Have you shown it to Dusty? Is Dusty going to do it?'*"

"When *are* you going to show it to me? I'm dying to read it."

"After the next draft."

"You are such a tease."

"There's still a few problems."

"There's *always* problems," she said, touching her wife's hand. "I'm sure it's *really good*, Allegra. You are *such* a good writer."

"I don't know," she said wistfully.

"Can you for once not minimize your talent?"

"I don't even know if I'm excited about it anymore."

"Here we go," said Dusty, rolling her eyes.

"Maybe I should just become a producer. Or an *agent*—"

"If you become an agent, I will fucking *kill* you."

"But maybe I'm not a *writer*, Bunny Bear. Not a real one, anyway."

"You know, baby, we're not real *anythings* until one day, we just . . . *are*. *Plus*, your hormones are totally going crazy. You're *pregnant*, Allegra! In case you forgot."

"I know—and I'm so fucking *grateful*. I really *am*, Bunnikin. For *everything*." She flipped again. "But if I'm not a *writer* or a *whatever*, is *that* what I'm going to be now? A mom? Is that what the Universe is saying? You know, that—that's the only thing I can be?"

"Oy," said Dusty.

"I'm going to be *thirty-seven*—"

"And I'm staring down sixty!"

"You are *not* staring down sixty, you're fifty-*three*. I don't know . . . I'm just starting to think maybe I took a wrong turn. I used to be *such* a good photographer—maybe I should have pursued that? And I have all these *amazing* ideas for design. For jewelry. I think I'm really gifted at that—"

"Then go make jewelry!"

"—and *hats*. I was reading this *insane* profile of Isabella Blow online—oh my God, Dusty, you *have* to read it, I am *totally obsessed*. There were all these pictures of her in these *amazing* Philip Treacy *hats* and I couldn't believe how *similar* my shit was! I mean, I was drawing these outrageous *hats* when I was, like, *twelve years old*. And gloves! Oh my God, I was *totally consumed* with drawing hats and gloves! Do you think—do you think I should go back to that, Bunny? Do you think I should try to create a line of gloves and hats?"

"If that's your passion, babe." She was kind of over it.

"Or start taking pictures again? I get so crazy!"

"Really?" said Dusty, affectionately ironic.

"But maybe that's what I *should* be: just a mom."

"Stop!"

"Maybe I'll find out *that's* what I'm genius at. Being an amazing *mom*—"

"I've *always* seen that in you, Leggy."

"—and that I won't *care* about being anything else. Why shouldn't that be enough?"

"*Nothing's* ever enough, babe: welcome to The Human Condition 101. Aw, sweetheart, I love you, but can we please find the frickin' 'off' switch for your head? You are such a *nut.* You're all *over* the place tonight."

"I know!" she said, as if snapping out of a trance. "And I didn't even ask about your movie day! Bun-Bun," she said, baby-talking, "I am *so*, so sorry. I'm such a spoiled girl! *How was your day how was your day how was your day?*"

Dusty finished her glass of wine and Cheshire-smiled.

"It was awesome. *Love* me this crazy movie. Bennett is *so inspiring.*"

She effused about *The Tonight Show* set and dished about Liam. The server brought more wine. They this'd and that, and for the first time, let themselves talk about baby names. Then Dusty said, "Oh! This *ginormous* Swiss conglomerate wants me to create a fragrance!"

"No!"

"They've been after me for, like, frickin' *years.* And Elise thinks it's a really good time to pull the trigger. She literally said that—isn't that such an Elise thing to say?"

"Oh, pull it! Love that! *Love* me a celebrity fragrance."

"El said they're kind of in the shitter—you know, for a while they were giving them to *everyone*. You could, like, be an extra on *The Big Bang Theory* and Walmart would give you your own scent."

"Amy Schumer should have one!"

"Amy has *enough* for a while, thank you very much. Ellie said there was this *backlash* and it all kinda crashed. But she said that doesn't affect *me*, 'cause the Swiss seem to think I'm *bulletproof*."

"*Love* her! *Love* Elise. Love me a bulletproof bunny. Oh, pull it! Pull the trigger."

"You could *totally* be involved in that."

"Ya think?"

"Think? Sista, I *know*." They were a little drunk, on top of having split a square of a cannabis chocolate bar before they left the house. "You are *so creative*—I totally wouldn't do it without you. I think it could be *amazing*."

"I love you *so much*."

They kissed, then Dusty went for a pee.

As she emerged from the toilet, a gal at the sink recognized her.

"I just wanted to tell you how amazing you are," she said, trembling. "I am *such* a huge fan."

"Thank you!" said Dusty.

The star's genuine warmth set the woman at ease. Another one came in while Dusty washed up. On her way to the stall, she said, "My sister's son was a gaffer on *Lone Wolf*."

Allegra's day was full.

Before lunch with Jeremy, she needed to drop by Samy's Camera to pick up a Petzval lens, a Sony Cyber-shot RX100 II, and the beautiful Rolleiflex—a belated birthday gift from Dusty that she planned to use for a book about celebrities and their newborns. She wanted to cruise Maxfield, to check out the millinery. It was like a museum there, you never knew what you'd find in those freakish vitrines. Everything was, like, hundreds of thousands of dollars . . . Then, if there was time, on to Barneys to suss out perfume bottles; she needed to be *au fait* with what Hermès, Margiela, Tom Ford, and the rest of whomever were up to. Tom was an old friend of Dusty's and was at their wedding. *Maybe email him?* The idea was to start making sketches for the Swiss—"prototypes." Kind of exciting! She had a five o'clock appointment with the midwife. Allegra wanted a home water birth and Dusty wasn't thrilled.

Jeremy was touched that she asked him along. Lately, for no real reason, he'd been feeling his outsiderness. Originally Dusty's bestie, he gravitated to Allegra in the last few years—they clicked. He was puckish and hysterical, with a bent, formidable intellect that provoked and inspired. And tender too: a soft, squooshy center. All heart. What she respected most was how he'd somehow managed to stay soulful and sane through the carnage of his life. He was a rock star and a survivor, all good for the baby's DNA. She aspired to be both.

Born Maurie Wojnarowicz, he shot experimental shorts in college under the "nom de Fruit of the Loom" Jeremy Prokosch, Jack Palance's character in *Contempt* (which he insisted on calling *Le Mépris*). In the nineties, he made an acclaimed documentary about Hemingway's transgender son, Gigi. Right after it won the Audience Award at Sundance, his mom and twin sister got T-boned by a drunk. It took them a week to die, which they managed to do just hours apart. Jeremy cut his avant-bohemian Red Hook life loose and moved to L.A., officially abandoning Art. At thirty, he became the most powerful casting agent in the business; none of his friends could figure out exactly how that happened. Then he dropped out again, "decompensating" in David LaChapelle's Maui guesthouse before reinventing himself as "Princess Liaison," a bridge between financiers and art house auteurs. There was an old connection to Megan Ellison, which was how he got Annapurna involved with *Sylvia & Marilyn*. He put the deal together quickly and became one of eight executive producers.

When he got the adoption bug a few years back, Dusty introduced him to Livia Lindström, the director of Hyacinth House. He knew the procedural hassles inherent in becoming a single gay parent but found the system—no fault of Hyacinth—to be sadistic "on the level of ISIS" and lost his stomach for the battle. When Allegra had the lightbulb idea of him being their sperm donor, Dusty felt dumb *she* hadn't thought of it. In an earlier attempt that ended in miscarriage, the seed had been random and anonymous, and now she was superstitious; there was something so right and so healing about inviting Jeremy to join their mythology. They asked him to dinner at the house in Point Dume and were mildly stoned when they playfully sprung the offer. He looked stunned and began to yowl—literally fell to the floor and started to crawl as the caterwauling became a bellow that imploded into deviant, cough-wracked sobs that were so outlandishly exaggerated that they took them for cruel, campy hijinks. When they realized it was ugly-beautiful-*real*, they joined in, a marathon sob sisterfest toggling with tears like an out-of-control scene from some hoary chick flick.

They became a family right then and there.

Jeremy was on time for lunch at Soho House. He wore a tie, something she'd never seen before, and pulled a few wrapped gifts from his Bookmarc bag: *Birth Without Violence*, *Water Birth: A Midwife's Perspective*, and one for coloring called *Our Water Baby*.

Such sweetness! And so *nervous* he was, about meeting the midwife.

"You're killing me," she said.

"Has Bunny met her yet?"

He was the only one who could get away with calling her that.

"*I* haven't met her yet," said Allegra. "Why would *Dusty* have?"

"I don't know, the celeb thing? Like, 'Hey! Where's the celebrity!'"

"Midwives aren't like that."

"*Everyone's* like that, honey."

"Not Khalsa. She's super-spiritual."

"The more spiritual, the more starfucky." He reached over and palmed her tummy. "Come on . . . *kick* for me! Kick! Kick! Who's your daddy!"

"She's sleeping. She gets her kicks at night. Like her mother."

"Wait. Hey! I think she's moving. Madonna's moving!"

"Do *not* call her that. Don't' even *joke*."

"Oh come on, wouldn't that be so hilarious? 'This is our daughter, Madonna.' Or 'Cher'!"

"Or *Liza-with-a-Z*. What fucking generation *are* you?"

"She can be Taylor Swift! Taylorswift—not *Taylor* but *Taylorswift*. One word! Even if it's a boy."

"You're insane."

"Or 'Spotify.' Here, Spot! Here, Tidal! Or Andy-Cohen, one word! Cersei! Khaleesi! No! You know what we should do? Give it *initials* for a name."

"She is not an 'it.'"

"Like . . . '*LGBT*.' I *love* it! 'Meet our daughter, LGBTQ!' LGBT-QIA!"

"Jeremy, stop!" she said, laughing.

Allegra ordered the octopus appetizer and burrata. He asked for the flat-iron steak, rare, and a Cobb.

"So. You gonna read my script?"

"Of *course* I'm going to read it. But you know what has to happen *first*, Lego? I know it sounds *crazy* . . . but for me to *read* it, you actually have to *give* it to me. It needs to be *physically* or *electronically* in my *possession*."

"Oh fuck you."

"What's it about again?"

"Oh my God, you *know* what it's about, Jeremy. The Children of God."

"Movies about cults are a tough sell, Lego. Cult movies don't even become cult movies. It's autobiographical?"

"Parts."

"You do *not* want to be the new Brit Marling."

"I love Brit Marling, so fuck off."

"Wasn't River Phoenix in Children of God?"

"Yup."

"Didn't River get molested by those people when he was, like, four?"

"So he said."

"Wish I could hot-tub-time-machine back and interview him. I'd molest the *fuck* out of him."

"He might not be up for it."

"So, Lego—did you get *laid* in that cult? As a child? I mean, did you have hot child cult sex? Were you a love child of God?"

"Not till I was six."

"I'm serious, though. Wasn't it, like, *policy* with those people? Wasn't, like, kid-fucking written into their bylaws?"

"There was a lot of weird shit going down."

"And what about Joaquin?"

"What about him?"

"Is that how he got his scar? From getting slapped in the mouth by cult dicks?"

"Jesus," she said, both exasperated and annoyed.

"Allegra! I just don't think you *fully appreciate* that the Phoenixes were the *Barrymores* of child-love sex cults!"

"The script is *really* good, Jeremy. And Dusty *did* say she would get it to Joaquin."

"Honey, *I* can get it to Joaquin. But it's kind of been there, done that for him, no? I mean, he kind of covered that in *The Master*."

"That movie is *so* different from what I'm . . . I just didn't—I didn't 'get' *The Master*. I mean, Joaquin was amazing, always. I *admired* it but I just didn't *get* it."

"Does Dusty want to be in it?"

"She hasn't read it yet. I've kind of been holding off."

"Clever strategy!" he said, sarcastically.

"Did you know Rose McGowan was in it too?"

"*Children of God?*"

"Uh huh. She's kind of talked about it publicly. Her dad was one of the heads of it? In Italy? They were really close. And I think she still kind of lives in Rome? We had a long conversation a few months ago, at a thing at the Hammer. I think she'd be into it."

"Rose is kind of amazing."

"*Love* her, *love* Rose. Love her Instagram. She's fuckin' fearless."

"I really don't think you need to cast actors based on their having actually been raised in the cult, Lego."

"I know," she said. "It *would* be interesting, though. Kind of meta."

"Can you *please* not use that word? I *hate* that fucking word. No one uses it anymore and the people who *do* are *pigs* who should *die*. But you want to know what's *interesting*? I'll *tell* you what's 'interesting'—"

He looked toward one of the couches at a man with a taut pink smiley face, frozen in a perpetual startle.

"Emilio Estevez's facework. Now, *that's* interesting."

He left the booth to go say hello.

A man on his knees, with his head inside an oven—

—the camera double for the Ted, as in Hughes.

Standing beside him is Larissa, Dusty's stand-in.

Dead quiet as the D.P. lights the set. The enforced, always eerie pre-shot stillness lends the *tableau vivant* a slapstick formality: *I Love Lucy* meets Buñuel. The pants belonging to the man with the hidden torso are down, bunched up above the knees.

The ass, in boxers.

When Dusty arrives on the stage she goes straight to video village, where Bennett is watching his monitor. She clocks the kitchen burlesque and giggles. The director smiles in his soft-spoken way but stays focused on the TV. "Let's try it with the pants up," he says into the headset. Then, "Grieg, can you go close on Sylvia? Can I see what that looks like?"

Larissa's face fills the screen, eyes turned downward in repose of humility—saucy, mournful, implacable—the tempered genuflection of a lesser god, in obeisance to her off-camera elders: *Kali, Durga, Shiva*. Dusty is again entranced. That hooded, impossibly ineffable gaze stirs in her a mystically erotic, unbearable melancholy worthy of ten thousand lamentations. The effortless smile, the acquiescent miracle of a stop-motion rose rising up from the cracked soil of their industry, blooms in an anthropomorphic prayer that drives its beholder to despondent little ecstasies.

The A.D. shouts, "First Team!"

On Dusty's way in, they cross paths. Larissa dares to say, "Nothin' says lovin' like hubby in the oven."

(The first words she's ever spoken to her star.)

The actress ripostes, "Preheat to three-fifty—the new foreplay."

Larissa laughs, touching her shoulder in a sisterhood of traveling innuendo. A charge between them as the double's eyes lock in and widen before she caroms off.

It's been a while since Dusty got hit on.

As she stands on her mark, a full-bearded Liam Neeson arrives to take the place of the Ted stand-in.

"Hi, babe," he says, winking.

"Oh my God!" says Dusty. His skin has a bluish sheen and his nostrils are stuffed with snot crusts. "*Someone's* ready for their close-up."

"My face isn't, but my ass is."

"People are definitely interested in your derrière, Liam."

"It's huge on Instagram. Literally."

Dusty chortles.

The First shouts, "Last looks!"

When makeup harpies descend, Liam asks if they've brought the Easy-Off. His team re-applies goop under his nose and touches up the spidery nostril webs of broken blood vessels.

The First says, "Okay, let's try one."

Dusty stands outside the closed kitchen door as Liam gets on his knees and ducks his head in. Bennett calls action. Dusty takes a breath, shouts "Ted?" then enters. Screams. Runs to him. Clumsily fishes out the body and cradles it in her arms. Liam is dead weight.

"Ted!" she bellows, shocky and distraught. "Ted! Ted! Someone help me! *Someone help me—*"

Thirty endless seconds of messy, camera-rolling anguish pass.

"And . . . cut!"

"Was I brilliant?" says Liam to Dusty.

"You were incredible."

"Self-cleaning too."

"Going again," says the First.

The cast and crew gathered for lunch under a tent, two stages down.

Usually the stars ate in their trailers but sometimes they went socialist, joining workers and day players at the long tables. Last week, when Larissa was scarfing fish tacos with the camera operator, Liam came with his tray and sat down, out of the blue. She had a hunch she might soon be sharing a meal with Dusty but understood the need for caution. The unspoken protocol was *Don't join them, let them join you*. The making of a film created an instant family, held together by the glue of a fanatically casual blue-jeans decorum and cordiality; it was easy to get caught up and forget one's place. The best bet was to be cheery and obsequious when not invisible. Larissa had a plan, though, and was willing to take a calculated risk.

She watched a P.A. sidestep the line to talk to a server.

"Dusty *loved* the seaweed and kale," she heard him say. "Do you think there's any way she could get a little more?"

"Absolutely!"

The caterer went about his task and the stand-in seized the moment.

"Hi, Rory!"

"Oh hi, Larissa!"

(Exclamation-point hellos were the coin of the realm.)

(It was her habit to establish "real" relationships with the crew of each film she worked on, a strategy that often paid unexpected dividends.)

"Can you do me a favor?" she whispered. She was arch and flirty, even though he knew that she knew he was gay. They got off on the goof.

"Totally."

"Can you get this to Dusty?" She handed him an envelope. "It's something she asked me to research. I didn't want to bother her."

"You got it."

"You're awesome."

"No, *you're* awesome."

"No, *you're* awesome."

They riffed like that a few more times and were cracking themselves up when the caterer returned with Dusty's healthful treat.

"You take such good care of me, Rory," said Dusty, as he set down her food. "Can I adopt you?"

"You can *so* adopt me. Oh my God."

"I love you."

"Oh my God, I love you for saying that!"

On the way out he turned back, having almost forgotten.

"And *this* is from Larissa." She was nonplussed. "Your stand-in."

Dusty took the note.

"Need anything else?" he asked.

"Nope, I'm *great*. Might try to nap."

Before closing the door, he shouted, "Bye, Mom!"

She pulled out the flyer. It was a schedule of yoga classes, with Larissa's name and a few yellow-highlighted class times. A Post-it read *My day job! Come—if you need to de-stress.* ♥ *L*

At her fourteen-week checkup, the doctor couldn't find a heart-beat. Apparently, that wasn't unusual but an ultrasound confirmed their daughter was dead. A few days after the D&C, Allegra was in crippling pain and kept bleeding. They did another ultrasound and couldn't believe the whole baby was still in there. She had a second D&C.

Dusty had been a few weeks shy of announcing the pregnancy; now she needed to do everything possible to hide what had happened. But there were too many variables and all she could really do was hold her breath. The shooting schedule was shuffled to allow her to stay home awhile with her wife. Bennett was the only one told. For everyone else, it became a "family emergency," related to Dusty's mother. She got a lot of mileage out of her mother in emergencies—about all Reina was good for.

It was awful. Allegra was crazed, distant, bellicose. Dusty got tired of the lashings and after a few days felt guilty for praying that she pack up her sullen histrionics and take them to the beach house, where she could lick her wounds in solitude. That never happened. She was glad to have withheld the suggestion because the image of her young wife walking into the sea had hauntedly taken hold. Marta, of all people, was the one to persuade Dusty to return to work a few days early.

Not to worry, said the housekeeper. I'll take good care.

God bless Marta.

She spent hours in the pool, soaking in amniotic misery. She wanted a home water birth; now she had a home water death all her own.

Whatever she touched turned to shit, sorrow, and dead ends—everything, that is, but Dusty. Dusty was her salvation, their union her miracle birth. Why, then, was she punishing the only one who ever loved her, loved and *protected*, bestowing shelter, status, and a fractured raison d'être? (Made an honest woman of her too.) Wasn't Dusty suffering as well? *Of course she was.* Well, maybe. *Probably* . . . — just now, Allegra didn't give a fuck, and for the most heinously juvenile rationale: Dusty was older, Dusty was rich, Dusty was immortal. Dusty was bulletproof because she'd already *had* a little girl, already had the whole full-tilt *Alien* experience of it, already watched the thing slither out and bloodsquall with life. That she basically never saw it again was just a technicality.

Before the Xanax, Ambien, and Percocet mugged her to sleep, she dodged her wretchedness by skimming the recently published diary of a righteous medieval executioner (a little light reading before bed). Allegra fixated on the passage that described his specialty: torturing robbers who used the severed fingers of infants as lucky-charm candles to light the homes they plundered at night. She drifted off the pages into a kaleidoscope of fantasies. She imagined herself buried alive, crouching in a sealed tomb while Dusty organized a rescue party . . . sitting with Anna Wintour at a fashion show while Allegra's famous, spanking new triplets threw epic, squalling tantrums . . . on the Rue du Faubourg in front of Chanel, having her YouTube head sawed off by Boko Haram schoolgirl recruit hotties. Maybe she'd just stop eating. Feeding the body seemed nothing more than a reward for infanticide—comfort food for an infernal job well done. She was tired of the whole eating/shitting game anyway, the one that turned everything into stink, poison, and sewage. She'd gotten a lemon for a womb, but her asshole was a fertile workhorse slated to deliver thousands of newborns right to the end. Even in her last moments on earth, her bowels would loosen—God would make certain she'd die in "childbirth," spraying one final citizen into the fecal world.

She thought of overdosing, which led her to a meditation on

media moms, all those trashy suicide fails who snuffed gangs of kids in their bathtubs. *At least they had babies to kill.* She reflected on sundry sash and doorknob hangings (Robin Williams, L'Wren Scott), wondering if she'd ever manage to grow the *cojones* to do the same. But how? When she couldn't even commit to third-draft screenplays, rip-off perfume flacons, and fucktard custom chapeaux? *Eight times* her beloved Ms. Blow tried in vitro—eight times! Toward the finish line, like some Wile E. Coyote *agoniste*, she'd variously flung herself off a bridge, rear-ended a truck, tried drowning herself in a lake—and after nothing worked, the bitch drank weed killer. (When the E.R. nurses didn't know who she was, Issie shouted, "Google me!") Now *that's* commitment! While the bonkers muse had a memorial fit for famous eulogizers and fashionista pallbearers, Allegra knew her own final wrap party was poised to outshine and outgun: the interment would blow Issie's out of the water, featuring a legendary cortège of Dusty-pimped thumbnail-ready griever-chic A-listers, curated to celebrate her uselessness, infertility, and defeat.

Chronicle of a life stillborn . . .

The thought of such inglorious pageantries made her want to vomit.

Jeremy tried to see her but she kept texting that she just wasn't ready. After two weeks he showed up unannounced. He was sweet and loving, but when she gave him nothing he soured.

"Goddammit! This happened to *me* too!" he blustered. "And *Dusty*, it happened to Dusty! It's fucking *selfish*, Allegra! And it's *mean*! Do you think you can just get *over* yourself? For, like, *ten seconds*? Because the line between *grieving mom* and narcissistic *cunt* is *really* thin."

She winced then let him come hold her while she cried. When he made a douchebaggy showbiz joke, she jaggedly laughed back to life, like the nearly drowned throwing up water.

Dusty and her manager shared a gloomy, superficial tea at the house.

The actress was glad that her wife and Jeremy were spending the long weekend out at Dume. The worst was apparently over but things hadn't returned to normal—not by a long shot.

"How was New York?"

"It was New York," said Elise. "It's always New York."

She was one of those classy, brassy, Big Apple throwbacks, a brazen widow-bachelorette, sprung forth from the Carlyle in a spangled pantsuit of sugar plums, tough love, and flint. She'd worked with Dusty since the late seventies, when she discovered her in an off-Broadway production of *Small Craft Warnings*.

"See any plays?"

"Want to hear my dirty little secret? I haven't stepped inside a theater in Manhattan since *Into the Woods*. That was 1987, can you believe? Lost my appetite. And schlepping my grandniece to *Book of Mormon* doesn't count. You know what? *Kinky Boots* just don't do it for me. Disney don't either, nor terrible revivals of not-so-great plays. I'm a snob for the heydays. I'm sure there are absolutely glorious things out there, but you know what? *Ain't interested*. Though I may see something when I'm in London."

"When are you going, babe?"

They loved calling each other *babe, kid, sweetheart*.

"In four hours. Straight from here."

"I'm jealous! What's happening in London, El? Did you sign Prince George?"

"Not *yet*," she smiled, then turned grim. It was time to talk about the baby elephant in the room. "Honey, I'm so sorry."

"I guess it wasn't meant to be."

"How's she doing?"

"Better. There's still a little bit of . . . *subtext*. You know—sometimes it feels like she thinks I went in there with a coat hanger and did the job."

"But why accuse *you*?" she demanded, playing the *outraged naïf*.

"Hey, it's not like it's rational," said Dusty, shrugging it off. "My shrink says it's sublimated *whatever*. Self-esteem was never Leggy's strong suit, *you* know that. And if she felt inadequate *before*, well . . ."

"Poor, poor darling."

"But I get it, I really do. I can take the hit." She paused to absorb. "It's just so sad, so awful."

"This too shall pass," said Elise. "And how are *you*?"

"How am *I*? When I run into myself, I'll ask."

"Are you going to—do you think you'll try again?"

"I don't know," said Dusty wearily. "It's our second miscarriage, Ellie. *And* she had one before, before we were together."

"Oh Christ," tsked Elise.

"All girls. They were all girls! Isn't that bizarre?"

Elise sighed deeply then touched her client's hand. "What about adopting?"

"Not my thing."

"Why not?" she asked. When nothing came back, she let it go. "Well, the Universe will sort it out. It always does."

"Yeah, well I'm not such a big fan of the Universe at the moment. It's my karma, El. My karma is *fucked*."

"Oh *bullshit*. Your karma is extraordinary!"

"Not in the *kiddie* department, my love. What's fucked up is, I thought—*we* thought, we really did!—*this* would be the *one*, you know, the one that would 'take.' I think it really would have grounded her."

"And what about *you*, Dusty? What would it have done for *you*?"

"I'll be all right."

"I know that, kid. But I never hear enough about *you*—"

"You know how tough I am."

"I *do*, and sometimes I wish you *wouldn't* be. So tough all the time. You don't *have* to be."

"I'm a survivor, Ellie."

"You can't hold the world up *all the time*. Pass the globe to your old friend, sweetheart. I'll put it on my shoulders while you have a good cry."

"I will, Ellie, and I *have*. You *know* I have—you've held it up for me plenty, more than anyone." She was really the closest thing to "Mother" Dusty had ever known. "But Leggy needs . . . *something*, to get her out of herself. A baby would have—*I* don't know. She's just . . . she's still not a woman in a lot of ways."

"Let me tell you something, a baby doesn't *poof!* save the day. Ask the gals with postpartum. Ask the special-needs moms. And a baby doesn't make you a *woman*, either, *you* know that and *I* know that. Want to hear Elise's deep thoughts?"

"Do I have a choice?" she said, with a smile.

"I think you need to start giving Allegra the freedom to find out who she *is*."

"That's *all* I give her, Ellie! All she *has* is freedom!"

"I'm not talking about the freedom that comes from being in-dulged like a *child*. Give her the space to find out who the *grown-up* is. I know there's one in there somewhere, just *dying* to get out."

"I thought having the baby would take care of that."

"*Maybe*," Elise said indulgently. "Maybe. 'More will be revealed.' But I think for Allegra, a baby might have been—God *bless* her, you *know* how much I love that girl—it may just have been another *project*. I don't mean that to sound harsh. Look: I'm not saying a baby was a *bad* thing. Of course not. It may still be the best idea in the world!"

"Yeah, well," Dusty said impatiently. "You know what? Raising a kid at my age wasn't exactly on my bucket list, either. I'd be collecting fucking Medicare when she got her first period. But—" She briefly closed her eyes to access something. "I was really starting to look . . . *forward* to it. I don't know. I guess I was starting to go to all these places in my head. 'Oh, the places you'll go!'" With a quick, cartoonish smile, she muttered, "Well, you know what they say. If you want to make God laugh . . ."

"To *hell* with what 'they' say! I've had my dukes up against 'they' all my life." Her grassroots psychotherapeutic tack having failed, she sloppily defaulted to Feisty Old Broad. "If you *want* it, Dusty, *go* for it, and don't let *anything* stop you. If at first you don't succeed, try, try again! It's a terrible cliché but it's *true*. That's what my mama always said and I say the same. *Words to live by*."

Set to music, it would have been one of those act-break show-stoppers Elise abhorred.

"We'll see," said Dusty, suddenly more depressed than ever. "We'll see."

"Okay, all right," said the manager, breezily putting a button on it. "Now: I know the moment isn't opportune, but we need to talk about the *Bloodthrone* sequel before I'm stuck on a plane for a hundred and forty-seven hours. It's a spectacular offer. They're up to five million for six weeks."

"*Shut the front door*. Are you frickin' serious?"

"Completely. Joss has been *wonderful*."

"*Love* Joss."

"He certainly didn't have to bend anyone's arm but he *did* tell Bob to make sure you were *very* happy."

"Aw! Isn't he a doll? And *so* talented. He's an *artist*. *Love* him."

"And Bob knew *Elise* had to be happy."

"Aw! Eliza Doolittle, sweet dragon lady!"

"They want you to do Comic-Con but everyone does Comic-Con."

"*Love* me a rock-star Comic-Con."

"So I can close?"

"Fuck *yeah*. And let's get something for Joss, don't you think? Maybe a BeoVision? Or a Tesla! Oh my God, Ellie, let's get him the new little Tesla. Let's get him *three*—he can give 'em to his kids."

"We'll talk about it when the check clears," said Elise, slyly. "How's the shoot going?"

"It's *heaven*."

"It'll get you nominated."

"Ya think?"

"Yup. One for love, one for money. That's the way we do it."

"Did Mama tell you that too?"

"You better believe it."

"But I want to do *three* for love and *ten* for money!"

"Greedy girl."

"I'm totally serious!"

"I know you are."

"'Cause I get worried 'cause I'm getting so *old*."

"You are *not* old. And only Meryl has the kind of career you do, so don't talk foolishness."

"I'll take Meryl's career and she can take mine."

"Ha! I'll put in a call." She stood. "All right, gotta go. I'm checking *in* with you from London, okay, Mrs. Wilding? And if I don't hear *back*, I'm going to *worry*. I want you to keep me in the *loop*. Tell me how Allegra's doing—and how *you're* doing. Got it? Ellie's orders."

Dusty Skyped her shrink from the trailer.

"I had the *weirdest* dream last night. I was on set, in the movie I'm doing now—kinda-sorta this movie . . . but no one was paying attention. To *me*. I was . . . *completely ignored*. Actor's nightmare, huh. I mean, I was . . . the only one standing still. Everyone was, just, *whirligigging* around me, with some sort of blind purpose. And I just stood there. I remember wanting to talk, but I couldn't. Like being frozen. Then I realized I was 'second team'—a stand-in—for *myself*! A camera double. They were all, like, getting ready for the 'real' me to arrive."

"Do you hear what you're saying?" said Ginevra, with a smile.

"Oh God. It's so transparent!" The epiphany embarrassed her.

"You said you were frozen. What is it that freezes us?"

Dusty let a few seconds go by. "Fear?"

"In your dream, you're 'on set'—you already have a purpose. The others have a purpose too, but they're 'blind.' *Your* purpose is *real*. Your eyes are open but you just can't see what that purpose is."

"Uh huh," she said, grasping at revelation.

"You're *so close*, Dusty."

"I guess losing the baby brought up a lot of old shit."

"Maybe some new shit too."

"Old wounds."

"Mother wounds."

"Do you know I haven't seen Reina in six months?" They sat awhile in silence while Dusty head-tripped. "It just feels so . . . *karmically fucked*. I was *ready* for this little girl, Ginevra! All the work I've been doing, with *you*, for *years* now, fucking *years*! I mean, an argument could be made that I gave Aurora *away*, but *this*—*this* one was fucking *taken* from me and I'm fucking *livid*, Ginevra!" She grabbed some Kleenex and blew her nose. "I can't start crying, we're about to shoot . . ."

"Talk about that—this place you go. That you 'gave Aurora away.' This so-called *argument*. Because it just doesn't sync with the reality of what happened."

"But I didn't try to *find* her, Ginevra! I *abandoned* her!"

"Who was abandoned, Dusty? Who? It was *you* who were abandoned."

"Oh, what difference does it make!" she said, disgusted. "It's—it's like that workshop I took on the Hindu gods. Kali . . . the Great Mother, Great *Destroyer*. Is that what I am, Ginevra? A great destroyer?"

"Not 'destroyer,' no. Great *Mother*, yes—"

"Bullshit! God! How can you even *say* that?"

"*All women are.* Honor that, Dusty! But you need to be that Great Destroyer too—to destroy all these terribly damaging *ideas* you have about what you *did* and who you *are* and how you're to *blame*. Those *ideas* will take you down if you let them. You're on a journey, Dusty, a hero's journey. And your mother—*Reina*—your daughter—*Aurora*—and the *baby* Allegra lost—that *both* of you lost—they're all *teachers*."

"O *God*, Ginevra, I am *so fucking sick* of teachers and fucking journeys! I just want to graduate already and get wherever the fuck it is I'm going! And be whoever I'm supposed to be . . . I am *so tired* of playing a *role*. Playing *roles* . . . I've been playing Mother all my life with everyone I love, even the people I *don't*! *Protecting* and *nurturing* and taking *care* of—"

"—*of everyone but you*. That's what your dream was saying, can you see? The 'real' you is about to arrive on set: 'First Team.' Isn't that the term? The phrase they use? Well, maybe it's time to go home. *Yes*, we've done a lot of work. *You* have—brave, hard work. Maybe now it's time to go home."

There was a rap at the door. They needed her on set.

"I don't even know what that means, Ginevra."

"I don't believe that."

"I don't know what home is."

"I think you know *exactly*. Because you're already there. Open your eyes and you'll see that you're home."

On Wednesday, they began night shoots.

She had a few errands to run. On the way out she found Allegra on a chaise by the pool, reading her script.

"Hey there," said Dusty.

"Hey now." She barely looked up.

"How's it goin'?"

"Okey-dokey."

"Wanna do yoga with me later?"

"When," said Allegra flatly.

"After lunch."

"I think I should probably wait."

"I thought the doctor said it was fine."

"He did but I think I should wait."

"Okey-dokey."

Allegra grinned and went back to her reading. The actress loitered, then said, "You know that perfume dealio? The Swiss thing? They agreed to meet on Sunday. Wanna come?"

"This Sunday?"

"Uh huh."

"Maybe. Where are they again?"

"Beverly Hills."

"Can I see how I feel?"

"Sure! I think we could both learn a lot. Be fun." Dusty nudged off a clog and dipped her foot in the water. "Positano when I wrap? Il San Pietro? Or maybe get a house for a few weeks?"

"*May*-be," said Allegra, playfully drawing out the word. She tried to make it sound like a yes, to take the pressure off.

"Or La Colombe . . ."

"Oh! I fuckin' *love* that hotel."

"*Or*—we could just hop in the car and head up the coast."

"Hippetty-hop on Highway 1."

"We've never stayed in one of those houses at Esalen. They're right on the cliff—oh! Know what I was thinking we should do? Get a place in the Lake District, for *Bloodthrone*."

"That would be awesome."

"Remember when we went to Wordsworth's cottage?" said Dusty, cracking herself up at the memory. Her effort was a tiny bit forced—she was trying to build some bridges. "That whole thing about Coleridge having a crush on Wordsworth's sister? With the wooden teeth?"

"*So* much fun," said Allegra. "Oh my God."

It wasn't going so bad now. It was pretty much the most they'd spoken since the miscarriage, and Dusty was relieved.

"Or did Wordsworth want to sleep with his *own* sister? Was that it?"

"I think that was it," said Allegra. This time her smile was genuine.

Adrenalized by the rapprochement, Dusty stage-peeked at her wife's pages. "Workin' on your script?"

"Kind of."

"I'd love to read it, when you're ready."

She'd overplayed her hand and Allegra got moody. Vibing that, Dusty said a hasty "Okay—love you!" then kissed her cheek and left. She refused to beat herself up for her hopeful exuberance, her *mothering*. That was the gift therapy had given her.

Allegra watched her go. She hated being a bitch but couldn't help it. She grimaced and said *fuck*, covering her eyes to suppress the tears.

They still came.

It was her habit to arrive late—to escape, or at least divert, atten-tion. (That's how she went to the movies, taking her seat during trailers.) Across the room, Larissa threw Dusty a *so-glad-you-came* wink, fetching and funkily assured.

Dusty set her mat down in the space closest to the entrance. Larissa wove among the sweaty, focused women, making small adjustments to poses while offering whispery encouragement. A few of them spotted the celeb but were quick to look away; this was Larchmont and it was no big deal unless you made it one. Larissa played it cool, in no hurry to approach. When she did, making a correction to the special visitor's *Uttanasana*, Dusty felt the same *frisson* she had on set, when Larissa touched her shoulder. The instructor moved on, careful not to overstay the moment.

After class, Dusty said, "Shall we share a cuppa?"

They sat in the shady backyard of The Elixir Traveling Tea Company.

The actress was a passionate studier of people. When she became intrigued by someone new, say, a civilian or below-the-liner, she was greedy to learn everything about them. Being famous, others already knew so much about her—not just from the Internet but through years of fishbowl living—and she thought it poor form if she didn't at least try to congenially rectify the imbalance. The flattered interviewees tended to be shockingly candid; conversations quickly became confessionals. For Dusty, the intimacy was erotic.

Larissa opened up about her divorce.

"He's a film editor. Work has definitely slowed but he still manages pretty well—*fairly.* Derek's a little older than me. Mostly, he gets jobs from directors he's had long relationships with. But they're getting older too—a lot are in their seventies now. They were kind of his mentors but really aren't doing features anymore. And the cable shows and Web stuff—everyone's *so much* younger. All the new technology, bla. He's kinda freaked, but he usually lands on his feet . . . though he's had sort of a dry spell. The *next* time he lands on his feet, he might need a walker!"

Dusty thought it was a funny line—no doubt a staple of the *routine.*

"Do you have kids?"

"Two. Our son's twenty-three. He's kind of on his own planet . . . or maybe he's just *orbiting.* But it's been *so* hard on my little girl—the divorce. Rafaela. She's thirteen. Our little 'surprise.'"

"What happened? With you and Derek."

"In *October,* he texted me that he's in love with his intern—*so* cliché."

"He texted you."

"He *texted* me! Oh my God, *such* a cliché, you know, like a *joke,* except when it's happening to *you.* And she's a *baby!* Our son's age!"

"Wow."

"Derek's *sixty-one! And I'm really doing okay.* But it's only *now* that

I'm, just, beginning to—it's been tough. I mean, for a while it was . . . fuckin' *brutal*. And poor Rafaela! She's in therapy now. Which is a *good* thing, apart from everything that's happened, because I'm a *total believer*, I almost *became* a therapist—still might! But he's losing his IATSE insurance and I had to really go after him to get him to pay. For her shrink. It just really hit her hard."

"I'll bet."

"'Cause she's very much a daddy's girl and she is *so angry*, Dusty. I mean, she really *gets* it and is so *pissed*, on so many levels. Because we had the whole family and lifestyle thing, right? I mean, we were always living above our means—hey, old L.A. tradition, right?— but . . . we were a tight-knit little unit, family unit. You know, us against the world and all that. And Derek and I were *best friends*. At least, I *thought* we were! And I think that for Rafaela, on some level— all levels!—it just didn't—*doesn't*—compute. (I guess it doesn't compute for me either.) We used to go away twice a year—Hawaii, Santa Fe, Napa. The whole ring-a-ding-ding deal. We had a pretty good life! Then: *enter the intern*."

"Maybe he'll come back. You know, once it's out of his system."

"I don't *think* so. I wouldn't *take* him back. At this point."

"Men are weird."

"Tell me about it! Hey, if I could have gone down your road, I would have."

It was said offhandedly but the innuendo was there and Dusty let it ride.

"Your daughter'll be okay."

"Oh, I know she will. She's a survivor, like her mom."

"Children are incredibly resilient. She's thirteen?"

"Almost fourteen—going on forty-two. Did you ever want kids?"

She was glad Larissa hadn't pretended not to know she was

childless. "I think there was a *moment*. Man, we tried. Recently, even." Her words surprised her; sometimes "opening up" went both ways. "I guess my career always seemed to come first. I never wanted to be one of those monsters you read about in some spawn-of-celebrity *tell-all*. You know, whose presence was defined by their absence."

"Then it's probably a good thing. That you didn't."

"Right? No kid, no memoir!" They laughed too hard, as if defusing a tension. "But hey, people do it—the kids-and-career thing—and do it *well*. So maybe I'm just . . . full of shit." They laughed again, then Dusty paused to silently reflect while the enthralled Larissa took it all in.

"Would you ever adopt?"

"We're not ruling it out . . . though I'm not sure that's something either of us have a passion for. It's kind of a crapshoot though, right? Like, people never seem to get one that becomes a doctor or a lawyer. It's always either *junkie* or *serial killer*—"

"Or both—"

"Or actor!"

Larissa practically belly-laughed. "Well, I guess we'll just have to wait and see what happens to Maddox and Zahara."

"Angelina's amazing, I have *total* respect. But it's not the little *African* babies who go south, it's the *Americans*. The white Americans!"

"You could always get yourself a little Russkie."

"Nun-*uh*. Fetal alcohol syndrome."

"China?"

"The holiday card photo always looks . . . awkward."

Larissa spit-taked her oolong tea then laid her head on the table in a summer storm of giggles. Dusty really liked this lady.

She dropped the actress at her car on a residential street behind the Yoga Center, thanking her for the "playdate." They were shooting tonight from suppertime till dawn and commiserated about the inverted schedule; it could really do a number on your body and your head. They lingered like that, running their merry mouths about circadian rhythms, fractured menses and aging *vessels*, and even while they spoke, Dusty mused how it'd been ages since she met a peer, someone who'd been around the block a few times but was still openhearted, still game, still *interested*. It was way sexy. The thought of fooling around crossed her mind—she could lean over and kiss her right now, just swamp her—but these days that was dangerous, for all kinds of reasons. The omnipresent, cockeyed slaves to fame were a-tweeting, and all the cocksure paparazzi were using drones. Plus, she'd never cheated on Allegra, not really, in any way that counted. There'd been the low-grade emotional affair or two (she took that as an elder's prerogative) and maybe that time in Pebble Beach when she let herself come during a massage. The masseuse never even knew it, though maybe that was just an absurd lie she told herself.

No, if she was going to be unfaithful, she'd feel better about waiting until her spouse wasn't so miserable, so vulnerable. It was just too easy.

Dusty waited in the car.

She thought Allegra had been holed up in the pool house for the last few days working on her script, when actually she'd been tirelessly sketching perfume bottles. She stepped from the house, in vintage Chanel (her version of a power suit), a green leather portfolio tucked in her arm. That touch—the portfolio—broke Dusty's heart.

"Do they know I'm coming?" asked Allegra.

"Of course they do," she lied. The Swiss were thrilled to be having the meeting at all. They wouldn't have cared if Dusty brought a mob of violent, mentally ill homeless people along.

The Bartok offices were just off Civic Center Drive in that leafy, oddball business park on the edge of Beverly Hills. An employee waited for them on the sidewalk. Their youngish escort, face flushed by the surreal proximity of a movie legend on a quiet Sunday, was charmingly beside himself. He shepherded them through a series of empty lobbies with a *wabi-sabi* aesthetic—Le Corbusier spaces and furnishings fit for a high-fashion *zendo*. They finally entered a vault-ceilinged room where a dozen elegant men and women sitting around an enormous ebony conference table instantly rose to their feet. It took a few minutes for the marrieds to shake everyone's hand.

Anton, a beautiful, sixtyish black with a suavely indiscernible accent, spoke up. "First off, we want to thank you for coming to see us during this very busy time—I am sure it is *always* a very busy time. But we are most grateful and delighted, absolutely. We welcome you!"

The group, smiling in approbation, deferred to the powerful chair, giddily holding themselves in check.

"No, no," said the honoree. "Thank *you*. I know it's taken *too* long for us to meet and I'm *so* thankful for your patience. Elise and I have been talking about this *forever*. And I just wanted everyone to know the delays weren't a diva thing. My schedule has been *out of control*."

"Not at all, not at all," said the chair—though more, a king enamored of a neighboring country's queen.

"We are *totally honored*," said an insanely stylish Frenchwoman with Gertrude Stein hair. "I was telling Dominic, we will wait forever!" With the last, she tapped her fist to the table, militant and nobly resolute, as if sealing a Rosicrucian blood oath.

"Well, maybe not forever," twinkled the chair.

"But *close*," said Dominic, a few seats away. "Not *forever* but 'for-*almost*.' I said we would wait 'for-*almost*.'"

The room laughed as its expansions and contractions began in earnest.

"I feel *so horrible* asking you to come here on a Sunday!" said Dusty.

"That you would come to visit on your day of rest from *filmwork* is really so much appreciated."

"'Day of rest' sounds so biblical," said the actress.

"But it's true, *mais non?*" said the Gertrude. "When you compose a film, you are making the world from Creation."

"I can only imagine how exhausting it can be," said the chair.

"The *exhausting* part doesn't happen until the red carpet! And the junkets. But I *do* feel a little guilty—you should all be at *home*. It's so kind of you to accommodate my sometimes ridiculous life."

The banter went on in that vein, the mutual praise and phony apologies, with shyer, lesser lights down-table testing the waters by volunteering a clumsily worshipful remark about the star's body of work and their general gratitude at being born in her time—*apart* from the incomparable joy of meeting her today in the *flesh*, breathing the same air, potentially sharing the same sewage plumbing, etcetera. Allegra wondered how high the bullshit would fly.

A stately woman in head-to-toe Missoni said, "I cannot remember when our team has been this excited about a fragrance."

"I'm excited too!" said Dusty.

"I like to tell Anton," said a raffish man, clearly a "creative," "that the Dusty Team is a bit like the Venus flytrap."

"Oooh!" said Dusty. "*Love* me a Venus flytrap!"

"I promise we won't close on you all the way," he added.

"It will be a velvet glove!" said Dominic.

The same smile had been slapped on Allegra since she'd arrived, and her face was starting to ache. She felt like a block of ice with teeth stuck in it; a rube and a loser.

The Missoni said, "You've been the Holy Grail around here."

"Aw!" said Dusty. "That's *so sweet.*"

"Welcome to the Bartok family," said Anton.

They spontaneously applauded and Allegra thought, *Oh my God, it will not stop!* They were so far up Dusty's ass you'd need a search party to find them. She wanted to rogue *out. I'm gonna spray this fucking room like the self-radicalized homegrown lone wolf I am!*

Dominic gushed about the most recent film she'd won an Oscar for—five years ago, already—and was echoed by a chorus of heartfelt, anachronistic congratulations.

"Aw, thank you!" said Dusty, as if she'd come straight from the ceremony. "You know, I always think of wanting to do a Woody and not show up. Can't seem to pull that off!"

"That was your third, no?" said the Missoni. "Bit of a rare club."

"Fourth time's the charm," said Dusty blithely. "Am I greedy?"

"We'll be there when you accept the fourth," said the chair.

"And the fifth," said the "creative." "And the sixth!"

"Let's talk about the *fragrance*," said the chair, down to unctuous brass tacks. "We are expecting to do *very* well."

"*You* are going to do very well," said Dominic to the star.

"Oh no! I can't deal with the pressure!" said Dusty melodramatically. "But I *want* to do well. Like, *White Diamonds* well!"

"It is our high hope," said Anton, "that it may be arranged."

"Dusty, we are *looking* at this on a White Diamonds scale," said Gertrude. "We believe we definitely have the same potential."

"She was my hero," said the actress, with a crestfallen little girl look.

"We used to go drinking in West Hollywood," said the "creative."

"Oh my God," she shot back. "Me too! At the Abbey? Why didn't we ever *see* you there?"

"You may have," he said coyly. "I might even have bought you and Dame Elizabeth drinks." He winked. "I am nothing if not discreet."

"You are so not!" said Gertrude, and everyone laughed.

Dusty turned to her wife and said, "It's important to me that Allegra is *very much involved*." The crew nodded, almost gravely. "Her *taste* and her *instincts* are *amazing*."

"Of course!" said Anton to Allegra. "You are in our family now!"

"Like mafia, one can never leave," said the "creative."

The Missoni ogled her and said, "Allegra, you have *incredible* style." The "creative" took in her biker jacket. "Rick Owens?"

"Yes," said Allegra, more stiffly than she'd have liked.

"I *love* Rick," said the "creative." "Rick and Michèle."

"Michèle?" said the Missoni.

"Lamy," said Gertrude. "His muse."

"I just saw them in Paris," said the "creative." "There's a huge *statue* of Rick in front of Selfridges . . . and the *furniture* he designs— my *God*."

They included Allegra in their space now, as if to cue her, and she hungrily took the bait, offering, "Aren't his furnishings amazing?"

"*So* genius," said the "creative."

"We have some in the Zurich office," said Dominic.

"I didn't know Rick was fabricating furniture," said the Missoni.

The "creative" swiveled toward her to enlighten. "Some of the pieces are . . . *promethean*. They're incredible! Museum pieces—literally. They always remind me of *Rodin*."

"We have a few," said Allegra, *très engagé*, her cherry taken at last. "At Point Dume."

"A bed in one of the guest rooms," said Dusty. "It's petrified wood, isn't it, Allegra? Like, *thousands* of years old. You don't actually go there to *nap*—you go there to *die*."

Everyone thought the remark was beyond funny.

"And *crazy* expensive," said the "creative." "I mean, *crazy*-crazy."

Some talk ensued about the scent itself . . . kudos to boutiques such as Le Labo and Byredo . . . the Osmothèque in Versailles. Legendary "noses" that might assist in creating DNA (none of whom Allegra recognized) were bandied about with cryptic, gossipy bluster, and even a little aside about Chanel No. 19 between Dusty, the Missoni, and Gertrude went over her head. The celebrity wife was at sea.

"Allegra's been working on some amazing designs for the bottle," said Dusty.

"They're very rough," said Allegra, adding, "They're in the conceptual stage." She thought that sounded dumb, but—too late.

"We'd love to see them!" said a bookish man who hadn't yet spoken. He wore a green tunic and a gold Aztec-y medallion around his neck.

"We eagerly welcome," said the chair, directing his comments to Allegra, "we *solicit* your help in this creative process."

"What do you think about 'Ecco'?" said Allegra boldly, to no one in particular. "With two *c*'s?"

"Ecco, Ecco!" said Dusty, in ludic enunciation, a bad actor "doing" an Italian. "I love it!"

"It *is* lovely," enthused the Missoni. "We wanted to use it last year, didn't we, Paco?"

"We did," said a cherubic, self-effacing down-tabler. "We had some hassles with the 'Ecco Bella' lawyers, so didn't pursue."

"Maybe open it up with them again?" suggested Dominic, knowing the effort would be futile. "Do some reaching out?"

"They were fairly adamant," he said. "But of course."

"Then what about 'Echo' spelled *E-C-H-O*?" said Allegra, in brainstorm mode. Fun! "Can you get around it that way?"

"I like your mind," said the Missoni, showing her canines.

"*That* belongs to a competitor," said the chair. "But—it's a process. Sometimes more of a process than we'd like."

"How about a movie theme?" The ideas were flowing. "Something related to the cinema?"

(Dusty, proud mama, thought it so cute that, surrounded by Europeans, Allegra invoked "the cinema.")

"Well, we *love* that," said the Missoni.

"Something like 'First Team'? Or 'Final Touches' . . ."

(Dusty saw that the names had been in Allegra's pocket all along— little secret weapons. Proud!)

"'First Team' might be a little sporty," said Dominic. "But its energy is rather charming."

"I *love* 'First Team,'" said the Missoni. "*And* 'Final Touches.' *Really* great. But I'm wondering if they convey the glamour."

"'Final Touches' *is* intriguing," said the chair, though in truth, more conciliatory than intrigued.

Allegra was heartened and said, "What about 'Last Looks'?"

"There's a lovely poetry in that," he said. "Though I think with both of these—'Last Looks,' 'Final Touches'—we wish to avoid anything too *funereal*."

Of course he was right and his clarity broke the bubble.

(He wasn't the chair for nothing.)

"'Scent of a Dead Woman,'" said Dusty, not making fun of but rather seeking to riff away her wife's defeat. "From Al's movie! That way, we keep the theme of *le cinéma*."

"Our first choice," said the chair, "—and of course we want to involve you in this decision, *both* of you, of course *nothing* shall be approved without your complete assent—our first choice is one that's been in the marketplace for years under many different *auspices*. Which actually gives us wherewithal in terms of trademark." He paused to make a steeple with the fingers of his hands. "We've given this a tremendous amount of thought and the feeling was unanimous: *'Dusty.'*"

Gertrude said to Allegra, "It is not yet *un fait accompli*."

"Not at all!" said the chair, realizing his announcement may have been premature, and slightly impolitic.

Dominic stepped into the breach. "It was one of those eureka moments. We said to ourselves, how could we call it anything else?"

The star tilted her head and gazed out the window, turning over the eponymous *nom de fragrance* in her head. With a half smile she slowly raised her eyes from the hem to the collar of an invisible sky.

"One of those forest-for-the-trees things," said the bookish man.

"If we can clear it, no one will remember its other incarnations," said Dominic.

"Oh, we can clear it," said the man in the green tunic, assassin-like.

"Clear the forest—for the trees," said Dusty.

"*Have* we cleared it?" asked the chair, suddenly businesslike.

"Yes," said an unidentified man, far enough away to be practically out the door.

"'Dusty' for women, 'Dustin' for men," said the actress, not entirely serious. Her thoughts roamed elsewhere.

"'Dusty Rose'?" said Allegra, startled by her own eruption.

The Walmart-y suggestion instantly made her cringe. She thought she saw the "creative" and the Missoni lock eyes. She was about to deflate her own idiocy with a joke about Dusty's white-trash fan base but fortunately had become paralyzed.

"That's owned by a competitor," said the unfazeable faraway man.

"And it's lovely," said Gertrude, ever charitable. "But they got there first."

"It *is* kinda downscale," said Allegra, rousing herself. "Plus, her middle name isn't even Rose."

"I could *change it* to Rose," said Dusty supportively.

Allegra died a little.

"So *much* of what we do is about getting there *first*," said the chair diplomatically. "And so much of what we do is . . . intangible."

The actress smiled and put a hand on her better half's.

She had been staying in the guest cottage but couldn't sleep. She walked past the pool to the kitchen in the main house, made herself a soup bowl–sized cup of champurrado, then stole away to the den with a bag of marshmallows and medley of books.

She tucked her knees into a cashmere throw and dug in. As was her habit during trying times, she picked through their library's shelves with messy, surefire alchemy to gather a healing wildflower bouquet. One of the selections was a strange meditation on loss-of-pregnancy grieving rituals, acquired just after her first miscarriage. The Japanese memorial practice was called *mizuko kuyō*. Wikipedia dryly informed that "mizuko" meant dead fetus but she preferred the book's claim of literal translation: water-child. It said the root—*mizu*—meant "lost" or "unseen." Allegra thought that beyond beautiful.

She plucked yet another flower and softly read aloud:

> There are no eyes, no ears, no nose, no tongue,
> no body, mind; no color, sound, or smell;
> no taste, no touch, no thing; no realm of sight,
> no realm of thoughts; no ignorance, no end
> to ignorance; no old age and no death;
> no end to age and death; no suffering,
> nor any cause of suffering, nor end
> to suffering, no path, no wisdom and no fulfillment.

The Heart Sutra was supposed to be everything you ever wanted to know about Buddhism but were afraid to ask, though it only made her think of her baby. Her *babies*—lullaby of things unseen and unsaid, things almost-but-never-were . . . maybe that *was* Buddhism—the presence of absence and the absence of presence. The aroma of nothingness might have comforted if only she weren't suffering so.

She pulled an anthology of Greek myths from the nosegay, remembering a picture book she adored as a little girl. Her mom got it at the Salvation Army just before they left the Family, right around when Willow began an affair with the itinerant, charismatic American guru named Gridley Wright. She joined his group, the Shiva Lila, and early one morning they all ran off to India, leaving the last of Allegra's American "stepfathers" behind. (Shiva Lila was a child-worshipping cult, though you wouldn't have known it, because a lot of the kids were never vaccinated and wound up dying of diphtheria.) Even as a six-year-old, she knew she was living inside an allegory—the word was almost her very name—and sought confirmation in the colorful storybook's exuberant grandeur: sheer escapism from the tawdry Olympus of dirty magic, delusional soothsayers, and beleaguered, narcissistic women who littered her adoptive communal worlds.

The hyper-sexualized child had obsessed over the story of Tiresias . . .

When he separated two snakes having intercourse in the middle of the road, the female became so enraged—Allegra the adult couldn't blame her!—that she punished his meddling by turning him into a woman. After seven long years, the transgendered Tiresias saw the *same snakes fucking* and somehow reasoned that if he interfered again, his maleness would be restored. He was right; his original form was bestowed. When Zeus and Hera squabbled over who enjoyed lovemaking more—man or woman—they asked Tiresias to judge, as he alone had experienced both sides. Strangely, it was Hera who insisted that *men* received the greatest pleasure. But Tiresias ruled in favor of the gentler sex, calling their ecstasies tenfold. Hera was so peeved at being contradicted that she blinded him. Being Tiresias was a bummer.

She thought it would make an amazing screenplay, abetted by the culture's ravenous appetite for all things intersex. The version in her hand (while sipping Mexican hot chocolate in the other) implied that Tiresias became a whore during his phallic exile, making Allegra even more passionate about the transgressive prospect of adaptation. But when the thought of her unfinished Children of God script swiftly intruded, inspiring winds poured through tattered sails.

She ruminated some more on that mad time. She hadn't been altogether honest with Jeremy about her early experience; there was much she was ashamed of and much she'd repressed. It was true that while Allegra remained mostly amnesiac about the Family's ritualized sex-play, she knew bad stuff happened in India for sure. A few years ago, to her dismay, a persistent childhood masturbation fantasy resurfaced, featuring a totem cock that sprung from her nine-year-old cunny like a genie when summoned. She could fuck women with it, and boys too. (Another memory: frottage was the prepubescent sleep aid of choice.) She vividly recalled what the thing *looked* like—the real, veiny deal. *Yuck.* It wasn't so much the Boschian precocity of the image of her bedangled cherub self that alarmed and mesmerized, but the ensuing speculation over the nature of dark materials, lost and *unseen*, that drove poor, gypsyfied Alice-Allegra through the looking-glans. A mish-mash of nefarious, arousing, troublesomely indistinct home movies played double matinees in her head throughout her late teens. If she'd blacked out their content for nearly twenty years, what else might soon be resurrected?

The myth of Tiresias was so compelling because it held the seeds of both punishment and a child's polymorphous perversity in hand. Yet no one would arrive to separate the snakes, no one but Allegra the Orgasmic Dragonslayer—for in her wild, ambivalent couplings, she dreamed herself to be the seer come to her own rescue, who would then be betrayed for telling the truth about the poisonous, anarchic power of sex. (Rendered blind, might she at least be rewarded with the power to un-see all that she'd seen?) Along with retribution for whistleblowing came the deep consolation of prophecy—a double bind the child would have eagerly embraced, because she'd have sacrificed the pantheon of gods and Mothers themselves to foresee how her story would end.

The set was cleared while Dusty and her co-star rehearsed for Bennett. Only the D.P. watched from the periphery, and Bonita, who would make a late entrance in the scene.

The lovers lay in bed. The Marilyn was blowsy, radiant, and real—like one of those JPEGs of what movie stars might look like if they hadn't died young. When the First shouted, "Very quiet! We are rehearsing!" the people milling around the soundstage suddenly deactivated, staring into their phones like recharging droids.

The director hovered over the actors as they ran their lines, occasionally watching through a handheld lens like a referee poised above wrestlers.

"Arthur's in a *major* fucking funk," said the Marilyn.

"Talk to me," said Dusty.

"At a certain point, *male artists* just keep going back to the well."

"You mean the *womb*. And not just artists! *All* men. Ted's been so depressed." Dusty paused. "He can't fuck."

"*Tell* me about it! Arty never *could*. Maybe if I wore a mask . . . of his face! The man would not eat pussy under threat of death."

"You could dangle a Pulitzer down there . . ."

"It'd have to be a Nobel!"

Dusty asked Bennett if she should do some business—drink a glass of water beside the bed or fuss with the Marilyn's hair. He said, "Whatever comes."

The scene resumed.

"Does he hate that you're doing a sitcom?"

"Sylvia, oh my God! *Hate* isn't even the *word*. And he's *mean* about it. He's always been a sadist, and that's on me . . . But you know what? *The Golden Girls* is the smartest move I ever made. Keeps me *alive*—and not just in the public eye. I laugh more on that set than I have in my entire *life*."

"And the ratings!"

"We're bigger than *Family Ties*."

She lightly kissed the Marilyn, avoiding her mouth—tongues would come "on the day"—then asked Bennett who he thought would be the aggressor.

"It's probably more interesting if it's Sylvia," he said. "I kind of think of Marilyn as the eternal bottom."

They rehearsed awhile longer (Bonita making her entrance) before calling second team. Larissa came on set. Dusty left an earring in the yoga studio and the stand-in had been carrying it around for a few days but hadn't found the right moment to give it back.

Dusty kibitzed with the Marilyn on the way out. Stepping into the sun, she was startled to see Marta and her daughter.

She'd completely forgotten.

"Oh my God, Marta! Was *this* the day?"

Marta nervously wondered if she'd gotten it wrong.

"You say Friday—today. It's not okay?"

"No, it's fine! I'm *such* an idiot, I didn't even think to look at what we were *shooting*." Her face scrunched to a stressed-out wince. "I'm just not sure if today's *appropriate*—but whatever." Her qualms vanished as she turned full wattage on the daughter. "*Hi*, Julia! Oh my God, *look* at you, look how *pretty* you are in your dress! And happy birthday!"

The Marilyn excitedly said, "It's your birthday?"

"Yeah," she said shyly, amending to "Yes" so as to be more adult-like.

"Come have lunch in my trailer!" said Dusty. "Though maybe you'll have more fun eating with everyone outside? That's probably better than a stuffy old trailer. Go! Go with Mama and I'll join you." She stage-whispered to Marta, "It's kind of an *R-rated day* . . . but she should be fine, to watch. For a *little*, anyway!"

"Hey, you'll both be in your birthday suits," said the Marilyn, in good humor. "How old are you, Julia?"

"Thirteen."

"It's *not* her *quinceañera*," said Dusty.

"Well, *duh*," she said, puffing up in contrived offense. "What do I look like, a dumb blonde? Don't answer that!" She turned back to the girl. "So you wanna be an actress?"

"Don't encourage her," said Dusty.

"Maybe," answered Julia. She'd never given a thought about acting, ever.

"Marilyn," said Dusty belatedly. "This is Marta, Julia's mom."

"Hi!" said the Marilyn, shaking Marta's hand.

"Her name is Marilyn, and she's *playing* Marilyn—Monroe."

"You look just like her," said Marta. She really thought she did.

"Aw, you're sweet," said Marilyn-Marilyn.

"Who's Marilyn Monroe?" asked the birthday girl.

"Good question!" said Marilyn. "I guess no one ever really knew."

"No one," said Dusty. "*Especially* Marilyn."

Another Sunday—

—so tired.

Overcome.

Riding on mid-shoot stamina fumes: etiolated blowback of all the emotions expended on her craft.

Dragging through the usual job/ego influenza . . .

Beat up—

—by the spikey, wrenching melodrama of Allegra's loss too.

Their loss . . .

At sixteen, when she gave up her child, she made a pact with a monstrous paradox: she would covet both fame and oblivion.

She wanted *nothingness*—if she did not exist, she could not be judged. She wanted *fame*—balm and anodyne to self-torture.

She would live (in her head) in a mirrorless tenement, in penance and atonement; but would live too in a palace (Point Dume, Trousdale, the Hamptons), for the ease of being found. When the orphan finally sought her, in the immensity of darkness, wouldn't it be best that the bejeweled glare of a golden seraglio light the way? She customized a mythology that justified fame's pursuit: to set the stage for the prodigal daughter's return. Aurora would find her way back by Mama's crisscross S.O.S. swordplay of movie-premiere searchlights . . .

It was always about *her*! The child she abandoned would seek *her* out! Such was the erratic fairy tale of this Mother Grimm—

The chronically torturous state of wretched anonymity and grandiose renown (with its cheap, glorified reunion fantasy) created a bottomless rage and confusion that unhinged.

A pregnant woman was in the news. She drowned her three kids then arranged them in bed with their arms around one another. Before jumping off a building she wrote a good-bye on the wall:

> *Bury us together We need to stay together I need to look after*
> *them and keep them safe A mother never abandons her children.*

She died for her kids—

—but *Dusty's* kid died for . . . *Dusty*.

The star had committed an act against nature, a primordial, pornographic sin. The Great Destroyer thought: *I am the demon's demon because I made no effort to find my child*. No effort! *None*: wallowing in the idolatry of fans, attended by a dirty mob of piss-gold statuettes— every prize bore a plaque with the gremlin's motto "Mother of the Year"—masking her cowardice with luxuries and accolades like a bulimic hiding vomit breath.

On a good day, she told herself she never wanted fame, that fame had come to *her*, occult and unbidden, a karmic fluke. The humility shtick she hustled on talk shows and magazine profiles was as big a lie as the childlessness she promoted to the world. That her mother could have bullied her into amputating her *issue* held some truth for a sixteen-year-old; she wouldn't have been the first to be cowed, manipulated, and ruined by a matriarch. Then how to explain her apathy, her religion of neglect in the decades that followed? What did that say about her as a human being? She'd done well in managing martyrdom. She was lucky; the perks of stardom were narcotic. Yet whenever the drug wore off, she conveniently lapsed into blaming Reina for the walking, talking abortion of her daughter (if, in fact, she were still alive)—*the devil made me do it*. But it was a dodge that invariably ended in violent self-contempt. The therapy-smart actress usually fell back on deconstructing the abandonment of her only-born as an obvious re-creation and consequence of the original sin of the absence of mother love. Dusty even floated the idea that Reina's spiteful stratagem possessed an erotic component: the woman got off on her own crimes. She sought affirmation from her therapist, but what good would it have done for Ginevra to give credence to her client's suspicions? To agree that Reina hated her daughter, which the therapist believed in her gut—everything she knew about the beast conformed to the sociopathic model—to endorse the theory that she took baleful pleasure in Dusty's torments and that Reina's wickedness was such that she may plausibly have considered murdering her daughter, in the end substituting a far more sophisticated, destructive act (the trapdoor disposal of her grandchild in order to secure the actress's admittance to purgatory)—well, Ginevra was of a mind there were professional limitations on candor. How could she concede to such outlandish horrors? Some things were better kept in shadow, else healing never occur.

Sunday—

—reviewing the week on her way up the coast.

Making a film was always a mixed bag. She lived for her time in front of the camera, likening it (naturally) to the attentive mother she never had while at the same time noting the poignant metaphor of a lens that could not touch, could not hold, could not love. She took that back—*could* love, but the manifestation of its embrace was deferred, subject to a director's intercession and an audience's diverse, subjective interpretation. Still, the *attention* given was unrelenting and unconditional, something she'd never had as a child. There was absolute purity to the mother-daughter relationship of actress to camera because in those fleeting, eternal moments of communion she lost troubled selfhood and risked only *feelings*—only!—not words, for they weren't *her* words, but another's, the screenwriter's, and as such meant nothing, no matter their eloquence. In that regard, she would always be making silent movies. What were words anyway, between mother and child? Only depth and profusion of feeling were essential. At the end of our lives, only feelings remain.

Still, there were complications.

Movie acting was like gambling in a burning casino. Dusty bridled at the small, sadistic window of time allotted each scene for emotional stuntwork. You prepared for months, weeks, hours, you tortured yourself, and when the day of reckoning came, suddenly you were in a shoot-out that lasted only moments, some kind of high noon showdown with eternity, though you were always outdrawn and outgunned. At best, your performance ended in a dignified, technically proficient, sometimes stirring death—but always a death. When things weren't going well she felt dumb, bamboozled, whorishly deranged, though probably more like a miner than a trampy clown; having experienced a thousand cave-ins, the old pro had learned how to breathe through the panic and find her way out. Now and then, her most critically rewarded work had been by rote— sometimes it went like that. Mother Lens would hold you when you were at your worst and see you through. Though not always—even now, at this time in her career, she got lashed to directors who sacrificed her on the altar of "making the day." The casino was burning daylight. Sometimes it went that way.

She yearned to be Frances McDormand, unglamorously formidable workaday actor's actor, but was marooned in the body of fabled Dusty Wilding instead, no more able to deny her showy iconic heft than the condemned could their crimes. Like the story she once dramatized on NPR about a torture machine that etched the transgressions of convicts into their flesh, she could never escape her glorious star chamber, its hidden walls graffitied with the classy *New Yorker* profile cant of her lies and unworthiness. It's been said that an actor is less than a man and an actress more than a woman. As one of the most famous gay women on the planet, Dusty sometimes still felt less than a man; by throwing away her child, her chance at feeling—*being*—more than a woman was shot . . .

—Sunday!

Past the midpoint on *Sylvia & Marilyn*, she got a second wind.

It was overcast . . .

Driving up PCH to see Reina.

All her work with Ginevra had led to this.

Leggy's miscarriage had led to this—

Maybe there was still a chance to be more than a woman.

But was the idea of finally becoming a warrior—*of showing up on her mother's set*—just another fantasy of a bravura role? It hardly mattered. The motivation behind entering combat, however chimerical or self-glorifying, would be quickly expunged by the act of warfare itself.

All would be bloodily forgotten, especially in victory.

The "memory care" home, formerly a private residence, lay at the end of a cul-de-sac on a high Santa Barbaran bluff. Straining, one heard the low, querulous static of the ocean.

She never called beforehand to announce her visits, few as they were.

Ninety-year-old twin sisters nodded on a couch while a man in formalwear tinkled a saucy, castrated version of a Nirvana song on the lobby's baby grand. As the staff caught sight of her, tiny seismic shocks of surprise jostled them one by one. Like a royal *incognito*, Dusty kept her head down but managed to dispense a few fleeting, undercover smiles as she floated toward her destination.

She stood at the door, looking in.

Asleep in her chair, Reina wore the robe Dusty brought a few years ago from Beijing. Deep blue, with an embroidered astonishment of yellow-gold swallows. The braided bun atop her head was a work of art; a hairdresser came each week and did the ladies for a small fortune. She instantly thought of retreating. Why not just have a cup of tea and catch up with the R.N.s? Then Reina's eyes opened and seemed to look at her—into her. *Devil.* So Dusty entered, dutiful and dignified, like a eulogizer taking the stage.

"Hi, Reina." That's what she called her, for years. "How ya doin'?"

"Well, I'm *doin'*," said Reina. "I am definitely *doin'*."

A not-too-far-off neighbor's voice cried, "Mama! Mama! Mama! Mama!"—battle cry of dementia and defeat.

Dusty kept the ball in the air for the usual amiable volley of nonsense: how long Reina had been sitting versus lying down, how beautiful her hair was, the beautiful weather, had she been to the beautiful beach, did the piano man play her favorite Bacharachs. A nurse brought Dusty's special tea (kept on reserve) then two more appeared and they all had a jovial visit in the queen's wing of the broken-memory palace.

When they left, Dusty sunnily asked, "Do you know who I am?" Reina looked askance, brow knit in disgust. "Tell me my name."

"Why should I?"

"Oh come on, Mom." The *Mom* just came out—she'd process that later, with Ginevra. *Interesting.* "What's my name? *You* can tell me."

"I'm supposed to do everything you say?"

"You've never done *anything* I've asked you to!" She had to laugh. "I'm *Dusty*, your *daughter*."

"Want to give me your autograph? Asshole?"

Scalded, she backed off and took a few yoga breaths before starting over.

"How are you, Reina?"

"Oh, just fine," said her mother, with blank kindliness. She was somewhere else now but Dusty wondered how much of it was an act. "I do a lot of dancing."

"Really?" she asked, humoring. "When? When do you dance? When do they have dances?"

"Every night, Josephine!"

"Wow. *Really.* Okay."

"*You* know that," said Reina, scowling.

"Cha-cha? Fox-trot? Do you fox-trot?"

"Well, I don't *trot*. I'm not a horse. Last time I looked."

The old woman smiled, bits of green food in her teeth. Dusty wanted to shove stalks of frozen broccoli down her throat until she choked—to flood her lungs with saltwater and organic juices till they ruptured.

"What about tango? Do you tango? Do you samba?"

"They don't allow that."

"Illegal, huh."

She was running out of things to say. She had come with a mission but everything was getting sweaty and fuzzy now.

"Have you eaten yet? Did you have lunch?"

"They don't serve lunch till six-thirty."

"They don't serve lunch till dinnertime?"

"That's right."

"Well, I'm not sure if that's the case, but okay. Maybe they do it differently here."

"I'm glad you approve."

They sat in silence. Her mother said, "So how's Big Movie Star?"

"Big Movie Star's great!" said Dusty, with bullshit bravado. "Makin' *shitloads* of money." Announcing her worth was her most toxic venom.

"And how's the little tramp?"

She didn't see that coming and contorted under the knife.

"She's not a little tramp and her name is Allegra. She's my *wife* and she's effin' fantastic."

"She's *stealing* from you."

"I don't *think* so, Reina."

"Why else would she be with you?"

"Good question!"

"She wants your *money*."

"She can have it, she can have *all* of it! In fact, I've already given her *millions*!"

For all her bluster, she may as well have been a crippled woman being chased down a dark field by a rapist with superpowers. Reina guffawed and wet-farted. "She's *cheating* and *stealing* from you because you're *old, old, old*. Look at your *skin*. The young do not love the old!"

Dusty walked from the room and out of the building. She moved listlessly toward the car and stopped. No: she would go back in— had to. She'd do what she promised herself then never return.

The twins on the couch were gone and so was the pianist.

An orderly in a hairnet had just brought a lunch tray and Reina was snarling that she wasn't hungry. Dusty was surprised when her mother asked her for help. A happy-faced R.N. came in and Dusty told her that Mom would eat later, they were going to visit awhile longer, it was all good. The nurse said *of course*, then, with comic flourish, reassured that "Your mother eats . . . whenever she wants to!"

"I'm sure she does," said Dusty.

The nurse said, "No one's on a timetable here."

Everyone left.

Dusty steeled herself.

"Mother," she said studiously. "I wanted to ask about Aurora."

There it was: the euphemism shot by a fainthearted cannoneer. Ginevra told her to expect nothing, which was understood. Therapist and client agreed to call it an *exercise*—just asking the question was an important step in *healing*. Dusty had even psyched herself up the night before by performing a visual meditation, linking this final errand to the closing of the lid of Reina's coffin.

"Can you tell me what happened to her? Years ago you told me she was adopted by a 'nice family'—Daddy told me that too. But you never . . . we never really *talked* about it. Ever! Why? Why didn't we?" The old woman remained quiet and expressionless. "But we can *now*. Can you tell me anything? About the details? Mother, is there anything you can remember?"

The trickster genius of wet brain lay in its oracular unpredictability; Dusty's arrows might elicit cyclopean rage, the flinch of nonresponse, or essential truths. Hope rose hard, like a hundred shuttlecocks in her chest.

"I'd like to know if you ever met them, that's all. The people who adopted Aurora."

"Oh, just *forget* it."

Reina put on her warty Brueghel peasant face—not a harbinger of good things.

"Forget it? I basically *had* to! I basically had to arrange my *entire life* around forgetting it—so don't tell me to forget it!"

"It's a movie," said the crone, with malignant calm. "It's just a *movie*."

"Didn't you ever want a granddaughter?" said Dusty, changing tack. "Didn't you ever miss not having a granddaughter?"

"Like a hole in the head."

"Because I know we had enough money . . ."

"*We* had money, not *you*."

Dusty was crumbling. "Daddy wanted—I know Daddy wanted a granddaughter—"

"Oh, is that *right*. And who *said* so? And don't tell me *he* did, 'cause he *didn't*."

"I *know* he wanted one!" She heard her voice become little girly and the eeriness of it frightened her. "I know he wanted me to have her . . ."

"You *know*, you *know*, you *know*! I am *not* going through this with you again!"

"What do you mean *again*? We have *never* gone through this!"

"Oh yes we have—"

"In your *mind*, maybe! *You* wanted to get rid of it! You *forced* me to because you didn't want to be . . . *encumbered*." Reina was actually laughing now. "You wanted to be *free as a bird*"—Dusty hated the antiquey phrase she'd inherited from her bitch mother—"so you could go out and do your *fucking* or *whatever* it was you were doing—"

"Look, you just better *shut up* because you're hogging the line! I need to keep the line clear."

"What are you *talking* about?"

"I told you! I'm waiting for a *call*."

"From who?" asked Dusty, in numb moratorium.

"Well, it ain't from *Baby Aurora*," said the old woman, glint-winking.

She leaned in and slapped Reina's face. Her mother immediately began to cry and Dusty leaned in close. She pinched her then quickly stopped, fearful of leaving a bruise. She whispered in her ear, gravely staccato, *"I am going to come in the middle of the night and strangle you and shove a knife up your asshole, you sick fucking monster cunt,"* and then, as a cover for Reina's distress, she went and told a nurse that out of nowhere Mom started raving about getting slapped around by the staff. Dusty tried to be a little funny about it until she saw the look of medico-legal anxiety on the R.N.'s face that her lie had evoked.

To defuse her remarks, Dusty lightheartedly improv'd, "She asked me to call Hillary Clinton and Ruth Bader Ginsburg! Has this sort of thing ever happened before?"

When she stepped through the door, a barefoot Allegra, gorgeously disfigured by a crying jag, padded over, startling her. Dusty was able to say "What is it?" before her wife's mouth ended the inquiry. She was overcome by the throaty, familial fragrance of Allegra's membranes, embargoed since miscarriage.

She towed Dusty upstairs, everything pounding, her hunger corny and romantic, yanking her along by sheer youth, the look on her face like that of a thousand movie action heroes risen from the depths to pierce the glassy sea, choking on oxygen under reclaimed citadel of sky. Blood-lungs aerated, they dove deep into bed, fastening mouths to deltas and coral reefs like parched divers buddy system—leeching on scuba masks—having their fill, surfacing again above breathless waters, now face to face, eye to eye, muzzles still other-dusted, on land now at last, tongues dancing round a bonfire made from waisted frictions:

Celebrants on a criminal's High Holiday.

On Saturday, Dusty threw a dinner party in Trousdale. The dislocation between them was still profound but the renewal of physical vows had kindled a semblance of normalcy—a tenuous cessation of hostilities, anyway, with a tang of the good ol' days. The get-together was a small coming-out of sorts (they hadn't really been social for months) attended by Jeremy, Larissa, Marilyn, Tuesday, and Dusty's forever hair guy Patrice.

Patrice had a passé but fun Heathcliff look, all broody-gaunt and windswept rocker, swathed in beat-up motocross leather. Jeremy said, "You look just like Artaud!" (He knew the reference would be lost but didn't care.) The laconic hairdresser possessed a vacant, guru-like open-heartedness that pulled guests into its gravitational field whenever a place opened up on the couch beside him. Marilyn's long, respected career in New York theater preceded her fairly recent successful run as a character actress in film. She was single at the moment, a tough New Age cookie known for her storied marriages to celebrated, difficult men, and reminded Allegra of the cracked, charismatic earth mothers she'd met in the caravan of her cultish travels. Marilyn and Larissa were the same age with the same kind of sunflowery, gregarious energy, though the stand-in, ever mindful of her place in the firmament, erred toward *holding back*. When Dusty joined the ladies for an impromptu boogie, Jeremy, in an aside to Allegra, said, "Those three broads are a real pussy riot."

It was the first time Tuesday had been to the house, and the guests were starstruck. Dusty liked throwing a wild card into her party mixes, like Dylan (a Point Dume neighbor) or J. K. Rowling (Dusty called her "Joey") when she was in town; she adored watching the look on the faces of the unsuspecting when she made out-of-the-blue, ultra-downplayed, homespun introductions to sundry unnerving, nearly mythic folk heroes. Allegra had a long-time Tuesday Weld fetish—Ann-Margret, Joey Heatherton, and Yvette Mimieux were satellites around that moon—and of course knew that Tuesday would be there tonight. (She was Dusty's old friend and sometimes joined the couple for dinner at Matteo's.) Allegra also knew how fabulously freaked Jeremy would be to meet her—he was more into Tuesday than she was, if that was even possible—and impishly withheld the surprise.

When he laid eyes on Ms. Weld, he went stone-cold giddy, inanely shouting "T.G.I.T."!—*Thank God It's Tuesday*—over and over.

Halfway through the party, he called Allegra into a bedroom. He'd snuck away to find a clip from *Play It As It Lays* but uncovered a crazy Roddy McDowall home movie on YouTube instead: Malibu beach, circa 1965. A bikinied Tuesday, around thirty but looking ten years younger, scrutinized a dragonfly on a windowsill with wide-eyed, virginal wonder. The very loaded Allegra couldn't believe the magical, soundtrackless majesty of what they were watching: a hairless Kirk Douglas lolled on the deck in a scanty swimsuit, a sunlit caliph, as the waves crashed behind him—endless OMG-miracle of the Internet!—as Lauren Bacall made an entrance in prototypical erotic/sardonic splendor—followed by a passel of towheaded surf kids then a bearded Paul Newman then Janice Rule and Jane Fonda—holy *shit*—a parade of shades and sylphs on a stolen prehistoric Colony afternoon, locked and loaded for futureworld's iMasturbatory viewing pleasure. And Jane was *still* getting it up for a party—Allegra sat with her and Taylor Schilling at a gala not too long ago, vaping hash oil, super-present and *alive* and going on *eighty* . . . still *sexy*. Allegra marveled at the *energy*, the *drive*. It was crazy! True movie stars were like vampires that way.

There was a noticeable lull when she and Jeremy returned.

Tuesday was sitting by herself, spacey and contemplative. She was past seventy now and grossly overweight. There was something reserved and melancholy about her, a quality of being mortal, spiritually wounded, spent, as if living on borrowed time since she'd solved the riddle of the dragonfly, and had the follow-up realization that nothing else would be revealed. Allegra was about to make an overture when Tuesday announced to no one in particular that she'd never had plastic surgery.

"I don't have any lines in my face because I'm *fat*. You lose wrinkles when you're fat."

Jeremy spoke up, his face shiny with disposable intimacy. A zealous serf in the kingdom of Future Anecdote, he decided to ask about Elvis. Their legendary alliance was well known, but when the fuck else would he get the chance to hear about it firsthand?

"I was at a party," said Tuesday, "and someone kind of grabbed me and walked me over. But Elvis didn't say anything so I got bored. I did what I used to when I got bored—went to the kitchen, opened the fridge, and let the cool breeze blow." Jeremy's eyes bugged from his head like an ecstatic devotee. "He walked in and said, 'Hungry, little girl?' I remember what I was wearing: toreador pants, sandals with heels, and a windbreaker tied around my neck. A tight periwinkle sweater. He wore black. I was sixteen."

It was a killer story, even if the details were too perfect, too rehearsed. Allegra and Jeremy traded glances with the same thought: *Did she write a memoir that we missed?*

Need to Amazon that . . .

Dusty and the others joined them. Marilyn caught the tail end and said, "*Sixteen?* Where were you *living?*"

Allegra thought it was a goofy question but whatever.

"The Hollywood Hills," said Tuesday. "With my mother. We had a split-level and I told her I needed my privacy. I was starting to *bully* her—you know, threaten that I wasn't going to *act* anymore. Her *ultimate nightmare* because I was the woman's only source of income. I told her I'd *leave* if she didn't build this *floor* over the stairs that led to the lower part of the house, where I had my room. To wall it off.

So she did—and I had a separate entrance for my friends! Lenny Bruce lived really close. We used to do peyote together. I saw Elvis at night and Lenny during the day."

It was almost too much for Jeremy to take—like one of those wack plays from the sixties where Jean Harlow meets Billy the Kid. (Allegra noticed Dusty's and the stand-in's arms "randomly" touching; Larissa had tangles of red hair there). He tried getting Tuesday to talk about Lenny but she wouldn't. She suddenly shut down; she was funny that way. An element of paranoia could drive her to abruptly curtail reminiscence, as if an invisible lawyer had told her to say no more.

The peyote mention got Marilyn riffing on mushrooms. She said that on the last winter solstice, she went "journeying" in New Mexico.

"That's amazing!" said Dusty, drunker than Allegra had seen her in a while. "I've always wanted to go to Burning Man," she added, apropos of not very much. "But I think I'm too *old* for that shit."

"My daughter wants to go," said Larissa. "She's been on a *campaign*. I said, When you're eighteen!"

"How old is she?" said Tuesday.

"Thirteen."

"Almost old enough for Elvis," said Jeremy. He was really high. Tuesday winced. "Burning Man is insanely great," he said authoritatively, as if to clear the air of flip sacrilege.

"I would *totally* go if you want to," said Allegra to Dusty, and she meant it. Going to Burning Man together sounded like the bestest, onliest idea in the history of the world.

"You would *love* it," said Jeremy. "We had a trailer and a driver— the whole thing was, like, four grand including tickets. For three of us. Or you can do the "Über-slash-Pinterest-camp-Sherpa-helicopter thing."

"What *is* burning man?" said Tuesday.

Jeremy sweetly broke it down for her à la the Idiot's Guide, as a kind of amends for being naughty about Elvis.

"I think it'd be *amazing*," said Marilyn. "We should *all* go; wouldn't that be so crazy? All my friends say it's *totally life-changing.* If you're over fifty, there's kind of a shame factor though, right? The Madonna Syndrome? I mean, no one wants to be *pathetic.* But *apparently* I still need to do my counterculture, rich-hippie thing."

"*Love* me a rich hippie," said Dusty. "So you did ayahuasca?"

"Not ayahuasca, *mushrooms.* I'm fucking *terrified* of ayahuasca! I do *mushrooms* with this amazing herbalist and *bruja*, in Taos. I try to do it every three years. You know, for a tune-up with the Goddess."

"On the solstice?" said Larissa, throwing in.

"Uh huh. It was *amazing.*"

"What *happened*?" said Dusty, eyes aglow and leaning in, leg pressed against Larissa's.

"Well, it's always—whenever I take mushrooms, there's always this *palace*, I kind of go to this *palace*, like, where the Goddess lives. I go into this palace, with all these *rooms* and *courtyards*, and—*festivals.* There's all these *festivals* going on . . . like Burning Man probably! Ha! But *oh my God*, these *festivals*, with this *music* and *drumming.* There was *one*—I remember there was one that had a *procession*, made up of this . . . *triumphant battalion of women* who never had *children*—"

Dusty didn't flinch but Allegra did. She figured Marilyn was too blazed to register her borderline faux pas, before quickly hypothesizing that the gal actually might not *know* about the miscarriage. Yet how would that even be possible? Dusty and Marilyn were obviously close—plus all those shooting days that needed to be rearranged when Allegra got "sick." Of *course* she would have known, or at least found *out*, whether Dusty told her or not . . . it suddenly felt sucky and appalling to Allegra that she'd been too self-involved to have bothered asking her wife about whatever cover story she'd decided to use—or if in fact she'd simply told everyone the truth.

"—which was, like, incredibly *healing* for me because I never had kids . . . some of the strongest, most beautiful women I know haven't. The Goddess was trying to tell me it's *impossible* to be 'childless'—you know, the moment a woman is born we already have countless children, like, even *before* we're born . . . countless children and mothers are contained within, you know, we're *multitudes*. But the world says we're *less*-than, if for whatever reason we *don't* have kids, which is *so* deeply fucked! 'Have'! And they have to be *biological*! If you don't have a *biological* child, it's just not *real*! Too bad for you, you're not a *real mother*! And I just, on the mushrooms, I just sort of dip into these *courtyards*, in and out of these *rooms* . . . these mush-*rooms*—they're like *kingdoms* or *battlefields*. And I remember there was this *province*—this 'protectorate'—that's a word I *totally* never used before this last journey; the Goddess must have given it to me—this *protectorate* of villages and *townships* or *whatever*, filled with those who cannot protect or fend for themselves."

"Oh my God!" said Dusty. "That is *so beautiful*."

"It's one of the most sacred places! I mean, it was to *me*. And it's—I was just *so honored* to be there. In that presence."

"I can't believe that you go and do this," said Dusty, in awe. "You are so courageous, Marilyn!"

"I'd never be able to," said Larissa.

"I didn't think I could either. But if you met my guide, you would *totally* change your mind."

"We should all *do it*!" said Dusty, with can-do cannabis-vaping energy. "Like, a women's workshop! Leggy, should we do it?"

"I *love* it," said Allegra. "We should go tomorrow!"

"I think it would make me sad," said Larissa.

"And after a meditation about *Mom*," said Marilyn, "I said to my guide—"

"How do you even *remember* all this?" said Dusty, still awed.

"I took notes! I had someone taking notes in case I said something good!"

"Amazing!"

"You're incredible."

"I said to the *bruja*—about my mother—'What a terrible bind she was in. What a terrible bind we're *all* in.'"

"You *said* that? That is *so incredible*."

"And the Goddess had me dance with my mother! It's like you're literally *dancing*. And in that moment I was a thousand percent certain the whole fuckin' deal with this crazy life began and ended with her. Of *course* it does, right? Because she's my *mother*, I came from her *body*, how could it *not*. But then my *father* cuts in—Daddy tapped my shoulder and took her place—then I'm dancing with *him* and suddenly I'm a thousand percent certain *he's* the one! *He's* the key to the mystery! So I'm dancing with Daddy then *Mom* cuts in again and I'm dancing with *her* . . . *everyone likes to have their dance*. I remember saying that, telling them to write it down: 'Everyone likes to have their dance.'"

Tuesday was the first to leave.

Patrice escorted her because she was worried about falling on the slopey steps. Dusty thought that by the time they got to her car he'd have booked a house call for her hair. Good—she could probably use a friend like Patrice, and a little styling wouldn't hurt either. Marilyn and Jeremy left soon after. Jeremy had a hot date with "a special boy" he'd been seeing. (She couldn't tell if he was being ironic.) She felt a tug of possessiveness.

Dusty took Larissa on a belated tour while Allegra stayed downstairs, sidetracked by email.

"Your house is so beautiful."

"It's a Neff. Took me *three years* to restore. I was going to flip it. Pink wanted to buy it, she *begged* me, but I couldn't bear to part with it."

"It's just so gorgeous."

"Thank you. You okay?"

She'd picked up on Larissa's distractedness.

"No! I mean yes!" They laughed. "I'm just—I guess I'm just a little nervous. Shy, maybe?" She squinted at her inscrutable hostess. "I feel a certain energy coming from you."

"And what do you think about that?" said Dusty, perversely reminding herself of Ginevra.

"I don't know," she said. "I'm not sure! I guess I'm not used to it. The attention?"

"Well, you should be. Because you're fucking hot."

"I am?"

"Oh come on, Larissa! You *know* you are. It's kinda criminal if you don't."

"I wish my husband would have thought so!"

"Not worthy, babe."

She continued her improbable docent chores as they walked onto the bedroom terrace—the architectural influences behind the unique bespoke balustrades, the months-long search for the perfect shade of ochre—but the fix was in and Larissa had gone deaf. Dusty took in the Trousdale sky and said, "Full moon." Larissa said, "Of *course* it is," and the heavenly body seemed to wink its endorsement of her imminent abandon. "I keep forgetting to give you your earring—" At the end of the ambushed kiss, Larissa still couldn't breathe. She sneezed a laugh like a cork blowing off, and thought the outburst ugly. Dusty smiled like a mystic and the double felt her own wetness. They came together again but this time the moon was indifferent, a chaperone on leave.

When Allegra got back, they were dancing. Dusty was still dressed but Larissa was topless; all night long the young wife had prepared for this, inoculating herself against jealousy. Seeing her, Larissa covered her breasts in modesty, taking some comfort in the assumption the duo had enacted this scenario many times before (she would never know how wrong she was). She knew she was in good hands. Allegra welcomed Dusty's maverick impulse because she'd been feeling so guilty over how she had treated her these last few months. There was something dangerously sexy about it too, because they were in uncharted waters. Sometimes bringing in another person was a point of no return.

Dusty changed into a robe while the others danced. Allegra kissed Larissa's neck, watching the carotid pulse like a samba-school *Carnaval*—fiftysomething virgins were the wildest of tigers. She moved to the double's mouth and got an amateur's sloppily passionate response. Dusty reemerged and stayed where she was, to observe. Allegra took their guest by the hand and led her to bed. She draped up her skirt, tugged at her panties, and ate her. Larissa literally shouted and staccato-wept. After a while, Dusty knelt by the bed and stroked Larissa's hair. She kissed her face and said, "It's okay, it's okay," like a hypnotist. "It's just a *festival*. Big festival in the palace . . ." Then: "What was the word? What was the word the Goddess gave Marilyn?" Larissa struggled to find it amid the butchery, finally whispering, "Protectorate." Dusty said, "Yes!" and kissed her some more and said, "A *protectorate* . . . it's just a *protectorate*. Can you hear the drums? Babe?"

The film crew alit in a cemetery.

Video village was tucked behind a mausoleum. Bennett sat in front of his monitor, waiting. Dusty and Bonita stood before the grave. Ted Hughes's casket was poised for a third-take lowering. (Liam wrapped three days ago and was already in Europe, on another picture.) Marilyn sat on a canvas chair near the director. She wasn't needed until the next scene, an insert of her surreptitiously watching the ritual from her car, but wanted to be there for Dusty's last shot.

Bennett called action and the mechanism lowered the casket.

Bonita threw a rose into the pit. "Good-bye, Papa."

The camera pushed in on Dusty as she declaimed a poem beneath her breath:

"Whoop dee-do, the oven's clean, of you and me and toddler shouts. Cooked too long, it all burned up—the swastikas and brussels sprouts."

"And *cut.*"

The director nodded to the First, who cautioned, "Checking the gate!" After a beat, the D.P. nodded all clear and the First shouted, "Ladies and gentlemen, Dusty Wilding is wrapped!"

Yips, applause, and whistles from the crew—Dusty got emotional. She'd been doing this a lifetime but was always surprised at how those traditional, cracker-barrel announcements moved her. "Oh my God," she said. "I'm so sad! I don't want it to end." She hugged everyone, saving Bennett for last.

Larissa hung back, ceding to awkwardness—they hadn't really seen each other since the palace coup—then made the immodest error of subtly stepping forward to be wrap-acknowledged as Dusty headed back to her trailer.

The star averted an encounter by stagily chatting up one of the pilot fish who was escorting her, and just kept moving.

They ate dinner at home. Dusty was brittle and quiet.

"Is there going to be a wrap party?" said Allegra solicitously.

"They're not done till next week."

(Leggy had the scary new feeling that Mama'd had enough of her. She talked to Jeremy about it; he said she was nuts.)

Best defense being a strong offense, Allegra said, "You know, I was thinking about the Lake District, for *Bloodthrone* . . . it might actually be kinda great"—the words emerging from that sly, lopsided grin that once so ensorcelled.

"I just don't know my dates yet."

"That's okay," said Allegra, laid back and accommodating, trying to be okay with Dusty being a cold, hostile bitch. "And, oh! I didn't tell you—I got an agent, for my photographs." (No response; the engine wouldn't turn over.) "Vasha Bowska. Do you know Vasha?"

"Nope."

"She says she knows you. Vasha's a friend of Riccardo? Tisci? I think maybe you might have met in Berlin? At the festival? Anyway, she wants to have dinner with us. Would you be cool with that?"

"Yup."

"Bunny, are you okay?"

"I'm fine."

"You seem so far away."

"I always get like this when I wrap. You know that."

Allegra bit the bullet. "Can we talk about the other night?"

"Do we have to?"

"*Kind* of. Are you okay with what happened?" It was her unadvised nature to sometimes barrel forward—another thing that once ensorcelled. "I know that a 'third party' isn't really something we've been into . . ."

"'Isn't really,'" said Dusty, tartly.

"I guess I was just . . . finally feeling in my body again."

"Well, good for you!"

"Hey, don't be like that."

"You don't have to defend yourself for having an orgasm, Allegra."

"I'm not defending, I'm just . . . *talking*. Look, I thought you were into her."

"I'm not 'into' anybody," she said, sideswiping.

"When I came in, you were already fooling around! I mean, I thought . . . you *knew* I'd be coming in. I thought that was something you *wanted*. And I'm not *blaming* you, Dusty—"

"Thank you!"

"—I know I've been *horrible*. I've been a total selfish bitch and I don't blame you for wanting—"

"Can we be done now? I *really* don't want to talk about this!"

"Okay," she said, pouty and stung. "Fine. I just wanted to tell you that *I* got into it only because I thought *you* were into it. It's not something I'm all that interested in pursuing."

"'All that.' Well, okay, *good*. Good for you! I mean, duly noted. Whatever. It's fine."

"—and I'm *apologizing* for my fucked-up behavior." Her eyes brimmed with tears. "Because I know I haven't been so easy to live with. And I just want to make sure we're okay."

"We're fine." She smiled, mercifully softening, and touched Allegra's hand. "And I *am* looking into the Lake District. I'm *on* it. Okay?"

"Okay."

When she kissed her cheek, Allegra laid her head on Dusty's shoulder and began to cry. Dusty caressed the small of her back, softly shushing.

She was being honored again, this time by Hyacinth House. When Livia asked for help, Jeremy reached out to friends for $35,000 buy-ins—the Katy Perry table, the Jada Pinkett Smith, the Annapurna, the Moonves, the bla.

Between calls, from the aerie of his Nichols Canyon office (it sat above a creek), he thought about his life.

I love him.

But what the fuck was he doing with a wonky little twink he met on Scruff?

Tristen was odd, prickly, smart. Jeremy supposed he was fathering the boy (in a fashion)—though he knew better than to call it mentoring, he insisted to himself that it wasn't *sick*. And anyway, the warmth of their love and the tenderness of their sex helped salve the heart pain awakened by the death of his baby. That's right: *my baby*. His shrink told him not to minimize it, even to say it out loud—*my baby died!*—to ward off the disconnect that, all his life, had come so easily.

The force of his grief wound up taking him by surprise—the mid-morning sobs and muttered daytime prayers. His subsequent, adamant resolve to try again made him feel virtuous and mature.

The miscarriage felt like some kind of payback on a karmic debt. In his darkest hours, it seemed a just punishment for not having taken full responsibility as a parent; his paternal excitations had been more those of a groupie looking forward to the endless, official perks of a permanent blood alliance with the Wilding dynasty. Fatherhood was only another word for sperming his way into a jackpot; postmortem, he felt stained—stained!—by the pride of provenance and all that went with it. As part of the healing process, he came to view such corrosive self-characterization as simply another indulgence. *It is what it is.* Everything happened for a reason. No matter how many cretins had said it, it was inalterably true.

Still, he was shaken. Moody. Aggressive. Weepy. The shrink got busy, tweaking his psych meds. Jeremy had a healthy fear of "the black dog" and didn't want to leave any food out for it. Twice it had chased him—once in college and once when his mom and sis were killed by the drunk. He never wanted to be running from the black dog again. Ever.

The reenergized mission of becoming a dad brought solace. He visualized his *offspring* (with alternating genders) at different ages— watched it being born—saw himself beside it during the scrapes, sicknesses, and convulsive tears of childhood, the travesties of adolescence, the heartaches and false starts of young adulthood—even imagining himself in hospice, cancer'd or by natural causes, chemohairless or wildly white-bearded, ministered to by the one he'd so stalwartly loved, shepherded, and nurtured with father's milk. The poignant slideshow made him feel part of that great collective: the family of man. He didn't want to approach Allegra about a do-over, not only because he sensed it was way too soon for her to go there (or that intuition told him she'd miscarry again), but for the larger reason that he needed to move *now*, in response to a sense of urgency he couldn't explain. Some sort of fuse had been lit and he was raring to go. What spun him was thinking about how awkward it would be when it came time to tell Allegra he was pregnant—he should probably let Dusty know first. Maybe he wouldn't tell *either* of them until the surrogate was six months along. That was probably the best strategy.

He headed to the Plummer Park A.A. meeting. He'd made plans to talk with his old sponsor, who recently had twins. He was walking toward the clubhouse when he saw them—travelers on a bench, basking in the sun.

The woman was in her thirties, lovely and plain, a blond hippie with grey-green eyes. Her companion was a bearded Scottish colossus, burly and red-faced, twice her age. She wore a threadbare cotton sundress, its brilliant colors faded. A bracelet of bells, much larger than they should have been for that sort of thing, was tied to her ankle with a leather cord like a medieval ankle monitor. Her dignified friend raffishly boasted—that would have been the word— an Edwardian morning coat over silken pajamas, an appropriate uniform, so it seemed, for his pastime of smiling toward the ether in divine abstraction.

Something drew Jeremy in.

Uncharacteristically, he approached to ask if he could sit with them. The woman said, "Please do!" The old man looked into Jeremy's eyes with kindness before directing his gaze, fervid yet impassive, back to sacred horizons. Joining them on the bench, he took in the Scot at a glance: the pasty, wasted epidermis, the greasy pompadour, the flecks of food in his whiskers, trapped like insect exoskeletons in a web.

The hippie lady said, "I knew you would come. *Knew* it."

"As a sitting, *active* board member—and all-around angel—the effect of the work she has done for the House and its children is impossible to quantify."

The evening's formidable director and hostess, Livia Lindström, was wrapping up her emotional remarks. Dusty had asked one of the fashion houses to loan her old friend a gown and Livia felt awkwardly glamorous. No one knew of her discomfort; she was a chic, vibrant sixty-three-year-old woman who reminded everyone how beautiful the species could look, *au naturel*. In L.A., the ones her age who hadn't gone under the knife were nearly extinct.

"Not just through her heroic fund-raising efforts—which in the foundation's early years literally sustained us—but through her unique and pioneering role in public education, raising the bar *and* public awareness for L.A.'s then burgeoning, now *flourishing* LGBT community. Please dim the lights!"

The audience focused its attention at the large screens to watch a montage of the actress interacting with the Hyacinth staff and challenged children, in private and public venues, down through the years. Celebrities and studio executives sat closest to the dais. At the "family" table were Dusty (backstage just now) and Allegra, Jeremy, two longtime volunteers, and a girl whose mother was in prison for molesting her while under the influence of meth. After parental rights had been severed, the foundation orchestrated the teen's adoption by a wealthy couple, who were at the table as well. The lights came up.

"Ladies and gentlemen," said Livia, "please welcome the most beautiful of Hyacinth's 'founding flowers'—our very own Dusty Wilding!"

All rose as the star made a luminously diffident entrance from the wings. Livia took a dainty, deferential step backward; Dusty warmly chastised by bringing her in for a hug before turning to face the cavernous room. She let them love her awhile, then pantomimed "sit."

"Nothing," she began, after dramatically gathering herself, "*is* or *remains* more important to me than Hyacinth House. I have been *privileged* to have grown up among *so many selfless people* who, with their sacrifice, their compassion, their consistency and single-mindedness of *purpose*, who with their *hearts* have been instrumental in transforming—*saving*—*thousands* of at-risk young people. Not just by providing them shelter from the storm—sanctuary from harm—but by literally *rescuing* them, *many* of them, rescuing this precious, vulnerable re-source from dangerous, often *life-threatening* circumstances beyond their control. And I want to say *very* clearly . . . that I have been a soldier, *not* a general. Hyacinth has nourished me and fed my soul. I've tried to be a good soldier . . . and a *mother* as well. And *I* have been mothered too—sometimes rescued!—by the amazing Livia and her extraordinary staff, by the amazing volunteers and amazing fund-raisers, by the amazing judges and attorneys—yes, attorneys *can* be amazing! (*laughter*) And most of them are women! (*more laugh-ter, applause, whoops*) I want to thank all of the 'friends of Hyacinth' too—I like to call them the garden where our flowers grow—who've worked *so* very hard and *continue* to perform miracles within our often very unmiraculous court and legal system." She steeled herself, in anticipation of the next few words. "And when I say I have been mothered, it was *by the children themselves.* They have enriched my life in ways they can never know. They have been my *lighthouse* and taught me how to love in ways I never could have dreamed, never could have expected. And are walking with me now, on my own jour-ney . . . (*the cryptic inference was meant for no one but herself*) So I'd really like everyone to stand—there are lots of 'flowers' out there, and I want them all to be seen. It's a beautiful garden! A sea of hyacinths!— can we please rise? Would everyone who belongs to the House in *any* capacity please stand? Come on—*everybody* stand. Everybody! Lights up!"

She suggested Livia drop by the house to return the gown, an impromptu feint that somehow lightened the burden of what she was about to reveal.

Marta brought them tea by the pool.

"Was the night a smash?" asked Dusty.

"Three and a half million dollars!"

"Isn't that wonderful?"

"That's a high-water mark. Because of *you*."

The actress waved that away. "Are we getting a new building?"

"That's a conversation I'd really like to have," said Livia. "You know, the *old* building isn't so bad! We can do a little cosmetic work and still have *so much* left over for things that just seem more real."

"Okay!"

"I keep thinking, *Why?* We're not a *hospital*, you know; we're not Children's Hospital, where there's a *need* . . . we're not *MOCA* or *LACMA* either. We can always use more space, there are people who want to *give* us space. But I've seen too many foundations take a tumble over real estate."

Suddenly something shifted in Dusty and her guest took note.

"What's wrong?"

"Livia . . . we've spoken about this over the years—not a lot, but we have. And you know there's some shame—a *lot* of shame—over how I've chosen . . . how I *chose*—to *handle* it. I've been so—I've tried to be courageous in my life, but this, this as you know, is an area where I've failed."

She knew straightaway what Dusty meant.

"But you *didn't*—you didn't fail. You *haven't*. You made a choice."

"—and it's okay. I'm okay with what I did, I really am. But I'm not that person anymore, the person I was when I made that 'choice.' Or whatever you want to call it. I'm not that sixteen-year-old girl any-more. Though sometimes I *feel* like her! Anyway, I'm making *another* choice now—a *real* one—because I think it's time. I've been with the House for twenty years—I've grown up with you. *She* brought me to you. Everything I do, Livia, everything that *motivates* me, in my *life*—has been because of *her*." She breathed deeply. "And . . . I think I want to find her now, Livia. I want to try to find her."

"Oh, Dusty."

Livia's smile belied her emotions. She resisted leaning in to hug her friend; she didn't want to whitewash the moment with sentimentality. She'd always looked up to her—Dusty was a great woman, a fearless woman—and felt so moved to be included in such intimacy.

"I know it sounds totally crazy but I actually do try to keep my life private. Some of it, anyway. *You've* seen that. And it's a lot of work! But I've pretty much decided that . . . I want to make this 'journey'—*hate* that word!—that I'd like to do it in front of the world. In front of a camera. *Total transparency.* And it's not an ego thing. I just think it might really help people. Not just the ones who're searching for their kids or for the kids who're searching for their parents— but for *anyone* who wants to speak their truth but can't find their voice. For whatever reason. That's why I want to document it. I have some ideas about that and I want to hear yours."

"Of course!"

The mood lightened, becoming almost festive.

"I don't know if it's an HBO thing or whatever . . . but I *would* like the proceeds to go to Hyacinth. And I want to do it hand in hand with *you*, I *need* you to be my *partner* . . ."

This time Livia couldn't restrain herself and began to weep. Dusty went to her and the two cried together.

"It'll be frickin' *scary* but I think it'll be *amazing*. I *know* it will be. I even reached out to Laura Poitras—the gal who did the Snowden movie? She's *amazing*. I'm not sure she'll do it but I think she's definitely *intrigued* . . . The timing might be good because she's kind of taking a *hiatus* from the *heavy shit*. Did you know she spent *years* worrying they were going to break down the door and arrest her? Though maybe the critics *will* arrest her, after she does our little film!"

"I think it's going to be really important, Dusty."

"Right? Ya think?"

"I'm just so honored."

"I'm gettin' butterflies! You've pretty much been my therapy all these years, Liv. You and the foundation *totally* paved the way for this—I really think meeting all those kids was like . . . a *rehearsal* for meeting *her*. And . . . some part of me thought she'd walk through those doors one day—I think that was in my head, for real. Isn't that funny? That I thought for sure one day I'd bump into Aurora . . . did I ever tell you that was her name?"

"No," she said, with a mother's tenderness. "It's so beautiful."

"Strange. That I never told you that."

She said the name again aloud, like a conjurer.

Tristen, twenty-three, a slight-of-build outlier type with acne scars on his neck, but *cute*—nonstandard-edition cute. A Crossroads alumnus who ran with the Brentwood/Palisades crowd before getting outclassed, outlapped, outed, and outrun.

(His folks, fringy showbiz aspirants/below-the-liners.)

Back in the Ritalin folly of youth, a genius troll who called himself "AssDoxxtorFill" online—definition of *doxx* (short for *documents*) being "to search for and publish the private or identifying information of individuals on the Internet, typically with malicious intent." He became a bandit anarchist on the 4chan imageboard's wild and woolly so-called */b/forum*, part of a rowdy nihilistic gang of hacks who called themselves "/b/tards." In the electronic havoc of finding others, he found himself.

Do not ask for whom the /b/tards troll; they troll for thee . . .

Tristen made his bones in mayhem and sundry Web *motherfuckery* way back in 2006, not too long after All Souls' Day, when a coke-bingeing teen 100-mph-joycrashed her father's Carrera into a toll booth (troll booth soon enough) on an Orange County highway, becoming a legendary Internet phenom after CHP dispatchers adventitiously leaked official photos of the gory results to the Web. Nikki Catsouras's goopy face, a work of abstract, accident-scene art in a pre-hashtag-days atrocity exhibit, had spookily retained its luxuriant hair, the superglued coiffure of a demon; her teeth cornrowed in the cranium's middle like a double helix. The steering wheel, a warpy airplane travel pillow, collared around her neck, her skull resembling a child's papier-mâché version of one of those spiritual bookstore half-bowl anthracite crystals. The dead girl was Tristen's christening, his ritual coming of rage as a player in the genre called "RIP" trolldom— using a filter to deepen his voice, he rang up her grieving parents and impersonated an official who claimed to be spearheading an investigation into rumors that unholy acts had been perpetrated upon their daughter's corpse by lady sheriffs and various family members of the coroner, and to assert that the body had been further, if virtually, desecrated by kinky Comic-Con aficionados, supposedly given access via premium morgue-camera pay-per-views.

Why did he do it? "For the LULZ"—definition of *lulz* being the trickster's version of *for laughs*, i.e., same as LOL, but with the pirate flag of motherfuckery flying.

The Catsourases were too stunned to hang up, which Tristen thought awesome, because it implied no one *else* had called, not yet anyway, and meant he was surfing the first-wave riptide of pranks that would keep pulling the bereaved under until the Internet End of Days. He spent a week lovingly accessorizing a mannequin's head *Fangoria*-style before sending it chez Nikki, having already mic'd a windowsill so that when Mrs. Catsouras opened the hatbox left on the porch (with a flowery card that implied it was a condolence from one of her daughter's anguished friends), she flipped as hard as Brad Pitt at the end of *Se7en*. Tristen posted the wailing soundbite, a caprice that, to his dismay, caused him to receive a small but significant amount of shit from his comrades, whose self-touted fearless amorality apparently had its limits. *Poseurs and hypocrites*—they were turning into body-snatched TEDxTeen pussies before his very eyes . . .

He got bored, vaulting over Nikki's cadaver to whitewater-raft the BitTorrents of spring—"spring" going by the name of Matthew, a thirteen-year-old who inexplicably hanged himself in Rochester, Minnesota. Valiantly struggling to process the senseless death, imponderable at any age but a jarring novelty to tweens, a clique of pubescent Matthew survivors crafted a poignant memorial page on MySpace, extolling their friend with charming ineptness, as if he'd been martyred to a cause. When they clumsily called him "an hero" (the eulogizer's heart, if not indefinite article, was in the right place), an inspired meme was born: to RIP trolls, the boy hadn't killed himself, he'd "an heroed"! So genius! The coinage should have been *Tristen's*—envy soaked the un-Google-able recesses of his encrypted heart. In consolation, he designed GIFs on MyDeathSpace of a Matthew-faced Casper doing a floaty jig on a grave while being violated by a Sambo-looking golem. For sheer technical wizardry of slapstick execution, Tristen received high kudos from the very merry band of shit-disturbers—all older than he, and handsomer in their own ways—that had recently shunned him. The sins committed against the Catsouras mom were now forgiven and forgotten.

Yet another period of ADHD boredom ensued, and after all his crazy lone-wolf shit, Tristen was disgusted that he'd subsequently allowed himself to be seduced into hacktivism by the older, more-handsome-than-he manboys. (Their energy and *scent* was responsible for his acquiescence.) Dutifully, he became a mouse in Anonymous—

a *rat*—all the while hating on the do-gooder, high-dudgeon politically correct exposés he got conscripted into: the sight of a Guy Fawkes mask was enough to make him gag. So he bailed again, holing up in his room at the parents' to explore newfound Web-sex thirsts (how he met Jeremy), his doxxing dormant but for sporadic video-design work, hyper-real porn goofs for a seditious, star-baiting website called Celeb Jihad . . . carefully crafting a Kate Upton/Kaley Cuoco-bukkake-facial here, an Ariana Grande/Aubrey Plaza-jerking-themselves-on-the-bed there—

Then came the quantum leap, for which he'd remain forever, happily unattributed: the creation of an event *whorizon*, the great celebrity selfie-porn scandal of August '14 AKA "the Fappening." (Impishly named after *fap*, the onomatopoeic root of jacking off.) Tristen's luck and good fortune astonished—so many others might have laid claim to that prize! So many others had *tried* . . . Embedded in the lining of the net, the Fappening's birth had been inevitable, yet fate and history had chosen *him* to summon the lava flow of exposed taboo bodymaps—Jennifer Lawrence's and lesser cousins'—that verily swamped Old Reality, engulfing the pristine, elitist coastal cities of the lascivious, clay-footed gods of TMZ. JLaw herself! Jennifer *too* had been chosen, but couldn't wrap her head around the perfection of being the figurehead on the evolutionary supership's bow, couldn't *fathom* the ultimate privilege of signifying that dichotomy. Vain and addled, she'd mistakenly believed that *Dior* and *Katniss* and David O. Russell would confer immortality, immunity . . . they *all* thought they could be private whores behind the gates of gilded Beverly Park playpens. But more than their arrogance, what enraged him was the grotesque ignorance of it, the *world's* denial of *spiritus mundi* and the shitstorm audacity of what was coming—what *he*, Tristen, had ushered in. They were all his age, yet still clung to the idea they could "own" their images, passwords, thoughts! The entitled, alt-precious, star-fucking Lena Dunham even delivered a warning (to her constituency of *Girls* and girly men) that to view the cell-phone images he'd unleashed would be at one's peril, for the act was equivalent to a sex crime. Her self-righteous Brooklyn shit was über-Orwellian: chubby, people-pleasing, exhibitionistic Little Sister Is Watching. Couldn't they see it was the HBO Medusa's gaze that would turn them to stone? And leave them in the dustbin of history?

He was consumed by the architecture of that consensual edifice called reality. Months after Tristen conjured his fake GIFs on Celeb Jihad, the net of the Fappening (there were many fishermen now) trawled an *actual* video from Aubrey Plaza's iPhone of her masturbating in front of a bathroom mirror with one leg propped on the counter—the real and the sham, the already-happened, the inchoate, and the never-was were simply different sides of a Möbius strip. He thought of the Baudelaire story of the man who delighted in giving counterfeit coins to beggars—was there really a difference? In the moment, joy was spread to giver and taker. He found the story in the *I Ching* (Hexagram 18—"Correcting the Corruption") even more instructive. In the dead of winter, a dying emperor asked for fresh roses. The armies scoured the entire country but found only one flower each day; the ruler's health returned overnight then plummeted in the morning when it began to wilt. Finally, the court magician presented him a rose that would never die, and the emperor lived to an old age. It was artificial . . .

Privacy wasn't dead, *reality* was—but it sure was tough to kill. His screen-refreshable quote of the moment belonged to P. K. Dick: "Reality is that which, when you stop believing in it, doesn't go away." It would take generations before the swashbuckling daring and seminal importance of the Fappening could be properly measured.

Someday, even his father would see, and be *awed*, and would *know*.

The Dusty Wilding kiss-off threw Larissa into a deep funk.

It wasn't the type of thing she could gossip about with friends. Most of them, anyway. Maybe eventually . . . She didn't have much of a career but didn't want to get blacklisted either. *Could happen.* It wasn't just that, though; it was pride. *I got dumped.* Of course, it wasn't so simple but that was how it felt. Dumped! By a movie star! After losing my virginity!

As if life wasn't fucking hard enough.

Her take on the actress had been so wrong that the heart-stomped stand-in began to question her judgment in general. She chastised herself for letting all those fantasies run wild. At the height of her crush, she imagined becoming part of a celebrity threesome— bellwether of a next-generation cultural trend of ménages à trois "marriages" soon to follow the humdrum glut of gay celeb conjugal couplings. (She even saw herself getting movie roles out of it.) Some of the reason those head-riffs were so compelling was the element of husband-payback. She could just see Derek, alone in bed after being ditched by his nine-year-old girlfriend, flicking on *Hollywood Tonight!* to catch Larissa leaving a paparazzi-swarmed restaurant with her crazy-famous lovers. Of course, *she'd* be famous too . . . *how frickin' great would that be?* The thought of her daughter's shock and embarrassment on learning the news wasn't enough to dismantle the scenario—after all, her dad, with his dalliance, had thrown the first, unsavory punch, and because Larissa's new friends were women, she was certain Rafaela would be more understanding. She had dreamed of the girl finally meeting them and loving them and being loved in return; a new, extended family that would heal her wounds.

Now everything was fucked.

New York Post headlines of her spurning intruded instead:

CAMERA-DOUBLE TROUBLE!
STAND-IN STOOD UP!
GIRLS GONE "WILDING"!
HUMPED-Y *DUMPED*-Y
DUSTED!—

The whole debacle was enough to drive a gal to Tinder.

Back when she was married, she heard hair-raising stories from girlfriends about their online exploits—one gave her the name of the hotel she was about to tryst at with a complete stranger. "If I don't text you in two hours, call the police"! Larissa was glad to be dodging that bullet.

But that was then, and this is what now looked like: only last week she found herself hooking up with a thirty-two-year-old gaffer, in an attempt to wash her brush with greatness (and greatness's hot young wife) from her system. When they kissed, she felt Allegra and Dusty's tongues fencing with hers, like out of some erotic horror movie.

The sound of a key in the lock interrupted her reverie. Now that *Sylvia & Marilyn* was over, she was back to worrying about her troubled son 24/7. Yoga class helped a little but the shame of being played for a fool in an on-set romance made her more susceptible to unease—about the boy's rootlessness, his reckless otherness, his deathwishy life.

Whenever he came to sleep in his old room, she regressed.

Tristen walked in.

She met Laura for an early dinner at Mr. Chow. She hadn't invited Allegra, not because of their recent hassles, though maybe that was part of it. Her "project" was really just too new, and still felt dream-like and precarious. So far, Livia was the only one she'd told—she needed to take baby steps.

"I know better than to ask why you're in town!" said Dusty, with a laugh. She knew the filmmaker probably found all the cloak-and-dagger jokes tiresome, but she couldn't help herself.

"HBO. We're sort of putting something together."

"I love Sheila."

"She's great. Steven's kind of *brokering* the deal."

The word was said ironically; Laura was fun. (A little guarded, yes, but fun.) Though her imposing career had been defined by the keeping of indictable secrets, Dusty found her warm, open, accessible. She was rangy and right around the actress's age, with a downturned mouth like Jeanne Moreau's. The overall effect was of an elegant pio-neer woman and fearless soul sister. Dusty loved her on sight.

"Don't you live in Berlin?"

"I do."

"Would that be a problem? If we—if you decide you want to do this thing?"

"I'm back and forth for a while."

"You know, I was actually kind of shocked you were interested—if you *are* interested, maybe you're not!—I was shocked that you called me *back*. Look: regardless of what *happens*, I'm just *so thrilled* to be having dinner with the amazing Laura Poitras."

"Well, thank you. That's lovely."

"I mean it. I am not worthy!"

"Oh come on now."

"I'm *serious*. After I saw your movie, I thought: *She's the one.* (I've been working up to all this for a while.) It was, like, everything—even my courage to finally decide to *do* this—everything *came together*.

Of course my *next* thought was, There is no friggin' *way*! She's Laura Poitras! And I suddenly felt *delusional*. You know, Oh, *right*! Like, she doesn't have better things to do! I mean, *important* things."

"This *is* important."

"You know what I mean."

"Yes, but everything doesn't have to be—my fundamental interest is in *people*. I don't think of myself as a polemicist or even as someone who makes *documentaries*. I make movies. I'm interested in all *kinds* of stories."

"We don't even know if this *is* a story. *Yet*."

"That's okay. I do a lot of my work like that. Shoot until something crystallizes. And if it doesn't . . ." She smiled and shrugged.

"The *other* thing I thought," said Dusty, "was that people would think it was *overkill*. You know, that having *you* do it would be like using an elephant gun on a—whatever the phrase is."

"Mosquito."

"Mosquito! That's me."

"Hardly."

"And because I'm so . . . *codependent*, I got worried about *you*."

"How so?"

"That people would say, *Are you serious*? You know, *Why?* 'Why on earth would she . . .' '—Oh *man*, from Edward Snowden to *her*?' You know, from this . . . *revolutionary*—to . . . famous-mom-searching-for-long-lost-daughter *Lifetime* movie—that people would think you were *slumming* or sold *out*. That it would 'damage your credibility'—"

"I'm not concerned."

"—because you were bitten by the 'celebrity' bug. Seduced!" Laura laughed and Dusty got embarrassed. "I'm sorry! I know! I'm crazy. But this shit *does* go through my head."

"I get it. But I don't think you should trivialize what you're up to, the journey you're beginning. The search. People will *always* have their . . . perceptions. I've never cared what others might think of my work and my choices. I can take care of myself."

"I know!" she blushed. "I know you can! You're Laura Poitras!"

"Look. Here's the deal. I like to film all kinds of things. I can't control what people think of me, or my work. I want to make the movies I want to make. So after we spoke, I thought: *hmmm*. Okay, *that's* kind of interesting. I let things come to me and, when they do, I pay attention. The truth is, Dusty, you're one of the most political people around, always have been. What you did by coming out—and coming out *when* you did—took an *insane* amount of courage. You're a warrior. And I really remember that moment. It was a huge one for the culture and a huge one for me personally. A lot of things shifted in my life because of what you did. That's why I'm here. And I have a feeling that what you want to do now is just as brave, just as powerful, just as healing—just as *political*, in its way—and that got my attention. Whether I can do this logistically or timewise is something else, but let's see. Does any of that make sense?"

"Yes," said Dusty, eyes welling with tears. "Thank you."

"Wow," said Allegra.

"I know," said Dusty.

"So how long have you been planning this?"

"I wasn't really 'planning'—you mean the documentary?"

"I mean, trying to find her."

She sighed and shook her head. "I think . . . I was just *running*—I ran, ran, ran, for *so* many years. It's . . . *complicated*, Leggy. And I know I never talked about it that much with you, because I couldn't. With anyone—but Ginevra."

"Which is perfect. I knew you needed your space, so it's not like I've been waiting—"

"I know that," she said warmly. "I really do. And I really, *really* appreciate it, babe. It was so important, for me not to feel that pressure. I don't know," she said, touching Allegra's cheek. "It's all so mysterious, right? But *everything's* mysterious. Right?"

"Might just be time to visit Marilyn's *bruja*, huh," said Allegra.

Dusty laughed and said, "*Oh my God, yes.* And have Laura *film* it!"

"We could show it at our own festival—Burning Woman!" They laughed, and it took the edge off. "So, how are you going to begin? I mean, to look?"

"Livia's quarterbacking, as they *say*. And *no one knows*—not Jeremy, not Elise, *no one*. So you gotta *zip* it, 'kay?"

"Of course! Oh Bunny, you are *so brave*, I love you *so much*." They held each other then Allegra said, "Did Livia say how long it would take?"

She shook her head. "I don't even want to *think* about it. I mean, we might not even be able to . . ."

Allegra let her wife's words trail off. "Did you—do you have any . . . like, information?"

Dusty didn't feel like getting into it, so she lied. (Plus, she didn't want things to sound bleak.) "Just the hospital and the time frame— I mean, Liv has access to—she's gonna start exploring what social services were happening back then—agencies or whatever . . . it was the sixties! Did you know she used to be a private eye?"

"*Livia?* Are you serious?" she said, with a shocked smile.

"Yes! A P.I.—private investigator. Still has her license."

"Oh my God, she is *so* Miss Marple!"

"Isn't that amazing? I friggin' *love* it."

"And it'll be for HBO or Netflix or what."

"You know, I'm not sure. I want to say probably HBO? But part of me doesn't want to get ahead of myself. I mean, it's kind of something not so much on my mind right now? I don't want to jinx it! I'm totally feeling superstitious."

"I can't *even*," said Allegra. She reached over and stroked Dusty's flat stomach. "Butterflies, huh. You're a butterfly girl, huh."

"*Beyond*. But they're not really *butterflies* . . . they're more like *doves* or *bats* or—"

"Cats! Does Bunny have kitties in her tummy?"

"With *claws*. No: *hawks*. Bunny has a belly full of baby hawks."

"Goshawks and eagles—little *eaglets*. Prob'ly some in your womb too, huh."

"Yup. That too."

"Tumblin' around. Like she's in there *kickin'* again. Mama's coming to find her and she *knows* and she's startin' to *kick*."

"I've had diarrhea for days."

Bed: Leggy iPads while Dusty coasts on 25 mg of Trazodone HCl, woozily meditating on her life.

Standing on a Greenwich Village balcony, age nineteen, surveying the windswept nonstop cerulean world. That jazzy sunkissed time of firsts: her first play—*The Miss Firecracker Contest*, and first big-city love affair—a *latina*, ten years older (Mark Morris dancer). Her face twitches as she drifts and dreams. How *blessed* she has been, how blessed she *was*—again! (*My precious baby will be born anew*.) *Journeying, journeying, journeying* . . . she envisions her daughter, their first embrace upon reunion. Though not wanting to think too much about how Aurora will look in present/future time: the color of her hair or how she wears it or how she'll dress for their meeting or the shape of her eyes or if they have the same freckles, moles, and skin tags or if she likes the same music or where she's been living all these years or if she's married or divorced and remarried . . . didn't want to over-think. And so, with her oblivious wife screen-scrolling beside her, Dusty flew back on R$_x$ wings to primal NYC scenes: all the tumbled, deflowery moments enshrined in a rush of scent and weltered sound—first subway ride, first fireworks, first sighting of a stinky *Oh my God, is he dead?* sidewalk vagrant . . . first crazy blizzard, first concert (Prince), first Central Park nighttime mouthfuck. She literally saw a bank getting robbed one day, and on another, Yoko leaving FAO Schwarz. And Robin Williams shooting *Moscow on the Hudson*, hey! . . .

Hey? *Say what*—now she's quit the Greenwich balcony, and hears a clamor of soft voices. Music? *Ahhh*: dance party in Brooklyn. No . . . New Orleans? Liam and Livia and Marta are there, and . . . *Martin Luther King*? WTF! Now someone's shaking her. Uh oh. Stop—

The clattering chorus becomes a single voice: Allegra's.

She blinks open her eyes. Her wife's hand is on her shoulder.

"Dusty, Dusty! It just said online that your mom died."

Soon after, a nurse from Sea Bluff called the house to inform.

It was "sudden," she said, and was Dusty coming up? Sometime tomorrow, the actress told her.

By morning, a bare-bones obit appeared on the *Time* and *Us* websites, and just a few others. Not exactly news of the century. Dusty got the expected emails and phone messages. The only one she answered was Elise's. She doubted if Ginevra had yet heard.

Allegra drove. Dusty spoke to her lawyer, who said that one of the kitchen staff texted her sister about the death minutes after it occurred, the sister put it on Facebook, and bla. Dusty waved away the notion of legal action. *Jesus, Jonathan, like I fucking care.* She called her shrink a half hour before they arrived; the conversation was brief. Dusty told Ginevra she didn't feel anything, but didn't feel numb either. As usual, when it came to Reina, she didn't know how she felt.

She went into the viewing room alone.

Her mother lay beneath a white quilt, on a table draped in white sheets, bookended by what looked like delicate miniatures of streetlamps from another time. They seemed borrowed from a prop house; the presentation was theatrical and unexpectedly lovely.

Reina's visage was unlined, bare of makeup. The hair had been brushed so that it hurried behind her, giving an effect of breezy repose. A fine white tendril of scar grew scalpward from each ear, soft-spoken evidence of face-lifts gone by. After those surgeries, no hair could grow on the high temples and the baldness there made for strange, denuded fields, like the tonsure of an anchoress. Her ears were enormous, as if drawn by a caricaturist. (Reina called them "rabbit ears"—that's why the actress bristled when Allegra first called her Bunny.) The lids of the sunken eyes were Rembrandt-dark and beautiful.

Death had fallen for her.

She reached out to touch the cheek she had slapped before stepping back to circle the body. Then sat, stood, and circled again, an antsy ritual of shock, relief, and acclimatization. She wanted her money's worth. She'd had the persistent fantasy that when this time did come, revelation would appear in a softening guise, forgiving and merciful. But there was none of that. Accustomed to editorializing when it came to this woman, she was already "writing" her impressions, crafting the raw, pithy commentary of what she would soon convey to Ginevra in session. Her mother could still wound her, no doubt, though no longer by the spoken word. Seeing the body was like the taking of an important beachhead or the demolition of strategic tunnels or the murder of a prolific sniper; many strongholds still needed to be captured before it could be proven the enemy had truly been neutralized. But it was a good start, and with that realization, Dusty came the closest she could to grace—an apprehension of peace that echoed the cadaver's stillness and signaled the potential end to a lifetime of predation.

Perhaps in such hopeful quietude love resided.

It wasn't lost on her either that the moment she resolved to find her daughter, Reina had died. *That* seemed like grace, real and cosmic. It was a time of inauguration and more: might it be that Dusty slew the dragon by her bold (albeit belated) resolve? It *did* feel like mythology—something she was anxious to talk to her therapist about. A bulletin from the Universe: *Your mother's power will die when your own mother-power manifests in the search for your child.* And when she pulled the sword from that stone, Reina drew her last breath . . .

She left the room to bring in her wife.

Allegra had always wanted to meet her, at least lay an eye on her, out of curiosity if nothing else, but Dusty would only laugh, saying, "That will *never* happen." She was sheepish until the actress took her by the arm and walked her close. She could see her wife in the dead woman's face and suddenly felt like a child, so inferior to these warrior gods, one fallen, the other at the forceful peak of her artistic and retaliatory powers. She felt weak and insignificant, but lucky too. Worthy somehow.

Dusty addressed the corpse with defiance. "You're finally meeting her, *Mom*." She turned to Allegra and said, "I should pry her eyes open and let her have a good look at you."

"Dusty!"

"Well, there she is, Leggy. And for once, she has nothing to *say*. Not an *unkind word* for *anyone*."

Allegra sat respectfully in a chair not far from the body.

Dusty pulled up a stool and spoke to her mother with fierce intimacy. "You'll never meet your granddaughter, Reina." It was like the beginning of an actor's soliloquy, which of course technically, it was. Allegra knew that she meant her grown child, Aurora, but it comforted her to imagine that Dusty was speaking of their own daughter as well—not the one they'd lost, but the one they might still have. "I was *never* going to let that happen when I found her." Adding, for good luck, "*When* I find her. *If* I find her." Then: "I wouldn't bring her to your *grave*. Though maybe I *will*—for a little dance. We can have a little dance and a *pee*—"

"Baby . . ." said Allegra, trying uselessly to settle her.

"Reina—meet *Allegra*. Allegra—meet *Reina*. Meet the young woman—my *wife in marriage*—who's given me *so much* pleasure, *so much* joy! A beautiful person who *knows how to love*. She gave me the joy you *took*. But that's done. It's over. I'm *free*."

On the way out, Dusty told an employee that the directive for cremation was obviously a mistake because her mother was terrified of fire. (A lie.) Obediently cowed by celebrity, the gentleman apologized and changed it on the spot. She said she'd call soon to make arrangements for Reina's ground burial, reconfirming there were to be no services or witnesses, at the deceased's request. (A lie.)

Then she upgraded the coffin to the most expensive, the one made of steel, because she wanted the lifelong claustrophobe sealed in tight for as much of eternity as could be guaranteed. Maybe you could still scream in the afterlife. Who knew? God was full of surprises.

Tristen used to walk, hitch, bus, and Lyft himself around town. He biked and skateboarded for a while too but that got old. Then, for his birthday, Jeremy bought him driving lessons and a new car. (Tristen didn't want to be anyone's sugar baby but accepted the gift as a goof.) He thought it'd be funny to show up at Mom's or Dad's in some doofussy electronic ride.

They drove to the DMV in a brand-new fire-engine-red Honda CR-Z. He passed all the tests. The whole deal made him think of Nikki Catsouras; he had fantasies of himself on a toll road, be-headed. The lulzy image cracked him up.

On the way home, they listened to Sirius. (The car came with it.) A man was talking about how he treated his sex addiction by per-fecting the technique of "masturbating without thought." That way, he avoided the trap of "cheating" on his girlfriend. "I let thoughts of other women come," he said, "but don't stay with them, don't 'own' them. They're just clouds."

Tristen laughed behind the wheel until he choked.

He didn't have a clue how or why he'd bonded with the runic couple from Plummer Park. Bonded with the hippie girl, anyway. She was actually thirty-five.

They'd really only just begun a conversation when the friend that Jeremy was meeting about the surrogate came along and he had to run. Devi asked for his email and he thought that would be the end of it, so it was a surprise when he heard from her. He invited them to an old haunt on Chautauqua, a quiet place for an early supper, and was delighted when she agreed. He found himself thinking it would be nice if she came without her cohort, and wondered what that was about.

She had an aggressively peculiar, somewhat archaic manner of speaking that both confounded and charmed. What was it about her—about both of them, really—that spellbound? It dawned on him that he was attracted to Devi physically. That occasionally happened with women; once or twice he'd even followed through, to mixed results. He wrote about the encounters in his journal, under the chapter heading "Miss Adventures & Other Ms.-haps."

"We were interrupted in the park," she was saying. "You didn't think you'd hear from me again, did you."

"That's true. I didn't."

"If you had the energy—if you *cultivated* what you already *have*— you probably would have known we were *fated* to meet."

"O-kay," he drawled, sweetnaturedly.

"You might *even* have known that this restaurant happens to be *very close* to where my teacher and I are staying."

"Interesting! And who *is* your teacher?"

"My guru!" she said, as if he were being silly. "My 'Sir.'"

"And what does he teach?" he asked, playing a little game of pretend that the Scotsman wasn't present.

"How to cultivate energy."

"Oh, I *see*. Well, I'd very much like to meet him."

"I *think* that can be arranged. He's right here at this table."

"I had a vague suspicion," said Jeremy, smiling at the "Sir." It was just the kind of bizarre back-and-forth he craved. He'd had his share of exotic encounters, back in his salad days.

"My name is Devi."

"I know that!"

"My teacher says it is of *utmost* importance to state one's name before one speaks . . . of certain things."

The oversized gentleman was eating, which seemed to be his favorite (perhaps only) diversion. Using a tiny fork that looked positively dollhouse-scale in his hands—mitts so large, swollen, and slow-moving they reminded Jeremy of Mickey Mouse's gloves in the Macy's parade—he was daintily in the midst of removing clams from their shells. There was numinous glee in the extraction; the outré smile of a mystic never left him. He began to wonder if the fellow was retarded and the girl possibly dangerous. He decided he didn't give a shit. It was all too deliciously outlandish and intriguing.

"I've been traveling with Sir for seven years now. My daughter would be entering puberty, if she had lived; more of that later. Myself, I was born and raised in Urbana-Champaign, Illinois. Father was a physician, Mother a housewife. I had a normal childhood, as they say. My single hobby was guitar. Laura Nyro was my favorite—I was a precocious student of the sixties! I was absolutely *possessed* by her 'Wedding Bell Blues.' I was all about the bells! (More of *that* later too.) I was *extremely* self-disciplined and drew consistently high marks. My plan was to enter medical school and join my father's practice. I was completely devoted to him—devoted to them both.

"As I was saying, my childhood was uneventful. Nothing exceptional happened and nothing exceptional in middle school either. I never rocked the boat. I was prudent in my daily life, blessed with a cautious but cheerful disposition. On graduating twelfth grade, I was accepted to Loyola and moved to Chicago. Leaving home was hard but my parents insisted. They wanted me to have a fine education. As you may know, Loyola was a Jesuit school—I wasn't at all religious and of course no demands were made in that regard. I was at the top of the honors list. I worked weekends in an E.R., helping the nurses as much as I was allowed. It was the happiest time of my life, until my second year of premed, when Mother died."

Jeremy hadn't expected that in the laundry list.

"She must have been so young!" he exclaimed, a little too eagerly.

The strangeness of it all had gotten the better of him. "What happened?"

"A house fire. She was forty-five. If I'd known that her death was only the beginning of my misfortunes, I would have put a bullet through my head. But of course I didn't know *then* what I know *now*."

"And what do you know now?"

"That it's the worst greed to yearn for a different destiny than what we're given. It's a sin, and the tragic flaw of man."

Then just like that, her monologue ended, as if turned off at the spigot. The Scotsman stuffed his face, oblivious. Jeremy had to admit that "Sir"'s glacial uninterestedness, his *not-thereness*, was immensely appealing. On second thought, there seemed to be a great presence behind it.

At this time in his life, feelings of doubt concerning his own judgment pursued Jeremy with fair regularity, and it didn't take much— say, impulsively inviting two freaks he'd met at the park to a fancy watering hole—to lead him to that most inane of philosophical questions, "Who am I?" (With its popular corollary, *And what the fuck am I doing here?*) Perhaps he intuited that Devi had the answer, or at least might be inclined to point him in the general direction.

She must have uncrossed a leg because Jeremy heard the tinkle— more a hollow clank—of a bell. He used its declaration to deflect a looming discomfort. "What are those all about?"

"They were a gift from my Sir."

"But they're so heavy! I saw the marks they made on your ankle. And people stare . . ."

"Do you know the poem 'The Bells'?" she interjected—as if to dismiss his inconsequential remarks.

"Poe?"

"That's right. When I first read it, I nearly blacked out. I'd just turned twelve. Suddenly, into that very ordinary life I described, came something *abnormal*, *unruly*, something fabulous, forbidding, exalted! To say I memorized it would be the palest truth; I *embodied* it, it resided in every cell. I *breathed* those stanzas, they coursed through my veins! That poem was the prayer that set me off to sleep—I recited it *in* my sleep, and awakened to its words upon my lips. During the day it was uttered with each breath, as pilgrims do their guru-given mantras. But *why*? I asked myself that just once and got no answer. For when one has a first love, there can be no interrogation.

"They told us in school that 'The Bells' was about a man who met *his* first love. He married her then witnessed her death by fire, and perished of grief soon after. The poem tells the story of what happened to my parents; it prefigured their deaths. I never thought of myself as morbid, but there's darkness in all children and some of that Gothic metaphor took hold years before it came true. Something *else* mesmerized me, though, less earthbound—I was like a young shepherdess, following the sound of the bells of a lost animal, one she thought was hers yet belonged to nothing and no one. That celestial sound belonged to Silence! My teacher told me that the instant I encountered the poem, I unwittingly entered the world of the esoteric, for which I was well-suited and predisposed.

"I believe that if Mother hadn't died, I would have fulfilled my goal and become a doctor, only to abandon the profession for the path of the *seeker*. (But by then, it may have been too late.) My Sir told me I was in search of *one thing only* since I was small—'the only thing worthy of discovery'—Silence. He said *true* Silence resides everywhere, except in one place: the very bells that seekers insist upon ringing! 'Bells entertain the monkeys,' he likes to say. (He's *very* funny, you know.) Many times my guru has told me that when he *sees* the energetic bodies of human beings with his *third eye*, they uncannily resemble the shape of a bell. The Source formed us that way—the

Source, who delights in that first wild clanging of shrieks that pour from the throat when we're born—the Source, who cries out joyously at life's end too, when the scream of Self and its tintinnabulation of vanities, having rung, pealed, tolled, tickled, tinkled, and gonged its alarum on our breath for a lifespan, returns to the Silence whence it came. So you see, it isn't at all true one can't unring a bell. We are *all* bells, yearning to be unrung—monkeys craving Silence!

"It's the habit of human beings to muddle a simple thing. Take a bell: we convert the *ineffable* into a crude call to faithless prayer, an echo of the ego, unable or *unwilling* to apprehend that its 'sound' represents an entreaty to *soundlessness* and nothing more. We leach out the *mysterium tremendum* of its instruction, for it's our blockheaded nature to make convenient signs and symbols from the Unknowable. The bell's original purpose loses its way, like a love letter in a littered ghetto—just as they say one cannot see a forest for the trees, we cannot see the face of *God* for the bells. We insist on *reminders* to summon us to worship, as if love is a mess hall to which we're subpoenaed only when hungry . . . My Sir has also made the comparison of a prizefighter: punch-drunk in the ring, we feint, wobble, and reel, each round marked by a profane cacophony of bells—and for what? What is the boxer's true prize? A bowdlerized Silence that gives rest from his struggles between rounds, in timed segments so deformed and desecrated they've lost all meaning. Money, power, and perverted love is what we hear ringing . . . The cracked clarion is even on our currency! We troop schoolchildren to see that golden calf: 'Proclaim *liberty* throughout all the land unto all the inhabitants thereof.' How true that is! Yet *still* we miss how close the broken bell is to the mark, for divinity sees glory in the fissure running through it. Would that cast-iron ruin was our sole legal tender—for a bell that cannot be rung is a cousin to Silence!

"The cliché of all seekers is to stubbornly believe that as long as they hear the airy, rippling magic of a bell, they're on the path. Its music, melancholy and light, is seductive no doubt, but the sound is mere incense in a temple. One may enjoy it, even be saturated in it, yet it will not lead to Silence. Like Judas, it may even lead one away . . .

"When I grew older, the poem stayed with me, even influencing the school that I chose. Loyola was Jesuit, and it is said that Poe, living in the Bronx, wrote 'The Bells' after hearing them ring in the tower at Fordham, a Jesuit college. When Mother died in that fire— Dad tried to save her but was overcome—the poem became prophecy, a mandala containing all things. My Sir said it was the compassion of the Source that allowed me as a little girl to perceive the bells as messengers of Silence, not harbingers of doom and sorrow; that would have been too ugly and cynical a burden for someone so young. But I wasn't strong and hadn't yet found my teacher. After the death of my parents, the ringing of the bells grew violent and too much to endure. The tinnitus would have been fatal but for the birth of my daughter, which quelled all sound—and the intervention of my guru, my teacher, my love."

Without segue, Devi cheerily asked Jeremy about his life. It was jarring. In an instant, the woman who'd channeled a daft, pantheistic discourse was gone. Caught off-guard, he confessed to the recent stab at fatherhood and his ambition to try again. He felt vulnerable and surreal, as if they'd been thrown together in a Red Cross tent, sharing intimacies amidst an unfolding disaster. Content to follow his nose and his gut (the only two organs that never failed him), he allowed himself to acquiesce, and let the mysterious goings-on guide the way. He really did sense something might be born of such lunacies.

When Devi told him that she and her consort had walked to the restaurant, he offered a ride.

As they drove up PCH, he expected to drop them on some forgotten Topanga utility road leading to a communal encampment. Perhaps they'd wash their faces in a stream before trudging into the helter-skelter woods. When Devi told him to pull into the driveway of a faultlessly manicured beach house off Malibu Road, he thought it was a joke—even when she produced a key that opened the front door.

That was when her cohort uttered his only words of the night.

"Two hundred and twenty-five thousand a month I give 'em! Ain't that a pretty penny?"

Tessa, the Marilyn stand-in, stopped by Larissa's for a drink. She was on her way to Pump because the man she was dating said that his good friend Lisa Vanderpump told him "Katniss" was having dinner there tonight. (Apparently, Jay-law was all about flaunting her serious reality-show love and insisted on chowing at Pump whenever she was in town.) He was a man of certain means who relished creating a mystique around his wealth—of the L.A. variety who liked to foggily "present" as billionaires. They wore the bullshit, self-aggrandizing rumor like aftershave and were legion. They chose Bentleys over Teslas. Teslas were for schmucks.

"How old is he?" said Larissa.

"Sixty-two."

"Oh my God! Your cougar membership has so been revoked!"

"Can't be. Member for *life*."

"Ha! How old was the last one?"

"Twelve?" Larissa laughed so hard she belched, which made her laugh harder. "Well, that's what he *told* me. Maybe he was fourteen. But I'll tell you something, Riss—until Mister Billion, it'd been a while since I saw hair on a man's back."

"Ask him to shave."

"That'd be like polishing a turd—an *old* turd. But actually, I kinda *like* it. It's kinda *animal*. It's old-school."

"Oh, fallen cougar! How's the *sex*?"

"No trouble in *that* department. Rich geezers need to *prove it all night*. It's like a campaign! I don't even think he takes Cialis! He really likes the *hard fuck*. But we cuddle too, we *do*. Pushes my 'daddy' buttons, I guess."

"*You* are fuckin' *hilarious*."

They were already drunk.

"When I tell him what a *man* he is, Mister Billion just *blooms*. All I have to say is, 'You a *rock star*! You a *gangsta*!' and he's hard like a motherfucker. Tell you somethin' else, Riss: when he's fucking me and whispering in my ear how I'm the most *full-on woman* he ever met, it's a *total* fuckin' turn-on. It full-on *works*. He tells me I have the perfect body! *Me!* Well, for *him* I guess it's perfect . . . tells me I have an ass like a black woman and I *love* it. I seriously *own* that pedestal he puts me on. Aren't we funny, Riss? How everybody lies to each other and it never gets old?"

Just then Tristen came in, barely acknowledging them as he scurried to his room. (Rafaela was on a sleepover.) Larissa made necessarily hasty introductions before excusing herself to follow the blur of her boy. After a minute she came back in, distracted.

"He's cute," said Tessa. "You okay?"

"My son has . . . a lot of frickin' *issues*. Know who I blame?"

"Dad?"

"Tristen always . . . I mean, he's his own person, always has been. With *incredible* gifts. He's a friggin' *genius*. Gets that from his mom, o' course—not the genius part but *definitely* the *go-your-own-way*. Derek always shit all *over* him—the way he *dressed*, the way he *looked*, his *sex-shoo-al-itay*. Everything! Rafaela was always the angel . . . our little one. But you know what's wild? And freakin' *unfair?*" She laughed spitefully. "I poured *so much love* on that boy! The *therapy* and the boosting him *up*. Daily. *So much!* In some ways, I'm closer to him than Rafi—I know it sounds crazy, even to me, but it's true. And *he* knows it, *Tristen* knows it. But you know what's unfucking fair? He *still* seeks that approval from his dad—"

"Wants the love."

"—fuckin' *masochism!* Keeps going back to that poisoned well." She finished her drink and got contemplative. "God works in strange ways."

"God doesn't fuckin' work at *all*, sista, nuh-*uh*. The man is currently unem*ployed*. Basically just sits around the house planning gore and *may-hem*. You know: tips and helpful hints for ISIS."

Tessa got a text. "*Fuck.* Mister Billion's running late."

"Mr. Hairy Man?"

"He's probably blowing his Bentley."

"Or waxing his back."

"He takes better care of that car than I do my vajine-jine . . . it's ten grand for a tune-up. Give me ten grand and I'll tune *you* up, *bitch*—hey, know what you should do to your ex?"

"Contract killing?"

"Post ads on the Internet with his *address*. You know, '*Cuckold seeking big black cock for wifey—drop by all hours.*'"

"Don't think I haven't thought of it. But I just read on *HuffPost* about a gal who just went to jail for that. Crazy story. She wanted to buy a place in Carmel Valley and this couple swooped in and bought it instead. She was so pissed that she went online pretending to be the new owner. Said people should just drop by for sex 'while my husband's at work.' Said if there's no answer, just push your way in!"

"Now *that's* the spirit. That's what ahm talkin' 'bout."

Tessa made herself another martini, which Larissa discouraged, because her friend always told her, "I'm a Cadbury—that's cheap drunk to *you*, missy." She was going to get shitfaced tonight and that was that. "I just want to puke in his vehicle. Or do I mean butthole. Or is there a difference." She swung the topic back to Larissa's love life. "Best way to get fucking revenge on that cradle-snatcher is to fuck one of his *friends*. If he has any."

"No way, Renée. They all have tiny dicks."

"Probably all *pedophiles* . . . you should tie him up and make him watch you get fucked by niggers."

"*Tessa!*"

"But seriously, Riss, you gosta get *out* there. Fucking well is the best revenge—who said that? Maybe it was Mr. Wonderful from *Shark Tank*. I frickin' *love* Mr. Wonderful!"

She was getting loud. Larissa shushed her, nodding toward Tristen's room.

"Anyway," she said, "I *have* been out there. *Sort* of."

Tessa immediately sobered up. "I knew it! Tell all!"

Larissa couldn't believe she was about to, but went with it.

"You cannot tell *anyone*, Tess."

"Oh my God, you *know* I won't!"

"But I'm *really serious*. Because it's—potentially—*I* don't know what, but you have to *totally promise*."

"Larissa, I *swear*. On my *kids*."

She took a dramatic beat then said, "I went to a party."

"*And* . . ."

"I totally wasn't expecting anything to happen—"

"*Expecting* . . . ? Larissa! This is *not* freakin' charades! Spill it!"

"The party was at Dusty's house—"

"*Oh. My. God.* I *knew* it."

"And I wound up sleeping with her *and* her wife."

"Oh my God," said Tessa, hand clapped to mouth. "Oh my God, oh my God, oh my *God*! I *knew* something was going on!" (Which of course she didn't.) Giggles became an avalanche, burying them both. "Was that—is that something you *do*?"

"It was *totally* my first time."

"You are *amazing*. I love you so much I want to *sleep* with you, *right now*! I'm totally jealous!"

Larissa shushed her again, raising an eyebrow as she gave the wall of her son's room the fisheye. She knew Tessa was kidding but said, "No *way*. Been there, done that. *Not* my thing."

"Well, it might be *mine*! So what *happened*? I mean, are you, like, *seeing* each other? Are you all, like, *seeing each other*?"

"No! She fucking fired me!" said Larissa with a forced laugh.

"*What!*"

"The day after, she totally ghosted me."

"Dusty? Or wifey?"

"*Dusty*. When we wrapped, she made it *very* clear."

"Oh my God."

"Can you *please* stop saying 'Oh my God'?"

"You mean, you guys fooled around the night before she *wrapped*?"

"Yep."

"I *totally* think I *remember* that! I mean, that there was something—I think I *totally actually* think I *saw* that *happen*—she walked right past you, right? At the cemetery?"

"It was *totally* kinda creepy. It was, like, *mean*."

"Rissa, fuck *her*. *Again*, if you can hahaha! No, but seriously. Okay. Do you know what you have to do? Do you know what you *totally have to do*? You have to, like, *blog* about it. Or go on Twitter or *Reddit*, whatever the fuck that is. Payback's a motherfucker."

"Tessa, I can't."

"If for no other reason than to fuck with *Derek*."

"That's not really me."

"But why *not*? It *could* be you, why *can't* you? You *have* to!"

She adamantly shook her head. "I'd never work in this town again."

"Who are you, Jennifer Aniston? It's not like you're working *now*, my friend. And this could *lead* to work—I mean, if you put it out there in the social *media*. Fucking *Instagram* and *Meerkat* it! *Periscope* it or *whatever*; my daughter'll *totally* help you! Larissa, I am *so serious*. Or, like, all you need to do is write one of those, like, little *essays*— like an op-ed for *Huff/Post50*! Or Jezebel or *wherever*."

"You read *Huff/Post50*?"

"*Fuck* yeah. And the AARP magazine too, *all* that shit."

"You're insane."

"Just *do* it!"

"And what about Rafaela?"

"What about her?"

"There's, like, a *shame* factor. You know, that her mom . . ."

"Oh *please*. Kids are *totally* fucking blasé about that shit. I have two words: Kendall and Kylie. I rest my case."

"Well, if I *do* write something, I'd have to wait. Her mom just died."

"Probably in a threesome with that cunt and Allegra."

"Tessa, that's terrible!"

"You fucking *have* to, Riss. It's not like it's going to hurt her *career*. No one's going to be *shocked*—"

"If no one's going to be shocked, then why should I do it?"

"For *you*. She wants everyone to believe she's a *dyke saint*, that she's so fucking *above it all*, but in the end she's just a user and a typical Hollywood bullshit power-tripper. Do it for *you*! And oh my *God*,

don't you know how fucking *hot* it would be? You'd get *so much attention*. It's total reality-show shit! I'll tell Mister Billion to talk it up to
Lisa Vanderpump!"

"Don't you dare!"

"Fuck *Derek* and fuck *Dusty Wilding*—"

"Already did."

"What was it like!"—in a flash, she went from rage to *naked need to
know*, and they both thought that was the most hilarious thing. "I'm
totally serious. I totally want details! I want to know how it fucking
smelled and who came *when* and how many hundreds of times!" Larissa
couldn't stop laughing. Tessa, sobered by her devilish curiosity,
clasped her friend's hands and stared into her eyes like a woman about
to ask a psychic the burning question of her life.

"Tell me! *How. Was. It?*"

"Pretty fuckin' *great*," said Larissa, with a seraphic grin. "Like, off
the charts, major *earthquake* great. Like, *insane*."

"Oh my God."

Driving over to Hollywood to see his dad, Tristen was all nerves.

There'd been so much drama around the divorce. Derek tried to
hide the existence of the twenty-three-year-old slut from Rafaela but
she found out by overhearing one of their mom's phone rants. The old
man went ballistic, even though he knew he was officially fucked.
Locked in a perennial war with his father—a war whose origin mysti-
fied him—Tristen lately adopted the strategy of vibing to Derek that
he was judgment-free, thereby forging a truce, or at least waving the
white flag of ceasefire. It wasn't in Tristen's nature to take a moral
position anyway, even if he *hadn't* been involved in a relationship mir-
roring that of his dad and the ho who practically shared his birthday.

Anyhow, he didn't give a shit *who* Derek climbed in bed with. (He'd called him by his name since middle school, when he'd been ordered to—which creeped his little sister out, inspiring Rafaela's contempt for Tristen, *not* their father.) He'd only seen him a few times since the breakup; Derek would get in touch if he had a particularly thorny PC or coding issue. Tristen felt warm and fuzzy that his dad seemed to trust him with his personal shit, in that Derek was well aware of his son's malevolent online history.

One of the puzzles of his life was determining the exact moment Derek began to hate him. There *had* been good times, though it felt like a hundred years ago. In Hawaii once, when he was nine, he remembered how they both started laughing, and when his mom asked what was so funny, he and Derek just looked at each other and kept busting up and Tristen could tell it delighted her, like she thought it was a good thing, a *nice* thing that she was being excluded from the sacred, mischievous fellowship of fathers and sons. And it *was* a good thing; it was good and it was new. A good, new, *special* thing . . . Then there was that time in the hospital—was he six?— when some weird infection swelled up one of his balls to the size of a mini watermelon and Derek sat bedside, feeding him grapes he'd put in the freezer the night before. They got warm in his mouth really fast, like sweet frozen marbles, and his dad kept them coming. All had been well with the world . . .

The receptionist told him to wait.

The editing bay of the YouTube reality show *Mental Real Estate* (featuring eccentric houses) was in a suite of post-production offices on Gower.

Derek was a Tesla freak and Tristen wanted to show him the hybrid. Not that one had much to do with the other. Anyhow. He knew he shouldn't have come without a heads-up but hoped the nature of the surprise would short-circuit his dad's knee-jerk pissed-offedness. When he finally emerged, he looked like some sick, emaciated bull entering the ring. It was pantshit scary.

"What the fuck are *you* doing here?"

"Uhm, hello to you too," said Tristen.

Something was wrong—maybe he was on drugs again. Opiates and speed were the daily vitamins of the editors of his generation but as far as Tristen knew, his father had been clean for years. He was way gaunt and sallow, though, with wet, stringy hair. Sounded like he was *wheezing*—

"I wanted to show you my car."

"Your car? Since when do you have a car?"

"Out front. I'll show you."

Derek hesitated. He looked like he wished he was dead or wished Tristen dead or wished both of them dead. He stormed out in disgust, as if to minimize a scene at the workplace.

And there it was—like a thing expecting to be petted:

The Honda.

"See?"

"Where'd you get it?"

"Just . . . with some money I made."

"Doing *what*?"

"Computer stuff. It was cheap."

"What'd you do, some bitcoin rip-off? You hack an ATM?"

"No-o-o-o," said Tristen, unfazed. He pointed toward the CR-Z like a model on a game show. "It's pretty cool. It ain't a Tesla, but—"

"You shouldn't have come by. I'm barely holding on to this piece-of-shit job *without* your little unannounced visits."

"Okay."

"Well, is that all you wanted? To show me your *new car*? If it even *is* yours . . . Are you paying your mother rent? Your sister told me you've been staying there again. Are you giving her rent money?"

"Yeah, I am," he stammered. "And I pay for groceries—not just mine, for the house. Anyway, I'm getting my own place soon . . ."

"Buying a little *casita* in the Hollywood Hills?" he said sarcastically. "You better not be into any illegal shit."

"I'm not."

"If you go to jail, my friend, you're on your *own*. Your mother and I ain't gonna rescue you. And you know what? I don't believe you bought this car for a *minute*. Who bought it for you, Tristen?"

"*I* did. I told you—"

"Because if some *man* bought it for you, some *faggot*, that's even worse than fucking *wire fraud* or *destroying people online* or whatever the fuck it is you're up to, okay? Because if a *john* bought you a *car*, that makes you a whore, right? Wanna be a whore, Tristen?" Derek walked over and tapped the trunk of the Hybrid. "You go, girl."

A young woman covered in tattoos raced from the building. She looked like one of those pale-skinned, blue- and black-haired porn stars Tristen knew from the SuicideGirls tube.

"Derek," she said urgently. "You need to talk to Manny."

"I'll be right in," he said. Without looking at either of them, he said, "This is my son"—like the introduction had been mandated by law.

"Oh hi!" she said, startled, then all happy-faced.

"Hi," said Tristen.

"I'm Beth."

He was too upset to give his name.

"That's Tristen—queen of the sporty hybrid," said Derek. He spun around and walked back to the building. Beth followed.

On their way in, Tristen heard her say, "Manny fucking *hates* the first cut. He was just, like, *screaming* at me. He's totally out of control."

It really did feel as if Reina was still alive, which gave some concern.

Her death seemed more and more like a daydream.

Dusty feared her mother had "won," that she would always walk the earth, haunting her in some form or another. If all the years of therapy meant nothing, if even her dying meant nothing, where did that leave her? Ginevra tried to console, drawing comparisons to those who were raised in a fascist country that finally lost a despotic ruler. There was much rebuilding to be done, not only of infrastructure but collective spirit. The therapist said that her feelings were normal and she needed to give herself time. But Dusty insisted she *had* no feelings. That was the problem.

The private line rang—Livia, with "some news."

Dumbfounded, she blurted out, "Did you find her?"

"No *no*! Not *yet*. I have *other* news."

"Related though?"

"Yes."

"Can I call you right back?"

A gal from Bartok was having a raucous hang with Allegra out by the pool, one of those casual, getting-to-know-you post-deal-signing playdates that were more about the fab house and the fab Dusty Lifestyle Experience than anything else.

She locked herself in the bedroom and curled up with the phone. "So what's going on?"

"A *few* things," said Livia, girding herself.

A week ago, when Dusty came clean about how she'd lost her daughter, Livia was stunned, and knew right away that finding Aurora might be impossible. Until then, everything that had been told to her over the years, or implied in glancing conversation, portrayed the case as a fairly typical adoption scenario. At the time, of course, Dusty had no desire to go further, so Livia didn't probe. By accepting what she'd been told, she booked passage on Dusty's leaky ship; she hadn't *enabled* the actress's false narrative, but rather conspired, in complete innocence, to endorse or at least subscribe to the history that was provided. But the facts she'd recently been apprised of— details Dusty blithely, wrongly presented as what Livia "already knew"—greatly disturbed. The storyline's fresh parameters fell far outside the usual avenues and networks of Livia's experience, and well beyond her sleuthhound capabilities. She *understood* the distortions and confusion of Dusty's recollections; because of the guilt she carried for losing Aurora, she'd been deeply invested in the somewhat sugary expository yarn her mother had initially imposed. Reina had inculcated, shaped, and molded, persuaded and propagandized, masterfully exploiting the teen mom's vulnerabilities. It made sense to her that Dusty would have cosigned whatever story she'd been spoon-fed at the age of sixteen, one that got reinforced over time—a wrenching tale, yes, but craftily commonplace (though in gross contradiction of the recently shared facts). Even if from early on Dusty was aware *subconsciously* that something didn't jibe, the details had hardened into a mythology that served her wayward heart.

It was imperative that Livia handle with care; Dusty was family. Outside help was now required and it was time to have that conversation. But first, she needed to soften the blow—to *give* her something.

"I found Aurora's dad."

"You found Ronny?" she said with a smile, not really surprised. She'd provided Livia with the full name. How hard could it have been?

"Yes. And you *did* say he never tried to get in touch with you?"

"Absolutely not!" said Dusty. "Wow. God. Ronny!"

In truth, she was only mildly curious, and a little nonplussed. *You found Ronny? Ronny Swerdlow?* That's the newsflash? Well, thanks for the memories . . . *But, like, uhm, really?* It made her bitchily wonder how Livia had been spending her time. Maybe the old broad had been in the general's tent too long and forgotten what she knew about hand-to-hand combat. Why waste time tracking down a man who was useless to the cause? Besides, *anyone* could have gone on the Internet and found him, Marta's *daughter* could have . . . but she needed to give Livia her due. The woman *did* know her shit.

Didn't she?

Perhaps more would be revealed.

"So did you talk to him?" asked Dusty.

"I would *never* do that. But I have an address and a home phone. He's married, with three children."

"Where does he live?"

"Provo."

"Is he Mormon?"

She was making conversation, to take the edge off her impatience.

"No idea."

"But what does it *mean* that you found him, Liv?" she asked, with a hard smile now, unable to restrain her contempt. She'd already shared the strong opinion that Ronny would have been clueless about their daughter's existence, because Dusty never told a *soul*—none of her girlfriends knew she was expecting, not even faraway Miranda. *Especially* not Miranda. So there was no way that he knew.

"How does finding him *help*?"

"He's a resource!" said Livia excitably. The declaration sounded hollow and straw-grabby, like the spin a wild-eyed publicist puts on a doomed project. "I've been doing this long enough to have seen some pretty strange things. The truth is always so much further out than we can even imagine. One scenario—and it's just a *scenario*—is that Ronny's parents stayed in touch with Reina. That wouldn't be unusual because in cases like yours, *both* sets of parents can become 'co-conspirators.' They bond over 'saving the day.' Reputations and futures. Maybe Reina told them *exactly* what happened—"

"I doubt that, Liv. But I'm still not following!"

"—then over *time*, everyone moves away, loses touch. Everyone gets on with their *lives*. And *maybe*, after however many years, Ronny's parents—or maybe just *one* of them, because the other one died, which would heighten the urgency—let's just say the mom finally talked to her son. To Ronny. Now this could have happened *years ago* or this could have happened last month. Maybe even triggered by Reina's death, by someone seeing that in the paper or on the computer, who knows? But what we *do* know is that there would be *guilt* from all those years of keeping *secrets*. So Ronny's mom or dad tells all. Blabs the *truth*. Maybe it's as simple as them just wanting to be *grandparents* . . ."

"*O-kayyy* . . ." Dusty felt like she was listening to a psychotic writer's pitch.

"So now Ronny *knows*. The big secret. Again, this could have happened *thirty years ago*. Because wanting to see your grandchild is compelling. And let's say he was able to *find* her, find Aurora, using the information given. The information Mom or Dad got from Reina. From the horse's mouth. Unlikely, *yes*, but *anything's possible*. It's a *scenario*. Remember, we're dealing with a giant puzzle right now."

"Let's go with the *scenario*," said Dusty, disheartened and unconvinced. "For argument's sake. Let's say he found her. Found Aurora. If he *did*, why wouldn't he have found *me*? Why wouldn't he have come to *me*. Why wouldn't he have told me?"

"Maybe he holds a resentment—"

"A *resentment*—Livia, this is crazy!"

"—it would have come as an enormous shock to him—that he had a daughter—and he may have been *so angry* that you never told him. Not to tell you he found her would be a way of *retaliating*. I once worked with a couple where the mom was reunited with the son and told him in no uncertain terms that his father was dead, when he was alive and well. It's more common than you'd think. Here's *another* scenario: that he found Aurora and *did* tell her about you—"

"Oh Lord," she said, exasperated. "Lord, lord, lord."

"—and Aurora wasn't *ready*, was still angry, wanted nothing to *do* with you—Dusty, I've seen it happen! Where children feel that when their parents give them up, they *forfeit that right*. They go through all *kinds* of emotions. Maybe Aurora *knows* but doesn't want to— didn't want to give you that *pleasure*." The flurry of hypotheticals made the use of tense problematic. "She might have thought—might *still* be thinking—that if you wanted to see her so much, you could just come *look* for her like her *dad* did."

"Livia . . ." she said hopelessly, unable to account for her old friend and advocate's delirium. "We're not talking about some . . . *flustered teenager* anymore. We're talking about a *woman*!"

"Who may still *be* that flustered teenager *inside*, we can't *know* what wounds she's carrying."

"It's like castles in the sand! It's *less* than castles in the sand—it's like castles in the *clouds* . . ."

"I know," said Livia sympathetically. "I know. But we're just beginning. And we're not dealing with the *rational*, it's *fraught*. And *if* Ronny found her—remember, there've been *far stranger things*—if he found her—years ago—and she *didn't* want to contact you, didn't want to know anything *about you*, then he probably would have honored that because he wouldn't want to risk losing her again." Dusty tuned out Livia's ramblings; she'd already made an executive decision to diplomatically cut her losses and go another way. "He may even have decided *not* to tell her that Mom was a famous person, because it had—has—the potential of making things *worse*. For Aurora. That she had a rich and famous movie-star mom who never tried to find her. Or—depending on her self-esteem issues, Ronny might have decided to withhold that information because it would be too overwhelming—you know, Mom's an overachiever and *she's* an *underachiever*—or *thinks* of herself that way, even if she isn't. Ronny might have been—might be trying to 'protect,' whether that's wise or not. There are *so many ways* to go with this, Dusty, and *believe* me, I've seen *every* variation. But the truth *is* out there. *Somewhere.* We just have to find it."

But who? thought Dusty. *Who can help me, who can I trust? How the fuck am I going to pull this off, where do I even begin? And I don't want to hurt Livia—I know she means well. But this is my life! I know she'll understand . . . she has to—*

"There *is* something else I needed to talk about."

"Okay," said Dusty, heartbroken, and spent.

"There's someone I'd like to bring in."

That took the actress by surprise—at least it sounded like a cry for help. "What do you mean, 'bring in'?"

"Richie Raskin."

Something in Livia's tone changed; the desperation was gone. What took its place scared her somehow. "Why does that name sound familiar?"

"He's had a number of high-profile clients, probably some that you know. He's a cold-case guy—*long* history with the foundation. He consults for us and probably will join the board next year. Dick's retired now but still takes on clients. As a private investigator."

"And why do you think we need *him?*"

"Well, you know, I've been flailing a little bit here, Dusty. I've done my best with what you gave me but haven't uncovered any agency records, private *or* public. *No records at all.*"

"What could that mean?"

Ominously, Livia said, "One thing we need to take a look at is the possibility that Aurora was never adopted."

"Really," she mulled. "Then, if she . . ."

Something inside her collapsed—for one catastrophic instant she lost her mind and her nerve. *Now* she understood Livia's wacko lead-in: how difficult and reprehensible it must have been to "position" Dusty for the infernal deduction.

"You don't think"—she couldn't breathe—"that Reina . . . *Livia!* Is what you're saying is that she—"

"I'm not saying *anything,* Dusty," she said, trying to cap the well.

"—that she *killed her?* Oh my God—"

"Dusty . . . I know this is hard."

"Oh my God! You're right! She killed my baby! Of *course* she did!"

"Dusty, *I need you to pull yourself together.*"

"I can't! I can't! Oh Livia, Livia, why couldn't I *see*—why didn't I *see* that? Why—how—how didn't I *know* that!"

"We don't know *anything,* Dusty, not *yet.* I *told* you, in these situations, whenever you *assume,* that *assumption*—whatever that assumption may be—is rarely *ever* the case. Whatever you *think* you know is usually *wrong.* So I need you to *stop!* Don't *go* there. It's all about *information.* Knowledge is power."

"But it makes so much *sense!*" she blubbered. "Livia! What *else* would she have done with her? The *monster!* Monster, monster, monster! Can't you see the *sense* it makes? You *do,* Livia; I *know* you do!

That would explain all his *letters*? Dad's letters? He kept *apologiz-ing*—I swear, Livia, the letters were fucking tear-stained! He kept apologizing for what they'd *'done'*—'we shouldn't have *done* it'—'I know we'll be forgiven in Heaven'—I thought it was his Catholic *bullshit* and alcoholic *dementia* but *that's* what he must have been talking about! But he *couldn't* have, *she* must have, oh my God, maybe he was in the same *room*, maybe she *forced* him to so she'd have *one more thing* to hold over him—*that motherfucker!*—oh Livia, *that* must have been why he tried to kill himself! Or maybe—maybe he walked *in* while she was—oh God, Livia! Oh my God, oh my God!"

"Dusty, *don't go there*. Not *now*. Because we simply *do not know*. But I *had* to talk about it because your eyes need to be *open*—*our* eyes need to be open, to *everything*. And remember what I said, 'everything' isn't true, only *one* thing is, and we don't yet know what that one thing will *be*. We don't *have* it yet, we don't have the *information*. But we *will*. And we'll face *whatever* it is, *together*. Okay? Can you hear me, darling? Are you listening?"

"Yes." She was traumatized, like an animal that knew it was about to be killed.

"*Good*. Then I'll call Richie and you'll meet. Would you meet with Richie, Dusty?"

"Yes."

"*Good*."

"What about Ronny?"

"What about him?"

"Do you think I should call him?"

She sounded like a little girl lost, and Livia stifled a great sadness. The whole world was lost and overrun.

"As I said, he's a *resource*. An important one, I think—an important part of your journey. Remember! It's about keeping eyes and heart *open*. And *reaching out*. You've done this on your own for too long, Dusty! And I think you need as many allies as you can safely gather."

Allegra offered to come with her to Provo but she wanted to go solo. The idea of a *Looking for Aurora* documentary was shameful and ludicrous to her now. She'd gotten a lovely letter from Laura anyhow, regretting her unavailability. Laura Poitras! What had she been thinking?

Here's what she did:

Cold-called Ronny—the wife picked up. Dusty was prepared for that and did a little acting. Used her down-home Middle America persona, which was closest to her real disposition, anyway—frank, sunny, gregarious. Gave her first name and was relieved the woman didn't joke the way folks on the phone sometimes do: "As in Wilding?" Went on to say that one of the old gang gave her Ronny's number at a high school reunion. (Mrs. Swerdlow was the type of nostalgic, homespun gal who was thrilled, not threatened, by that sort of development.) Dusty apologized for the weirdness of the call, said she'd just lost a mom and found herself reaching out to all kinds of people from back in the day. Well, that further endeared her to the missus. *But Ronny isn't here just now.* He was in Montana with some clients. Dusty asked what he did for a living, and Sam said—she really did *sound* like a Sam—he was a professional fly-fisherman and guide. Dusty said *Wow* and meant it. Well, she said, I think I'm going to actually be in Salt Lake City soon and thought it might be fun to come see y'all. When Sam unexpectedly asked what *she* did for work, Dusty hesitated. She hadn't thought *that* one through at *all* and impulsively threw caution to the wind. "I'm an actress." It took Sam about two seconds to half rhetorically ask if she was Dusty Wilding, but with a laugh because how *could* she be? Part of the laugh wound up covering Dusty's *Yes*, so again, she averred, "Yes, I am." Sam was sweetly flabbergasted. *Ronny never told me he went to school with a movie star but isn't that just like him? He's going to have some explaining to do.* In the wake of the reveal, Sam hit a speed bump of self-consciousness. Dusty asked when her husband would be back and Sam said tomorrow. *I'll call again, if that's okay.* They chatted some more about this and that, just normalizing and making nice, and by the time they wound things up Sam was back to her regular self. She ended the call by insisting that when Dusty hit Salt Lake she make a field trip to the house for dinner, to meet her girls—they'd be over the moon. *Lord, I think they loved Bloodthrone more than The Hunger Games and that's saying a lot.* Dusty had no intention of talking to Ronny on the phone but wanted, strategically, to leave her number so she gave Sam the dummy-decoy line, the one that silently rang through. The dead line that her mother had all those years.

Three days later she flew private to Provo. (She never planned calling back. She'd try her luck and just drop by.) It felt like half a fool's errand but she didn't care anymore. She was biding time till she met with "Snoop" Raskin, Livia's mucky-muck shamus.

High in the air, she remembered . . .

Tustin, where she grew up. County of Orange. He was a few years older, a football player. Gorgeous. He'd been after her awhile, all the boys were but she never put out. One time a jock called her a dyke and Ronny got him in a headlock until he begged apologies through rank, ugly tears. Dusty had a top-secret girlfriend, an Australian foreign exchange student, and was aloof to such chivalries. It was the year of *Grease*; when she and Miranda were in bed they used to laugh about which of them was John Travolta and which was Olivia Newton-John. Boy oh boy, that Melbourne girl swallowed her *up*. It was the first time Dusty ever came with anyone, and the volcanic force of that brand-new unconfused knowledge of who she was at the core of her being scared her shitless. She nearly died when it was time for Miranda to go home. Out of shame, loneliness, and desperation, she ran straight to the football player's arms, and let him do all the things boys do (which was almost nothing, compared to Miranda). She never came with Ronny, not once, but didn't stop trying, right up to when she got pregnant. Her mother pulled her from school before she started to show.

How she wanted that little girl . . .

She knew Reina wouldn't be moved by her entreaties so she cried to her dad but he didn't stand a chance against that woman either. He was the cuckold in a film noir, his life having effectively ended upon an arrest for exposing himself to an undercover cop at a public toilet in Mission Viejo. Reina somehow—*somehow*—saved his job as branch manager of City National in Newport. (Dusty wouldn't have been surprised if she'd slept with someone at the bank to make that happen.) Now her mother had him where she wanted him, which was where she had everyone.

She read Dusty's diaries and stole the hidden cache of overheated letters from Miranda. One night, when father and daughter attempted a final, tender plea to keep the baby, Reina exploded with rage and said they were perverts that filled her with disgust, she would *never* abide her grandchild being raised by a faggot mom *or* a faggot gramps, and if they dared bring it up again she'd publish the diary of what Dusty'd done down under and the pornographic letters too, she'd dump a thousand xeroxed copies on the schoolyard before marching into City National with Arnold's arrest record, so all the world could see how much she'd suffered, living under the same roof with two weak, conniving, promiscuous queers.

It wasn't until years later that she learned her father had taken an overdose of pills a week after Reina's screed; Dusty was told he'd been hospitalized for heart problems. Eventually they separated but never divorced. (Reina had a lover all those years—a Mormon!—who called her his "sister-wife" and assured that he would know her in the afterworld by "Sarah," her celestial name. She drunkenly told Dusty all about it, the day after Arnold died.) Even before she got famous, Dusty would send him money. God, he wrote the saddest letters. It was pretty much all he did in those last few years, apart from slowly dying of liver failure—write sad and beautiful letters to his daughter from the Skid Row SRO where he would *succumb*, at fifty-six. She wondered what she'd done with them . . .

Provo—

The neat grid of houses sat on the hem of a serious mountain, as the neighborhoods tended to. She didn't want to just pull right up. She asked the driver to stop so she could walk the rest of the way.

The streets were empty and the residences large and well-kept, with Disneyfied lawns and facades. The Swerdlows' had a rustic frontier theme, the only home on the block that departed from the generic. She smiled to herself; that actually struck her as "kind of Ronny."

Powering through her trepidation, she strode up and rang the bell. The door swung open and they just stared. He beamed at her through his startle.

"Well, hey there! Sam told me you called."

"Hi, Ronny! I am *so sorry* to drop in on you like this!"

"Not a problem! You know, I tried calling you back but it just kept ringing."

Oh! The free-fall sorrow of it killed her and she started to bawl. He hadn't really figured out why she'd gotten in touch but knew *some* of it probably had to do with being of the age when life sandbags you—suddenly, you're a forced enlistee in that army of brave, conflicted, slap-happy souls not yet ready for the finish line but sure as shit chagrined to have caught a glance of the endgame's blazing lights not too far off, like a fatal, glittering Oz.

As they held each other, she heard the delicious, tumbling sound of life behind them. Dishes and voices jostling . . .

His tiniest girl shyly snuck up and peered.

"Why is she crying?"

"Aw, she's just tired from her trip."

(She loved that he actually said *Aw*—like Jimmy Stewart would have.)

"Hi there!" said Dusty, yanking on the throttle of acting chops, to pull out of her tailspin.

"Aggie, this is *Dusty*. We went to school together. Say hi!"

Aggie retreated behind her dad—then Sam popped up.

"Well, look who's here! Welcome!"

The other daughters scrummed to the door wide-eyed, to Mom's laughing reproach. Sam hooked her arm in Dusty's and led her in, adding that most beloved of moviedom tropes—

"You're just in time for dinner!"

The girls were aflutter—the oldest was seventeen—and anxious to know when to expect the sequel to *Bloodthrone*. Dusty said *soon* but swore them not to tell. If they Instagrammed or Snapchatted or even *talked* about it she'd be *fired*. The warning got them excited and they promised that her secret was safe.

She lied about being in Salt Lake for *Sylvia & Marilyn*, as if anyone cared—they were so happy to have her as a guest in their home. The girls couldn't get over their dad knowing her; he definitely rose a few notches in coolness. It wasn't Thanksgiving but sure felt like it: the white tablecloth and platters, the sweating, burnt-orange turkey, the corn on the cob, biscuits, mashed potatoes and perfect gravy, the effortless care and generosity of spirit. It wasn't even put on, because they didn't know she was coming! She wondered if that was a "Mormon country" thing or an archetypal American thing or just the bountiful way that certain people—kind, decent, giving people— chose to live their lives. She never had that experience as a child, remotely.

Aggie asked if she was married and got swatted by one of the sisters. When Sam said, "You *are* though, no?" the eldest rolled her eyes. The actress said yes, she was, and the middle child piped up, "To *Allegra*. We saw the wedding online." Dusty said, "You *did*?" and the older girl said, "Big Sur! We couldn't really *see* anything—I hope you don't think it's rude that we watched!—but you *could* see the people *arriving*. Sort of. *Some* of them." "They should have used a drone!" said the middle one. "They didn't *have* drones then," chastised the elder. "It was *before* drones." Sam told the girls not to talk so much but Dusty was utterly charmed. When Aggie asked, "You're married to another girl?" the ponytailed brood pounced. "You are *such an idiot*, you *know* that she's married. To a *woman*, not a *girl*."

After dinner, while Sam and the girls cleaned up, Ronny showed her the den where he did his fly tying. As if in mid-surgery, some of the lures were clamped beneath magnifying glasses; others sat in tiny jewel boxes, each in its own compartment. Dusty thought they looked like miniature rings and broaches created by an aficionado of outsider art.

The mystery of her visit hid in plain sight. It wasn't the right time, and they both knew it; so many questions would have to wait. The suspense was tolerable because Ronny took the lead—as always—and led well. He was a "true gentleman," modest and even-keeled, a gracious antidote to her panic. He'd always been that way. Still, she found herself having the somewhat grandiose fantasy that his serenity was born of the delight in her being there, the fateful, miraculous culmination of all the years he'd spent dreaming of this very moment. *Narcissism dies hard*, she thought, half comically.

He said that he met his wife when he turned forty, coming off a rough divorce. But the kids were theirs. "Babies just never happened till Sam."

She couldn't even begin to wrap her head around unpacking that remark.

"How long are you in town?"

"Just a few days."

"It's really good to see you, Dusty."

"It's great to see *you*. Oh my God, it's *beyond*."

"Tell you what. We *probably* have a few things to talk about," he said slyly. "Why don't you come to the house tomorrow at six."

"For dinner?"

"In the *morning*, kid," he said. "I'm gonna take you fly-fishing. Ever been?"

"No! I'd like that very much."

"I've got waders and everything you need. I have a feeling you're going to be pretty good at it."

He was in the driveway, loading equipment in the truck. She was glad. She'd been stressing about the earliness of the hour and wasn't looking forward to knocking on the front door.

They rode for about forty minutes, mostly in silence, which felt fine. They drank coffee from a thermos and laughed about his kids,

especially Aggie, the youngest. Ronny was easy to be with. *Old times.*
When they got to the river, he helped her into the waders. They were
Sam's—she and Dusty were about the same size. He had all sorts of
gear clipped to his vest—lures, feathers, delicate pliers—like some
fly-fisherman action figure. Grinned like one too. They finished their
coffees while Ronny decided where he wanted to cast. A few anglers
were already on the water, one on the bank, the other standing in the
middle of the wide stream.

"Our dad used to take us here in the summer. Taught me everything I know. He was kind of a legend. He doesn't come out too
much anymore, but when he does I still watch him. He'd get his eye
on one—they don't travel too far—and just stand, for hours. *Total*
focus. He was a freak. My brother and I were pretty good but not
like the old man. We'd catch half a dozen fair-sized ones and be all
puffed up because Dad didn't get any yet. Then just before we went
home, *blip*, he'd land it. A fucking *beast*. The one that he wanted.
That's what I shoot for when I'm out here, that kind of focus and
purpose. That *stillness*. The art of that. It's what I aspire to."

Then, like his father before him, he hooked the monster—at least
that's what it felt like to Dusty when he asked, "Did you ever want
kids?"

She stared at the ground and gathered herself.

"I got pregnant once. With you."

Smiling affably—disconnected, as if on tape-delay—he said, "Are
you kidding?"

"That's why I disappeared. I got pregnant and my mother took
me to get an abortion."

"An abortion?" he said, uncomprehending.

"But I never had it—the abortion. I had the baby. A little girl."

Then, with only slight modulation, he said: "Are you fucking
kidding me?"

"No, Ronny," she said, still looking down and shaking her head. "I'm not."

"Where is she?" he said, with hollow urgency—a desperation that hadn't yet coalesced.

"I don't know."

"What do you *mean*, you don't know?"

"We think—I think maybe—there's a chance that she's dead."

She knew she sounded like a mental patient but there was nothing else to do than lay it all out. Ronny fought through brain freeze.

"I'm not *getting* this! What are you fucking *saying*, Dusty?"

"I told you—"

"You *told* me?"

"I had a little girl—"

"And it's *mine*? How do you even *know*—it's mine? It's *mine?*—"

"It was yours—*is* yours. But I think she—we think there's a chance that . . ."

"You show up at my house, like, *forty fucking years later* to tell me we had a *kid* together? A little girl? And you don't know where she *is* but you think that she's *dead?*"

"I don't know that for sure. I'm trying to find out."

"You're trying to find *out*?"

"Maybe I shouldn't have come."

She hated falling back on that, it was a dumb, cowardly, cliché thing to say. But just then, she wanted be someplace—anyplace—else.

"Damn *straight* you shouldn't have! Who do you think you are, Dusty? Who *am* I to you, one of the fucking *little* people? The little people the celebrity *deigns* to drop in on? 'Hi! Thought I'd walk into your shitty little *life* and give you some horrible, shitty fucking *news* before I go back to my *fame* and my *money* and my *bullshit'*—"

"Ronny, it's not like that."

"Oh, it isn't? It's not like that? Then what *is* it like? You know what, you don't know *me*. You never knew *me*. And I sure the fuck don't know *you*—I'll tell you something else, I don't *want* to. You're *sick*, Dusty. You're fucking sick to come here and tell me this shit."

She was calm and emotionless. She'd left gaping holes in the story, it just spilled out that way, and his gears kept slipping. (Hers too.) Who could blame him . . .

"How long did you *raise* her? How could you have *raised* her and not *told* me about that?"

"I *didn't* raise her. She was taken from me."

"At what *age*?"

"Three months—when she was almost four months old."

He let that sink in, then grew imperceptibly settled, because four months was "better" than whatever he'd been thinking. It was still insane but *less* insane.

"*I can't believe this.* We have a *kid*—or *had* a kid!—and you *knew* about it and never told me . . ."

"I was sixteen, Ronny."

"And now you're *fifty-three*. And you kept this a secret? For forty fuckin' years? *Why*, Dusty? What *is* that? You didn't want people to *know*? Because you thought it'd hurt your fuckin' *career*?"

"It's more complicated than that."

"*Bullshit.*" He started back to the truck, muttering, "Yeah, it's *complicated*. It's *fuckin' complicated*."

She chased after. "Wait! Ronny, wait . . . *please*. Just—*please* wait. Can you please just listen?"

There wasn't much of a choice—he'd been thrown down a dark well and she was the only one with a lantern, weak as it was. Grudgingly, he followed her back to the bank, where she asked him to sit. The onshore angler had vanished during the argument. On their

return, the remaining one threw them a look of reproof and reluc-
tantly kept fishing.

"Do you know about those women whose babies die in their wombs
and the doctors say they still have to carry them to term? That's what
it's felt like *every day* since she's been gone. Except she was *alive*, and I
held her and *nursed* her and *loved* her. And I'm sorry I never—if I had
kept her—if I'd been allowed to keep her, I—I *know* I would have found
you, Ronny. I would never have deprived you of that. But when I lost
her . . . I was—it just, it *destroyed* me and I—I was ashamed, and . . . it
took *all those years until now* to even begin to *look* for her. And I feel
horrible about that too, that it took me so long! So *please* don't judge
me! Because *I've* judged me every day! And it's not *about* me, Ronny,
I *know* that, but that's how I *feel*! When that *bitch* died last month—
Reina, my mother, I . . . it—I guess I couldn't, until she—even though
I'd already kind of started putting things in motion *before*, something
was *stopping* me—"

She broke. The angler looked over and shook his head with disdain then waded to the opposite shore and left. They sat and listened
to the sporadic plashing of trout. With the river as their stage and
the embankment their proscenium, they began an operatic duet, a
fearful, star-crossed give-and-take without promise of grandeur or
resolution. Tenuously, Ronny's rage subsided.

"My parents sent me to my uncle's," he said. "In Ogden." Each sentence was marked with a sigh. "A few weeks after you disappeared.
Suddenly I was in fucking Ogden, away from my friends, and I didn't
know why. None of it made sense. I never went back to Tustin, either.
A month or so later they sold the place. Then we moved to Provo and
I've been here ever since." He threw a rock into the water. "I kept in
touch with some buddies back home. A few guys from the team. For
a little while, when I first got to Ogden. No one knew what happened

to you. Now I'm wondering if my parents knew. They must have. Or
who else in the family did."

"Reina took me to L.A. for the abortion. I was super-cooperative—
I think I even told her I was glad to be getting rid of it. We were at
a motel and I went down the hall for ice and never came back. Stuck
out my thumb and climbed in the first car that stopped, a guy going
to Arizona. So I went to Arizona. My daddy used to give me spending money that Reina never knew about. I saved it and probably had
a few hundred dollars on me. Got a job waitressing in Wickenburg—
that's a big rehab town now. Might have even been one back then.
It's, like, the hottest fucking place in the *world*, it was a hundred and
twenty when I got there, but I was so, *so* happy . . . to be away from
her and still have my baby. I knew Reina was going to do everything
she could to find me but I was safe there. I felt safe in the desert . . .
My little girl was safe and that was the only thing that mattered.

"I was kind of taken in by these . . . lesbians. They were sort of
wiccans—you know, hippy-dippy witches—but to me they were saints
and angels. I could tell them *anything*, and I did. And they just *loved*
me, like big sisters, and they *listened*. I told them all about Miranda—
remember *Miranda?*—and all about *you* and my cunt mother and
poor, sweet Daddy . . . and they totally *got* it. They were on my side,
a hundred percent. It was like I'd stepped into a dream, a paradise.
You know: Honesty World. No Secrets World. *Unconditional Love*
World. They mothered me, I never had that, I didn't even know what
that *was*. I tried to seduce them but they weren't going for it. They
were righteous! I was *terrible*. But they knew I was just a child, wanting to be loved. When I was seven months, they made me stop working at the restaurant and took care of me. They took *such* good care
of me. And—they knew a bunch of midwives, and I had Aurora at
home in a tiny swimming pool. They cried as much as I did when she
was born.

"But something happened . . . when she was about three months old. I started getting homesick. I missed my daddy, I mean, *really* missed him. He was such a gentle, tortured soul! And he couldn't *defend* himself against her . . . I loved him *so much*. I just wanted to protect him. And I guess I missed 'home' too, no matter how fucked up it was. It's pathetic but that's how I felt. So I started secretly thinking about going back. To Tustin. It just totally started to preoccupy me, to you know, go back with my baby—and part of it was a *Fuck you*. A fuck you to Reina. I am woman, watch me roar. I mean, like, what could she do? What could Reina do? What was done was done. That's what I was thinking: What could *she* or *anyone* do? The sickest thing is that *part* of the fantasy was that Reina would *welcome* me! I know that was in there somewhere . . . that she'd welcome *us*. You know, that once she saw Aurora, she'd be able to see the error of her ways. How twisted is that? I guess I kinda brainwashed myself—and they *warned* me, my angel-witches warned me. A leopard does not change its spots, they said. But I was young and hardheaded, and one day I just split. Got on the bus to Cali, I was finally going home. And Aurora was *so beautiful*. That's what I named her, after the Northern Lights. Oh my God, Ronny, she was *so*, *so* beautiful. Madonna and child were going home. Supergirl and Superbaby—in matching capes. I had a lot of strength but too much innocence.

"And she *did* welcome us. But Reina was only doing what I did that time we went for the abortion. Playing a role. One morning—I'd only been back a week, hadn't even taken a *step* outside the house—I went to her crib to feed her and Aurora was gone. Like *that*. Can you imagine? She wouldn't tell me where she was, all she'd said was I'd never see her again. And I *know* it doesn't make sense, that I didn't go to the police or just *tell* someone—"

"What happened?"

"She said she 'arranged' for a family to take her—a couple who already had kids but really wanted to adopt a baby and could care for her and give her a 'proper' life. She said it had all gone through the county and was totally legal and there was nothing I could do, that it was the only way and to just shut up about it. Shut up about it! Of course with my adult brain, I know her story was bullshit. 'The county'! And the woman who's helping me . . . find her . . . thinks there's a—possibility . . . that Reina may have caused her *harm*. And I know she was *absolutely capable* of that."

"Jesus."

"The morning after she 'went missing,' I took an overdose. My father did the same thing a few weeks later! They pumped my stomach and Reina said that was *further evidence* I was unfit to be a mother, that she always knew I was unstable and that was why the baby couldn't—"

"I'm so sorry, Dusty."

"—she said Daddy overdosed because of *me*! Because of the *baby*, that I bullied him so much about keeping the *baby* and made him feel so *worthless* that he wanted to take his life! That was like putting a knife in my heart! But *now* I think he did that because—because he might have known what *Reina*—that he *knew* what she *did* . . ." Ronny put a hand on her shoulder while she cried. "That was when we sold the house and moved to Carlsbad. And I *never* forgave myself for continuing to live with that woman—for three more years! *Three more years* before I got the *balls* to run away to New York! I told myself I stayed because of my dad but that wasn't really why. I stayed because of *Reina*. I guess I still wanted her to love me, as *sick* as that fucking sounds. I've spent a thousand years in therapy trying to figure it out. It was like I was married to her and was the battered wife."

Neither spoke for a while.

"I thought about you," said Ronny. "Did you think about me?"

"Of course I did."

"I've seen all your movies. Even the awful ones," he smiled. "Sam was all over me for never mentioning you. She was flattered too—you know, that she got the man who got Dusty Wilding."

"The man who turned me gay?" They laughed.

"I told her that we had a little thing. She pried it out of me."

"She's pretty amazing, your wife. She's beautiful."

"Hey, don't make a move on her. She might go for it."

"Ha."

"She's tough," he said, admiringly. "Wouldn't have got through half my crazy shit without her. You know, when I saw you on talk shows, and on the covers of magazines . . . I was actually really proud. Not just about your career but how you've conducted your life." She laughed again at the irony of that, and cried some more too. He drew her close. "I used to trip on what things would have been like if we'd hooked up and got married. I mean, even with the gay thing. How my life would have been different. You know—Mr. Hollywood! Then I'd think, *Naw, that wouldn't have worked*. 'That ain't me.' Oh, I had the whole deal going on in my head though, for real. Even included a few kids."

"Are you serious?" It touched her.

"Maybe my life wouldn't have been so different after all. We'd probably have hung in there a while because of the . . . *children*, then split up. I'd have let you have custody—"

"How kind of you."

"—even though the judge would have sided with me because of the, you know, the gay thing. Times were different then."

"You're too much."

"Maybe you'd have thrown a little palimony my way . . . ho *ho*! Then I'd've probably walked into a bar somewhere and met my Sam.

You know what's funny? In my head, the kids we had were all boys, you gave me sons. And I was tripping on that *before* I had my girls. That was always the fantasy. It's fuckin' *amazin'*—these thoughts we have, and they're all bullshit! 'I think this, I think that. I'm fantasizing this, I'm fantasizing that.' All these years I'm tripping on us having sons, but we made a little *girl* together, no lie. You know, I *did* think about trying to get in touch with you. Just to say hey. But you were rich and famous and I guess I thought it might be too weird. What would I say, anyway? What would I have said? I'd have felt like the world's biggest loser. Which I was, for a lotta, lotta years. You had this big life and at the time, mine was kind of falling apart. I was a drinker. *Bad* drinker. But then I met Sam and got sober, got 'in the middle' of A.A. I have twenty-three years now—it's crazy. There's a guy I know in the program who walked out of his son's life. Knocked a girl up and vamoosed. When he turned forty, he decided to find him so he could make amends. His sponsor said, *Don't do it.* 'Don't you dare.' What he meant was, you fucked up his life once and you don't have the right to step in and maybe fuck it up again. Let *him* find *you*. Otherwise, let it go."

Dusty wondered if that story was for her—or just a story. Then she said, "Hey, Ronny. Think we can fish?"

"I know *I* can," he smiled. "Can you?"

They waded in. He caught one right away. He held it and stuck a small plastic siphon into its mouth.

"What are you doing?"

"Pumping its stomach."

"Oh shit, it O.D.'d!"

"I want to see what's on the menu today." He pulled out the tube and squinted at the bugs in the see-through pump. "What they're hungry for—sometimes it's the usual, and sometimes it's a little more exotic. You think they're eatin' hamburgers but they managed to find caviar. If they're having *caviar*, they won't bite if you're baiting the hook with a Big Mac. You'll be here all day and go home with nothin'.'"

He reached into one of his boxes and pulled out a nymph. He put it on the line and showed her how to cast the lure. In less than a minute, he shouted that she had one (Dusty wouldn't even have known), then talked her through as she reeled it in. She held the fish in her hand while he removed the hook.

"I'm going to find her, Ronny—dead or alive. I'm going to find out what happened to her. I owe her that."

It sounded like a line she once said in a movie, and he responded in kind. "I believe you will, Dusty. I believe you will."

He told her to put the fish back in the water and she watched it swim away. When they reached the truck, he helped her out of the waders. They sat in the cab and finished what was left in the thermos.

"Will you . . . be there?" she said plaintively. "If I need—to talk? If I need you?"

"You know I will."

"I'm so sorry, Ronny."

"It is what it is. I just hope she's alive. That your mother didn't do that terrible thing."

"Thank you."

"And that's a beautiful name—'Aurora.' I didn't tell you that."

They drove off. Dusty got weepy again. "You were just a boy but you were so good to me. I think I even finally told you about being in love with Miranda! I was crying all the time when she left and you kept asking what was wrong, so I told you . . . I can't believe I *did* that, but it shows how much I trusted you. You cared about me."

"I loved you."

"And you didn't judge. You were like a man that way. Or how a man should be."

It was cold and beautiful and the sky looked so heavy. He suggested they go for breakfast.

"Ooh, bacon!" she said. "But *hey*: we shoulda kept that ol' trout and caught some more. Coulda fried 'em up."

"In this part of the river, we throw them back."

"Oh! That's cool. I *love* that."

"'Catch and release.'"

Before Dusty left for Utah, Allegra told her about the nightmares she'd been having about the miscarriage. Her wife suggested a support group but Allegra was reticent. *Then why don't you try Skyping with Ginevra?*

The therapist was in her early fifties, chicly Euro, kind of hot. (Allegra didn't know what she'd been expecting but it wasn't that.) At the beginning of the call, Ginevra informed the young woman that because Dusty was her client, this would have to be a one-off—but she was happy to help in any way she could. Allegra already knew the ethical drill and wasn't looking for a shrink anyway.

"So how are you doing with everything that's going on?"

"Oh! I think I'm actually doing okay. But there's a *lot*. There's a lot going on. I mean, *man*, the whole *daughter* thing with *Dusty* . . . she's *so amazing*. She's been through *so much*. And I know she likes to—not really *minimize*, that's not the word, the *right* word—but *diminish*, or whatever, her mother—her mom's death. I mean, even though she *hated* her, Reina was just *so big* in her life, and I think that her death, it just—oh, *I don't know* what I'm trying to say."

"You're saying—what I *think* you're saying—is that grief is complicated and it's important to honor all of its aspects."

"I *guess* . . . though it's been so hard for me *personally* to get to that place. But the whole thing with her daughter—trying to find her—is more about—not *more* about, but—I think on some level she's just so angry with *herself*—totally not that she should be! But you know she kind of pointed the finger at her *mother* all those years—and Reina *was* a total monster and I'm *totally* not judging Dusty—but I think she maybe *knew* her mom was going to die? *Sensed* it? And that if she didn't try to find her kid, there wouldn't be anyone left to blame but herself? So she finally put it all in motion to, you know, finally go *looking* for her. Because I think that was something she wished she would have done a *long* time ago. So what she's doing now is so amazing and incredibly *brave*. I try to put myself in her place and just can't imagine. I don't think I would have had the courage."

"You'd be surprised. But let's talk about *you*. And *your* loss."

"Yeah."

"Does it upset you that Dusty has a daughter?"

"What do you mean?" she asked, preparing to be offended.

"Well, the two of you have been trying. And now you're dealing with the grief and I'm wondering if you feel alone in that process. If you resent Dusty for going off and looking for that *other* little girl."

"Not really. I don't *think* so. And she's been great. She's been there for me. I just think because—maybe because she's older, it maybe didn't affect her in the same way. Or maybe it *did* and that's even a part of what motivated her to—you know, go looking for her kid. I mean, along with Reina's death, maybe the miscarriage gave her another . . . push."

"Let's talk about the nightmares."

"Usually, it's the same one. I'm in bed sleeping and there's a baby crying somewhere in the house. Kinda obvious, huh. And I just lay there trying to figure out where it is . . . you know, is it in the library? Is it in the living room? The laundry room? The kitchen? And I sort of start mapping out the house in my mind—going through each room. And my ears are, like, *aching* from trying to pinpoint it. Then I start to think, well, maybe it's *outside* . . . by the pool or in the cabana. And the only thing that gives me *some* little form of comfort is that I know at least *Dusty* is with it. You know, Dusty's taking *care* of it. And *that's*, like, the moment in the dream where I can actually breathe. But then it occurs to me—and this is the *shock* and the horrible part!— that Dusty isn't even *home*, she's on location somewhere in *Havana* or wherever . . . and *that's* when I hear the baby again and now it's, like, *screaming*, it's totally screaming. I mean, *shrieking*, right at the foot of the bed! And all this is happening, you know, with the incredible speed that shit happens in a dream. Like, the dream could be a half hour or could be, you know, like, *three seconds*. And I try to get up but I'm paralyzed—of *course* I am! I mean, what would a nightmare be without total paralysis, right? And I *totally* can't move my arms or legs and the screams are getting louder and louder and that's when I realize—this is the *second* horrible part—that *this is how it's going to be*— you know, the baby screaming and screaming and maybe probably *dying*, and me just laying there *listening* to it—with both of us not being able to drink or eat, and no one finding us. And that's just *how it's going to be* . . . until Dusty comes home."

Jeremy didn't feel like going, but was compelled.

He wanted to be there for Allegra. And not just because he knew the loss of the child had put stress on her marriage; he didn't want to sweep his own feelings under the rug either. He needed to fully honor the experience—the death—that had brought him to the emotional breakthrough of meeting with a surrogate. Still, it felt like his mourning period was on the wane, supplanted by the dream of trying again. Allegra's seemed only to be beginning.

Yet who (he asked himself, with self-loathing malice) had suffered more? While an incubus cast its malevolent spell on the expectant mother's womb, what had *he* been up to? Shopping online for designer onesies and pricey Belgian prams; immersed in the real estate porn of lazy river penthouse pools, private automobile elevators, and houses made of rammed earth; buying a car for his friend-boy. Signing mass emails "Mrs. Dusty Wilding the Second." (In preparation for going public with the birth announcement.) While they vacuumed out the little bones, he was having his Tesla detailed at Soho House . . .

The church basement support group reminded him of a scene from *Fight Club*. Sad, sad group of people! Like a small circle (and circle-jerk) of Hell: infinity loop of parents grieving over children unborn. The format wasn't like A.A., where everyone did their three-minute spiel; it'd be tough to tell someone in the middle of a dead-baby crying jag that their time was up. They went *on* and *on* and *on* . . . Allegra fought back tears the entire hour while Jeremy zoned. He thought about sex with Tristen (he was always thinking about sex with his "twist"), about projects in various stages of development, about Devi and Sir . . . he'd been asked to dinner next week in Malibu, at the "pretty penny" house—

Emerging from his reverie, he caught the words of a mousy woman in her mid-thirties. The faint, decaying man beside her was apparently her husband.

". . . and I just wonder when it's going to *end*. I know even *thinking* that way is so *selfish* . . . I just worry that I'm living with too much pain—that it's become an addiction, and that *chemically*, I'm becoming a different *person*. That I'm in this *hole*, and can't climb out. Because this was almost *two years ago* and it feels like *yesterday*. Like *today*, it feels like *today*! And a lot of people say that when we're *pregnant* again, that's when I'll be able to—that's when we'll be able to move on. But a lot of them say the pain never goes away too . . . and I don't want it to! I don't want it to go away! Because that would be like losing our baby a *second time*! They say that you . . . *integrate* it. But Calvin and I—we tried—and it's—they said—*so many doctors* we went to said it was impossible for us to get pregnant . . . and that's why Jarett really *was* a miracle baby. You always hear that, 'miracle,' but he *was*. He took eight years! So when he died . . . so I'm— we're really looking at the possibility it may never happen. Again. And every time I think I'm okay with that, it brings me to my *knees*. But I actually felt better the other night. And this is *so terrible*, we were home watching *Gravity* and it got to the part where Sandra Bullock is telling George Clooney about how her little girl passed away. She said something like—she said it was something so stupid, like she slipped and hit her head on the curb, on the way to school. That's what she said when she was talking about how her daughter died, she said, 'It was the stupidest thing.' And I actually felt better for a little while because I thought, *That can never happen to Jarett.* You know—he can never grow up and have something awful like that happen to him, like fall and hit his head on the way to school. And die. That cannot happen to him *ever*. And I just—that made me feel so small! That Sandra Bullock's grief, even though she was just a *character* . . . that it would make me feel good to *hear* that, made me—"

She convulsed in tears while pathetic Calvin stroked her back.

Proletariat regurgitation of sentimental pop-cult movie moments was one of Jeremy's bêtes noires. Watercooler snippets from *the national conversation* always gave him the creeps—and made him feel like a schmuck for being one of the "content providers" to the scary, useless, brain-damaged world.

"Well, *that* was a supposedly fun thing I'll never do again," said Jeremy.

They were back at Soho House, where he seemed to live.

"Thank you for coming. I know it bummed you out, but I really appreciated it."

"Oh please," he said, reversing himself. "I *wanted* to. It was actually kind of beautiful. *Depressing* but beautiful. I mean, we're suddenly in this *tribe*. It's a fucked-up tribe, but it's *ours*. I guess!"

"It *did* make me feel better. In a *way*. Or maybe it's all the crying."

"It's just going to take time, Leggy," he said, reverting to the seasoned Wise Man tone he used when shutting down the dreams of showbiz strivers. "I know it's the worst cliché, but time will heal."

Just now it felt insanely callous that he'd spent the entire day mulling over whether he should tell her about the surrogate. At dinner, after the grief support group no less!

She felt so close to Jeremy. She would have felt the same even if he disclosed his plan; it'd have hurt but Allegra would have understood. It was hard for her to imagine getting pregnant again. Losing a baby like that really did a number on your womanhood—you were raised with all these presumptions and expectations, that you were the cradle of life and propagator of the species, your whole sexual identity was inextricably bound up with fertility. When you didn't pass muster, everything went to shit and got thrown into question. Just who and what were you? People adapted to pretty much anything and women who couldn't bear children were no exception; Allegra knew her fair share of contented, barren ladies; over time, surrender came, often in the form of the gloating declaration that they'd never wanted kids in the first place. All the mushrooms and *brujas* in the world conferring eternal motherhood couldn't get Allegra to believe it.

"What's going on with Bunny?" he asked innocently.

"Nothin'. Jus' chillin'."

"How's she doing with the Reina thing?"

"It's *heavy*."

"Ding Dong! The Witch is dead."

"I think heavier than she likes to put *out* there, but she's doin' okay. I think she's actually doing very well." She longed to blab about Aurora but knew that if she did, it would come back to seriously bite her in the ass. "Man, it's fuckin' *complicated*, Jeremy. I know there's *relief* there, for sure. But I think there's also . . . I think she's really, like, *sad*. I mean, she'd never *admit* to that, but they did that dance for *such* a long time."

"For real. You get used to dancing with the devil and suddenly it's, like, 'Hey! Where'd the devil go? Where's my devil, I want my devil!'"

"Right?"

"Was there a funeral? Why wasn't I invited to the funeral?" he said, in mock outrage. Half a mock, because suddenly he was in a huff about maybe having been excluded from something.

"Nope—*nothing*. She wanted to be scattered at sea but Dusty overruled her and put her in the ground in Santa Paula!"

"Well, *good for her*."

"But can we talk about something else? What are *you* up to?"

"Same old. Projects, bla. I might do something else with Megan. There's a Xavier Dolan thing, but the script's four hundred pages. Bla."

"*Love* Xavier. Love that little genius boy."

"I'll probably see Angelina when I'm in London."

"When."

"Whenever."

"I didn't know you knew Angelina."

"For, like, a hundred years. And I've kind of been thinking of maybe directing again."

"That is so *awesome*, Jeremy. A documentary?"

"Feature."

"Oh!"

"I haven't really figured it out yet. I'm circling. Circling the *drain*, probably. Hey, I read your script!"

"Oh my *God*."

"It was *excellent. Really*, really good, Leggy."

"Jeremy!" she squealed.

"I was kind of surprised."

"Uhm, gee, thanks," she harrumphed, still glowing.

"No, I mean, in the *best* way. Not that it was better than I *thought* it would be but that it *definitely* doesn't read like a first-time script."

"Jeremy, *thank you*. Oh my God, that is *so nice*. But did it make *sense*? I mean, could you *follow* it? 'Cause I made some choices—I was worried people wouldn't be able to follow it."

"*Totally*. You totally pulled it off, Allegra. That's what was surprising and kind of amazing."

They were in the middle of riffing about the next step—whether to focus on directors or actors, engaging in that style of spirited, pre-production élan favored by the town's doers and dreamers—when a striking redhead strode up. They went blank.

"It's Larissa!"

"Oh my God, hi!" said Allegra.

"How *are* you?" chimed Jeremy, with a convincing spin of authentic interest perfected by years of glancing industry social encounters with those who could do nothing for him.

"Really good!"

(The rejoinder being L.A. shorthand for making shitloads of money—a socially acceptable substitute for not being famous. Of course, etiquette required both parties to believe the assertion. In the moment, anyway.)

"Wasn't that party so much fun?" said Jeremy.

"*So* much fun," said Larissa, eyes dilating Allegra's way.

Jeremy's naughtiness sensors beeped.

"Tuesday Weld," said Allegra. "Oh. My. God."

"I *love* her," said Larissa. "And those *stories*. Elvis! Lenny Bruce!"

"What have you been *up* to?"

"*Working, writing*, doing *yoga* . . ."

"We should all get together again," said Jeremy, like some lame-o rapscallion.

With a caregiver's concern, Larissa asked after Dusty. "I was so sorry to hear about her mom."

"She's good, and thank you," said Allegra. "She's totally doing well."

"Say hi for me?"

"I will!"

"Well, I need to get back to my friend. I just wanted to come say hello!"

"I'm so glad you did!"

When she left, Jeremy said, "I think she's really *hot*. You and Bunny tap that?"

"Are you serious?"

"That was kinda the *vibe* just now . . ."

"No way. She's *totally* straight."

"*No* woman is totally straight. Which means you totally tapped that!"

"Totally *didn't*."

"Well, if you *haven't*, you *should*. I didn't know you and Bunny were even into that."

He was fishing now.

"Would you shut the fuck *up*? And what's going on with *you*, romantically? How's your little boyfriend? Did you get *secretly married*—"

"Are we *deflecting*?"

"Come on, Jeremy, don't be boring. Are you still seeing him?"

"Uh huh."

"And?"

"I think I might be . . . in *love*."

"Shut the front door."

"Shut the front door? Who *says* that anymore?"

"You are *so* not in love."

"I bought him a car," he said sheepishly.

"Oh my God! You *are*! If you bought him a car then you *are*."

"He has . . . *issues*. But, oh my God, Leggy, it's *so tender*. I just want to take *care* of him. And he's *brilliant*—I mean, *so much smarter* than me. He reads, like, *everything*. He *discourses* on—he knows who *Bergson* is! And Thomas Bernhard! He fucking plays *Gymnopédies* on an old *Casio*! He's, like, smarter than *Josh Cohen*! And he's a *total* film snob, oh my God, Leg, he's *so* much worse than I am! And he's twenty-three! He's twenty-three!"

"What's his name?"

He paused, to mark the closeness of letting her in.

"Tristen."

"*So* beautiful," she said. "I'm so happy for you!"

"And now I have to *go*. My *friend* is waiting for me at home."

She asked *who domesticated who*, before excusing herself to the downstairs WC while Jeremy took care of the bill. (She knew Larissa would see her go.) She lingered at the sink and washed her hands, pretending to be surprised when the stand-in appeared. The bathroom was empty and they backed into a stall, mouth to mouth.

Larissa was startled by the ferocity of her own desire. The more experienced Allegra hit pause and said, "Maybe we should do this another time."

"Oh—sorry!" said Larissa, embarrassed. "I just thought it was okay. Was it not okay—?"

"*Totally.* It's fine, it's *great.*"

"I'm really sorry!"

"Don't apologize, you're *amazing.*" Gusts of heat poured from Larissa's throat, and all kinds of scent. She was still in the throes. "And I *love* that you came and found me. But it's . . . complicated."

It felt like she'd been using that word a lot lately.

They left the metal playpen and, side by side, threw cold water on their faces. Larissa couldn't believe her sudden lie; it erupted from her as if something—some*one*—had taken possession.

"Dusty's been coming to yoga. It's *so much fun* having her in class."

"Oh, great!" said Allegra, flustered.

"She's *really* advanced—she should be teaching! But I think she feels comfortable there. You know, like a safe haven. Everyone leaves her alone—they're all too self-obsessed to notice her! I hope she comes back soon. I know she had a big loss but it really helps to lean on your practice. To get grounded and back in your body again."

"She just needs a moment," Allegra said automatically.

Larissa had written her number on a card upstairs; she slipped it into Allegra's hand. Trying to make up for her boldness, she discreetly insisted Allegra "go first," and return to Jeremy alone. After she left, Larissa loitered in the alcove behind the marble steps, pondering her spontaneous artifice—and the plot, mysterious even to her, that was busy being born.

After Reina died, they resumed sleeping in the same bed. No sex, but lots of cuddling—a comfort to them both.

Allegra told her she ran into her camera double. Dusty gave the tiniest of shrugs, as if it wasn't worth acknowledging. When she said Larissa talked about hoping to see her again at yoga, Dusty scoffed.

"Uhm, not gonna happen."

"But she said you loved the class."

"I only went once, honey."

It peeved Dusty that Larissa even *mentioned* they had that off-campus moment. Everything *about* that woman peeved her.

Allegra left it at that but wondered, *Why would she lie?*

That night she had the dream, but this time the baby was dead. The woman from the support group stood at the foot of the bed and held it in her arms.

She looked down at Allegra and said, "Is this an intervention?"

When Jeremy walked in, Tristen was working on his laptop at the kitchen table. It was nice coming home to someone—it felt like family. He kissed the boy's cheek then let him get on with whatever he was doing. He liked to show that he wasn't the smothering type.

Jeremy put on the Brahms channel and ran a bath. It was raining; how he loved that. He thought about the support group, comparing and contrasting its high emotion with his apathy. Long ago, the sudden, violent erasure of his family by a drunk (who, of course, was himself unharmed) had inured him to grief. With that event, any presumptive expectations of an orderly, linear life underwent a deep and disorienting transformation. Up until then, the *a priori* world, even in its supreme, shambolic splendor, had adhered to the inviolable three-act structure—a beginning, middle, and end—whose literal translation, as it happened, became the foundation of his career as a story editor and creative executive. Like a high-ranking cultist, he *understood* the three acts, becoming their scholar and servant, their trustee and executor, their henchman and trusted lieutenant. He learned much from them. They embodied divine symmetry—the syncopation of life and death. Like God, they saturated all creation, bringing comfort, reason, and solace. They were ancient. They shone like the sun and darkened with the consistency of night. He was a joyous laborer in the garden of the three acts, pruning and tilling the soil, designing pathways, caring for all its living things. And then his loved ones were obliterated and he awakened in a secret garden where nothing grew but the present moment. He was a terrible horticulturist now—how could you water *that*?—yet he was free.

The other day he watched a mini-doc on YouTube. An English barrister with an aggressive cancer enlisted his grandson to film his last few months. They went to the cemetery where he would soon be buried and took beguiling footage of a walkabout amongst the graves. After supper, he sat by the fire musing about the end, only weeks away. It played well to those who hadn't experienced the unfathomable riddle of sudden death—like an ad brought to you by the Three Acts Corporation.

A newborn dies minutes after being delivered, without awareness of having existed; an ebullient Florida tourist is taken out by a 350-pound manta ray when it leaps on deck; a barefoot bride poses for a wedding photo in the shallows of a river. Water creeps up the gown and she stumbles on the embankment—the soaked dress, now heavy as concrete, makes rescue by the photographer impossible. A posh barrister, fatally diagnosed, has ample time to reflect on life's mysteries before morphine companionably hastens his death. What did any of it mean? In a world of drowned brides and murderous, bitch-slapping flying fishes, it meant nothing. He felt asinine even posing the question, even thoughtlessly having the thoughtless thought . . .

Jeremy only prayed that when his moment came, he'd be quickly absorbed into the masterpiece of dark matter and infinite nebulae—of black holes from which neither light nor three acts could escape.

At midnight, just as she turned out the light, Larissa's cell lit up with SHITHEAD.

(How Derek was listed in her contacts.)

Her gut clenched. *He's drunk.*

When she picked up, a woman very tentatively said, "Is this Larissa?"

"Who's *this*?"

"Uhm, Beth. Derek's in the hospital."

"What happened?"

"He had the flu but now they think maybe it's his heart? They're transferring him to the ICU. Uhm, did I—? Sorry if I woke you."

Larissa stewed. The asshole made the girlfriend call his mommy! Unfuckingbelievable. Then she laughed, imagining how the doctors and R.N.s probably kept asking if she was the granddaughter.

Larissa got out of bed, empowered by her abrasively carefree assessment of the situation—it really was liberating to feel *nothing*. No way was she going to get in her Uggs and race over there.

It started to gnaw, though, as her thoughts turned to Rafaela.

"ICU" never meant anything good . . . if the piece of shit upped and died and she never woke her daughter, she wouldn't hear the end of it.

Seeking clarity, she had herself a pee.

She crept to Rafaela's room, softly calling her name. Turned on a light. The sleep-confused girl yelped when Larissa said her daddy was sick and had been taken to the hospital and that they probably needed to go. When Rafi asked what was wrong, she snapped, "His girlfriend wouldn't tell me." On the way to UCLA, she regretted the snark.

Her daughter whimpered the entire ride like some puppy outside Starbucks. (She should have given her a Xanax.) They stopped at a light before the final turn. A woman at the intersection held up a sign.

> I failed
> Now what?
> HOMELESS
> Can you help?

He was still in the ER when they arrived.

They sat for a moment before a volunteer came to escort them back. Larissa demurred and told Rafaela to go by herself. Mom said *try to be calm* but it was no use.

Larissa scanned the waiting room for the g.f.

Just as she returned to her seat, a slender gal emerged from the ladies' room—emo wallflower with a twee trunk of retro tattoos covering her arms, petering out at her jawline. They smiled at each other and knew. *Well, that's sorta interesting,* she thought. *Definitely not his type—though maybe she is . . . good on ya, Derek! What do you call that, a frickin' millennial?* At least she didn't look like what Larissa feared: a 2.0 version of her younger, voluptuous self.

Her anger dissipated as the girl timidly approached.

Larissa smiled and extended a hand—a grownup's power move. "So, what *happened*?" she said, trying to colonize her with a *WTF*, big sister vibe.

Beth smiled wanly. She was disarmed—she'd prepared herself to be ambushed by a flurry of hostile innuendo. It had been such a very long day.

"He had—he's had this *fever* for, like, three days. I told him not to go into work but we had this really important deadline. He was *breathing* funny. I tried to get him to go to the ER but he wouldn't."

"Sounds like Derek!" she said, with a smile that overplayed. The collision of her vanity with the lover's *callow youth* (she felt so old!) made everything go large. She couldn't help herself.

"What freaked me out was that he coughed up *blood*."

"Oh shit."

"When we got him here—we've actually been here since *six*—I wanted to—I thought I should call someone, I thought I should call you, but he wouldn't *let* me. But they said his lungs had fluid in them and his heart was, like, *really racing*. I think his pulse was, like, *two hundred*—"

"*Whoa.*"

"—and I kind of started to get scared maybe something was going to happen? I think they think it's like a really bad upper respiratory infection? Someone even said asthma? But they're checking his heart. One of the nurses said there wasn't enough oxygen in his blood."

Once Beth finished relaying the essentials, it got awkward. Things went quiet until a flurry of Tessatexts came to the rescue. She was at Pump and fully drunk, urging Larissa to GET YE BISEXUAL GINGER ASS OVER HERE RAITCH NOW because an Eddie Redmayne lookalike was there with a hottie WHOS PUSSIE YOU WOULD DEF LIKE TO LICKK. Larissa laughed out loud and texted back guess where i am? While she waited for a response, she considered sexting Allegra, but thought, *Nope. Too soon.*

As another tessellated bulletin came in, Rafaela stormed toward her, in tears.

"How's he doin', babe?"

"Not good!" she said, falling into her mother's arms.

Beth hung back, which was smart.

"Tell me what's goin' on," said Larissa, cool and steady and *interested*. For her daughter's sake.

"They're saying they need to test him for a stroke!"

"Fuck."

"Mommy, is he going to die?"

"I don't *think* so, sweetie."

"I don't want him to die!"

"He's going to be *fine*, okay? Daddy's *tough*, he'll pull *through*. And he's totally in the best place if something goes wrong, okay?"

"Something already *has* gone wrong!"

"There's no better place for him to be. They're going to figure out what's *wrong* and they're going to *fix it*. Okay?" She drew a hand over Rafaela's hair. "Let me go see what I can find out. Want me to, babe? Want me to go talk to someone?"

"Yes! Yes! Please, Mommy! Please!"

The poor thing was in a state.

As Larissa stood, her daughter said, "He *really* wants to see you, I *know* he does. And he said for you not to tell *Tristen*. He said he didn't want to deal with *Tristen*."

Richie "Snoop" Raskin was a virile, dapper, imposing figure—what they used to call a "gent." Pop culture had bestowed upon detectives a colorful rep as snappy dressers, men's men who weren't afraid of a little bling, but Dusty never saw anything quite like *this*: the cologne that reeked of fathers and forest gods, the wedding ring that was the broadest gold band on the thickest finger she'd ever seen, the old-school Brioni suit (courtesy, so he informed, of the ancient haberdasher Sy Devore), the vintage "Los Angeles Railway" cuff links fastening crisp, blindingly white sleeves . . . The old, swinging dick veritably hydroplaned into the room on buttery John Lobbs, a soigné king of forensic flatfoots and Hollywood fixers gone by. That he was *host emeritus* of an Emmy-winning cold-case series called *The Spirit Room* only further burnished his legend and general legerdemain. He'd been a confidant of Sinatra (of course he had), having met the Chairman in Vegas when he was just nineteen; it was Frank who'd christened him "Snoop." (Of course he did.) Their relationship forged his career and forever changed his life.

"I acquired the name long before Mr. Calvin Broadus Jr. was born," he said, referring to his more famous namesake, Snoop Doggy Dogg. "Though Mr. Dogg *does* defer, when we're together sociably—I call him Snoopy and he calls me Snoop. He's actually a client of mine. Good people. Hardworking, honest, *very* savvy. Smokes a bit too much of the funny stuff but to each his own. I've helped him out of a few jams," he winked.

Marking time, she reminisced about her own run-ins with Sinatra and a few other folks they shared in common. Dusty was glad she'd asked her wife to sit in, not just for support but because she didn't want the rift between them to widen, not if she could help it.

He could tell she was anxious—through Livia, he already knew the actress was convinced that her baby had been the victim of foul play. As if sensing her dread at wading in, the detective gently informed that, for now, he had all the facts he needed. Instead of homing in on "the case," he spoke with discerning intelligence about her filmography, with a hobbyist's emphasis on the obscure.

Apparently, he used to frequent weekend screenings at Liz Taylor's (another client). "Liz told me, 'Keep your eye on that girl. She's the one to watch.'"

Dusty was moved by that.

Livia's instincts were spot-on: he was the man for the job. Dusty felt a rush of hope, like an end-stage cancer victim being told that surgery and chemo wouldn't be necessary to effect a complete cure— just a change in diet.

"Do you know Joni?" he asked. "Joni Mitchell?"

"Yes! Not super well—I haven't seen her in . . . a *long* time."

"She's had some hard times lately but she's still with us. A tough old bird. Brilliant."

"I *know*. I feel so *awful* for her. It was an . . . aneurysm?" He nodded. "*Love* her, *love* Joni. I could listen to her for *hours*. Not sing—I mean, that too!—but *talk*. She's an *amazing* talker. *So* brilliant! Knows *everything* about *everything*."

"I think she knows a little *too* much," he said mischievously. "And she likes to let you *know* that she does. And that *you* know too *little*."

"We had a period where we kind of hung out, before she got that weird disease."

"*Morgellons,*" said Snoop, with amused disdain. "I have a whole opinion about that—some other time! The reason that I asked—if you knew her—is because there are similarities."

"Similarities?"

"You know she gave a daughter up when she was twenty."

"I *did* know that."

"You lost Aurora at about three months?"

"Yes."

(It was interesting to hear a stranger say the name and the detail.)

"Well, that's about the age Kilauren was when Joni put her up for adoption."

"Really! That, I didn't know."

"And it's curious: I *think* she was exactly your age when Joni decided to see if she could find her little girl."

"Wow," said Allegra. "How weird!"

"The minute the search went *public*, gals started coming out of the *woodwork* to say, 'You're my mother!' 'Hi, Mom!' We had to put everyone through a fairly rigorous screening process."

"I can imagine."

The conversation rambled—shared friends and timeworn anecdotes from his end—before he circled back to Aurora, in regard to his fee. It had been a long while since anyone spoke directly to her about payment of services. Again, very old-school, and she loved it.

Before Snoop left, Dusty wanted to know how he became a cold-case maven. As it happened, he was a pioneer in the field, long before it was a cultural and living-room staple. Initially, the work had called to him because "like Elvis, I had a twin who died at birth. Not to get too psychological about it, but I think part of me is always *looking*—for that other part, that other *me*. The thing that will make me whole."

Standing at the door on the way out, he doffed his hat and said something so crazy that after he left she had to ask Allegra if she'd heard him right.

"Did he say *dig up the yard*?"

"I *think* so," Allegra said grimly.

"What *exactly* did you hear him *say*?"

"He said—I *thought* he said not to worry—that he'd find her—'we'll find her . . . *even if we have to dig up that yard*.'"

They used to smoke weed, hop in Joni's red Mercedes 280SL, and drive through traffic just to blow people's minds. She could really make Dusty laugh. It embarrassed and surprised her that she didn't know more about the singer's whole adoption deal. It was a famous story that she hadn't followed too closely, which in itself was deeply telling. Because after all, Joni was *looking*—and Dusty wasn't. Probably struck too close to home. Why would she have been interested in the journey of an artist and a peer who had the guts to do what she herself wasn't capable of?

They lay in bed, watching a YouTube interview from a while ago. (Allegra'd been Google bingeing; Patti Smith had given up *her* baby girl around the same time Joni did. WTF!) Joni wanted to clear the air because she was tired of people saying she'd put her kid up for adoption because of her career. Looking elegant and patrician— matrician? mortician?—probably in her early sixties at the taping, she defended herself by explaining how she was young and poor, and the father of her child had left three months after the girl was born. It was freezing cold and she had no prospects; she knew she couldn't make a home for her daughter, let alone a life. The *presentation* was so plausible and forthright, she was so *articulate* and made such *sense*, but, still, Dusty was uncomfortable. Why couldn't Joni have just said *she wasn't ready to be a mom*? Wouldn't that have been cleaner? Where was the sin? What was wrong with saying you weren't *ready*? Because if you *were*, you could overcome *anything* . . . couldn't you? Joni told the interviewer that it was a different time, a different, harsher time, but what did that even mean? A time when mothers gave up their daughters *en masse*? She hated and loved Joni, forgave and condemned . . . because wasn't *not searching* for Aurora the very same as having *voluntarily given her up*? If only she'd taken the singer's sensible, guilt-free path! She'd have been spared so much.

Joni was saying how she watched from a balcony as her daughter arrived for the first time. "It was like Romeo and Juliet." In another clip, Kilauren said it felt like she was coming home after being away just a short while. Supportive, famous friends of Joni chimed in, taking note of how the genius's demeanor, her very *face*, had changed upon reuniting with her lost child, that she'd finally come full circle in her life and her work, the whole both-sides-now thing—paradise regained. If only I can have that chance, thought Dusty. *Please, God, give me that chance!* It didn't matter a whit that Kilauren's boyfriend sold pictures of the reunion to the tabloids or that Joni and the foundling ended up "divorcing," with "incompatibility" being cited . . . didn't matter that Joni *allegedly* slapped her daughter in the face during a disagreement at her home in Bel Air, and police had been called—

None of it mattered!

Because, oh! What she would give to bring her own daughter back! And a *granddaughter* . . . oh! It astonished her that the very idea of a grandchild hadn't occurred until now—

What she would give!

What she would give, for a daughter to slap, or be struck by, hard across the face! To break skin and teeth, and draw welts! What she would give for a daughter whose passions commanded the police to be summoned, lights flashing, sirens blaring—SWAT teams, stun grenades, bomb-sniffing dogs!

What she would give, what she would give, what she would give!

On Fridays, Dusty had a standing poolside lunch date with her assistant. Their little ritual—savories, gossip, and talk of old/new business:

Jimmy Fallon wanted her for a lip-sync battle. One of the young stars of *Bloodthrone* was hosting SNL and Lorne called to ask if she'd make a surprise walk-on during his monologue. Did she want to go to an investment conference in New York in November? "Hunh?" she said. The assistant informed that it was at the Met, happened every year, and Sir Paul ("not *RuPaul*") was the last musical guest. Dylan was supposed to be doing it—that was the rumor anyway. "If you want, I can reach out to Bono. He usually goes. You could fly on the Google plane." "I need *Bono* to fly on the Google plane?" she said impishly. "That's not what I meant!" he said, laughing. "Then what *did* you mean? And I'm *kidding*." "Google would be *totally thrilled* to have you—*everyone* would be thrilled." "Now you're digging yourself deeper, bubba." She liked to goof on him. "Just let me know if you're interested," he said. "I mean, whenever. But sometime in the next two weeks!" Moving on, he said there'd been "whispers" she was up for a Kennedy Center Honor. "Whispers!" she said. "Whispers! I love it!" She put on a pixie face and mused, "I wonder who votes on *that.*"

He turned his attention to the nonsectarian. "I got an email from a very sweet *elderly* person who said she knows you. Ida Pinkert. Ring a bell?"

"Ida Pinkert, Ida Pinkert . . ."

"She used to be a neighbor? In Tustin?"

"Ida Pinkert! Oh my God! She must be a hundred and seven!"

"Let me pull it up," he said, scrolling his phablet.

"She was a *'friend'* of Reina's—the neighborhood *spinster*. Lived catty-corner from us."

He stared at his screen, muttering, "Why can't I find it?"

"I'm sure she's sending condolences."

"I actually don't even know how she got my email—oh, here!"

She took it out of his hands to read.

"Okay," she said, blankly. "I'll take care of it. Are we done?"

The old woman's email had been sent via library computer, "with the help," she wrote, "of a very kind young man." She apologized for the intrusion and expressed sadness at her mother's passing ("I'm most certain you had mixed emotions") before inviting Dusty to visit her home ("If you find you may have time in what I am sure is your very hectic schedule"). The caveat IT IS MOST URGENT leapt incongruously from the screen, like a message, both hidden and decoded, meant for Sherlock Holmes. She had probably asked the very kind young man if he could underline the words for emphasis; he would have said we do that in caps these days. Ida wrapped things up with more apologies for not "giving you a ring," as a phone call was precluded by deafness.

Dusty hit the road again, which seemed to be the theme of the hour—intimate, introspective journeys, far different in flavor from those of the carefree, location-jumping itinerant life of her profession. She thought about the fish they released into the river . . . and let the freeway carry her like those ineluctable waters. Softly, she began to cry—

And then suddenly, like a dream, she'd arrived:

Home.

The house on Mimosa Lane . . . listed on the National Register of Hysteric Nightmares—vortex of her wounding, and sacred burial ground too. (Thanks, Snoop!) Sitting in the car, she got infested by a gooey, revenant stillness.

Salutations of the dead—

As she stared out the window, the image-repertoire encroached: her girlhood self on a ten-speed . . . a smiling, lawn-watering daddy— her Arnold, so handsome, in the silly orange bermudas that she loved . . . Miranda, on the Fourth of July . . . the cat that got killed by a pit bull . . . nursing her little one (*her* little one! *Aurora*) in the bedroom upstairs. The house had been redone—spray-stuccoed and generally face-lifted—so she felt less of a charge. Shifting focus to Ida's ramshackle one-story, she watched herself grow numb. Dusty knew what was happening: the organism was protecting itself. Systems were shutting down. Yet as the blankness receded, she felt a certain exultation, because suddenly she saw herself *surviving*. (She loved declaiming "I'm a survivor!" during sessions with Ginevra. Hadn't she earned that right?) She could absolutely visualize herself—one day soon, maybe sooner than she imagined—moving *on*. Free as fuck. She sensed that coming-to-wisdom place, a complete *understanding* that she was merely an instrument played by the Universe, a servant of God's will, a magnificently insignificant player—an actor!—in the great mystery. One needn't be a guru to have such a revelation; on a good day, albeit a *very* good one, anybody could see that life was but a dream.

The front-seat epiphany left her open to embracing the Narrative, only this time that of her own—not mother's, daughter's, wife's, not *anyone's* but hers. She would hold in her hands (and heart) the gloriously random, still meaningful, still *unique* Saga of Dusty Wilding. That's what this ghostly place was telling her: it was time to live her story, without encumbrance. She needed only be awake enough, *aware* enough, to watch it unfold *this moment* (impossible to have any other), as she sat in *this* car on *this* street, the street upon she once lived, and once died too—where Janine (her birth name) and Aurora Whitmore, or at least her *idea* of them, died, together.

How could any of that be a problem? To jump from one cosmic narrative to another? How a problem, to be fully conscious? To acquiesce to what *was*, what *is*? To have the veil lifted and finally see? How a problem, to know nothing could be altered, nor would one wish it to be?

Ida Pinkert would say, "Yes, it's true. Your baby was murdered," *and I'll be okay with that.*

I'll be okay.

Because I'm a survivor.

That's what I *do.*

After a few minutes on the porch, she thought she heard a small voice. Bending to listen, it *seemed* to be saying, "Come in! Come in!" She turned the knob and pushed through.

There stood Ida, giddily encaged in a walker.

She took hold of Dusty's wrists. "You look *wonderful.* Oh, I had no *idea* you'd get my note and I am *so pleased.* There were *so* many times I was going to call you over the years, Janine, you *must* forgive!" Her face scowled with worry. "Oh, I called you *Janine.* Do you *mind?* You don't mind if I call you Janine?"

She led them to the kitchen, where they sat at a table strewn with bills and reminder notes. It was obvious Miss Pinkert spent her waking hours there. A relic of a television was on, sound muted.

"I went to see *all* of your movies until it became *just too hard* to get around. A girl comes once a week; she drove me to the library. I asked Griselda—that's her name, she's from Salvador—I asked if she knew how to send something on the computer but apparently she did not! She doesn't speak English very well, though I think she speaks it better than she says. She certainly seems to *understand* it well, *very* well. I think she's *lazy* . . . I thought she would know how to do the computer. I thought that if you have one of those *Apple phones*—which she *does,* even her little *girl* has one, how they can afford it *I don't know*—I thought if you have one of those Apple phones and you're *young*, well, *relatively*, then you would *know how to send a message on the computer*. But you see she didn't. So a young man helped me. Oh, he was *wonderful*.

"The last time I visited your mother was, good Lord, I want to say five years ago. Could it be so long ago? At that *lovely*, lovely place. That was a *lovely* place you found, but so far away! The gals at church used to take me, they were *wonderful*, I paid their gas, well, *offered* to, but they wouldn't take my money. Not at first! And I don't know *why* I visited your mother because once I got there, well, sometimes she *just wouldn't say a word*. She could be in a *mood*, you know—oh, she was famous for her moods! But I suppose I thought it was the right thing, she was all alone, I don't think many people *talked* to her, it was always difficult to be her *friend*, for *Reina* to be a *friend*. If you can't *be* a friend, then you won't *have* too many. That's the general rule. I don't even think the *staff* talked to her! Not that much, anyway. She didn't have an easy time of it there. *I* don't think she had an easy time of it *anywhere*. So I suppose I was trying to 'lighten her load.' We'd known each other so long! Good Lord, *too* long. And that is what—I believe that is what a friend is for. You can't always have *reciprocation*.

"Well, it got harder to get the ladies to take me but eventually they did because I insisted on giving them money and they just had to take it. I paid their gas, plus twenty dollars, which eventually became *forty* dollars, gas plus forty dollars, but that was my limit. I am on a fixed income! Then, well, I suppose it just became too much because people have their own lives, they have children and husbands and all kinds of things. And they could only drive me on weekends—they worked— and I suppose they wanted the weekends to themselves. Who could blame them? No one wants to cart an old lady up to Santa Barbara for twenty dollars. *Or* forty dollars. Because that was what I eventually gave them. Maybe they wouldn't do it for a *hundred* dollars! And I wanted to reach you, Janine—oh, for years!—but I just didn't know *how*. Reina wouldn't *talk* about you. When I asked if she'd seen you, she would not say a *word*. And I daren't ask for your telephone because she would have been *suspicious*. She was a little *paranoid*, you know. So one day I got *very* bold and did a *terribly* sneaky thing. I told one of the nurses—they knew I was 'the neighbor,' and a harmless old lady, which I *was* and still am!—they could *plainly* see I knew the lay of the land—that you and your mom weren't 'close.' So one day I took one of the nicer ones aside and told a little white lie. I'm *calling* it that but maybe it was a *big* white lie! I said that you and I spoke *every day* but I'd had a terrible flood—there were those awful, heavy rains at the time—and the telephone people were at my home trying to fix every-thing and all of my *papers* with all of my *phone numbers* were just *soaked* and I was worried you would might be trying to reach me and that you wouldn't be able to . . . would they *please* give me Janine's—*Dusty's*—number again? 'Again' I said! Pretending that I already had it, or had it *once*, which of course I didn't. Oh, that was *terrible* of me. I didn't even *think* to ask for your *computer name*. Lord, I felt like a criminal! Just shaking like a *leaf*. Well, I don't know if they believed me! But they were *so* kind to give me your number, and even a way to reach you on your computer, which *I could not decipher*. I *called* a few times but there was never an answer. And it just kept ringing so I couldn't leave a message . . . I thought they must have given a wrong one, just to get rid of me!"

"Ida," she said, calmly touching the old woman's hand. "Did she kill her?"

"Did she—"

"Ida . . . I *know* that she killed her. Isn't that what you wanted to tell me? Isn't that what was so 'urgent'?"

"Oh—no! No! No! Good Lord, no . . ." she said, aghast.

"You can *tell* me now—you won't get in trouble." She felt grounded and alive. "Because it's *over*. Reina is *dead* and it's *all over*. It doesn't matter anymore, Ida, so don't be afraid."

"But she didn't! No no no, *no one* killed that little girl! Oh, mercy! Oh, you poor, poor thing! Mercy, mercy, mercy! And it's my *fault* for not *calling* you—I should have called a *long, long time ago*! Oh, Lord have mercy on our souls!"

Dusty caressed the spinster's bruisy arm, and flashed on paramedics invading the house; Ida's end of days.

"Your mother told you that your little girl was adopted—she told *me* that—but it just wasn't true! She gave her away! She paid a girl to take her away! I saw the woman and her man-friend steal it. Steal the baby! I watched from my window! Arnold—your father—the *dear* man—this was *years* later, just before he died—he used to write me the most beautiful letters—your father told me—oh and it broke his heart!—that Reina *paid* the gal to take her. He *begged* her *not* to do that, Arnold said, 'Please take the little thing to a hospital! We dasn't do this, please!'—because he knew it wasn't *right*—but she—Reina— wouldn't—well, you *know* what she was like! And you *knew* the young gal, you *knew* her, she *sat* for you, and oh Dusty, I just never thought the gal was *fit*. I thought she was *unbalanced* and somewhat of a—well, she was a *whore*. She had different men at the house when she looked after you, *many* men, you were so *little*, and Reina turned a *blind eye*, but I *watched* from my *window*. I just don't think that gal was *fit*, and I don't see how she could *ever* have been fit to be a mother to that—to *your little girl* . . . I always thought she was a *very disturbed young lady* and *could* not understand—I *could not understand* how Reina let her in that *house* the way she did, to look after you! And none of it was *legal*, you see, I would have had *no trouble* with an *adoption*, no trouble at *all*, it would have been the *best thing*, but *this* was not *legal* and *that* is what has *bothered* me all these years! And that is why I wrote to you, to tell you, and clear my conscience. Oh Lord have mercy! It was not *legal*. You see it just wasn't *right*, and should have been handled quite *differently.*

"One must always obey the law."

Ida's news dismantled her on a number of levels.

After the shock engendered by Livia's inference of homicide had subsided, Dusty experienced what she could only describe to her therapist as a feeling of intense relief. The grisly "solution" of her daughter's murder tied everything up in a silver bow, letting Dusty off the hook. It no longer mattered that she never went looking for her baby—in fact, she was far better off for having done nothing. An added bonus was the shower of fresh blame she could unleash upon her mother's corpse, a pastime that always rejuvenated. With the polished stone of rage born of the terrible suffering both had caused, she killed two birds: demon mother and martyred child. It was a win-win.

But now she was robbed of such closure. That familiar, lifelong fetish of self-hatred, only recently banished, rose in her throat like vomit. She excoriated herself for "wishing" her baby dead—her Aurora! Her beloved, whom she'd recently disinterred, rhapsodizing over her corpse with Ronny! Aurora: holy grail of her rapturous quest for motherhood, mother love, completion! She had looked spinster Pinkert right in the eye, so *certain* that Baby Rory was dead, *daring* her not to tell her otherwise . . . The hubris! Her revulsion was unbearable. *Reina* once said it and Reina was right: *she, Janine Whitmore, was unfit to be a mother*—or anything else.

In an instant, the burgeoning, self-proclaimed hero of her own story was covered in horror and shame, less than human.

Again.

She regressed and became undone.

Dusty told her wife that she needed to sleep alone for a while. She stopped sharing information with Allegra about the search. The actress was amicably distant. Allegra thought she knew why.

During this time of withdrawal, Allegra began seeing Larissa. She was playing with fire but felt justified. She strongly suspected Dusty and the stand-in were having an affair—that would explain so much.

She was on an information-gathering mission, or so she told herself.

Today, instead of the invisible Miracle Mile IHOP where they'd had a few rendezvouses, they met at Larissa's house in Mar Vista. Even though they hadn't fooled around since that time at Soho, Allegra knew it was dangerous. The irony of a covert dalliance with Dusty's "double" wasn't lost, amplifying the frisson of guilty arousal; if nothing about it felt right, it felt *sexy*, and she didn't want to overthink. (She wasn't thinking at all.) Apart from the *fact-finding* aspect, the clandestine get-togethers with her wife's probable lover were an antidote to Allegra's jealousy, furor, and confusion. Besides, there could only be consequences—real consequences—if her suspicions were unfounded. Which they weren't. Because why else would Dusty have lied about seeing Larissa in the weeks following the notorious ménage?

If she couldn't confront her wife, her wife's stand-in would do.

"Are you having an affair?"

They were on the couch in the living room of the modest Spanish bungalow, whose furnishings and general vibe had seen better days.

"With Dusty? No!" protested Larissa, in dinner theater–style outrage. "Allegra, *please*."

"Well, I think that you *are*," said the guest, determined to hold ground.

"We have *tea*. After *yoga*. We *talk*."

"What about?"

"Just . . . *stuff*. Oh come on, Allegra! I think she's just *lonely*."

That hit her like a fist in the stomach because they used to talk all the time, about *everything*. *Bunny + Leggy—Best Friends Forever* . . .

"Stuff like *what*?"

"I don't know, just . . . *things*. We just talk about—*I* talk about—my *son*. Or my *ex*, who almost just *died*."

"What does *she* talk about?"

"Her life . . . her *mom*. *Stuff*."

"And you don't sleep together?" she said pitifully.

"Absolutely *not*." Larissa subtly gamed it to sound like a lie, even though it wasn't. "And if we *did*, I wouldn't be seeing *you*."

Allegra sighed—out of words.

"She *has* seemed a little distracted, though," said Larissa, gently testing the handle on a new trapdoor. No need to yank it open just yet . . .

"When did you see her?"

"Uhm, I want to say . . . last week?" The iffy, laid-back delivery hit its mark. "She's probably just, you know, *massively processing*. The mom thing's a pretty big deal." It was important to stay vague yet believable about her nonexistent encounters with the actress.

"Did she tell you?"

Larissa smiled, all squinty-eyed naïve. "About—?"

Allegra decided that even if Dusty *hadn't* told her, no harm could come. Anyway, it was *her* body.

"The miscarriage."

In a flash, Larissa *got* it. "Yes."

"What did she say?"

"Just . . . that she's—sad," said Larissa, wading into perilous waters of improv.

"God!" said Allegra, pissy. "She never talks about it with *me*. She just packs me off to fucking *grief groups*." A deep sigh, then: "Everything's just so *fucked*." The young wife was beyond tears. When Larissa touched her arm then began to massage, Allegra felt a sleazy jolt.

"Wanna feel better?"

"No—"

"Oh come on, Leggy. Come on . . ."

There was fussiness and cajoling before Allegra allowed herself to be ushered to the bedroom. Larissa kissed her neck, her cheek, her lips.

"I can't, I can't," said Allegra. "Too much guilt." She was lost.

"*She* wouldn't feel guilty."

"Then you *have*—you *fucked* her, you were lying!"

"No! I *told* you, we *haven't*. But I didn't say we *wouldn't*—it's *possible*. Anything's *possible*. I think she's definitely *attracted* . . ."

"Ugh ugh *ugh*—"

"You know, sometimes you need to step outside the relationship," said Larissa, in (sex surrogate) wisdom mode, "for it to heal. Then you come back to it. Maybe *that's* what she's doing—I mean, not with *me* but maybe with someone *else*. Those are your instincts, right? Or maybe you're *not* thinking that . . ."

"You *are* fucking her! You are both so totally fucking!"

"Allegra, *stop*," she commanded. "*Whatever* she's doing, if she even *is* doing anything, it's not with *me*. I *promise*." Her aggressiveness shut the poor girl down. Then Larissa grew pensively co-conspiratorial, nearly rubbing her chin. "I *kind* of had that same feeling too . . . that maybe she's—maybe exploring. I guess you got me thinking—power of suggestion! I'm so totally *suggestible*. But you know," she opined, "a lot of time that's not the *end*—of a marriage—or a *relationship*—it's the *beginning*. For both parties. A chance to start over. *Can* be. I *know* from whence I speak. Been there, done that, with Derek. *Firsthand experience*. I didn't do it with a *woman*, but I did it with a man. And it kinda worked."

She kissed her neck again.

"Ooooh," squirmed Allegra, playing the gamine, as her composure slipped away. "I just don't like to lie . . ."

"Sometimes you have to. As long as you're not lying to *yourself*." Her quarry needed more tenderizing. Radically inspired, Larissa shot the moon. "Why don't you just tell her? That we're seeing each other? Not 'seeing,' but that we've *gotten together*. Tell her you *called*— or we ran into each other at Soho or *wherever*—and that you just really needed someone to *talk* to. Which is true! Because *she wasn't available*. And you don't need to go into any *details*—because it's *kind* of none of her *business*. You're a *human being*, Allegra. She isn't your *whole world*. Or shouldn't be. Maybe she needs help *seeing* that. And you know what? You just might be *surprised*. Maybe she'll think it's a *good* thing that we're hanging out, maybe she even *wants* that. *Wants* you to have a friend, a 'mutual' friend. Or more . . ." She stroked her cheek as she kissed her on the mouth. "Maybe all of us together again would be *her* healing."

"I don't know—" said Allegra, still needing a bit more of a finesse.

"Okay," said Larissa, backing off. "Scratch that." Rising to the challenge, she masterfully chose a new vector. "You know, having kids ain't all it's cracked up to be. It's a fuckin' *heartache*. I know it doesn't *feel* like it right now, Allegra, but I think at this time in your life, with all the shit that's going down, some of which you don't even *know* about, but most of which you *do*—I think you dodged a serious bullet, for *real*. But you can still have one, you'll *still* have one, you're *young*, I *know* you will. 'Cause I'm *totally* psychic about baby stuff. And it'll be even *better* when it happens because you'll be *ready*. You'll be *so ready*, Allegra! Because you'll have really *fought* for it and it will have been *meant to be*. I *totally* wasn't ready when I had my son. The girl was *easy*—everything *about* her has been easy. But I'm much more like my son. I don't think either *one* of us was ready for this world!"

Her finger traced Allegra's hipbone then drew tight circles around the belly button before moving downward, like the logy legs of a sea spider. Allegra relaxed into it, even as her pulse quickened.

"What are their names?" she asked, trancelike.

"Rafaela and Tristen."

"Tristen?"

"Uh huh."

"Tristen? He didn't just get a new car, did he?"

"How did *you* know that?"

"Is he gay?"

Larissa stammered, "What the *fuck*—"

"Oh my God," she said. "Your son is dating Jeremy!"

"Jeremy—?"

"My, like, *closest friend*—from the party, the Tuesday Weld party! From Soho House!"

"Are you *shitting* me?"

"Totally not!"

"*Jeremy's* the international man of mystery? *Jeremy?* That is fucking *hilarious*! Allegra, that is so *crazy*! Because I wondered about the car and I *asked* him who he's been seeing, and it was, like, *radio silence* . . . he's not a creep, is he?"

"Oh my God, totally not! Jeremy is *amazing*. You've *seen* him, you've *met*!"

Though there didn't seem much point in keeping it from her—she'd already given away so much—Allegra decided not to share that he was her dead little girl's donor-dad.

"It's beyond small world," said Larissa. "How *old* is he?"

"I wanna say, like, fifty? Fifty-two?"

"Oy vey! Well, as long he's 'amazing.'" They shook their heads in wonderment like a couple of stoners. "I think that probably . . . you shouldn't tell him," said Larissa, "that you know his boyfriend's *mom*— oh my God, that sounds *so weird*—'his boyfriend's mom.' I guess what I *mean* is, everything's kind of messy enough, right?" The stand-in had reasons of her own, beyond those of discretion. "What's that great line from *No Country for Old Men*? 'If it ain't the mess, it'll do 'til the real mess gets here'—"

"*Love* that motion picture," said Allegra.

"I don't know," said Larissa, moving another chess piece. "I guess it doesn't really matter. *Fuck it*, I guess you *could* tell him, if you *wanted* to—"

"Of *course* I'm not going to tell him! I don't want *anyone* knowing about us."

About us—Larissa took that as her cue.

It was three hours before they were done.

Tristen's father had been home only a few days. His girlfriend said she had to go to Portland to see her parents but Derek knew she'd burned out on the caregiving, minimal as it was. What did he expect? She was twenty-three and he was a sixty-two-year-old loser who had to be put in a coma when his O_2 dipped into the 80s. They replaced him on the craphouse reality show he and Beth were cutting and fired her too. Good riddance to all.

The "medics" (how Derek annoyingly referred to them) had trouble figuring out the problem. They thought it was some kind of leukemia, which bummed him to no end, but when an MRI caught a stroke caused by a clot, they shoved a camera down his throat and found staph growing on the valves like mold on a pipe.

Tristen sort of took over for Beth, cleaning house, running errands, and—miracle of miracles—just hanging with the old man. A ceasefire was declared. Derek (miracle upon miracles) seemed grateful.

They grooved on watching *Snapped* and *Forensic Files* marathons. The half hours were crazy dark. In one episode, a serial killer was arrested after his dental impressions were matched to bite marks on the chin of a dead woman. The pathologist said he'd never seen a bite mark there, usually they were on breasts and stomach—the theory being that the killer became aroused by looking into her eyes as he bit down on the chin while mutilating her genitals with a knife.

"I don't really see a problem with that," said Derek. "Ya gotta take it on the chinny chin chin *some* time."

"*Bite* me," said Tristen.

"Don't mind if I do."

It was heaven to just sit around eating popcorn and Red Vines and shoot the shit over a bit of the old ultraviolence. Then out of the blue, Derek pushed pause on the remote.

"They say I need a heart transplant."

"For real?"

"Can you fucking believe it?"

"Uhm, whoa. Not really."

"Some kind of *infection*. They can't even nuke it with antibiotics. It's, like, *done*."

"Jesus. Shit! *Fuck.*"

"The medics say I've got an *abscess* in my heart. A fuckin' *pus pocket.*"

"Whoa—!"

"I'm about to go on the list. Heart transplant list. Mother*fuckers.* And here's the *best* part. Are you ready? My fuckin' *IATSE's* about to expire—next *month.* How 'bout that?"

"Your insurance?"

"That's *right.*"

"Can you, uhm, get you, like, COBRA?"

"Can't fuckin' *afford* it. And what's the *point,* paisan? How the fuck am I going to survive a *heart* transplant? 'Cause I'm *not.* It's, like, a *joke.*"

"It's no big thing anymore, Derek. I mean, they have it *down,* they've had it down for twenty *years.* I just read about a guy in *prison* who got one, some bank robber. Cost a million taxpayer dollars."

"Great! Then *that's* what I'll do—go rob a fucking bank. That'll probably get me bumped to the top of the list. Maybe they'll throw in a hair transplant and a *penile* enlargement. Widen the girth."

"I read that when they execute prisoners in China, they use their organs for transplants. You could get one of *those.*"

"Chinese take-out. No *ticker,* no washee."

Tristen over-laughed . . . *good times.* Sometimes all it took was a crisis to get back to where you once belonged. Derek unpaused, and they fast-forwarded to the next *Forensic.*

"Slow down, Twist!" said Jeremy (what he occasionally called the boy; Tristen now and then called *him* "Nobodaddy," after Blake).

Tonight, in the driver's seat, coolly navigating the wavy road, the kid lived up to the sobriquet. Jeremy was starting to think they should maybe have taken the freeway instead of Sunset.

"Y'know, a lotta people have *died* along this *boulevard of broken dreams*, Twisterella. Jan *Berry*, Ernie *Kovacs* . . ."

"Who's Jan Berry?"

Jeremy vaped his weed and coughed. "Jan and Dean—'Little Old Lady from Pasadena.' 'Dead Man's Curve.' Ernie *Kovacs* died over by Whittier. Me *thinks*. Know who Ernie Kovacs is?"

"'The Nairobi Trio.'"

"*Jesus*, you fucking *do* know! Of *course* you do, you fucking *brainiac*. Ernie Kovacs makes Louis CK and all these so-called geniuses look like Jay *Leno*. All these Apatow *genius cunts* with their *oh so amazing series and specials* and Madison Square Garden *bullshit*." He was in a merry mood. "*Tina's* the only genius. And Lena. *Maybe* Lena—no, just *Tina*. Maybe Lena'll *get* there but she ain't there *yet*. Though I do like Amy, gotta say. *Parts* of her. (Schumer, not Poehler.) If she can make it intact through the *canonization*. People even got shot watching her bullshit *romcom*—hotties too! How lucky is that? You're *nuthin'* till kids and hotties are killed at your movie. *That's* the big time. And who's that *friend* of yours? What's-her-name? Your *friend* who died right *here*, on this very stretch of *road*."

"*What* friend? What are you *talking* about?"

"You know—what's-her-name, *Dead Internet Girl*. The one who lost her head over a handsome Porsche. Right here on Funset Boulevard."

"Nikki *Catsouras*?" He knew Jeremy was high, and being playfully absurd. "That was in Orange County, bitch."

He *was* high—and happy. He'd just come from a meeting with the awesome Heather. She was in her late thirties, which worried him until he got educated on how that was a common age for surrogates. (She had four kids of her own and three more from IVFs.) It was all about the paperwork now, which was going to be hassle-free—Heather was already vetted by the agency, the same one she'd worked with when carrying his friend's twins. The whole deal was going to cost about a hundred grand. She'd clear about twenty-five thousand, more for "multiples," but he *still* couldn't fathom why a woman would want to have a bunch of babies for strangers. When he probed, Heather said, "I just love the way I feel when I'm pregnant."

"You seem awfully *chipper* tonight, Twisteramakrishna." They curved around the Lake Shrine Temple, a few minutes from PCH. "I'm going to have to start calling you Sunshine."

"It was a pretty good day. Hung out with my pops."

"Oh yeah? How's he doing?"

"He's actually *super* fucked up. He's trying to get on the transplant list."

"Kidney?"

"Heart."

"Are you serious?"

"It's crazy."

"I had no idea."

"It's one of those rare kinda irreversible deals."

"My nightmare. Maybe you should, like, *back* him a heart."

"Hey, if I could, I would. But I have an almost better idea."

"Do me a favor," he said with a smile, "and don't *tell* me about it. I don't want to be an *accessory* to any *inseminating information.*"

In preparation for the evening, he gave Tristen a précis of the ballad of Devi and the Sir, and was glad the boy had the savvy to appreciate the peculiar genius of the encounter. Jeremy liked showing off a little of the ol' anarchist brio that was a lion's share of who he was; showboating his psycho-historical DNA made him feel virile and adventurous, still relevant. And Tristen gave *Nobodaddy* props because he wasn't monetizing or script-teasing the couple. He was just following his Dadaist nose.

When she opened the door, her lustrous beauty overwhelmed. She'd morphed from street hippie to bohemian-cum-socialite, and vanity begged Jeremy to wonder if Devi's anticipation in seeing him had anything to do with primping her ride. When they kissed (that was a first) her skin smelled like cannabis and troubled sleep. They gathered in the overqualified kitchen and smoked—the Gaelic guru's whereabouts unknown—while Devi cooked up a storm. She moved with the alacrity of a five-star chef amongst the elegant dishes she was preparing. Maybe it was just a chemical thing but the socially awkward Tristen got on with her right away. Learnedly *au courant* without being pedantic, the hostess riffed on Trolls as Authentic Heir to Coyote Tricksters. The blasted boy was charmed and at ease, something Jeremy had yet to see, at least not in mixed company. It gave him intense pleasure.

He left them and walked to the vast terrace that overlooked the crashing sea. On the way, he was startled by three figures whom he thought to be guests before realizing they were employees. They smiled at him unobtrusively as they tended to the open-pit fire and busily set the stage with a profusion of scented candles, Persian pillows, and dark cashmere throws. He noticed a southern gate and went through it. Without fanfare, he found himself in a garden of dumbfounding sweep and breadth. He strolled, insensate, through a dusky, virtual meadow of ghostpipes and creeping myrtle, monkeyflowers and bursting heart, coatbuttons, toadflax and old man's beard.

Another gate led to the beach and he stumbled toward it.

He took off his shoes and walked onto the sand. The sorrowful wisp of a Santa Ana, broken off from the herd, brushed his face consolingly and reminded him of Devi's greeting.

The refrain of late—*who am I, why am I, where am I*—played just beneath the wave song, with its choral variation: *And what if I die before I know?*

He looked toward the soft lights of the house and heard laughter . . . Tristen, laughing! His wild child, blue-eyed boy! Would wonders never cease? He ambled back to the patio, where servers revolved with platters, delicately setting dishes on driftwood tables round the fire. Others brought carafes of water, juices, and wine. After a few minutes Devi emerged and dismissed them.

Suddenly the three were alone on the deck, gathered by the colored flames:

Storytelling Hour!

"Do you remember where we left off?"

She jumped right in, her method to a tee, which suited him fine. Tristen was already wolfing his food but paying strict attention.

"I was talking about the bells—always the bells!—and the fire that took my mother . . . I've been thinking about *all of it*. The only thing I haven't put to mind is my daughter because I knew I was going to tell you about her tonight. It's an extraordinary gift to have found someone to talk with—*organized by my Sir and the Source*—for I haven't spoken of this in so long. My guru says it's my fate—*our* fate, yours and mine!—to have found each other, just as it was *mine* to have found *him*. We don't know what 'the bells' have in store for us yet, do we, Jerome? Isn't that exciting? We forget so quickly that it's already written, and can *be* no other way. Mind if I call you Jerome? I like it so much better. Well, not *so* much better, but I do like Jerome. And I'm *thrilled* that you brought your friend!" Tristen grinned, his mouth half full. "It's always a good omen to have a witness, *particularly* since the Sir is dead to the world. (If we're *very* quiet, we might hear him snoring.) We've had *such* a long day and he needs his rest.

"Now, I've told you Mama died in a fire, and Papa followed just a few months later. His lungs were scarred by the heat and smoke when he carried her out. He held her so close that his skin became hers; I can see them emerging from the conflagration of that house like figures in a great fresco of Rubens—or something in the *American* style of Thomas Hart Benton . . . where her skin was no more, *his* stood in, like a graft. I've found that detail (*not* a metaphor) to be worthy of any of Poe's creations."

Jeremy noticed the boy had stopped eating and was completely rapt. He presumed Tristen's awed attentions had something to do with his recent role as caregiver to his own father, and the looming mortality of the aggrieved man who had brought him into this unquiet world.

"Before he died, my father made me promise I'd return to school (I'd taken a sabbatical to nurse him) and resume my studies. I was to inherit his practice—the only legacy he had to give. I told him I would and meant it, but after the fire it was impossible. You see, he never cared about money. His finances were in shambles. We'd been living in a motel since the holocaust; he'd forgotten to pay a bill and the insurance on the house had lapsed. The bank foreclosed.

"I told you at the restaurant that after their deaths, the clanging of the bells became too much—'a fatal tinnitus,' remember? I returned to Loyola and promptly went mad. I lived for months in a hospital associated with the school but that's another story. The *short* version being, I became pregnant there. A boy I knew from campus, prone to violence. He'd been placed on seventy-two-hour hold. They put him in the lockdown ward and he smuggled me in—as I say, another story! I knew at the very moment I lay with him that *she* had been born. I knew her sex and even what I would call her: Bella!—my beauty, my only, my Bella, my 'bell'! And in that moment of conception, the world stood still. Everything stopped ringing too . . . every-thing but my love for my daughter and this mysterious blue planet and the starry places beyond. I left the hospital immediately.

"I rented a room above a garage belonging to a former teacher of mine who pitied me. She thought I could have my child, come to my senses, and return to my studies. Because, you see, I was 'filled with promise.' In that tiny space above the carport, with Bella at my breast, I was so happy, Jerome! Time stopped, and with it, all worry. I took a job as a waitress. The teacher's mother lived in the main house and was delighted to look after the little one while I worked.

"I won't talk about what went wrong with Bella's body, in her fourth year. The details. Please forgive that omission . . . it's too painful. Though my Sir has said that one day I shall be able. It won't hurt at all, he said, the time will come when I'll be *eager* to remember those awful, terrible things—though I admit I have trouble *imagining* such a time, so do forgive my faithlessness!—but my Sir says they won't *be* awful anymore, they'll be as beautiful as the memory, the *truth*, of her eyes, her hair, her skin—that I'll wish to remember *it all*, the closer I come to seeing her again. For *that* is where we are going, my guru and I: to that place where she resides, that place where my Sir will see those dear to him, whom *he* once lost as well. The wife and son that he loved, and loves still . . .

"While she was at Children's, I took long walks. I was there, of course, for all treatments and procedures, holding her hand, kissing and fussing over her, taking on her pain as best I could, never leaving her at night. They kept a cot for me right beside her. But when she napped (often with the help of medicine) I took walks because I was starting to hear the bells again; walks were the only thing that muf-fled the noise. You see, if one is not in the proper frame of mind, if one isn't *ready*, the sound of the bells can be *very* unpleasant. For they're

not the sound of bells as *you* know them . . . On those meanderings,
I'd pass a homeless man, surrounded by heaps of rags and discarded
things, who begged for coins from his carpet of cardboard. I wouldn't
go by him *all* the time—it depended on which route I took. But when
I *did*, he searched my eyes in such a way that eventually I chose to
force the encounter. Each time I grew near, I slowed on the approach,
until one day I broke through my shyness and spoke to him. I'm telling you, I was in a horrible, shambling state! Yet the moment I was in
his presence, something strange occurred . . . I didn't realize until
half an hour later that *the bells had stopped entirely.* He cleared an edge
of cardboard and asked me to sit on some shag he had requisitioned
from a dumpster. I felt no shame. Pedestrians walked by, hardly giving notice. No shame! You see, *I'd come home.* So I poured my heart to
him and told *everything.* About the fire and the bells—and my Bella.
Jerome, never in my *life* had I been listened to like that! The tenderness! Had his tenderness stood of itself, without my anguish to balance it, I think it would have been too much to bear. I'd have died
from such kindness."

Tears hung in her eyes, and Jeremy thought he saw them in the
boy's as well; his own became wet by contagion.

"And we talked like that—*I* talked like that—for hours and hours
and hours, until there was no more sorrow, rage, or yearning to be
shown. Then one day, my Sir said—of course I didn't yet *know* him as
'my Sir,' 'my guru'—my Sir said, 'It's all over now'—said it under his
breath, as if talking to himself—but I *heard* and I *cringed* because I
thought he meant my poor Bella! *It's all over now*—God, the agony
when I heard that! (And he was right, about it being over for her,
though, you see, he meant something entirely *different.* I'll tell you what
he *really* meant in just a little while.) 'It's all over,' he said, louder this
time, and looked me dead in the eye. 'It's over because now they *know.*

I made *certain* of it—the "contract" is *magnificently broken.'* I thought, What on earth could he be talking about? *What* contract? I hadn't a clue. What strange words from a sidewalk saint, this rumpled, roly-poly, Rumpole-looking dervish who sent everything whirling! Before I could gather my wits and *ask*, he seized my arm and said with an urgency that thundered:

"'Let's see about your daughter now!'"

The flames in the pit suddenly brightened, letting loose a *crack* like gunfire—man and boy jumped from their skin, but the unsink-able Devi didn't stir. She just sat there smiling, cool and inscrutable.

"On the way back to Children's, we walked in silence—*Silence.* Did you know that Silence has a sound? One day you'll hear it. I have no words to describe—there *are* no words—isn't it funny that it even has a name?—'Silence'?—the closest I can come is that it's like the sound of a *single, extended heartbeat*—within a . . . *cathedral.* Not a *human* heart . . . and we're *enshrouded* by it, it belongs to the Source . . . and not that it can belong *anywhere*—I know I'm not mak-ing sense, that's *my* fault, not yours, but one day you might have an *inclination* of what I'm trying to tell you." She stared directly at Tris-ten, who appeared both unnerved and ennobled. "*You* will under-stand, young man! You already *do*." She brought her gaze to the other, so as not to neglect. "And *you*, my dear Jerome, are on *your* way! *Well* on your way!"

She refilled their wineglasses. The ocean roared and quieted, roared and quieted, as if it too were restive for more talk, more spir-its. Devi leaned to stoke the fire, which had also grown ornery; at her nourishing touch, it regained equilibrium.

She had the full attention of the elements again.

"The quality of our reception at the hospital was, shall we say, *guarded.* Ha! My 'friendly giant' was wild and unkempt, carrying

with him the ambrosia of the streets. Until we arrived, I hadn't considered how we'd be greeted. When I saw the fearful look on their
faces, I only hoped they wouldn't be *too* rude—see, I didn't want to
offend them *either*, because those nurses had been Bella's *angels*, and
mine too. I think I debated whether or not to announce him as
my child's *father* or *godfather* or grand pa-*pa*—I remember being wary
of doing anything to insult my big Sir. But he wouldn't have cared
at all! It wouldn't have mattered *who* I said he was! He wasn't of
this world! You see it was all *new* to me, so I dared not presume . . .
I suppose as well that I simply didn't want to tell a *lie*—in the face
of this formidable creature, any subterfuge, no matter how small
or expedient, suddenly seemed like a sin. Of course, in *his* world,
there *is* no such as *sin*—or a 'lie' . . . nor is there 'truth.' Only Silence!
I didn't know that yet, any of it. It was all so completely new.

"The oncology ward is sacred ground. Pain, unutterable sorrow,
and resurrection live there; it is a cradle, like an infant's, of the Source.
Bella was just awakening when we came in. By then, the man who
would be my teacher, who already *was* though I didn't yet know it . . .
we had both donned the required surgical masks and gloves—
shimmering raiments of Silence's heart!—and my *human* heart broke
when I saw her, and saw *him*—witnessed the care he lavished on my
baby. 'The divine interplay.' He touched her head with his hand
so *softly*, that bearish hand that had already spent a thousand
lifetimes ringing the bells of this world and of worlds beyond—I
couldn't stand it. I was about to *faint* when a spate of bells clanged
me to life. I was startled, for those clangorous sounds had abandoned me from that first moment I sat with him on his shaggy patch
of sidewalk—remember? But now I *heard* them again, was *jolted*, just
as that crack of fire jolted *you*—twelve times, they rang, a dozen
percussive strokes, for it was high noon, and the tower, only blocks

away, was tolling. My Sir kept his hand on Bella's head while he turned to me, his eyes blurred by— . . . he once told me that *tears of Silence* are rare as an owl's, and if one is *very* lucky, one may hitch a ride on such a raft of teardrops, all the way to the Source. With the most beautiful smile, he whispered, 'The little one has now broken *her* contract as well. How magnificent! Come, Cathy, come! Take her in your arms!' (I was Cathy before he named me Devi.) 'She's leaving now! Hold her while the bells ring out!' And I held her and they *kept* ringing . . . later, one of the nurses said that a mechanism in the tower went awry, so the cycle of twelve kept repeating, ten times in all, *a hundred and twenty tolls*, ceasing only upon my daughter's last breath.

"Sir made the funeral arrangements. He showed me a napkin sketch of a mausoleum, like an elegant confection, with a filigreed entryway and little benches inside where one could sit. Construction would begin the next day—but how? I never asked, never questioned the phantasmagoric speed with which he made everything possible. On the day of her burial, trucks delivered beds and beds of Million Bells. Do you know the flower? *Calibrachoa.* We have some in our garden—you walked through it on your way to the beach—I carry seeds around in my purse. Oh, it was a gorgeous celebration, not a funeral but a wedding! My Sir said that now I would hear bells no more—and the ringing would only resume when Bella and I were together again. He told me I'd see her soon, 'soon enough,' that's what he said, and somehow I knew he wasn't talking about the after-life. I'd see her soon in *this* world, or something so much like it that I wouldn't be able to tell the difference . . . she used to be *here*, he said—but *there* was where I'd find her. 'We will go to the place she now finds herself.' That's how he put it. 'I'll take you.' I believed him—and believe him still. *That* was where we were—are—traveling.

We were on our way to the place of 'a million bells' when *you* interceded. When you came to sit on that bench . . . *dear* Jerome!

"*You* are the reason we stopped, and now find ourselves *here*. That's what my teacher told me tonight, just an hour before you came."

The rest of the evening was spent shaking off the spell cast by her wrenching, cockeyed illuminations and they danced for their lives to a mixtape of one-hit wonders: "Come On Eileen," A-ha, the Easybeats, "Spirit in the Sky." With amazement, he watched Tristen become utterly transported (Jeremy was almost ashamed by his failure to believe the gyrating boy could have been capable of such elegantly frenzied *interpretations*) before turning his eye to the house. There, a massive robed figure rummaged through the Sub-Zero like some burgling, Edwardian ringmaster. He left his friends to their ecstatic, giggly contortions and went to have a look.

He crept in through the pantry and was about ten feet away when the Great Scot swiveled to face him, holding an enormous drumstick in his paw—*gluttonous interruptus.*

"Ho ho!" he shouted. His sparkled being seemed to ratify *some* version of the woman's more unorthodox claims. "My Devi wouldn't be glad about my raiding the fridge—she's worked herself into an awful *swivet* over my expanding girth."

"I think you carry it rather well."

"You're too kind! Has she been telling you our story?"

"She has. I've never heard anything like it."

"Of *course* you haven't. But she tells it with *panache*, no? All curlicues and oddities being the same, and the occasionally queer yet always quirkily charming turn of phrase."

"Yes yes, she tells it *very* well. But I can't say I *understand* it all . . ."

"I can't say I understand *any* of it! Please, then, to accept my invitation—the *Source's* invitation—to the Society of the Uncomprehending. I'm delegate *and* chairperson, at your service. *Go straight to the Source and ask the horse.* Or perhaps I mean the other way around." He went back to his rummaging. "A reg'lar Scheherazade she is, that girl, no? Or do I mean *ir*-reg'lar."

"Is there more?" he asked. What Jeremy meant to say was that he wanted to hear "the Celt's tale"—the old man's side.

"More? I should say! *For another time* . . . go now! Enjoy the dance! In the end, that's all it is. A pataphysical *rumba.*" He laughed uproariously then robbed the "cold drawer" blind. Without looking up, he said, *"You're* dreaming of a child as well, no? That's what *she's* doing— she doesn't know it yet—that's why you've *met.* 'A dream of children.' Lovely! Both of you suffered a great loss; it's piffle to say whose was the greater. All that *comparisoning* is the downfall of man. 'I go, and it is done; the *bell* invites me . . .' Thank Mr. Shakespeare for that one. We can thank him for nearly everything, no? Though I suppose at least we should try to . . . She's talked a lot of the bells, no? Got bells on the brain, that one. Oh, you'll *find* those children again, both of you—no worries in that regard! But first, you must dance."

Dusty passed on to Snoop everything Ida Pinkert told her. It was the sort of lead that made a gumshoe's day.

Her name was Claudia Zabert. The old woman hadn't a clue where Reina found her, and other than the generic sluttiness that Ida alluded to, Dusty couldn't remember much about her either. The babysitters were neighborhood locals—except for Claudia, who'd been imported from God knew where. She was probably about sixteen when she began working for the Whitmores, around the time Arnold was arrested and hospitalized. Dusty would have been ten. The actress remembered Claudia having boys over and sometimes even leaving the house with them after giving her hush money. Probably just a few dollars, but hey, none of the *others* did that. Come to think of it, she had tons of sitters—Claudia was the one Reina used the least. Maybe because she was hardest to get hold of.

Her parents often spent nights away. It was strange because until Ida's revelation, she'd never given much thought to the whys and wherefores. It wasn't hard to guess what her dad was doing—most likely haunting public johns and gay bars in Long Beach, San Pedro, or wherever. And Reina had her Mormon paramour . . . Dusty assumed there were a lot more where *he* came from (though not necessarily Mormon). The boss at her father's bank was a prime candidate—how else would Arnold have kept his job after a charge of public lewdness?

Maybe Claudia was the daughter of one of those men . . .

She shared a few names and theories with Mr. Raskin.

It was a time of upheaval and great promise—*shifting sands*, as Ginevra put it—and the only thing that mattered was keeping her shit together. She sought balance in hyper-vigilant attention to body, mind, and spirit. Self-care was the theme of the hour: yoga and journaling workshops, colon cleanses, meditation-spa retreats. (She even got in touch with Marilyn about shrooming with the *bruja*.) It was essential to be awake and aware, ready with open heart for whatever pesky festivities the Universe had planned. The trouble with Allegra was put on the back burner; this was *Dusty's* time. Besides, she'd had enough therapy to know that what was good for *her* would be good for the marriage.

She decided to visit Chakrapani, the renowned vedic astrologer. Her first session was a long while back, before she came out. Dusty remembered him being harsh, plainspoken, and unguarded; all of his predictions had come true. She'd been frightened to see him again, but now it was definitely time. She couldn't afford to have fear in her life. About anything.

"You are at the end of a *Ketu period*. Ketu is the beginning of change taking place—it has been this way for the last three years."

He worked from the guesthouse of a mansion in Hancock Park. Chakrapani must have been ancient but didn't seem to have aged. Though he possessed that timeless, sprightly, lit-from-within guru energy, he still managed to give her the willies.

"Thereafter, you are in the Ketu-Jupiter. I'm wondering how the Ketu-Jupiter is going to react, because Ketu and Jupiter are not in *harmonious conditions*. They have the tendency to create some stress and anxiety. I'm wondering in what way it's going to manifest for you, physically, mentally, psychologically. There is a tendency to create *tension*. It can also bring some traveling. Is it possible you will be traveling?"

"Yes—to England, for my work. I travel a lot for my work . . . but there's nothing just now. Is it bad? To travel?"

"It's not a question of 'good' and 'bad.' You'll be *prompted* to do the traveling. It has the tendency to bring the *possibility* of traveling, *going* places. And Jupiter is *aspecting* the rising sign *very strongly*. Jupiter is also in aspect with Mars—Mars and Jupiter in mutual aspect, which can bring you *organization*. Doing things and getting things done, which is considered very good. I am also wondering if it will bring *opportunity* to bring entertainment and positive energies, and take life a little easier. *Those* kinds of things it can create. The nature of Jupiter is to be taking it easy. To spend money only on good causes. Not to take too much *stress* in doing things, which you used to do in the past."

It was all a bit bland. Dusty wondered if he'd lost his touch, his edge, his whatever. He was known for not pulling punches, with celebrities, powerhouses, or anyone else. She remembered randomly mentioning him to Amy Pascal a few years ago and to her surprise, Amy went for a consult—which Dusty almost regretted, because apparently he foretold all the Sony craziness and a fall from grace. Not that there was anything Amy could have done about it.

"What else do you see?" she asked. She knew it wasn't a crystal-ball/storefront psychic situation, but hey. "You can tell me anything. I promise not to flip out."

She wanted him to drop the hammer, *any* kind of hammer—a sledge, a mallet, a gavel, even one of those little red rubber reflex dillies that doctors use on your knees. It was her Season of the Hammer and she implored the gods to *bring it.*

"From the point of view of the Ketu, Jupiter is *not good.* But from Jupiter *itself,* it is not *bad.* Jupiter is *well placed* in the Ninth House, it is aspecting the Rising Sign *very strongly* and in good relationship with Mars. What else do you want? But Jupiter is *not* a benevolent planet for people born with Virgo Rising. Your Rising Sign is Virgo. Jupiter is a *malefic* for people of that sign."

"A malefic?"

"It is *not* good. That is why it does not bring you a certain amount of *happiness* in the area of *relationships.* That has not been that *great,* true? Looking back in your life? Jupiter is occupying the constellation of Mars and is not a benevolent planet! And Mars is *aspecting* in Jupiter so it brings a certain amount of *aggressive nature.* Anyway, this Ketu *as a whole* is not that great a planet. It's *okay.* It keeps you in an 'unconventional' state—not in the state of doing one thing in particular, but doing *many* things. Jupiter lasts for *one year* but Ketu will go *two more years*."

"So you're saying there's 'potential for difficulty' in the next two years?"

"Not *difficulty*. Potential for *diversification*. Life changes in so many ways . . ."

"Oh my God, Chakrapani!" she said, in mock aghast. "That is *so vague*." When he started to giggle, she was charmed, in spite of herself. "I read an interview that you never tell people someone they love is dying, if you've 'seen' it in their chart—you say, 'Be kind to him,' instead!"

"I cannot 'see' or *know* such things," he said. "It is *possible* to know, but not for *me*. I have not climbed that high!"

"So what are you *really* trying to tell me? What are you *hiding*?"

He tittered but she wasn't kidding around anymore.

"I know that *difficulties* are always—they're always *there*, that's part of *life*. But Chakrapani: are you saying I'm entering a *particularly* difficult period?"

"Particularly *unconventional*. A time where *opportunity* for *unconventional types of activity* arise. We don't have 'future,' we only have 'now,' so what are you going to do? You don't *know*—today you are okay, tomorrow you may be something *different*. Who you are, what you are going to do, where you are going . . . these are all tendencies reflected by *Ketu*. That is why it is *stressful*: you can't see 'future.' *Jupiter* has created the problem! Of the relationship with your wife, it is over."

Say what?

The hammer!

"You may not accept *today* but it indicates strongly . . . the difficulty you will experience in the next two years is not about *relationship*. It is about *everything*. Ketu is more mystical and philosophical than it is material. Ketu is *not* good for material things. It is good for the *spiritual*, the *psychological*, *all* other aspects of life. As an actress, if you are working and making money, you will continue to. You are okay. It is not affected so far. What's affected is your *state of mind*. When your *mind* is occupied by 'ABC'—which is temporary!—things *appear* to be difficult. When it is temporary, it will be *difficult for you*, because when things are 'permanent,' we are *accustomed*, we are *attached*. The 'permanent' is familiar. But when *temporary* things show up, which *appear* to be new, ah! It can be difficult, frustrating, challenging. 'I don't know how to make the adjustment!' That kind of thing."

"What happens *after* this two-year period? Does it get worse?"

"No—the *best* period begins, best in twenty years!—until you leave the planet. You are okay thereafter, nothing to worry! You're in a transition just now. Ketu is a planet of transition, intermediary. Ketu is a node, a magnetic point. It does things in *exactly* the way that it wants! Jupiter is the enemy of no one—but is *not* your friend. Jupiter is one more year. Jupiter is death of 'home,' death of mother, death of marriage—"

"Chakrapani, I don't *see* my marriage dying!"

"'Relationship' means difficulty. Your marriage is tumultuous."

"But it *isn't*. I mean, not *really* . . ."

"You must remember, a relationship is not the best situation in your chart *as a whole*. Relationship is not able to give you greatest satisfaction. *Not marrying* is the best solution for you! Because this solves some of your problems. Jupiter is not *swallowing* you—it's making you *practical*! Jupiter represents the Seventh House, the house of relationship. Pisces is ruled by Jupiter. Relationships do not make you 'even.' Either you're up or down or you're agitated or not—that sort of thing. But that's no way to live."

"You're saying it's not great—not good for me to be married? Or in a relationship?"

"Oh, but that's not possible! Your work has not failed you but *work* is not *relationship*. Look back at your life—at your 'love' relationships *so far*, how they've *treated* you, and *why*. That is due to Jupiter! There's no way to overcome this, no *need* to. *Just take it as it comes.* 'Relationship' really means 'trusting companionship,' trusting partnership. *That's* a relationship. You trust for anything and everything. *That* is a relationship. All other 'relationships' are give and take. It is a *business*."

"Okay."

Jesus. Shit. *Fuck*.

"Things will get easier in two years! That is when Jupiter ends, and Venus comes. Venus is the planet of *love, creativity, music, art*. You don't have complete happiness and satisfaction in relationships— you have *never* had it in your life and may not even know what it means! Normally, I will not talk like that, because people are so much attached to 'relationship' that when I throw cold water on it, that is *not good*. When you go into Saturn, something changes. Still a tough period, not easy, but it may not be as tumultuous as Jupiter."

"So in my case, it goes from '*very* difficult' to just '*difficult*'?"

"No—some of your best years will be coming."

"It sounds like you're just trying to make me feel better!"

"Ha ha! No! Not at all! I say this because Jupiter is *exalted*. When a planet is exalted it gives good things, even if it isn't 'friendly.' What these things are, we don't yet know. Your losses—mother, wife— maybe *not* wife! But if you lose the wife, *Jupiter* is doing this—you can find another! When Jupiter is exalted, it rules more than *relationships*. You'll make it. You will. You're not going to die, I can tell you *that*. I do not see death."

"Well, I didn't *tell* her I was sleeping with her wife. I just kind of *implied* it."

"Oh my God, I *love* you, you are *evil*, I want to *be* you!"

Larissa and Tessa were in the Butterfly Room at Cecconi's, courtesy of a reservation booked by the ersatz billionaire.

"You *totally* fucked her in the bathroom that night at Soho, didn't you!"

"Nope."

"You *did*, I *know* you did! You are *so hardcore*. Come *on*, Rissa, you can *tell* me . . ."

"We *didn't*. We might have *mauled* each other a little bit, but we—"

"*Slurp slurp slurp*. But *now* you're fucking her, right?"

"*Only once*. I mean, we've only done it once, after the *ménage*. The other day was the first time *solo*."

"O *solo* mio! What was it *like*?"

"Really . . . *intense*."

"Oh my *God*, and she's so fucking *hot*."

"She *is*, right?"

"*So* hot, Rissa."

"She's *young*."

"Not *that* young."

"*Young enough*. Does that mean I get a Cougar Town zip code now?"

"There goes the neighborhood. So *tell me, tell me, tell me*: how did it *start*? Did you *call* her?"

"*She* called *me*. Apparently, she needed someone to talk to."

"Slurp slurp slurp."

"Stop that!" said Larissa, swatting her.

"And now you have her thinking that you're sleeping with Dusty?"

"I don't even know why I *started* that, Tess, it's *crazy*. And last night I was up at, like, four a.m.? Watching *Dangerous Liaisons*? On Netflix? Which is *kind* of what I suddenly realized I was *doing*. Have you *seen* that?"

"Dangerous *what*?"

"Liaisons. Glenn Close is so genius."

"Is it, like, about a *ménage à foie gras*?"

"*God*, you're fuckin' funny."

"'Cause that would *totally* make an amazing friggin' movie, right? The *Star* . . . the *Wife* . . . and the *Camera Double*—oh my God, *Rissa*! You need to start writing *right now*."

". . . I guess I'd feel worse about everything if—it's not like I held a *gun* to her head. 'Cause *she's* the one who called, right? And I know Allegra's playing the payback game, so I guess I'm kinda being used. *Again!*—"

Tessa drunkenly sang, "*Girl*, you just keep on *using* me . . . till ya *use me up*—" while Larissa continued her experimental hyperloop train of thought.

"—Allegra's really *sweet* and *vulnerable* and I *know* that Queen Wilding treats her like *shit*."

"Well, duh. It's all about who got duh power, honey."

"And I don't even know anymore why I got so *pissed*—"

"Because *Star Whore* took a steaming dump on you and that *never* feels good. Though maybe it *does*! Hairy Man would prob'ly know."

"I mean, it was just a *fling* with a *movie star*, and it was *fun*—"

"Until it wasn't."

"Because hey, you know what? I'm a big girl. I can do a one-nighter. Like, no problem! I can be the *whatever* who saves your marriage and I can be the whatever who blows it *up*. I can be whatever you *want* me to be, whatever you *need*. I can do it *all*, but just, like, treat me with *respect*. Treat me like a human being, okay? Right? You know, like, don't make me feel frickin' *used*. And I *probably* should've known better. I guess I got sucked in. You know, the *lifestyle* sucks you in every time."

"Dusty Wilding is a cold fucking cunt."

"She is, right? It was, like, *abusive*. And I think I *am* going to write something about it—"

"*Yass!*" said Tessa, with a fist pump. "I *told* you, Riss, *anyone* would publish that. You could get serious *magazine* money from a—even maybe, like, *Vanity Fair*. Oh my God, *Vanity Fair*! Like, it doesn't have to be *The Star* or a shitty tabloid. Payback *is* a motherfucker. You got *laid*, now get *paid*."

"No, I don't want to do that. And nothing online. I'm thinking of something *so much cooler*—like a novel, like a *Fifty Shades of Grey*. Or even *classier*, like a *Dangerous Liaisons*, which I Googled by the way and which happens to actually have been a 'pistol' novel written in *1782*. You can *totally steal* from novels written centuries ago. All the copyrights have totally expired."

"Oh my God, *Fifty Shades of Grey* made *a billion dollars*."

"I could sell it to publishers as a *roman à clef*."

"A what?"

"It's French, for a novel based on real people."

"I *love* it! A reality-show novel!"

"But without—I wouldn't necessarily have to come out and say who the real people *are*. You hire *publicists* to kind of spread the word."

"But your *name's* on it, right? Like, written by you?"

"I don't know . . . I think maybe 'Written by Anonymous.'"

"Larissa, you *can't*, you *have* to put your name on it. You can leave *theirs* out—even though I think that'd be a *huge mistake*—but it *has* to have your name on it. 'Le Ménage à *Twat*, by *Larissa Dunnick*' *has* to be in *huge letters* on the cover!"

"Mais *non*, cheri . . ."

"But why? Otherwise people won't know you *wrote it*—"

"I don't even know where this is *going*, contessa."

"Did you just call me a cunt?"

"It totally may not be going *anywhere*. I'm just making it up as I go along."

"But that's what a *novel* is. That's what *novelists* do, they make shit *up*."

"All I know is, I'm just gonna do whatever I have to, to maybe come out of everything with a book. And right now, it's *weird* but it's *fun*."

Tessa begged to hear more but Larissa wanted to talk about Mister Billion instead.

"What's going *on* with you two, anyway?"

"I don't know," said Tessa. "I think I'm kinda *over* it. He says he wants to take me to Turks and Caicos. I call it Kikes and Jerkoffs . . . he has this *boat*. Or *says* he has a boat. So far, all I've seen are fucking *pictures*. On *Instagram*. He takes more pictures of that boat than he does of his dick. Whatever."

"Turks and Caicos on a private yacht sounds kinda awesome."

"Fuckin' *hate* me a boat, Riss. But if you're *very good*, I *might* tell you something I did that was *naughty*."

"Oh my God, you *better*—after what I told *you*? You *owe* me like a motherfucka!"

Tessa *slowly* finished her wine (she'd been drinking on top of the Xanax) then scofflawed an American Spirit. Larissa snatched it from her lip and hissed it out in a glass of Perrier.

"Now *fess* the fuck *up*."

"He paid me for anal. *Paid*. Twice. No—three times."

"No shit."

"Pun intended. 'Cause I made sure I was clean as a whistle."

"Did you ever do that before?"

"Ever do anal? Or ever get paid for it?"

"Both."

"I have. Done it. But only a handful. Assful? Never got *paid* for it though. Not *exactly*."

"How much did he give you?"

"Five thousand."

"Whoa! Each time?"

"Yup."

"Nice!"

"It started as a goof. Like, he kept talking and talking about it? Kind of pressuring me? And girl, you *know* Tessa don't like bein' *pressured*. And I think he thought I'd like just keep saying no . . . like, I'd be all Betty Ford—*Just Say No!*—the Betty Ford of anal. Or was that Nancy Ray-gun. But maybe he was gettin' *off* on me saying no. So when I finally said, 'For *ten grand*, you can wear it like a turtleneck,' it was sorta like he was up shit's creek and I finally handed him a paddle."

"I thought you said five though. That he gave you five. Was it ten each or five each?"

"Girl, don't you watch *Shark Tank*? Apparently, *Mr. Wonderful* felt my valuation was too high, but was in love with the *product*. I gave him *back-end points*. Hey: a good businesswoman never wants to hear Mr. Wonderful say, 'I'm out.'"

They went to Crossroads to see their daughter in *Legally Blonde*. Rafaela played one of the Delta Nu sisters—a small part but she really shined. Derek sucked O_2 through a nasal cannula during the show.

For the past few weeks, Tristen had been crashing on his dad's couch in the cluttered Hollywood apartment. With Beth gone, Derek needed help. He was too weak and too bummed to resist the boy's overtures, and signed a provisional truce with the ex as well. Thanks to the *medics*, there was no shortage of Percocets and grass; getting loaded did wonders for his level of interpersonal tolerance. He'd lost most of his bark, and all of his bite—he was scared. He was on the organ wait list but had been designated "Status 2," the least needy of recipients. They said it could take months, even years. Derek saw that as a death sentence.

Their shit was upside down. They still owned the house together but in twenty years the mortgage hadn't budged. They were half a million and change in the red, plus a hundred and thirty-three thousand in credit-card debt, plus a hundred and sixty borrowed against the property. (And another ninety grand in back taxes to the IRS that he hadn't even told her about.) She cursed their spendthrift ways. They'd lived like delusional pimps—the Barneys shopping sprees, the celebrity doctors who eschewed insurance, the horse-shit weekend getaways at the Beverly Hills Hotel. All for the look-good, what Derek called "keeping up with the Jewses." And now she was old, a grifting wannabe dyke with just $16,000 left in her secret savings. She looked into the future, the *near* future, and saw a dried-up widow, a stinky hoarder living in borrowed rooms, on bor-rowed time.

During intermission, she brought him a tea because seeing him mingle with the parents—if he'd even had the energy to walk to the lobby—would have embarrassed her. He was sallow and gaunt, strug-gling.

"Did you know Bobby Altman had a heart transplant?" asked Larissa.

"Bobby Altman? Who the fuck is 'Bobby' Altman? What were

you, a *family friend*? It's *Robert* Altman. And he had *money*. If you got money, you live. If you ain't got, you die."

"I was searching transplants online. Tracy *Morgan* had one."

"A heart transplant? From the car accident?"

"Kidney—way before. His girlfriend gave him one. She thought if she gave him a kidney they'd get back together, but they didn't."

"That's what they call 'donor's remorse.' Ol' *Tracy* don't need any handouts, either—nigger's *rich*. Walmart probably gave him a hundred mill."

"You knew *Cheney* had a heart transplant, right?"

"Heart Vader! Ol' spotted Dick. Had his pick of donors at Gitmo too. And all those *'black'* sites . . . now *there's* an unkillable motherfucker."

"—and this golfer who had, like, *two* heart transplants."

"Yeah, one of the nurses was talking about him. He was probably Status 2, like me. But they took a look in his wallet and said, 'Oh! Rich Sports Guy! Need a heart? There's a *fourteen-year-old girl* in line before you, she's been on the list for three years, but fuck her, *she* won't mind, 'cause you're Mr. Rich Sports Guy! Oops—body rejected it? So sorry, sir, here, have another, our treat! 'Cause you're Mr. Rich-As-Fuck Sports Guy!'"

Derek could be funny when he was mad—which was pretty much 24/7. She loved that about him for the first few years, before everything got old.

"Have you seen Tristen's car?"

"Yeah," he snorted. "He was gonna get a Tesla but apparently they go for five thousand blowjobs. The Honda was only five hundred."

She just shook her head and asked how "the sleepovers" were going.

"They're going."

"Well, they've done wonders for *him*. He's sure been a happier camper lately."

"Been making hisself useful, anyway."

"So sorry that Beth—your *other* slave—escaped the plantation."

"Easy come, easy go."

"What do you have him doing over there, crushing up your pain pills? Putting a polish on those nonexistent editing awards? Fielding offers from J. J. Abrams?"

"*Nope*. Got him hacking into the IATSE system. He's goin' North Korea on it. Goin' rogue. Goin' Putin."

"Are you serious?"

"Creating a dummy employment file so we can keep our insurance."

"Oh shit, Derek," she said, with a mixture of caution and pride in Tristen's wayward expertise.

"No other option, babe. Look at the bright side—once he's locked us in, you can get your eyes and neck done. Have that titty reduction you always wanted. Hell, have an augmentation *and* a reduction. Spoil yourself! The tummy tuck's on *me*, the ass lift's on IATSE. Get your teeth and bunghole whitened. Shit, you can build yourself a hymen—get back that new car smell."

"Fuck *you*," she chuckled. "But can't we get in trouble for that?"

"Not 'we,' babe. It's on *him*."

"Oh, *great*. Why do you fucking *hate* him so much?" She ignored his dagger eyes. "He *loves* you, Derek. God knows you've never given him a reason to, but he does. He *loves* you and you *hate* him."

"I don't hate *him*," he said jauntily. "I hate *you*."

"Well, get *over* it. He's your *son*. Goddammit, it's heartbreaking."

"My *son*?" He coughed up a scrap metal resemblance of a laugh. "No *shit* it's heartbreaking. Tell me about it. My heart's so broke I need a new one."

In her twenty-eighth year, not long after winning her inaugural Oscar, Dusty Wilding came out to the world. The effect of that avowal, so thinkable now but unthinkable then, lends itself to clumsy metaphor—say, pick *tsunami*: waves of public acclaim receded at the announcement, exposing a naked, drawnback shore of flotsam, garbage, and gasping, outrun grunion; a perplexion of outraged starfishes and nationally stunned disbelief. After shocky abeyance, a hundred-foot-high wall of murderous *judgewater* raked in from the heartland, destroying everything in its path on the way to both coasts (and the continents and land masses beyond). Nothing could have prepared the actress for the initial, sustained violence of cultural response, the mad ugliness of it, the innumerable FBI investigations of mayhem and threats of mutilation and death, the mockery, vandalism and hate riffs of the country's best comedians. Against her will, she submitted to invasive shifts of bodyguards until one day Dusty'd had enough. "The tide cannot be held, let it come." She watched from higher ground as the villages of her spirit, her soul, her very being were drowned and reordered. Most of those whom she considered friends went missing; the cats all died; only her dogs remained, limping and three-legged. *Yes* she had her tribe, vociferous and militant, tried and true blue, but they were outliers too. They were fragile, and died hard—many were swept to sea in those first chaotic days, weeks, and months . . . *so many tree trunks, startled by their own amputation*, a confusion of desecrated bodies and debris, with no Internet (for better and for worse) to damn the flood. Yet in all such catastrophes, one may note the photo of the single church that survives, alone and untouched, magisterially indifferent amid the ruins, a day-after symbol of Christian love and renewal—Dusty and her heart were like that. She held fast until houses and new life sprung up around her.

And became a religion unto herself.

And eventually her followers were legion.

A pew within that lone church was forever reserved for none other than Diana Vreeland, who, during that season of hell and high water, had taken the young actress under her wing. The gimlet-eyed Garuda told her early on to "go with your heart," and whenever Dusty flinched she need only direct her gaze to wise doyenne Diana, who never learned how to blink. (She loved that Diana injected her pillows with perfume-filled hypodermics.) She couldn't number the hours she spent on the phone being firmly/gently talked down from the trees by that woman. Around the same time, D.V.'s dandyish grandson Nicholas, who resembled a softer, nebbishier Jerry Seinfeld, underwent a notable refurbishing himself (more a going in than a coming out): from womanizing apprentice-photographer to humble monastery-living monk. Handpicked by the Dalai Lama to become the abbot of an important tenth-century monastery in India, he was also director of the Tibet Center in New York. Dusty met "the Geshe" in 2005 (and many times since), courtesy of Richard Gere.

When the actress heard he was on his way to L.A., she decided to throw a dinner party. She thought it might be healing.

She reached out to the usual Maui Wowee bohos, spiritual *simpaticos* who enjoyed laying bread on the cause. (Of course Jeremy came, and Elise, who was on fire with beginner's-mind excitement over TM. The gal was full of surprises.) Invitations were last-minute, so she couldn't snag Jim Carrey, or her old friend Jeff Bridges, who texted love and *namastes* from Fiji. On a lark, she reached out to Laura Poitras, who sent regrets from Rio. But she was glad Shandling could come—he was a bit of a recluse, and no one made her laugh like Garry.

A hundred years ago, Mike Nichols introduced her to the comedian at a dinner in Paris, and the three wound up taking an impromptu trip to meet Thich Nhat Hanh at Plum Village in the Dordogne.

Rounding out the group were her Point Dume neighbors, the Ruschas; one half of the sisters Rodarte and one third of the sisters Haim; Donna Tartt; and Michael Imperioli, who drove in from his Santa Barbara home—they'd met through Jim Gandolfini, whom Dusty actually roomed with in the early New York theater days. She didn't know Michael that well but was surprised to learn he was on the "Vajrayana path" under the guidance of a man called Garchen Rinpoche. (Maybe Richard had already told her that.) The soirée was padded with enthused fillers as well—a sweet girl from Annapurna and an agent from UTA, both active in David Lynch's foundation. Joan Halifax, who'd been giving a lecture in a private home in the Palisades, came halfway through dinner, all apologies. (Dusty met *her* through Eve Ensler.) Joan was a live wire, a charismatic, politically active Buddhist who, Dusty found out, via a Wikipedia refresher, had received "transmission" from Bernie Glassman *and* Thich Nhat Hanh. She was the abbess of a monastery in Santa Fe. There was something posh about her and Dusty called her Downton Abbess, which always got a laugh out of Joan.

The night was funny, spirited, messy, and profane. Per usual, Jeremy played court jester, the heterodox, half wiggy *wag* who relished his role as goad, gadfly, and sometimes churlish upender of the status quo. In other words, the man was fairly deep in his cups. Tonight, Joan was the one to get under his skin. (There was always *somebody*.) After she went on a bit about her favorite subject—the suffering of Afghani women—Jeremy suggested her concerns were "a little *nineties*." Good thing she was a tough broad with a sense of humor. What *really* galled him was when she said it was "okay" to want to die for a moral cause and went on to invoke burning nuns as if self-immolation was something *everyone* should aspire to. In the same breath, he admitted there'd be something immensely appealing about watching Cara Delevingne, Kendall, and Gigi Hadid set themselves on fire in real time on BuzzFeed.

He got laughed at, laughed with, and forgiven.

"I was just in Hawaii with Ram Dass and Bernie," said Joan. "And we had this whole conversation about Buddhism not being *fun*. So, *that* was my New Year's resolution—make Buddhism more fun!"

Jeremy couldn't help compare the haughty glibness of the head-shaven *grande dame* with that dangerously deranged couple, Devi and the Sir. What a gulf separated the parties! Queen Halifax was of the entitled, huckstering American Buddhist Hall of Fame ilk—serenity profiteers—that so enraged him, whereas "the travelers" were unfathomable, unpredictable, *unfriendly*, with the innate ability not only to astonish but (he sensed) *transform*. Now, *that* was crazy wisdom . . . It gave him a pang to wonder what they were doing, *this very moment*. He hadn't yet made arrangements to see them again.

After supper they sat in the living room campfire-style and told ghost stories. Garry's was about a friend who bought a home in Upstate New York. He set about enlarging a pond to make it suitable for koi. The day it was drained, a woman in monk's robes knocked on the door. She said she lived there twenty years ago and wasn't sure what compelled her to visit—she hadn't been back to the place in all that time. He invited her in. When she noticed the wimpled waters of the pond outside his library window, she revealed that her little boy drowned there. After his death, she sold the house and took her vows at a Buddhist monastery up the road. Garry's friend said it was obvious that by disrupting the waters, the child's spirit awakened, calling to its mother.

Geshe Nicholas Vreeland, who was incredibly learned, was prompted to speak of the River of the Dead in Kusatsu's Sainokawara Park. He said that a god called Jizo lived there, guiding the lost souls of children to save them from demons trying to prevent their passage. He spoke of reptilian creatures called *kappas* that lived in ponds and rivers—dirty tricksters who kidnapped toddlers and drowned them. They liked to fart a lot as well. Apparently, they were adept at stealing the *shirikodama*, the soul essence "that lives in the anus." (Jeremy muttered, "Been there, done that.") Ironically, Nicholas said, the *kappas* could be quite friendly and were famous for their almost compulsive sense of decorum. If an enemy bowed, they couldn't help bow back, even knowing such formalities left them vulnerable to fatal attack.

Half of the Rodarte sisters listened with great intent, as if drawing future inspiration for a textile pattern; a third of the Haims was similarly entranced, lost in the acoustic, compositional mists of a nascent lullaby that might one day feature their bestie Taylor Swift.

While studying Indian folklore, Donna Tartt learned about women who die in childbirth during the Hindu Festival of Lights. She said they became a *churel*, a ghost known for its bloodcurdling scream. The *churels* sought revenge on family members who didn't properly care for them during pregnancy. Other ghosts were called *ubume*—also spirits of women who died giving birth. When the babies grew up and cried in their sleep with longing for their mothers, the *ubume* comforted them with gifts that by morning turned into dead leaves.

"Amazing stories for sure," said Mr. Imperioli humbly. He asked the author if she'd read Lafcadio Hearn, and Ms. Tartt said that she had. "Of *course* you have," blushed the actor. "I forgot who I was talking to! You're a great, great writer, Donna. My wife read *The Goldfinch* three times." He quickly added, "I loved it too. And *The Secret History*."

Jeremy thought Michael charming and without conceit; he marveled at the witchcraft of actors, of *this* one, who could reach into himself, or *out* of himself, and bring his seeming antithesis— "Christopher Moltisanti"—to savage, gangstery life.

"This isn't really a ghost story, though maybe it is," Michael said. "A 'hungry ghost' story, anyway. Those tales of ponds and rivers made me think of it. A friend of mine asked me to go with him to a retreat, up past Ukiah. This was a while ago, when I was in California. A few years before *The Sopranos*. A Rinpoche was going to be giving a talk. A *tulku*—I'm sure a lot of people in this room know him. Chökyi Nyima Rinpoche." Joan and Nicholas nodded in assent, telegraphing that they knew the man personally. "His father was Tulku Urgyen Rinpoche, the great Dzogchen master. Anyway, my friend and I were going through some hard times—not with each other, but separately. I'm not even sure what was happening in my life back then, but I was . . . kind of unsettled, in mind and spirit. Body too! Though I *do* think he was a bit more troubled than I was. My friend. At that time.

"Like so many of us, he was a lifelong seeker. He'd been a monk— he'd shot ketamine with Ginsberg, in *Benares*—did the whole Kumbh Mela nine yards . . . been through all kinds of phases. Jesus, I think he was even a Scientologist, a pretty high-up one too. For a while, he tried his hand at being a guru. Had a piece of land somewhere. He actually had followers! We went to college together—took different paths, but were very close. He was like a brother to me in a lot of ways; we had that connection. And I hadn't heard from him in a while, maybe ten years, until that phone call. When he asked me to go to Ukiah to hear the *tulku*, I said yes, no hesitation. It was good to see him again—I really *loved* this guy. It was like no time had passed at all. Being with him, being together. And he gave me this kind of *warning*, he said he didn't want to talk to anyone when we got to the retreat! (Not that it's mandatory.) Told me he'd had enough of people, didn't want to talk to anybody. He was always a little eccentric. But as you *know*, it's not so unusual for people to do that. On retreat. To want to do that, to choose not to speak. So we drove up the coast, and when we got there he put a little sticker on his shirt that said 'Silent.' *I* didn't care. But the thing *was*, I couldn't quite understand why he wanted to go on the retreat in the *first* place. Because there seemed to be an undercurrent . . . of *cynicism*. Still, I thought, 'Good for him!' You know, he's cynical or he's whatever, maybe he's hip to that and he's working shit out. I was happy to be of service. And I was probably a *little bit smug*—you know: *he's* cynical and *I'm not*. But I didn't want to be there under those auspices—you know, the Skeptic Brothers, the Skeptic Twins. So I was watching myself kinda carefully. Because I was way past wearing that particular outfit. So I thought.

"So we made the trip to Ukiah and it was good. On the drive, we cut up old times, caught each other up on who was dead, who was divorced, who'd gone off the rails—sex, dope, jail, whatever. All that. Turns out one of the casualties was his wife, which pretty much stunned me. Because I knew Meghan, fairly well. But I *didn't* know they'd stayed together (whatever together is), stayed married all those years. He was her first love, her only love, and she hung with him through the craziness. And there was a *lot* of craziness. Meghan was always there when he came back home from wherever—you know, to dress his wounds before he returned to battle. He didn't say how she died and I was almost afraid to ask because a voice kept telling me she'd taken her own life. What shocked me even *more* was the way he talked about her. You know, when he said that she died, that she was dead, there was *very* little emotion. I remember he picked up on my reaction, you know, my reaction on him not having a reaction.

But all he would say was that he was at peace with what happened. (I *still* didn't ask him for details!) And that sorta made sense, really, that he was 'at peace,' because for all that time, he'd been *with* her and *not* with her: the man had a lot goin' on in the ladies department. So maybe his equanimity was healthy, I don't know. And maybe enough time had passed anyway, for him to have reached that point, because it wasn't like it just happened. I think it was maybe five years before. That she died. Anyway, I wasn't his therapist.

"When we got to Ukiah, we didn't even go to register, we just went straight to the river and jumped in. It was incredibly beautiful, super hot day, in the hundreds, the water was cold, clear, *perfect*. We swam a while then sat on the bank, recovering from the long drive. Grooving. Starting to feel *really good*. A little full of ourselves—you know, Zen studs, spiritual good ol' boys, too cool for school. Like, 'this ain't our first rodeo.' Top guns.

"So we're tanning ourselves when this fat guy waddles toward us. And my friend and I kinda look at each other with a wink because he's our 'first victim'—the whole silent-retreat ruse. And I'm the straight man, *I'm* the one who's going to have to tell the guy that my friend *ain't talkin'*. (Because we're shirtless and he doesn't have his 'Silent' sticker on.) The whole set-up's a bit *passive-aggressive* for my taste. A bit lame. You know, I wouldn't have felt that way if my friend had been sincere . . . or if the guy waddling up had been some beautiful *woman*. It felt a little disrespectful, a little bullshitty, but I remember not wanting to get heavy about it either. I thought maybe I was just projecting my own shit onto it, and that would be one of my teachings for the weekend—to lighten up and not care what my friend or anyone else was up to. To just focus on my side of the street and get clarity that way. So I was able to sidestep those feelings.

"This fat guy waddling toward us—he looks like a Dutch banker, some kind of big fat sweaty tourist. And at this point I'm in *full judgment* mode. He's *pink* and *absurd*, and *slathered* with sunscreen. Awkward, comical. A Miami Beach Sancho Panza or whatever, an easy target—and he's wearing this *sombrero*! He starts asking all these questions, with this thick *accent*, Dutch or German or whatever, he's just being *friendly*, that's all—he wants to know where we're *from*, how we *got* here, how long we've been *practicing* . . . and my buddy's kind of *vibing* him. He is *not* making Sancho feel very welcome! He's looking at Dutch Boy like he's some kind of dumb, nasty *farm animal*. Then my friend looks at *me*, with a crooked *smile*, like, *See why I don't want to talk to these assholes?* And I have to say it's a little contagious, you know, the rudeness and entitlement are contagious. Even though I'd already been practicing for a while—meditating, doing *sesshin*—'lovingkindness' flew out the fucking window. So it didn't *feel* great, see, because I still had enough awareness to be *watching myself.* And I was really starting to feel like an *asshole* so I kind of cleaned it up, tried to clean up the mood. So I told fatso we were beat up from the drive and that maybe we could have more of a discussion at dinner. To kind of get him to go away. Which he did. And I could see the schmuck was bummed from the encounter. The whole thing got very uncomfortable—for *me.* I could have just said, 'My friend's on silent retreat,' and *engaged* a little with him. But I didn't. Because by then, it was kind of Us vs. Them. It got twisted. What made it worse was, the guy's first questions were directed toward my bud, *right at him*, and he wouldn't answer. Without the explanation of the silent retreat, it must have seemed very rude and very weird. Which it was! *Not* a great way to begin a long weekend with Buddhists! Or maybe it is.

"So after he walks away, the 'banker' waddles to the shore and dives—no, *cannonballs* into the river, you know, the classic fat-guy move! That killed us. And my friend starts to imitate him, cruel, but funny. (The guy's far away enough that he can't hear.) *Vare are you frome? How deed choo learn of diss place?* 'San Franciskie! Did you drove or did you flew?' Remember that character Eugene Levy did on SCTV? I busted a gut but it still felt . . . wrong. We took a nap and I managed to shake it off. I figured I'd see 'sombrero' later and make things right. Or not.

"The first lecture was in the evening. A *beautiful* hall, just stunning. And I felt *great*—you know, that magical feeling you get before hearing a dharma talk. I was rested and had put the earlier minor *debacle* behind me. Chökyi Nyima Rinpoche comes in, filled with light, with this *chestnut* energy. *You* know what he's like: mischievous-looking but warm, and at the same time very *serious* too. Like a frog, a frog prince. You just love him right away. His translator was by his side—the Rinpoche spoke English but not very well, at least that's my memory. That was my impression. My friend was wearing his silent-retreat sticker, at last! For all the world to see! And the *tulku* said, 'Ask yourself, after five years of practice, ten years—*fifteen, twenty*—"Do I treat my enemies in the same way that I do strangers and friends?" Yes or no?' That hit a nerve for me, in terms of our encounter with the fattie. Because it was still gnawing at me, I kept replaying the tape during his talk, you know, our bad behavior, *my* bad behavior. My *participation* in it. Just reflecting on it throughout the talk . . .

"Anyway, he went on about the 'nine sublime qualities of an authentic dharma master'—how the foremost teacher is the one who exposes your faults. I really felt he was doing that with me right then! He talked a lot about death. I remember him saying there were two hardships put before us: those related to poverty, disease, adversity—and those related to luxury and fame, popularity and ease. That hit a righteous nerve too. He said fame and luxury were the far greater adversaries, and when I heard that, I thought *whoa*. He said that if fame, wealth, or position—if good *fortune* comes naturally, try to accept it, the impermanence of it, so that when it goes, it doesn't hurt too much. Because we may die suddenly, he said. 'While talking or walking, happy, angry, or sad.' I'd heard those concepts before, but this time they sunk in. They really stayed with me.

"A lot of the *tulku's* chants began with the word 'Kyema,' which for me was new. The translator said it meant sadness, weariness, *wariness*, some sorrow. The way he put it was, 'Oh. Oh my! Okay.' He was fuckin' *brilliant*, that translator. I'd sat for *many* satsangs, *many* talks and lectures, before and since, but *this* guy was unforgettable. You know, I usually have to try and get past the translator—they're *obstacles*, or perceived obstacles, because most of the time they're . . . not so wonderful. And that can become part of the experience, part of the teaching. Of the workshop, the weekend, whatever. Navigating *through* and *around* those guys is almost like a meditation in itself because your mind grabs onto whatever you feel their *inadequacies* are and it impedes you, it tries to subvert you from listening to the guru. And I accept that. *Most* of the time! You know, if they're nervous or hyped up or just plain scared . . . I've seen it all. And sometimes they're not fluent in the language, they're filling in or just doing the best they can, like everyone else. That's a pretty big burden. But *this* one was different. Clearly, he'd been with the Rinpoche a long, long time. Traveled the world with him. I assumed he was a serious student of his as well, that would be pretty common. *So* fluid, *so* elegant, but . . . *scientific*. Poetic! He was, like, the Glenn Gould of translators! Chökyi Nyima would talk for, say, five minutes at a time, and then he'd pause, with this devilish smile on his face, you know, like he was *challenging* the guy—but playful. 'Translate *that*!' And the guy *did*, you know, no problem, just seamlessly summarized. Even my 'silent' brother was flabbergasted.

"That night, in our log cabin—we were right on the river—my

old friend was in a somber mood. I thought it was because of the Rinpoche's talk. Because so much of it was about death and impermanence, and I had the idea that Meghan might have been 'weighing heavily' on his mind. But it was something else . . . and at the end of each talk, getting further into the weekend, he became more and more quiet and reflective. I was pissed at myself for not having as rich an experience as *he* was having! Then he said something that took my breath away. Completely leveled me.

"He asked if I had noticed anything 'unusual' about the translator. Right when he said that—*bam!*—I *knew*: the translator was the 'sombrero'! Sancho, Fatso, Dutch Boy! Schmucko the Tourist! The cannonballing *'banker'* . . . groomed and hatless, he'd been unrecognizable in his cantaloupe-colored robes. And I just kind of took in that *new reality*. Just sat there, shaking my head and *tripping* on it, and when I looked up I saw that my friend was in *tears*. He looked like a *saint* in the middle of having a *vision*—the tears were coming from a well so much deeper than a place of contrition or embarrassment. Tears from some distant place . . . some—*river*.

"That fucked with us *hard*, because the translator and his teacher were the same—the same! No difference. *No difference.* We'd pissed on them both in that encounter by the water. In the very first hour we were there! Pissed on the teacher! That really got me, but it hit my friend like a ton of bricks. He finally took off his little 'Silent' sticker, I don't know why, because it wasn't like he was going to talk to anyone anyhow—and nobody was going to talk to *him* either. People pretty much keep to themselves on retreats, writing in their journals, meditating, what have you. I think he did it out of respect. He was *raw* and *open* now, but very *contained*—something shifted in him. I could see it, feel it. Something shifted in *me* too, though not as dramatically.

"On our last day, Sunday, we were out by the river when we saw the *tulku* jogging toward the hills. In his Nikes, with his entourage, the whole deal—I'd heard that he loved to run. 'The jogging Rinpoche.' We saw the translator again too. (*Not* jogging.) My friend approached him. He put his hands on the translator's shoulders and they spoke. I never asked him what was said.

"But the moment—the lesson—ingrained itself. And that's the first time I've told that story. I guess it was a little long. Thank you for listening."

"That was *so* beautiful, Michael," said Dusty.

"Yes—lovely," said the guest of honor, heartfelt.

Its aftereffect washed over the gathered. Following the Geshe's lead, everyone closed their eyes in contemplation; deep sighs became a single, collective breath. The room grew quiet as a *zendo*.

At some point, Jeremy caught the tail end of Allegra vanishing up the kitchen stairs. The guests began talking, in low tones, about the novella-like lushness of Michael's "fable." Garry and Donna took bathroom breaks. The Ruschas strolled onto the sand for the night air and stars. The surf, louder with the sliding doors open, was like a raucous prayer.

The Haim and the Rodarte spoke animatedly amongst themselves. Then one of them asked, "What happened—to your 'silent retreat' friend? Are you still in touch?"

He cleared sadness from his throat.

"I never saw him again. For a while I got postcards, from all over the States—he was still in America, which for some reason surprised me. I thought he'd have gone back to India or Asia, even South America. Because that was always his thing—to get on a plane and go as far as humanly possible. Get *way* out of Dodge. Then once he got to the end of the line, go even *farther*—trekking, climbing . . . Chökyi Nyima has a brother, Mingyur—Mingyur Rinpoche. And I read that Mingyur left his monastery in Bodh Gaya a few years ago to become a wanderer. Left with no money and only the clothes on his back, told his students there wouldn't be any way to reach him. Said he was going to do it like an old-school yogi, you know, a mendicant without fixed plans or agenda. It was kind of big news in the dharma. He wrote a farewell letter to the *sangha*, and when I read it I thought of that time by the river and wondered about my friend. That maybe he'd chosen that path as well.

"In his last postcard, he wrote, 'I am almost there.' He said—he said he'd be with his *wife* soon, with Meghan, which I thought was . . . strange. I got afraid for him. 'I am almost there' . . ." The actor stared out the window, over the dark waves and their undercarriage of lambent moonlight. "It was haunting."

"What do you think he meant?" asked Jeremy.

"I don't know. All he said was that he was going to a place called Summerland."

When he found her, she was crying in her cozy bolt-hole. (Her moodiness had distracted him all evening.) He sat on the duvet, stroking the small of her sweatered back.

"Puppy, what's the matter?"

"Jeremy!" she snot-blathered. "Everything is *so fucked* . . ."

"What is it? What happened, pup, what's wrong?"

"She's *seeing* someone!" (Which set off a string of sobs like ugly firecrackers.) "She's seeing someone!—"

"Who?"

"That woman Larissa! Her camera double . . ."

"*What?*"

His wheels were spinning—he couldn't get traction.

"Dusty and I had this *thing* with her the night we had that party. After everyone left—"

"*Really,*" he said sarcastically. "I would never have guessed."

"—I only did it because I thought it was something *she* wanted, that they were probably already *into* it—that Bunny was getting bored with *just me*. Oh, Jeremy!" she pled. "It was like she set it *up*, like she totally *planned* it so she could *dump* me! She *knew* what she was doing, *you* picked up on it, didn't you? How they were sitting together, with everything touching?"

"Leggy, you are *losing* it."

The sarcasm was gone.

"*Bullshit*, Jeremy! They were climbing all *over* each other, it was so *obvious*. And I don't even know when it *started* or if there's been other *people*! And I guess I was feeling—I've *been* feeling insecure and I guess part of me was just happy she wasn't trying to *hide* it, you know, that she wanted to *include* me. And I know that sounds pathetic but I thought maybe it was even something she was doing to, like, try to start it *up* with us again."

"Okay, and so? You all fucked each other. And *so*?"

"But right *after*, like, the next *day*, everything got so *weird*, it was like something *totally changed* between us, Jeremy, I can't *explain*, it was so *radical*, like, suddenly—well, not *suddenly*, because the fucking *bed death* has kind of been going *on*—but it was like she just wasn't *into* it anymore, with *me*. Into *me* anymore, at *all* . . . it was like the light *totally went out*. And Jeremy, you *know* how hard that was—with the baby—I was, like, *suicidal* and wasn't feeling in my *body* and I *know* I was a total bitch. But then I was slowly *feeling* better and starting to *reach out* but it was just too *late* . . . and now I *know* it's too late! She's, like, *completely moved on*. And I was, like, *wondering* if she was seeing someone and then I found out it was Larissa—"

"Found out *how*? What'd you do, read her *journal*?"

"Just *listen*! That night we saw her at the Soho House . . . after you left, she came over to the booth and we talked." She fudged the truth, but the details were the same. "She said that Bunny was going to her *yoga classes*, the classes she *teaches*, like, she'd been going a *lot*. Which totally didn't make sense to me because, like, a week after we all fooled around, Bunny told me she couldn't *stand* Larissa. I couldn't even, like, bring her *up*. I mean, Bunny *totally* went out of her way to trash her. And now I see that the lies were *deliberate*. It was a setup . . ."

"Dusty went to yoga and didn't tell you—so? She has a life, Leggy. You're not her mother."

"*No*, Jeremy, they're *sleeping* together! I *know*—"

"Are you having your period?"

"—because *I've* been sleeping with her."

"With . . ."

"*Larissa*."

"What the *fuck*, Allegra?"

"I know, I know! It's *insane*, I *know*—but you don't understand how *weird* Dusty's been! And when Larissa told me about her going to *yoga*, I decided to . . . a few weeks later, to, like, *call* her—to call Larissa—you know, like, hoping she'd tell me *more*. I just wanted to find out what the fuck was going *on*, Jeremy, because I was feeling so totally *gaslighted* or *gaslit* or *whatever* . . . and it just—I needed to— and then—I don't *know*. And with me and Larissa, I don't even know who seduced *who*. It just—whatever happened, just *happened*—"

"Whoa."

"—I saw Bunny's *earring* in her *bed*! I *gave* her those fucking earrings, Jeremy! What do I *do*, what do I *do*?"

He hushed her as she sobbed. Buying himself a moment, he reverted to a campy old standby—"Why do I feel like I'm trapped in an Almodóvar movie?"—before growing scoutmaster serious.

"It'll get sorted out, Allegra, one way or another. It *will*. I *know* Dusty loves you, she *does*, I *know* that. She's just going through some changes. In her *life*."

"What about me, I am too! And I *know* she is, Jeremy, I *know* she's going through shit. There are things I can't even *tell* you."

"Good! And please *don't*. Because I've heard enough for one night."

"*Really heavy things* I can't even *talk* about." She dried her eyes and said, "But should I tell her?"

"Tell her what?"

"About Larissa? That I've been seeing Larissa?"

"Are you out of your *mind*? Allegra, why would you *do* that?—"

"Because I *just can't deal* anymore! I am so *angry* at her, Jeremy, I feel *so betrayed*!"

"*You* feel betrayed? *She* has a fling and you seduce the *flingee*?"

"I know, I know, I know!" she said. "And I *do* feel *really horrible* . . ."

She covered her face with her hands while rocking on the bed like a penitent in *petit mal*.

It was time to get firm. "Now *you* have to listen to *me*, okay? Okay? Are you listening, Allegra?" She nodded, still shielding her eyes, ready to take her punishment. "You have *got* to stop seeing Larissa. Okay? *Call* her and *tell* her that you're just not *comfortable* anymore. Or you can fucking *text* her . . . and then hope to God she doesn't tell *Dusty*, which I strongly doubt she *will*, but you never know, that train may have already left the station. Just *call* her, Allegra—or *don't*! You could just *cut it off* and *ghost* her . . . though maybe that's not such a great an idea." He was thinking out loud. "Just *email* her, okay? And find your friggin' jollies *elsewhere*. All right? Okay? Leggy? Are you taking this in?" She nodded in anguish. "Look: *all* couples go through this, right? But the general rule of thumb is, *don't shit where the other person is temporarily eating*! So you just have to *stop* because, aside from anything else, it's totally self-destructive! Ultimately, right? Because you're not just hurting *Dusty*, you're hurting *you*. I mean, look how fucked *up* you are, girl! And I *know* the whole deal was fucked up to *begin* with—or *has* been—and I *understand* how it happened with Larissa—*kind* of—but Jesus, Leggy! Here's another fine mess you've gotten yourself into . . ."

She threw her arms around him and held on for dear life. He melted.

"Come on now, it's gonna be all right. We've *all* been through a lot, puppybunbear. But it's gonna be okay."

"Is it? Is it, Jeremy?"

"*Yes.*"

"And you won't tell anyone?"

"*Of course* I won't."

"I'm sorry, Jeremy! I'm *so, so sorry* . . . I know it was stupid. I *knew* it was stupid when I was *doing* it. I so *hate myself* for letting it *happen.*"

"Well, *don't.* Because hating yourself's only going to make it worse. You're *human*, okay? And people do stupid things—that's pretty much *all* they do. Now, *freshen up* and come back downstairs."

"I just want to sleep!"

"You'll sleep when you're dead," he chided, leading her from the bed. "Go splash water on your face, you need to make an *appearance*—come one, it's just a bunch of Buddhists and celebrities, it's *perfect.* That's about as good as it gets, ever! And stop being such a drama queen or she *will* get tired of you." That set her off and he had to majorly backpedal. "I'm *kidding*. She won't—she *isn't.* She *loves* you, girl. For-*evah.*" Though he wasn't so sure about that anymore. "But you know what? You need to let her go through whatever she's going through. And you need to let *you* go through whatever *you're* going through. It's a *moment*, Allegra, a moment in *time.* And whatever happens, you guys'll be totally stronger."

"What do you mean, 'whatever happens'?"

He hushed her again, steering her to the bathroom sink.

Waiting for Allegra to emerge, Jeremy stood in the hall doing mental gymnastics. Life was growing stranger by the hour.

Poor Allegra!

And Jeremy knew more about Larissa Dunnick then he'd let on . . .

After their encounter with her at Soho, he went home and took one of the most satisfying bubble baths in the history of mankind. Emerging from those healing waters with a powerful sense of gratitude for the unexpected gifts this short life bestows, he was encouraged to plumb Tristen's depths in more ways than one. That was when the boy recklessly opened up (in so many words) about his mum, unpacking the darker intimacies of her CV: the youthful arrests for check-kiting, the more recent for doctor shopping, and even *more* recent for shoplifting, from Kitson on Robertson. Since the divorce, she'd stayed afloat as a Jill-of-all-trades—yoga teacher, masseuse at Equinox, Neptune Society sales rep, and occasional "featured movie extra." When Tristen almost pridefully informed that on her latest studio gig his mother got an out of left field "bump" (production asked her to sub for Dusty Wilding's ailing camera double), a gobsmacked Jeremy managed to hold his mud, and refrained from disclosing his ties to the actress and even the film itself. He wasn't sure *why*; true, he'd been way circumspect with the boy about all things showbiz, though not because he was paranoid . . . it was more an experiment in taking the focus off *himself.*

Some sort of instinct bade him hold back.

But still, shit, *Jesus*—

—Dusty's *stand-in* was his boyfriend's *mom!*

The whole freakish *Welcome to L.A.* synchrony of it was one of those too perfect cosmic nuggets he'd normally have shared with the actress via email or text, *ASAP*. For some reason it became yet another instance in which he *failed to disclose*. *Hmmm . . .* Clueing her in about Tristen and Larissa would have been irresistible (*normally*, that is), and clueing *Allegra* as well—though naturally, he'd have told Mama *first*, because Dusty liked to think she owned the worldwide serial rights to exclusives on Jeremy's X-rated bromances, not to mention his everything else. He *still* wasn't sure what made him clam up. Anyway, he was glad to have kept his piehole shut because some weeks ago he'd made the resolution to turn a new leaf with his new love and rein in his sloppy, tell-all ways. Which meant generally gossiping less and *especially* not gossiping about the heartbreak kid and whatever it was they had or he *thought* they had, not if he could help it. This latest self-improvement regime employed what 12-Steppers called "contrary action," and Jeremy struggled to keep the fledgling relationship close to the vest. He was tired of putting his business on the street, of killing his darlings by letting the world pick the lock of the diary of his careless heart.

Was there any upside in revealing Tristen's provenance? He couldn't see any. The situation was already too sticky by half. On the Night of the Living Tuesday Weld, Jeremy *had* sensed something afoot and abreast and a-everything else (that hint of Sapphic appetizer he called *amuse-bush*), not just between Dusty and her double, but all *three* mouseketeers, a suspicion duly confirmed when Larissa slid into their booth for her sleazy sohello. Breezily letting Dusty in on the fact that he happened to be dating her stand-in's son would start a "conversation" about the players, at minimum, and who knew where *that* would lead. If Dusty *was* having an affair with Larissa (sure sounded like it), she probably knew everything anyway—and whether she did or not, Dusty might interpret Jeremy's reveal as icky or grandstandy, some kind of faggoty brinkmanship. It *definitely* would look like he was fishing.

Thank you, no, he'd sit out the incestuous quadrille for now. His dance card was full.

Contrary action . . .

In light-speed lucubration (still in the hall, while Allegra washed and dried, douched and cried), it hit him like a stun grenade: though he'd taken pains never to mention Dusty Wilding to his boyfriend, or anything *else* about his career—an absurd game he found dumbly refreshing—what sort of madness had allowed him to pretend Tristen didn't *already know everything about his life*? As if an *atom* of his world could be hidden, and from *Tristen*, no less—the *Kill Bill* bride, the Crazy 88 of Internet trap queens! Jeremy was continually surprised, galled, and shamed by his unrepairable naïveté; the generational blind spot that made him oblivious to the avalanche of files and thumbnails that rendered a jittery, fossilized portrait of him as exacting as a Chuck Close for anyone who cared to look. Of *course* Tristen knew about his decades-old alliance with the film star! Of *course* he did—and of ten thousand other dark and minuscule things about himself that Jeremy'd long forgotten . . .

Suddenly, he wondered how much Tristen had told his mother about their affair. He imagined that oedipal relation to be miscreant on the level of Vera Farmiga and Freddie Highmore in *Bates Motel*— why *wouldn't* they share all, routinely enlisting one another in the gory details of their mutual degeneracy? Jeremy *did* trust the boy yet in the moment let his thoughts run wild, shuddering as he fantasized about mother and son's salacious comparing of notes (he wouldn't have been at all surprised if Larissa told Tristen that she'd become "friendly" with the movie star *and* her wife), two Sherpas celebrating the amazing karma that had helicoptered them to Mt. Annapurna base camp for a grand expedition into the larcenous unknown.

But what *manner* of larceny?—

He heard Allegra flush the toilet.

An arson of sinister thoughts lit up his brain and threatened his hair; as much as he wanted to put out the fire, he wanted to watch it burn . . .

If his insurgent speculations were true—that Tristen and Larissa were thick as thieves—then what was the meaning, the *strategy* of the boy having delayed sharing that his mommy was Dusty's camera double? *Because he would have known from Day One.* And when he *did* finally mention it, Tristen was careful not to acknowledge Jeremy's relationship to the star, the movie, or anything else. The kid *could* have said, "Isn't that bizarre, Nobodaddy? And I know you don't like to talk about it but you're one of the producers on that film, right? Aren't you and Dusty Wilding, like, *really close*?" But, no—he just let it ride . . . and Jeremy definitely didn't get the feeling he'd done that out of respect or discretion. So the question remained: *why withhold what he knew all along?* And on a *more* sinister note, wouldn't it stand to reason that *Larissa* would have told *Allegra* (who, after all, was her *lover*)? You know, "Your friend Jeremy's *boyfriend* happens to be my *son*"? And if she *had* told Allegra, why hadn't Allegra shared that savory morsel with *him*? "Oh my God, Jeremy, you'll never believe this!" He could understand her not wanting to get into that with him earlier because she wouldn't have wanted to admit she was seeing Larissa—but now that she'd *confessed*, why wouldn't she have mentioned it right then, on the Night of the Living Buddhist breakdown? Might the omission have something to do with what Allegra said about Dusty while they sat on the bed? "There are things I can't even *tell* you"?

First things first. Assuming Ma Barker and protégé *were* in absolute control—that Jeremy and Allegra were their puppets, being made to dance on strings—what *was* it, then, that they were *up* to? Something criminal? Twisterella's Web-hacking motherfuckery already pegged him as a spectrum sociopath, albeit a harmless one—at least harmless when it came to *Jeremy*. (Or so the old mark thought, or *used* to think, anyway.) Clearly, moral turpitude, embezzlement, and flim-flammery were the building blocks of the Dunnick family DNA . . . all that kiting and trolling and five-finger discounting. And yet what, *now*, were the duo conspiring *toward*? And if they *were* conspiring, why would Tristen have even tipped his hand by laying out his mother's rap sheet for Jeremy's gratification and delight? He had the sudden, minatory thought that the boy's throwaway bulletin about her job promotion (to Dusty's double) had been a ruse—a game, a sort of *test* organized by Larissa, and that her son's mission was to report back Jeremy's reaction, with further actions *to be determined*. He wondered now if it had been a mistake not to have headed Tristen off at the pass with the immediate retort of, "Oh! Isn't that funny? I'm old friends with Dusty and I'm producing *Sylvia & Marilyn*!"

Allegra's film-noir words came back to haunt him: *"It was a setup."*

But if it *was* a monstrous strategem—to what end?

One last ominous question stuck in his craw. If Allegra *did* know that Larissa's son was his lover—which she *had* to have!—why the *fuck* wouldn't she have mentioned the meta-connection to Jeremy right away? And if for some unbelievable but still feasible reason she hadn't yet gotten around to divulging it, what would have prevented her from just spitting it out as she cried in his arms at the Geshe's soirée, when she was utterly raw and defenseless? What was there to *gain* by pro-tecting such intel? Unless she was a . . . *co-conspirator*, involved in something *truly iniquitous*—no! How *could* she be? Leggy was too much a naïf, too *dumb*, really (*ah, there: he said it*) to be so clandestine, so Machiavellian. *Wasn't she?* He wondered if he was reading too much into it. Maybe the explanation was simple. Maybe Allegra *not* disclos-ing that their lovers were mother and son was merely a result of her spectacular narcissism—a princessy self-involvement that trumped the possibility of any revelations that were off-point (*herself* being the *only* point), no matter how striking or singular.

Allegra emerged from the powder room and Jeremy walked her down.

Rejoining the group, she faked it pretty well, falling back on all that familiar, funky flower-child Eros, hanging mostly with the half Rodarte and the one-third Haim (too intimidated by the whole Tartt) whilst muttering spotty apologies in regard to her absenteeism and general agita, courtesy of an alleged stomach bug—though she really did have the runs. Dear Jeremy stood close by for support.

Dusty came into her room around two a.m., naked and stoned. Allegra had planned to confess everything but said nothing, sublimating rage, confusion, panic and fear into bodylove. Dusty knew something was wrong, even *very* wrong, but was energized by the demolition of language and analysis. Their love was potentiated, and for a moment, the niceties of psychotherapeutic dynamics among couples were forgotten.

They lay in a field of golden land mines that went off one after the other, leaving them eyeless, limbless, heartless—dead and alive all at once.

△

She hadn't left her favorite suite at the Gansevoort in three days.

She came to New York alone, a sort of getaway, half for the birthday party Meryl and Bill Irwin were throwing for Edward Albee's eighty-eighth, half to see Todd Haynes about a film project.

She had planned on staying a week but things changed.

When Ginevra heard from her—a disjointed rush of torn, hyper-ventilated syntax—she asked her to come to the office straightaway. Dusty balked and the therapist went over to the hotel instead. She answered the door in big movie-star sunglasses but the disguise nobly failed. Like a victim in a cerebral European horror flick, the skinscape and very bones of her face had already begun to meta-morphose into something unknown and misbegotten. She returned to the couch where she'd been living.

"There's tea," she said, nodding at a pillaged room-service table.

"Have you spoken to her?"

"No."

"Is your friend still here?"

"No." A long pause, then: "They both left."

Two days before, on a bright, freezing Sunday, Livia had called. (As it happened, she was in Brooklyn visiting a just-born grand-child; she'd learned through Allegra that Dusty was in New York.) She needed to see the actress—a "personal matter," which seemed to rule out any news about the search—and would rather it didn't wait until they were back in L.A. An hour later, her old ally arrived at the hotel with Snoop Raskin. The news came quick, like a rogue wave.

"I was able to locate the babysitter," he said. "Claudia Zabert."

"Okay," said Dusty with a generic smile, too disoriented by the incongruity of their sudden presence to even know she was afraid.

"And—this is going to be difficult."

His entire face blistered and lurched like a satellite photo of a surgical strike, before returning to a blank composure of unbombed grids.

"Your daughter is Allegra."

"What?"

Livia tensed and moved closer, self-deputized into suicide watch.

"It's—Allegra. She's Aurora. The one you've been looking for. They're the same."

Dusty tried to say *what* again but slurred "Grallegwa?" as if in the midst of a stroke. Sinatra's boy soldiered on.

"It's my understanding that your mother—*Reina*—gave Ms. Zabert five thousand dollars for 'expenses,' and after leaving Tustin, she and the girl—whom she renamed Allegra—spent time in Northern California. San Bruno, San Francisco, San Rafael. They lived in campsites and motels and with various acquaintances of Ms. Zabert's. There are at least five recorded arrests for panhandling, vagrancy, and prostitution—it's actually somewhat remarkable Ms. Zabert was able to maintain her physical 'custodianship' of the girl, such as it was. There may have been an involvement in a cult known as the Children of God or 'the Family,' but I believe that would have been something she dabbled in on an *expedient* basis in order to procure food, clothing, and shelter, and have other needs met. Ultimately, they settled in a commune near the Salmon River—this would have been 1981 or thereabouts, when the girl was age three. The commune was located in the Siskiyou Mountains and fairly remote; Ms. Zabert may have been seeking to avoid or escape certain legal pressures and predicaments. She and the girl experienced the communal lifestyle for approximately six years. Toward the end of their stay she joined a second cult, in a less *casual* way than she had before, and left the commune—with the girl, with 'Allegra-Aurora'—travelng extensively in Asia, India, and other regions where the members of that group may or may not have had 'affiliations.' I'm of the understanding they were living in the U.K. when the girl returned to the States at age fifteen, accompanied by an adult female who, to my knowledge, had no relationship with the cult *or* Ms. Zabert. I'm fairly confident that at this point in time, Allegra was a runaway. Ms. Zabert did not choose to follow her and remained behind, working as a housekeeper for a family in Knightsbridge."

She looked into Livia's eyes, imploring her to be allowed to awaken from this nightmare. But all the woman could manage was to tenderly say: "Dusty . . ."

She turned to Snoop—pleading now with her executioner.

"Is this some kind of joke?"

"I wish it were." He'd been careful not to go off-book but allowed himself that improv. "The degree of certainty is one hundred percent."

What could anyone even do with such information? The profusion of detail and deadpan *Dragnet* delivery belied the sheer horror. It was like trying to parse the meaning of a massive heart attack or a bullet to the brain. The shock was so great that Dusty wasn't even sent reeling; instead, she felt something akin to being catapulted into space and embalmed at once. A second opinion would be futile, as it didn't seem possible the detective could make such an assertion without already being in possession of invincible documents, inalienable proofs. To present anything less than an *airtight case* would be a recklessly unpardonable moral and professional sin, because if he *was* wrong . . . no—he couldn't be. Snoop Raskin wasn't a foolhardy man, nor was he prone to career immolation.

She saw it clearly now. On learning the truth, he and Livia put their heads together and seized the moment. With Dusty in New York, far away from the daughter-wife, the stage had been perfectly, fatefully set.

So they flew in from L.A., the detective with his Enigma machine in carry-on. Its decoded message, like the face of God, was fatal to behold.

She thought she'd lose her mind—perhaps she already had.

In the days that followed, she was consumed with the idea that Allegra *knew* she was her mother all along, and their marriage had

been a premeditated act—the capstone of an abandoned child's un-
speakable plot of bloodlust and revenge. She stubbornly promoted
this theory in a series of crazed, jaggedly hysterical late-night phone
calls to the detective, who, in turn, patiently attempted to defuse. He
argued that Allegra could only have learned of her origins through
her guardian, which was most unlikely; the street-smart woman
would certainly have been aware of the legal consequences of her
criminal act (the technical abduction of a child for financial gain). To
bolster his rationale, he suggested that by the time they landed in
the mountain commune, Claudia would presumably have been a fugitive from other crimes, and even more keenly motivated to retain old
secrets.

Each time his deftness of logic delivered them to solid ground,
Dusty lost her footing, and Snoop had to grab her by the wrists to
keep the poor woman from being sucked into a vortex of insanity. He
shot at clay pigeons and plugged leaks when they sprang, tap-danced
and puddle-jumped from one muddy foothold to another, and chased
runaway trains of thought—for example, derailing his client's idea
that the babysitter from hell had gotten in touch with her mother
for additional funds. The "profile" of the sadistic matriarch that
Dusty had provided led the detective to deduce that Reina was
likely holding something over Ms. Zabert's head that would have
made contact disagreeable, if not outright dangerous to her health.
Furthermore, he voiced strong doubts that Claudia knew of Dusty's
celebrity (which presumably would have been added incitement for
a cash grab), not only because the actress changed her name early
on—by the time she started getting noticed in movies, Allegra and
her guardian had already left America—but from everything he'd
gleaned of their impoverished, insulated life in a hermetic overseas
cult, exposure to the movies and gossipy ephemera of Hollywood pop
culture would have been effectively nil. There seemed little chance

she would have had an awareness of Janine Whitmore's cinematic transformation.

Dusty wasn't going for it.

In fact, she thought it was *lame—because all Claudia Zabert had to do* ("Out of sheer *curiosity!*" she crowed contemptuously) *was Google "Janine Whitmore" and* voilà: *mystery solved.* She had a point, but Snoop stuck to his guns. He counterpunched by proposing that even if Claudia *had* been aware of her fame all along—if she'd improbably followed her rise to stardom and become Dusty Wilding's biggest fan—why would she have shared her knowledge with Allegra, risking jail and/or the wrath of that gunslinger Reina Whitmore? Having spoken to certain individuals privy to Claudia's history (Raskin's resources were vast—just forty-eight hours before the Gansevoort summit, he had visited Ms. Zabert at a trailer park in Vallejo. She was "profoundly damaged"), he uncovered no evidence that she'd maintained any relations with Allegra after the girl returned to America. He convincingly theorized that *no one* knew of the orphan's origins by reason of the simple fact that in close to forty years, the movie star hadn't been contacted *once* in that regard, or in any other, not by Ms. Zabert or anyone else, for the most compelling, timeless motive of them all: blackmail. Dusty fought him on that too. (The vortex was always near.) *But what if Claudia was feeling guilt over what she'd done,* she forcefully suggested. *What if she just wanted me to reconnect with Allegra?* (She couldn't bring herself to say, let alone think "my daughter." She couldn't even bring herself to use *Aurora* yet, though *why* she couldn't made no sense; it should have been *so* much easier than *Allegra.* Everything was a nauseating jumble.) *Wouldn't that be a reason for her to have told Allegra everything? She could have told Allegra, then kind of just faded out of the picture.* His categorical response was, "Well, *did* she? Did she tell Allegra? *Did you ever get that call?*"

Dusty shouted back, sardonic and crazed, "In a sense!" but Raskin talked emphatically over her. "*No, you didn't.* Because *Claudia never knew*, and Allegra doesn't *either*. I can assure you of that."

Her therapist agreed with the detective. (When Dusty wasn't talking to the one, she was talking to the other.) "Look," said Ginevra. "The idea that Allegra *knew*, that Claudia *told* her—and I agree with Mr. Raskin, because who else *could* have told her—if Allegra *did* know, you have to ask yourself *when, when* would she have known? Claudia would have waited till she was older, to tell her. *Hypothetically.* Because why tell a six-year-old? Or an eight-year-old? That just complicates Claudia's life. Telling Allegra—Aurora—at *all* would have complicated her life! And that woman's life was already complicated *enough.* So let's just say for the sake of argument that she waited until they were in Europe and told her *then. Which* she didn't— but for argument's sake, okay? Let's just say that when Allegra ran away from England or wherever when she was *fifteen* and came back to the States, to New York—let's say that by then she *knew*. She already knew. Let's even say that's *why* she came back, why she ran away. Because now she knew who her real mother was and she wanted to 'come home.' Okay? The *idea*, Dusty, that she's *back in America*, that she's a *teenager*, probably desperate and flat broke, scared—the kind of *life* she's been living, so *chaotic*, like a gypsy—and now she's back in the States, in *New York*, *knowing* that her *mother's* a rich, famous *movie star*! Which gave her even *more* motivation to come back to the country . . . she's *here* but she doesn't get in touch with her mom? With *you*? Dusty, it doesn't make any *sense.* Because a fifteen-year-old doesn't *operate* that way! *Twenty*-year-olds and *thirty*-year-olds don't operate that way *either. No one* says, 'I'm going to get back at

her for what she did by making her falling in love and marry me!'
No—as her *mother*, at the very *least*, you'd be her brass ring, her ticket
out. She'd say, Help, Mom! Give me money! Give me love! I want to
move to Hollywood! I want to be rich and famous too! *That's* what a
fifteen-year-old would do, but she *didn't*. She didn't, Dusty, because
she *did not know*. This 'possibility'"—the shrink wouldn't give it more
weight by calling it otherwise—"this *possibility* that you've been obsessing over . . . well, it *isn't*. It's a possibility that simply isn't. That's
what I'm trying to say. Do you see?"

Dusty thought, *Everyone's insane*, and had to laugh. *They're all just
having a splash and a wallow before leading me to slaughter. Just doing their
jobs, being professional—grabbing the bullshit by the horns, trying to be
aggressively cool and proactive in the macabre funhouse of my looming insanity and death. Before they ditch me* . . . Her head took little time-outs but
at the end of each benumbed smoke break she'd get crushed again
by the nuclear reality of her predicament, berating herself anew for
the futile, addictive impulse to keep wishing it was all a dream.

"Ginevra," she said softly. "What do I do? What do I do? What
do I do with this?"

After a solemn beat, the shrink said, "You have to tell her."

The blows kept coming.

"But *how*?"

"We can talk about that. And I'll *be* there—right by your side. If
you need that, if you want me to be. You *can't* do this alone, Dusty.
Allegra's going to need some help as well—"

"'*Some*'!"

"—because she can't do it alone either."

"Oh God! Oh god oh god oh god, it's a *nightmare* . . . what did I
do, Ginevra? What did I do! Why has this *happened*, why has this
happened to me? Is it karma?"

"*You have to tell her the truth*," she said, staying focused. "Because anything *else* would be *cruel*. You've *seen* what secrets do—let this be the last. It's not one you would have wanted or imagined but it's one you cannot keep."

"It's more *complicated* than that."

"How so?"

"Ginevra, you're being naïve!"

"Tell me how."

"Have you even *thought* about it, Ginevra? *I* have! Do you *under-stand* what will happen when this becomes *public knowledge*? What the *Internet's* going to do with it? I'm not even talking about the fucking *tabloids* and the *talk-show* jokes—have you thought about what the *world* is going to say? The ridicule and the hatred? The *death threats*? I will get death threats! I still *do*! *I* went through that *once* and I'm not going to go through it *again* . . . *she* will get death threats, Ginevra, she will be a *target*—for some *lunatic* to just . . . *take a gun* and *pick her off*. This country is so *fucking sick*. *Her* life—*our* lives will be *over*! Destroyed! Destroyed! Destroyed! Destroyed!"

"Then you're worried about a leak?"

"Am I *worried*?" she said, her features contorted in contempt.

"Putting the question of talking to Allegra aside—are you concerned that Livia might share the information?"

"No! Not *Livia* . . . but *I* don't know who Captain What-the-Fuck—I don't know who Snoop *Raskin's* already told, shit, *I* don't know who he has working for him . . . probably a whole fucking *army*—"

"Then that's a conversation you need to have. And soon."

"—he *said* he did it alone, all that old-school confidential 'trust no one' bullshit, but how is that even *possible*? I don't believe in one-man bands, *no one* does it by themselves, Ginevra, no one *can*. And every-thing gets found out *anyway*! Every *text*, every *email*, every *everything*. We so fucking *know* that! Ask Laura Poitras! It's all just sitting there on the shelf in some . . . *Amazon warehouse, waiting* to be found! I can't even fart in a *restaurant* without someone recording it on their little fucking *Apple watch*—the *haters* . . . so either everyone *already* knows— I mean, right *now* while we're sitting here *talking about it*!—or they're *about* to in a *nanosecond* . . ."

The rant stopped, supplanted by the home invasion of a new fear.

"Ginevra, am I going to be arrested? Could I be arrested?"

"But how? You had no knowledge—"

She stared into the distance like an impotent philosopher. "Is this really happening?" Her laugh was pathetic and unconvincing.

"We'll get through this, Dusty."

"*You'll* get through it. I won't."

"Yes you *will*."

"No I won't," she said hauntedly, thinking aloud.

"You don't have to decide. About telling her. Not now, not *today*. But you *need to ask yourself*, what is the alternative? *Not* telling her . . . could you live with that, Dusty? Could you take that away from her? Could you take that away from Allegra?" The actress struggled to understand. How could she take anything away from Allegra, when she'd already stolen all the girl had? "Could you take that away from you *both*?" She let Dusty breathe before going on. "What has happened . . . is impossible to comprehend. But there is—something *extraordinary* . . . there is—a beauty in it—"

Dusty spat out "Beauty!" in a seizure of rage.

"*Yes*, there is *something*, you just have to *see* it. You *will* come to see it. And you may choose *not* to. You may choose not to. But it's *there*, *believe* me it's there. Now I've told you what I think. And no one's going to force you to do anything, no one *can*. I'm with you—*either* way. And I want you to know that. If you think you can live with it, don't tell her, Dusty. Just let it be. Have a 'breakup,' just break it off and divorce, tell her it's just not working and that you haven't been happy. Whatever. Let it *be*. If you think you can live with losing her again."

She flew private, back to L.A.

In rattle and thrum of cabin she willed the plane to go down, but thought, *I'll never have that luck.*

Then:

This must be hell! Yes.

I am in hell.

She'd been disparaging Snoop Raskin in her head for no reason other than shoot-the-messenger. Truth be told, she was touched that he'd flown out to deliver the news in person—an act of great kindness. It was the right thing, and rare, because people no longer cared about the right thing, if they could even locate it. Livia had been wonderful too, sleeping over on that baneful night (though neither slept much) to minister to her despair and mutilated maternity.

There was so much Dusty had to actively repress, taboos within taboos: the home movies of their mouths from only a dozen days ago, infernal circus of fingers, tongues, cunts, and anuses—no! Whenever the sights, sounds, and smells rocketed up they were instantly neutralized by the Iron Dome defense of self-preservation, and instincts of motherliness as well. But how long could she keep that up? How long before all her cities were laid to waste? Gentler impressions rose to the surface . . . for example, the press had always commented on the physical traits they shared (complexion, timbre of voice, willowiness, the way they laughed)—the world seemed charmed by such proof of soulmatedness. And that time they were antiquing in Vermont when an older shop owner mistook them for mother and daughter. That used to happen in the early years of their romance, before they became known as a couple.

She thought of the names—the names! *Aurora/Allegra* . . . the baby-sitter's alteration was just enough to echo and obliterate, to memori-alize the dead twin.

She kept circling back to the outlandish notion (though in context, "outlandish" had lost all meaning) of Allegra having targeted her own mother for seduction. Talk about revenge porn . . . The sophistic the-ory didn't really hold water, though, as the girl just didn't seem to have the right stuff to carry out such a diabolical scheme; Allegra had always worn her unconniving heart on her sleeve. And yet, in the very breath that followed such a repudiation, Dusty would think it *was* pos-sible, that Allegra would be capable of *anything*, of *course* she would, *especially* that which appeared bizarre, violent, or implausible—because in the end, wasn't she Reina Whitmore's granddaughter? As long as one had membership in that accursed, calamitous bloodline, one would never be exempt from all manner of devilry. There was no escape.

She tried to recall everything Allegra had ever shared of her vag-abond childhood. There wasn't much. Not a single toddler or family photo—only the thin, dinner-party-ready repertoire of exotic, darkly sardonic anecdotes hinting at cartoonish scrapes with death and the law in far-flung, Wild Wild Eastern corners of the world. It perplexed Dusty that she had never been more *curious*—or curious at all, really. She'd never really questioned Allegra's upbringing. When she said that her parents were dead, Dusty just accepted it, *no problem*, she swallowed everything whole, closing that door. Was that even nor-mal? To be so weirdly uninquisitive about the one whom one loved, whom one chose to make a life with? It seemed a little extreme, even for a narcissist. What could she have been thinking, to have appar-ently so not given a shit? With devastating logic, the lacuna became one more example of crimes against motherhood, of the high treason she'd committed against all children. Snoop had dredged up Chil-dren of God, a cult she was familiar with through her work with

Hyacinth. One of the shittier, more sinister groups when it came to child sex abuse . . . of course, Allegra had written that script where she'd changed the name to "Ellipsis." She couldn't remember ever asking where she got the *idea* to write about C.O.G. in the first place; she was so skittishly sensitive about her writing abilities that Dusty thought best to leave it alone. But now it all made sense—even *more* sense why Allegra had been so hesitant to show her the pages. She was certain that "Ellipsis" was completely autobiographical and wondered what terrible secret things were revealed . . . she probably didn't want her to read it because it was the True Story (names changed to protect the guilty) of an angelic little girl abandoned by her bitch movie-star mother—

A pocket of turbulence dislodged her thoughts, making room for a strobe-stink of incestuous images that gutted rather than aroused. She fought them off with recollections of how they'd first met.

Allegra was studying at Lee Strasberg, waitressing part-time at the Hotel Bel-Air. She was a server at the patio party Dusty was having for Lauren Bacall. When they saw each other, it was, like, *Oh. There. There she is.* Dusty was with her Gen Y galfriend, a New York fashionista. She whispered her number to Allegra, saying, "Memorize it." Throughout the lunch, Dusty whispered it four times; a sly, erotic joke. Allegra told her girlfriend at the time that she'd just met Dusty Wilding (but not that she memorized her number). The girlfriend was a superfan but Allegra had only seen maybe two of her films. She waited a week before getting the nerve to call. When she drove to Point Dume, they communed like old souls. Old friends and old souls and old

OH

There.

There she is—

And *now.*

The *horror* . . .

The hallucinatory karmic godlessness of it!

More turbulence. The plane shook shook shook. She threw up then dosed herself with another round of Ativan and Percocet. Closed her eyes and floated back to Mimosa Lane circa 1978 to nurse her baby but Reina was there, skulking in shadow, like an avenging Bunraku puppet-ghost . . . so Dusty recalled a different sanctuary, before there was even a child to be taken—her prenatal idyll with the cabal of witchy midwives and phabulous phreaks in Wickenburg, AZ. The smell of Sonoran campfires and the woof of javelinas suffused, and a watery, topsy-turvy diorama too, for the legendary Hassayampa—"upside-down river"—flowed through there, disappearing underground.

Its sandy legend sang

> *Those who drink its waters bright,*
> *red man, white man, boor or knight,*
> *girls or women, boys or men,*
> *Never tell the truth again.*

They woke her twenty minutes before landing in Van Nuys.

Texts awaited, from Allegra and Ronny Swerdlow.

Ronny's said, The girls miss you & so does Sam. (me too) Come for dinner + troutfishing in America soon

Leggy's said, oh where oh where has my little bun gone oh where oh were can she be? ♥ ♥ ♥

She didn't go home. How could she?

The car took her to the Presidential Suite at the Ritz-Carlton in

Rancho Mirage. She needed the proximity of people, the infrastructure of service and care. Elise had been trying to reach her, leaving
worried messages. Dusty finally emailed that she was on a secret
spa holiday and would be offline. Jeremy was texting and emailing
too and she wrote him the same. Livia offered to come to the desert
(she was the only one other than Ginevra who knew where she was)
but Dusty declined, though they *did* talk for hours on the phone.
Livia was an advocate and a good sounding board. When Dusty
told her about the shrink advising her to tell Allegra everything,
Livia respectfully disagreed. She said, "You should just *end it*," that
Allegra would survive a breakup "*beautifully*, you'll see." That it
would be the ultimate kindness to spare her the truth—"a mother's
sacrifice, if you will." Dusty's first impulse had been the same, and
because she trusted her old friend's instincts, the argument gained
authority. Livia judiciously granted that she could see the merit in
either telling or not telling but leaned toward nondisclosure, which
"favored healing, on both sides." A large part of Dusty agreed,
though she had trouble determining if her bias was inspired by
stone-cold pragmatism or stone-cold fear. There was a quality of
priggishness inherent in her colleague and confessor; playing devil's advocate, she asked herself if Livia's convictions were informed more by old-fashioned rectitude than common sense. (Probably
a goulash of the above.) *Whatever.* As deeply crazy as the current
situation was, it just felt good to be *talking*. If hell, among other
things, was a vacuum, Dusty was grateful to at least be having the
debate.

She emailed with her daughter only once—a text would have felt
too intimate, a phone call anathema. Dusty said she'd been working through "some unexpected issues" in the wake of Reina's death
and that Ginevra, whom she saw in New York, was guiding her in

the painful process. She was taking some "quiet time" in Big Sur. Dusty balked when Allegra ventured to ask, *Are you at Esalen or Post Ranch?* "At a house," she answered.

She only left her rooms at night, when she took long drives, parking in quiet, affluent neighborhoods before going on a ramble. Just after sunset, the desert was cool and divinely aloof. The choppy, analeptic winds spoke to her, and brought strange succor. She felt disembodied, as if watching herself with a drone's hovering eye, a demigod looking down upon that soft, sad ambulatory machine called Dusty Wilding—martyr, warrior, abomination. Slouching toward Trousdale with no plan in sight, she prayed some sort of liberation was at hand. She wanted to blame Jupiter, who, according to Chakrapani, was exalted; she wanted to blame Venus, the planet of love. She was tired of blaming herself . . . Maybe the stars and planets had aligned to rape her into selflessness and resurrection. She needed an illusion of *purpose* because anything was an improvement over the brimstone damnation she now suffered, the exquisite nonstop hurt whose insult she had begun to believe she might grow accustomed to, and even endure.

As she walked, she told the winds she'd break it off. *I'll end it and she'll kick and scream but then she'll understand. I'll sell the house on Carla Ridge and give her Point Dume, and anything else she needs or asks for—it's hers anyway, all hers. Yes, that's what I'll do . . . I'll go see her and we'll talk and talk and it will be all right, everything will be all right, and we'll find new loves. Eventually. Both of us. We'll find ourselves and be set free. And in time, we'll come together again: friends and old souls, just like we've always been. I'll be there for her like a mother (like always), and it won't even* matter *if I'm the only one who knows—*

But the winds shouted her down.

"Tell her," they said.

She was in a state.

On the day that Dusty left for New York, Allegra went back to tracing a whorehouse of *parfum* miniatures in her sketchbook, in an attempt to conjure the winning silhouette of the vessel entrusted to spray the pheromones of her bitch lying wife onto thousands of women's bodies.

She felt like a pimp; she felt like a cuckold.

At night, she dreamed of owls killing barnyard mice.

She took solace in a book of Sufi parables—one of them drove her to tears. It was the story of a wealthy merchant who kidnapped a songbird and kept her in an emerald-encrusted cage. The songbird grew to love its captor. One day, he was leaving on business to the very place she was stolen from. He told her that if she wished, he would search for her family and pass on a message. "Tell them I am with one who loves me," she said. "And my heart is full and I want for nothing. The one who adores me sees to my every need." The merchant went to that faraway place, and when his work was done found her brother on the high branches of a tree. He shouted up the captive sister's message. After listening, the bird fell dead from its perch. When the merchant got home, he went straight to the cage of his beloved with the unhappy news. "I told your brother you wished him to know that your heart was full. And that you wanted for nothing because the one who loves you saw to your every need. He listened, then fell from the tree and was dead." At that very moment she tumbled lifelessly off her golden perch. Horrified, he opened the door to revive her but she flew from the cage and straight out the window.

The peerless songbird circled back for a parting word.

"My brother showed me what it would take to be free."

But Allegra was not free; she hadn't the courage yet to die, so she might live.

What must she do, to take flight? It was a pretty metaphor but she was no Persian peacock, no mystic songbird—she was a Looney Tunes buzzard, feeding on its own flesh. If she died *this moment* she'd have no interest in reincarnation; why would she want to be reborn into the miscarried, adulterous world? When she thought of killing herself, the comfort—the *hopefulness*—came in the notion of remaining dead.

Jealousy, bewilderment, and fury had made her psychotic.

During yoga meditation, she heard a voice: *You must embrace the sovereign indifference of Love.* Why not just let Dusty be? Perhaps that was the answer! She and her wife were holy, sovereign creations with discrete sovereign paths. Those paths would naturally diverge but their love, if it were true (and she sort of knew it was), would endure.

Yet each time she inched toward the bejeweled cage's door, she froze.

She went on long drives and took solace in churches.

A pastor in Sylmar recited Ruth's words to Naomi—

> *Entreat me not to leave thee or turn away from thee, for whither*
> *thou goest, I will go; and where thou lodgest, I will lodge; thy*
> *people shall be my people, and thy God my God. Where you die,*
> *I shall die, and there I will be buried.*

She wondered if it were possible for a person to truly surrender, in utter humility—maybe it wasn't, maybe it was just an eternal ideal—then mused over whether an imperfect but sustained acquiescence would be sufficient to set one free. And when does the very idea of "forgiveness" no longer matter? When does the act become an ethereal concept, finding its proper place in the sacred, no longer earthbound, dream . . . because shouldn't a person be able to go beyond such a thing? I mean, if one was able to truly forgive something awful, it would seem that one might have advanced far enough, and had evolved to such a . . . but how, how to forgive Dusty for what she'd done? Only weeks ago, she couldn't even have imagined her wife having an anomalous emotional affair, let alone actively being with someone else . . . what was "forgiveness," anyway? Allegra scoured the Internet for those courtroom videos of families acidly dressing down prisoners after verdicts were read—the "victim impact statements" at the end of a trial. The cathartic public shaming when mothers and daughters and fathers and sons formally vilified those who took away that which was most precious. The clichéd, hectoring redundancy of the futile rebukes was heartbreaking; there were only so many ways to say *You will have Christmas but my husband will not* and *I hope you rot in hell.* Now and then, a family member faced the unrepentant monster and said, "I forgive you." I forgive you—for raping and strangling my bride. I forgive you for sodomizing and burying my child alive . . . and here am I, whining because Bunny came with Larissa! (And God only knows how many others. And I don't *give* a shit if that makes me look like a fool, because what she's done is the same as murder, it's the same, the same, the same!) Some of the convicted showered their forgivers with threats and obscenities. Others cried and said they were sorry. (There were only so many ways to say, *If I could give up my life so that he could live, I would.*) Sometimes the forgivers actually went to the jails for special meetings and tearful embraces. Allegra imagined herself in court. *I forgive you for sleeping with her and lying to my face like I was a piece of shit. I forgive you for filling your heart and your holes with her fingers and cunt juice and for obliterating my name and my memory with your wanton whorefuck treasons—*

She wondered how to make ready for such a choice—to "forgive"— if it even *was* a choice. How does one prepare? And how hard, how desolate, how barren was the land on which the road to forgiveness, that royal road to the sovereign indifference of love, how long and how wide, how impossible to cross, was the avenue that led to the songbird's destination?

That snaked its way toward that travesty of a word: *freedom* . . .

"Imagine wearing the outfit of 'Whole Foods customer,'" the pastor was saying, "and they don't have the item you want in the cookie section. So you take off that outfit and go elsewhere. You run into a friend on your way to Trader Joe's and that friend hands you a gift—the very cookies you were shopping for. So you take off the 'Trader Joe's customer' outfit and put on the 'friend' outfit—and receive the treats. And if you grow vegetables in your garden, the 'customer' and 'friend' outfits come off and you put on the outfit of 'self'—and harvest the food. *You take it from the Universe.* If we allow God to move through us, using more than just the roles and outfits we're comfortable with—good son/bad son, miserly man/generous man, lover/hater, Christian/Muslim/Jew—the congestion clears. *Thousands* of outfits are available, we *design* them! As a young man I did missionary work in India and tried on many. Savior, tourist, seeker, student, teacher, American, consumer . . . I was *always* wearing something. And all that we're trying to do with these outfits is *express love.* But we get *stuck.* By getting stuck with *twenty*, with ten, with three, even *one*, we limit ourselves. In trying to make those outfits work as *expressions of who we are*, we end up hurting people."

What was her role in the marriage? What were the outfits she wore *now*? "Wife betrayed," "the abandoned innocent," "she who lost her religion"—because Allegra had always been certain it was *God* that brought them together, it was *God* who'd arranged their union, she *knew* it was so! Yet what could the consequences be, what was the *meaning* of such divinity, if not that of redemption bestowed by the

sovereign indifference of love supreme? Surely God could be interested in nothing else! What *was* it she'd been seeking all these years?
Security? Status? Ownership (of another)? And with what costume
had she insisted her *wife* be adorned? Had she really expected
Dusty—either one of them—to be faithful, forever and always? How
to even begin to *define* "faithful," "faithless"? No—it was time to lead
by *example*. She must be steady, impersonal, godly . . . If Dusty could
see her wife stripped of the will toward judgment, shorn of everything but all-encompassing love, indifferent and sovereign, she'd
have no choice but to become naked as well. And if she chose to reply
to such selfless virtue by trying on something else—"divorcee," "elder
free spirit," "she who fell out of love and is now with another"—what
difference should it make?

When days passed without Allegra hearing from her, the mi-
graines she had as a girl returned.

She raced down PCH to a laid-back new urgent care in Malibu.
The doctor said, "Do you need a big shot or a little shot? I can give
you a shot then top you off with a second. If your experience is that
doctors take a look and say, 'She's so *shrimpy*,' and don't give you
enough, we can give you a big shot. Have you ever had Dilaudid?
I'm not the narcotics police. If you come every few months, we'd *love*
to see you. If you come every *week*, that's a problem. We have *lots* of
lovelies who come in and we make them feel like princesses. Do you
know what the lovelies all say? That compared to Saint John's, we're
Heaven! Because we don't make you wait and wait and wait. We
give you a shot, then off you go to have your princess time at home."

She finally had lunch with Jeremy.

They hadn't seen each other since she'd spewed her sordid chicaneries at the beach-blanket Buddhist bingo party. He *did* leave a voicemail blaming his MIA-ness on work, which was "super-jammy," plus his boyfriend's dad being back in the hospital and maybe dying, yadda yadda, but Allegra thought it was all jive. She knew she was a little *crazy* right now and that Jeremy had a life, *everyone* (but Allegra) had a life (a wife?), though it sure the fuck felt like the whole world was *conscientiously* saying its good-byes. And *yes*, she was working on being okay with that, getting comfortable with her new outfitless outfit, but she just couldn't get the thing to fit. It didn't go with any of her shoes either.

Oh well . . .

She'd been out of touch with Dusty for almost two weeks now, which had never happened, *ever*. After that bullshit email about quiet time and the "house" in Big Sur, Allegra ate a lot of Adderall and embraced her inner Nancy Drew. First she called Esalen and the Post Ranch Inn, asking for Dusty by her road aliases—Beatrix Potter, Eve Harrington, Jonah Feldstein—before covering NYC: the Mercer, the Lowell, the Mandarin Oriental. (Even the Gansevoort.) She phoned Buvette, their fave romantic spot in the Village, lying to the maître d' about Dusty maybe having made a reservation in the hope he'd say she was there the night before or had just left or was there right *now*. "Allegra, hi! Yes yes yes, we have her down for lunch *tomorrow*—you're going to surprise her? Of *course* I won't tell her you called. And how *are* you!" She didn't dare get in touch with any of their mutual friends but obsessively checked the Internet for sightings, comments, images. There was nothing. Tried the aliases again with Ten Thousand Waves in Santa Fe (disguising her voice because all the employees knew her and she didn't want anyone thinking something was amiss) and was about to start on Europe before saying *fuck it*. Smoked some dope and ate a giant blueberry cobbler from

Sweet Lady Jane instead. Topped it off with a chunk of Reddi-Wip the size of a preemie. Disconsolate, loaded, ruined . . . crying and moaning, staccato-burst *yelping* like some favela street mongrel after a hit-and-run. Faced the corner of the room à la *Blair Witch* and meditated to calm her breath. Thought of maybe emailing Elise, then got a brighter idea and left a vmail for Ginevra. Micro consult session aside, she would *definitely* rate a courtesy callback. But a few days went by—nada. How rude. I mean, she *was* still Mrs. Wilding.

Wasn't she?

"Hey now."

He was already sitting in the booth.

"Hey, stranger," she said, with a bite.

"Aw, don't be like that, Lego."

"Like *what*. I've been chasing you for weeks."

"I told you, Tristen's dad is *dying*. He's been a total train wreck."

"*Whatever*."

"Whatever?" he said, zero to sixty riled. "Okay, 'whatever.' Don't you already know everything anyway?"

"What's that supposed to mean?"

"Don't you already know the details? I mean, doesn't Larissa, like, *fill you in* on shit?"

"I don't talk to Larissa. And what the fuck do you *mean*, Jeremy?"

"Oh! Are we going to pretend you don't know that *Larissa* is my boyfriend's *mom*?"

"What? Of course I knew—know. And we totally *talked* about that."

"Excuse me?"

"We totally did."

"As in *you and me* talked about it? Jeremy and Allegra?"

"That's right."

"*Bullshit* we did!"

"Did we not totally discuss how weird that is?"

"Uhm, *no-o-o-o*. What's *weird* is that we *didn't*. Because you never even *mentioned* it."

"I'm sorry. There's just been so much . . . *shit*—"

"I've been, like, 'Of *course* Larissa would have told her. Why hasn't Allegra *said* anything?'"

"It wasn't *deliberate*, Jeremy. Why would I *withhold* that?"

"*I* don't know," he said, with a sly twist of the mouth. "Why would you?"

"Well, fuck *me*, I'm *sorry*. It wasn't like it was this *big topic of conversation*. It just kind of *came up*, she said her kid's boyfriend bought him a car and we just kind of figured it out from there. What is the *problem*, Jeremy?"

"No problem at *all*. I just assumed that since you and Larissa *share so much*, she'd probably already have *mentioned* her ex being at death's door. You know—pillow talk with the mistress."

"Fuck you!"

"Thank you, sir, I'll have another."

"Why are you being such a queen?" She teared up but he wasn't having it. "I mean, why are you being so *weird* and *mean* about this? Anyway, I did what you said and broke it off, so I don't even *talk* to her anymore. And I'm *sorry* I didn't have a big discussion with you about the bizarre genealogy of our *twink* family tree. Because I can *see* how fucked up you are over it, for whatever reason."

"Whatever."

"You know, I've got a lot on my plate right now! It's not like I wake up every morning thinking, 'Oh! *Larissa* is Jeremy's *boyfriend's* fucking *mother*! Oh my God, that is so, so *interesting*! That is, like, the most *interesting* and amazing thing that's ever *happened* in the *world*! I need to go write a fucking *book* about it!'"

"Let's drop it, Allegra."

"It's *Hollywood*, Jeremy! It's a tiny little *town*, shit like that *happens*. It just *happens*, what is your fucking *problem*?"

"*You're* the one who's acting like the one with a problem, darling."

"I'm sorry," she said, with a measure of sincerity. She dabbed at her eye. "Okay?"

"Sure."

"Can we please start over?"

"Love to." They took a moment and manned up; they'd lost the energy to brawl. "So what's going on with you and Dusty?"

"I haven't talked to her—*at all*. She doesn't return my emails. You?"

"Same," he said. "Incommunicado."

Jeremy was used to movie stars and their impetuous vanishing acts—the royal prerogative. When confronted by close friends and dependents about the havoc created by their absence (*cf.* romantic intrigue, drugging, wanderlust, or a combination thereof), they tended to offer the flimsiest of excuses or the most solemnly earnest; in the end, none of it mattered because the injured parties always forgave. But the situation was far more serious than he'd suspected.

"It's kind of become obvious what's happening," she said. "I feel like *such* a clown, Jeremy. I tried turning the other butt cheek or whatever, like you said. And I'm not blaming you, I actually thought it was *really* good advice, still do. But I mean, like, *fuck* her to treat me like this! Right? Right? It's *so* disrespectful. Man, if you're seeing someone or you've fallen out of love or *in* love or what-*ever*, just, like, have the fucking *decency* and *courage* to tell me to my *face*. It's so fucked *up*, Jeremy! Right?"

"And you definitely think it's Larissa," he said flatly, like an IT tech assessing a software issue. The familiar rhythm of gossip comforted, because he wasn't looking forward to what he was going to tell her.

"Probably—*I* don't know. Larissa never really came out and *said* it. But she sure didn't *deny* it. And there's *no* fucking other way to explain that *earring* in her bed. *I* don't know . . . maybe Dusty's been into that all along—seeing other people. Maybe she's some kind of secret psycho sex addict. I mean, her demented *mother* was a sick fucking cheater and how far can you fall from the whatever? Maybe she's—maybe she's been fucking Michelle Rodriguez, for all I know. Strapping it on for Maria Bello and Tatum fucking O'Neal. She could be out there sleeping with *men*, with *whatever*. Dogs and horses! And you know what?"

Her rage slammed into a wall of tears and the words wouldn't form. He put his hand on hers, drawing sweet little circles over her knuckles. Then Selma Blair appeared, gushing hellos. Allegra quickly recovered; if the actress noticed anything amiss, she didn't let on. When she asked after Dusty, Allegra said, "She's great! We're great!" Selma girl-pleaded, "I want to come *see* you guys, we need to *see* each other, when can we *hang*?" and was gone.

"It's so surreal," said Allegra, sadly pensive. "I never thought this would happen. Not like this. I thought we'd be together forever."

"Maybe you will . . . it *isn't* over, Leggy. Maybe—"

"It *is*, Jeremy! It's over for *me*. It can't just be over when it's over for *her*—she can't just say, 'It's *over*! It's *not* over! It's *over*! It's *not* over!' She can't expect me to sit here *waiting* for whatever *she* wants. It's not *fair*, Jeremy, I'm too fucking *vulnerable*!" She cut herself off and went dead—disgusted and resolute. "I guess I really don't want to talk about it anymore. But thank you. Thank you for listening to my endless bullshit."

"So what are you going to do?"

"I've made some plans."

"Can you stay at the beach for a while?"

"I'm making plans," she said noncommittally.

"Listen," he said, with a small adjustment in posture. "I know this isn't a great time but there's something I wanted to tell you."

"Are we getting a divorce too, Jeremy? You can't divorce me!"

At least she was laughing. "Nope. Not gonna happen. *Never* gonna happen."

"Well, *good*. Because *that* would *definitely* send me over the edge. I'd refuse to sign the papers."

"No worries. But here's what's going on." He took a breath. "Since the thing . . . with the baby— . . . I've been really thinking. A *lot*—you know, that I'd like to try again, try to be a dad. So I've been talking to a surrogate."

"A surrogate. Really."

"It's not that I didn't want to do it with *you*—'do it' sounds funny— but I—I didn't know where you were at, in your head."

"It's fine, Jeremy."

"Maybe I should have talked to you about it but I was pretty sure it was something you wouldn't be into, at least not this soon."

"You're probably right."

He read it all on her face: the relief and the hurt. Yet by her tone, he knew the worst was over. She'd become luminous, filled with grace.

"I can't explain it, Lego, but I just felt this *urgency*."

"So did you find someone?" she said warmly.

"I did. She had twins for my old A.A. sponsor."

"Okay," she said, in forlorn approval.

"And I just—it came together much faster than I thought. I mean, everything just . . . fell into place."

"Thank you for telling me."

"Can we talk a minute about 'Children of God'?"

"Sure."

As they spoke, he saw that he was losing her; Dusty was swallowing her up, like that YouTube clip of the anaconda digesting a cow.

"I think Kristen Stewart would be amazing as the mom—she's a friend, and she'll read it right away. My first choice for a director would be Lisa—Cholodenko—but she takes forever. I'd still like to get it to Sean, Sean Durkin. You know—*Martha Marcy May Marlene*. But I *really* want to get it to Kelly—Reichardt. Kelly would be *so* genius. She did *Night Moves*? With Jesse? Eisenberg? Have you seen it? Oh my God, Lego, you haven't seen *Night Moves*? You will *love* it. Dakota's in it? It's *totally* the best thing Dakota's ever done, she's as good as Liz Olsen in *Martha Marcy May Marlene*, she's *better* than Elizabeth. Kelly is the fuckin' *shit*, and *Night Moves* is *totally* about a cult! Or culty *behavior*, but not like so dead-on, like *Martha Marcy May Marlene*. It's *much*, much subtler. But I'm really surprised you don't know about Kelly. You *have* to see it: *Night Moves*. Kelly's totally great."

In the morning, Dusty texted where are you? It jolted Allegra's heart and she struggled against texting back. She almost answered fucking your girlfriend but didn't. An hour later, after the violence of emotions settled, she got another: u there, leg? She went to SoulCycle and shut off her phone. After, she saw that Dusty had called three times and left a voicemail. She just sat in her car, her whole body vibrating.

She put the message on speaker.

"Hi, honey. I'm back around four and wanted to know if you'd be home. Can you be, to talk? Sorry I've been so unreachable. Hope you're good and let me know if this afternoon or tonight works."

Dusty spent her last few hours at the desert hotel Skyping with her shrink—part pep talk, part general rehearsal of what was to come.

"This is your *daughter*," said Ginevra. "Not your wife, not your lover. Those are *nametags* describing someone you don't know anymore, someone you can't place. Someone who no longer exists." She sounded like a hypnotist. "You'll find that in time you will never miss that person, not for a *minute*. Even the memory of those nametags will cease to exist."

"Tell me *why* I have to tell her again, Ginevra?" Her courage kept flagging. "What if she can't *handle* it? *I* can barely handle it! Why can't I just 'break it off'? That's what Livia thinks I should do . . . she'll be *hurt* but at least she'll be able to move *on*—how can she move on from *this*? At least if I tell her I'm seeing someone . . . she'll be *devastated* but she might be able to fall in *love* again. 'Again'—!" She spat the word, turning her face to the sky in delirious contempt of the cosmos. "I keep thinking of the last scene in *Stella Dallas* where Barbara Stanwyck's standing in the rain, watching her daughter through the window as she gets married . . ."

"She *will* move on," said Ginevra, stone-faced. "You *both* will. But that *cannot* happen, Dusty, if you lie. You have *got* to live in your truth and create that *space*. You have to *allow* it . . . we've talked about all this. To deceive Allegra would be cruel. And remember, there's *no shame* in what happened—*zero*. None. And it *isn't* a movie, Dusty, you can't just shout 'I don't love you anymore!' and ride off into the sunset. You can't *wound* her like that and expect either *one* of you to come out unscathed. It may work in the movies but not in real life."

"*Real life!*" snarled Dusty—for reality had betrayed her; she lay vanquished. She sighed and grew melancholy. "I know, I know. You're right. It's just so *hard*."

"It's the hardest thing you'll ever do, bar none. And I would *never* minimize that, not for a moment. Wouldn't even try. *Reina* wouldn't have been able to do it, if you'll pardon the godawful analogy—what I'm *trying* to say is that Reina would have *lied*, like she lied about *everything* in her life, lied to *you*. Dusty, you've always talked about breaking the cycle and now you *can*. Not to tell Allegra—not to tell *Aurora*—who you are—who *she* is—isn't very loving. That isn't love. I don't know what it is but something tells me it isn't love."

On the way back to L.A. she distracted herself with practical matters.

There was so much to be undone . . .

Obviously, they needed to divorce. *Irreconcilable differences*—just like Joni and Kilauren! It would have been funny if it weren't so savagely, utterly grotesque. A backdoor revelation of "extraordinary circumstances" would allow for an annulment but what was the point? Anyway, *delineating* those circumstances, even with the highest degree of confidentiality, would only heighten the risk of a leak. No, divorce was the only way.

But something else was bothering her; a troubling flaw in her therapist's design . . .

The plan was that as soon as Allegra had been told, she would begin therapy with Ginevra *tout de suite*, an "emergency," stopgap measure, concomitant with the search for a "specialized outside practitioner." The shrink was convinced that her daughter's reaction to the unsettling news would be gradations of shock and anger followed by a "transition toward joyful integration." But Dusty thought there was something condescending and almost laughably glib about the presumption that Allegra would be even *temporarily* amenable to baring her rage, confusion, and fear with her mother's shrink. The

projected outcome was a little too tidy in an *Oprah* kind of way, and
Dusty had the feeling it wouldn't go down like that. Maybe Ginevra
was in some kind of denial and needed professional help herself; her
colleagues no doubt would find the whole case one for the books.
Even more controversial was her proposed injunction, shared with
Dusty (*overshared*, as far as the actress was concerned), that Allegra
not disclose the nature of her relationship with her mother to *anyone*
outside the therapeutic bubble—at least in the initial weeks or months
of however the fuck many years of counseling might be required to
bring *joyful integration* closer at hand. (It was Ginevra's opinion that
healing could not take place if her client was buffeted by powerful
and unpredictable outside forces. A "safe house" was required.) To
Dusty, this seemed quixotic on a number of levels. What if Allegra
was rebellious, combative, and unwilling? What if she went a little
(or a lot) crazy behind the revelation and was compelled to confide in
her besties—Jeremy, or some drunken Zoosk hookup, or whomever?
And wouldn't that be her *right*? Even if she found herself *joyfully
integrated* at the very instant she was given the news, wouldn't it
be her prerogative to tell anyone she damn pleased? To shout it from
the rooftops or take it door-to-door if she so chose? Wouldn't that
be the healthy, *human* response—to cleanse and renew, to *transform*
oneself by reaching out to the tribe, to the family of man? Wasn't it
fallacious, hypocritical, and controlling of Ginevra to believe—to
rule—that the truth be kept hidden under the rubric of therapeutic
expedience? And what about the bugaboo that "secrets kill," what
happened to *that*? Wouldn't a *second* conspiracy of silence be everyone's undoing?

Dusty reeled at the fiasco because in her gut and her heart, she
knew what she knew: the world *would* find out.

She pushed that fatal thought away and tried to imagine what a
happy ending might look like—one where a newly empowered mother

and child with an obscenely checkered past *clandestinely* followed
their bliss and lived in their truth, with the whole family of man,
woman, and Internet being none the wiser. Maybe Ginevra was right
and that after a rocky intro, all'd go smooth as silk. Allegra would
graduate from therapy summa cum laude then eagerly enlist in a P.R.
charade that would promote the split as sophisticatedly amicable,
with the gals remaining loyal *confidantes*, and best of friends. *We're even
closer now in so many ways.* Her old friend Diane Sawyer would do an
exclusive; in the weeks and months after the two-hour with Di, they
would cannily downscale to hipper venues like Kimmel, Colbert, and
Fallon. Though maybe not Colbert. Photos of the uncoupled couple in
supermarket weeklies and social media would be ubiquitous: the caring and charismatic divorcées being "spontaneous" in kitchen and
living room, on pool deck and seashore, mouths open in evolved mid-
laughter, with nothing to hide and nothing to proclaim but the genius
of their unashamed, no longer bed-sharing, modern love.

Role models!

*. . . Aurora will get her own therapist but then we'll probably start joint
sessions with Ginevra—maybe Allegra will even* request *that,* demand *it,
and it'll be very intense, tough at the beginning, then beautiful and so amazing. I'll ask Livia if she'll come bunk with us at the house—Aurora might
want to stay elsewhere in those first turbulent days but maybe not, maybe
she'll be very brave; they'd just have to wait and see—because Allegra loved
and trusted Livia, she was kind of the grandmother that Reina obviously could
never have been. Livia will be a wonderful buffer and liaison, a surrogate
maternal presence until Aurora can start to accept me as her own. What a
complex and rich and scary and amazing time it will be! With Mom and
daughter spending their days sequestered in Point Dume or Jackson Hole or
the South of France or the Cotswolds (it could be as long as a year before we're
ready to deal with the press and the whole shopworn but still relevant conscious*

uncoupling cover story), or anywhere really, we'll go anywhere and do any-
thing we want as we get to know each other all over again, really just a process
of deprogramming and resensitizing, probably approximating the few things I
know about behavior mod. The ratfuck Joni Mitchell scenario—losing Aurora
all over again—is definitely not part of the plan, though it's true I can't predict
or paint a rosy picture and that it just may happen that Aurora has a period
of adjustment where she does some drugging and sexing and acting out, which
would/will probably be a healthy, "normal" response (as long as it doesn't go
too far) . . . the year will pass and by then she'll be living in her own place and
both of us will have found some (a lot?) equilibrium. We'll do our decoupled
dog and pony show for the press, our story will be that we hit a rough patch and
went traveling to see if we could mend things but it didn't work out and we're
sad but strong, and after three or four months the attention will die down and
then just like that I'll find out Aurora's been seeing someone, and it's serious.
Maybe an older rock-star chick like Kim Gordon (if she were gay; though
Kim's probably a little too old) or an Amal Clooney politico-type or a studio
exec of the caliber of Nina Jacobson or even Megan Ellison (wouldn't that be
a goof?). Then I'll learn that Aurora's pregnant and this time the baby would
take, that would be the karma. I'll be a grandma! Oh! Wouldn't that be some-
thing? Wouldn't that—

She wondered what her own life would bring . . . saw herself
being alone for a long, long while and was okay with that. Not lonely
but alone. She envisaged entering a kind of monastery built from a
rededicated devotion to work and career, a devotion to *self*, for now
would be the time in her life, the time *of* her life, when all came full
circle and she ripened to the spiritual experience. (With still a full
quarter century remaining before death—who knew? She might
go another forty years. Even Chakrapani implied she'd have a
long life.) The *idea* of it, the plangency of the vision made her shiver.
She saw both of them years later, having a Norman Rockwell

Thanksgiving (with Ronny and his wife Sam as guests—and their daughters—Allegra's half sisters!): Aurora with new wife and child, and Dusty announcing she too had met someone special. The couples would go on vacations together with the kids (Leggy'd have *lots* of babies) and—

    —NO. I cannot tell her. I can't—I won't*! How could I? How can—*

Her heart fluttered as she pictured them—in just a few hours—in the living room up on Carla Ridge, its stage set for the full catastrophe. She'd allow herself a glass of wine beforehand, maybe a Vicodin—*no!*—better to be sober, *essential* to be sober. She would clear her throat and say, "I met someone," then let the chips fall where they may. Let the mirrors and all the boughs break . . . If she could only find the courage to fire that first assassin's shot—*and* survive the recoil . . . It'd be bloody, maddening, apocalyptic, but yes, in the end it would be for *sure* the best, the *only* thing. (It seemed almost insane to her that she had *ever* entertained the idea of proclaiming, "I am your mother.") After *I met someone*, Allegra would be cowed, leveled, traumatized into silence, and that was when Dusty would tell her she'd arranged to give her fifty thousand a month for two years, five years, ten years, forever—a *hundred thousand* if she wanted. Throw in the Point Dume house as part of the settlement (though the pendulum kept swinging because with all its memories she was thinking the place might prove too burdensome for her ex). Aurora might try to talk her out of it, talk her out of *not loving her anymore*, might say something like, "No no no! I'll wait for you, I'll wait, let me wait! Until you get this new love out of your system! *Just please don't end it, Bunny, please don't end it, please don't end it—*" That would be a dagger in Dusty's heart, but of course she'd still be forced to pull a Stella Dallas, shouting, "I don't love you, Allegra! I don't think I ever *did*. I want a *divorce*—I want to be with *her, her, her*! We're *finished*, do you hear me? We're all washed up!"—

NO!

No no no no no . . . how can I do that? How can I do that to my baby, how can—

To keep from screaming she told herself that Allegra was a survivor, over and over she thought it, then said it aloud, hoping to convince herself it was so, and that's why it would all be okay—because Allegra had the family blood, *survivor* blood, Wilding-*Whitmore* blood—and that her darling would take a hard fall, of *course* she would, then be able to get up again and stand tall, head held high, until she found *another* love, a *big* love, bigger than life, real and unperverse, the love she was *meant* to have from the beginning. *Your mother was just a starter marriage . . .* that's what Dusty kept telling herself as she sped through Covina astride her faithful pendulum—now fantasizing about what would happen if she told Allegra the truth, and mother and daughter united to share their reality with the planet. Would that really be the worst of worst things? Would it really be the end? Might in fact *transparency* be the solution—to everything? Why *not* tell all? The shockproof social media zeitgeist devoured the daily *commedia* of anarchy and annihilatory transgressions with all the fuss of a whale inhaling plankton. The yelp of an accidentally incestuous marriage, even a beloved faggot movie star's, would hardly be discernible among the twittering cries and whispers of the Web, a restless organism that greedily homogenized crowdfunding, dicpix, pandas, and beheadings. Dusty replayed the fantasy tape of a P.R.-spun divorce (whether or not they fessed up the truth, the mature and loving lesbian breakup narrative would still remain the same) but *this* time Dusty mixed in the yucky, high-opera, mind-blowing admission. There would be initial public scorn and revulsion, but she foresaw the unstoppable backlash of popular acceptance and compassion, the metamorphosizing of fear and loathing into profound respect for yet another worthy *Profiles in Courage* addition to the American freakshow canon. The mutant couple might even finagle a *Time* Person of the Year! All families had monsters in the cellar born of *deliberate* misdeeds—why should a national treasure worry if she and her child, *innocents*, were temporarily sacrificed, martyred to the cause of dark and hidden things? They'd practically be performing a public and cultural service! And before long, they would be martyrs no more, but mavericks—heroines and outlier pioneers, marching into the history books.

There would *always* be haters . . . She and Allegra were used to being vilified for their privilege, cougary union. So maybe it *would* be best to face the music: then she might truly earn the name Mother Courage. Some fool once said that irony was dead. How genius would it be to declare that shame itself had died?

Twenty minutes from Trousdale, her brain played more scenes from the phantom, psychotronic, *Keeping Up With the Wilders* HBO doc—the one where Laura Poitras points the camera on Dusty as she tells Allegra, "I'm your mom." How would the girl react? What would she say, what would she do? Would she bolt? Or—after a moment, an hour—would she rush toward her? Cleave to her blood? What an embrace *that* would be! Would she cry, "Mama!"? Was it obscene that Dusty actually yearned for such a sentimental, middle-class result, so saccharine a cliché? (She wondered.) And why *would* they hug each other, why should Aurora even *want* that? Wouldn't the aberrant nature of their *involvement* forever preclude such a "natural" impulse? Yet, knowing everything that she knew, Dusty ached with the thought of not being able to wrap her arms around her baby . . . and if she *couldn't*, in that raw *moment*, that moment of courage and sacrifice and honesty, when *would* they be able to hug, when *would* she be able to shower her child with a mother's kisses—when would the moratorium end? How much time must go by before what transpired between them would be neutralized? *Could* it be? Might it be possible they never touch again? That the terminus of their physical contact turned out to be the violent lovemaking of weeks ago on the night of the Buddhist soirée? What a horror! It was easy for Dusty to imagine things falling apart, once they had their "talk." Doomed! . . . and if that *was* to be the case, what was the point in telling her the truth? If, in the end, the result was that they never touched again—that Ginevra's theory was unsound, and on Dusty's revelation, the scales of the serpent's tail didn't fall away but multiplied . . .

Lovers no more, nor mother and daughter could be—

With the lights of downtown L.A. finally visible, all her fantasies collapsed like scaffolding in a fire.

Allegra was standing at the open door of her car, poking around in the backseat. When her wife pulled in, she pretended not to notice.

Dusty parked and walked over, heart going wild in its cage. She said a smiley, too boisterous "Hi!" Allegra took her in with a side-glance; face subtly imploding, she returned to hassle some luggage, removing a Goyard tote that was resting on a duffel. She plunked it into the front floorboard.

"What's goin' on?" said Dusty.

"What's goin' on? What does it *look* like?"

"Where are you going?"

"Where am I going? Where am *I* going? Where are *you* going? Where have you *been*?"

"You know where I've been—"

"Really?" she said derisively. "I know where *you've* been? Fuck *you*, Dusty!"

"I don't understand—"

Even though the situation was ugly and volatile, Dusty found relief in realizing that her abominable mission, shaky and amorphous as it was, would most likely abort. She numbed out.

"You disappear for *two weeks* and now you don't *understand?*" She skirted around to the driver's side and got in. "You're *fucking* someone *else* and you don't *understand?*"

"What are you *talking* about?"

"Oh please *stop*. Stop! Please!"

"Allegra, I am not *sleeping* with anyone!" she said, belching the words like some cheeky she-devil—a sinister kink in the script had forced her to declare her faithfulness.

"Fuck *you!*" shouted Allegra, crying now. She slammed the door and screeched a reverse arc while Dusty jumped from harm's way.

"I need to talk to you!" yelled Dusty. Allegra jerked the car forward, waiting impatiently as the automated gate crawled open in slo-mo. Dusty ran up and hollered through the closed window. The driver stared ahead, ramrod and tear-streaked.

"Allegra, please! We need to talk!"

We need to talk—she was in hell again, a cheap disaster-movie, condemned to repeat a trite line ad infinitum. And she hated what she had to say next but there was no way around it, if there was any hope in assuaging:

"I am not seeing anyone else!"

The insanity, the Byzantine contortions, the absurdity of it!

Allegra rolled down the window. "I *know* that you're fucking *Larissa*—"

"What?"

"—because *I've* been fucking her too!" It was the only weapon Allegra had and she hurled it with full force. "Who *else* are you fucking, and for how long?"

"I am *not* fucking Larissa or *anyone else*, goddammit!"

She peeled into the street and was gone.

Sometimes a boy was just a boy.

That's what it felt like as he held the sobbing Tristen. He wasn't a thing for sex play; he wasn't a wickedly brilliant shit-disturber; he wasn't a stoner orphan needing to be saved.

Nothing but a boy . . .

Though "sobbing" was euphemistic, for he was in the grip of a primal woundedness that was awesome to behold, a blowup of near epileptic proportions. Eyes glued shut, he clutched and windmilled, fighting and flighting for his life—Patty Duke to Jeremy's Anne Bancroft—pounding on the door of his lover's chest like a panicked repentant child locked out by punishing parents on a haunted forest night. The superheated bellows of his stomach pumped and furiously spasmed during the embrace yet Jeremy remained deserted by Eros. It was as if he'd become a leading man overnight, an understudy no more—a father now, fully present, seasoned and magnificent, in no need of rehearsals, dressed *or* undressed. The role felt so new and so old at once that its effortlessness astonished and pleased. The inconsolable boy behaved like a fugitive fresh from a first murder (one that might well have been his own), but interestingly, the details behind his misery failed to intrigue the *padrone*. Anyway, Tristen would have been mute if queried, he was beyond language, and of course Jeremy knew it had to do with the dad who lay in hospital, cardiac cosmonaut on the launching pad of ruined atria. Holding him now as he did, in a stuttering, slow jam boxer's ballet, Jeremy was disgusted with himself for daring to question Tristen's character in the last few weeks, that he'd tarred him with Larissa's brush, when in fact the boy had done nothing but bestow inestimable gifts—he was certain Tristen had endowed him with the courage needed to have chosen the surrogate path—and was honored young Twist felt safe enough, cared-for enough, loved enough (with father-torn spirit and his own failing heart) to collapse in Jeremy's arms just as natural as could be. He had learned so much from this boy! He'd never been so open and inspired with any of his young men.

What would never be revealed, at least not *directly*, to Jeremy or anyone else (though suspicions would be raised), was that Tristen had stumbled upon an email that effectively destroyed him. When his father's girlfriend unexpectedly returned from Portland (Derek had been on a quiet campaign to get her back), she usurped his quality time with the old man, and Tristen got pissed. So he hacked Beth's phone, archiving her banking/medical records plus the usual mix of quotidian/scandalous texts, cock&tits selfies, and lo-res videos (a four-minute one of Beth blowing his dad)—before coming across a note written some months ago, from Derek to Beth while he was stoned and unguarded. He said the boy wasn't his, that Larissa had a one-night stand early in the marriage but for ten years had passed "bitchboy" off as theirs, and that when Rafaela was born, his wife finally confessed. *it was like a fuickin grim fairey tale,* he wrote. *one day you go to your kids room to wake him for bgreakfast and there's a WHOREPIG there instaead. A filhy nasty fucking WHORPIG and you justthink about-KILLIN it and EATING it and feedint it to your family and expecially too that bitch you want to see her choke her on that bacon LOL i got a peternity test on raffi, she's MINE & you cn tell, she got my EYES (not my tits) and she HOT like her old man USED to be but you still like riding that cock, right girl??!?!?*

That was why he clung so fiercely to Jeremy—the only man who loved him, the only one who ever had or ever would. And when the anaphylactic siege was over (he self-hated for flashing that he was in *Derek's* arms, not Jeremy's), Tristen stole to the den to gather his thoughts. He swallowed a handful of pills and read the email again until he felt nothing. An hour passed and he left without Jeremy knowing.

He was on his way to kill him, Beth too if she was there, and then himself.

Beth needed help—Derek's breathing was labored but he wouldn't let her call 911.

To make matters worse, she thought he'd been doing blow. She had no idea where he would have gotten that, probably an old stash. With his heart the way it was, doing coke was the same as suicide, which is what she was beginning to think was the plan. Before Larissa rushed over, Derek had been fixating on whether the IATSE insurance hack would "hold," and kept calling his son. When he finally got through, he said Tristen went all crazy and hung up on him.

Larissa wasn't in such great shape herself.

A few weeks ago, while orgying with Tessa and the putative billionaire, she got a text from Allegra saying she was "uncomfortable with what we've been doing." Too blazed to respond, she shut off her phone. In the morning, Larissa wondered if she'd imagined it, but no: Allegra was breaking up with her. Which probably meant she had already confronted Dusty about having betrayed her with the camera double . . . the earring in the bed, the this, the that . . . *ugh* and *oy*. A friggin' nuclear situation. While part of Larissa was glad (she seemed to have reached an impasse over what to do with the monster she'd created), she was devastated too because one bright, euphoric morning she awoke to realize she was head over heels in love with the movie star's old lady. She wondered how the fuck *that* happened, but there you have it. When Allegra blindsided her, she grew sleepless and obsessive, stalking the house on Carla Ridge. What began as an impromptu goof—an angry, nutzoid, bizarrely innovative payback for how Dusty had scorned her—had seriously backfired. She was grievously wounded and painfully alone.

She was in bed when Beth called, spooning room-temp Häagen-Dazs Rocky Road into her mouth and masturbating to the nightlight of an MSNBC *Lockup* marathon. She decided not to wake Rafaela because she wouldn't be gone all that long—they'd drive Derek to the hospital and that would be that. The paramedics might get there before she did, anyway. (She called them herself when Beth said Derek had forbidden her.) Tristen was at his boyfriend's. The idea of alerting him only occurred in light of the men's recent détente, but she demurred; as much as it warmed her, she didn't trust all the happyface fence-mending, at least not on Derek's side. When Beth later mentioned something about Tristen raging on the phone at his dad, Larissa was actually heartened. It was about time he got angry.

Maybe he was growing up.

The next evening, he kept his appointment.

This time they were by themselves, as her guru was recovering from a head cold. She chose Denny's because she said they had the best fried chicken and she loved the Googie architecture. When Devi asked after "the marvelous boy" (who had also been invited), Jeremy said he had tried to reach him. He really had; but Tristen was worrisomely out of touch.

Without much ado she offered a summary of her fateful encounter with the portly sidewalk saint, succinctly recapping the history of all that led up to it—culminating in the long walks taken while her daughter lay in the hospital. When she first discovered the man who was to be her guru and protector, he was at rest upon a swatch of cardboard, hard by the fashionable Gold Coast establishment known as Mandry's. They spent time together and she told him about her life. Then one day he cryptically announced, "It's all over, because now they *know*. The contract is magnificently broken," and in the next moment the two were at her precious Bella's bedside, where the poor thing died soon after. She recounted the mysterious ease with which "my Sir" contrived a burial that was both humble and fitting for a princess—its million bells resounding—at costs marked paid and unknown.

"I've sat at his feet now, as I've said, for seven perfect years. He's given me life and shown me death and now we are leaving for that third place—I should say *he* is leaving and I hope to have courage enough, *silence* enough, to follow. Like myself, Sir is an inveterate rover, yet on a Promethean scale. In his day he thought nothing of swallowing hundred-mile walking tours whole; alighting in whatever far-flung city where his business had taken him, he'd set out on more compact versions, to shake off the crampiness of planes, trains, and automobiles. On one such restorative jaunt in Chicago, destiny brought him to Mandry's, a hip neighborhood gastropub of the type summarized in local guides by the symbols of crossed knife and fork, martini glass, and triple dollar sign. While my Sir is and always *has* been a teetotaler, he's a prodigious observer of *people*. He was drawn to the place; more about that in a minute. If you're curious about his 'background,' well, so am I, and I'm afraid I can't help you much. I know little about his life as a 'householder'—it's not something he dwells on, so I don't either. He *has* told me that he used to reside in Minnesota with his wife and only child. I believe they were married thirty some-odd years. Their son was mentally impaired, though as gentle a soul as one would ever meet. Again, Sir told me this himself.

"On those urban walks that I described, it was my guru's pleasure to dodge into watering holes of both high and low character. Once inside, he'd lean against a wall and people-watch, smiling at whoso-ever passed by while formulating some astonishing new idea from which hundreds of jobs and untold millions in revenue would soon be created. On the final night of his trip to the Windy City, it was close to two a.m. He was on the dregs of a ramble that would be his last before returning home; as he turned into Mandry's, a bouncer barred his entrance. 'They've called it,' said the man. 'You can't go in. *Last call.*' Wishing to defuse the surliness and even potential violence he perceived were at hand, my Sir lightheartedly said, 'Oh, that's all right, I'm not drinking.' 'You better *believe* you're not,' said the thug. 'Not tonight!' And with that, he leapt in front of my guru and barred the door, snarling, *'The last time I let you in, you asked every woman in the bar if they'd fuck you.'*

"I won't dignify such ugliness with a rebuttal or defense of my teacher's spotless character. I *will* say that until that evening, he'd never laid eyes on Mandry's *or* its tactless guardian. But what is of paramount importance *here* is that for the first time in his life, Frank MacKlatchie became so enraged that he entirely failed to recog-nize the man—himself!—who, as a result of those ill-spoken words, directed the blast of a high-pressure fire hose tirade at the bully who'd so casually slandered him. (I had almost forgotten that my Sir encouraged me, in telling this story, to use the name he went by *before* he was 'transformed'—Franklin MacKlatchie, Esquire.) Now as it *was* last call, customers began to pour from the front door; the bar was on a corner so that cars were poised at the stoplight and their passengers watched the embarrassing altercation for sport. It may have been just the sort of 'colorful' rowdiness that would have cap-tured my guru's attention himself, had he not been a star player in the spectacle . . . and then suddenly, as if deflated by a pin, the accuser dared to apologize! Without looking Frank MacKlatchie in the eye, he begged pardon, humbly admitting that it must be a case of mistaken identity! Which was the same as trying to unring a bell that'd been struck by lightning. The remorseful *thug* went on to remark upon the uncanny *physical resemblance* between my noble, my delicate Sir, and some other terrible fellow who'd made trouble some while back.

"Well. As Mr. MacKlatchie's remonstrations began to shrivel and he felt himself returning to his body, as it were, he became aware of the small, drunken crowd that had gathered to watch the 'fun.' When the fireworks ended, they lost interest and dispersed. My teacher left shortly thereafter. He went to bed but tossed and turned; humiliated and angry, he was unable to sleep. He felt an awful fool for losing his temper and handling the situation so poorly. He finally made peace with himself and drifted off. But in the morning, he was shocked to find that his rage had returned, white-hot and undiminished! He canceled his trip home and phoned the club, demanding to speak with the manager. He was surprised when the fellow got on the line and even *more* surprised when he coolly said, 'I know what this call is about— you're the gentleman from last night, no? I was in back of the club when it happened. I heard you arguing. Right after you left, Marcus came directly to me and admitted he'd made a horrible mistake. You see, a guy came in about a year ago who was *very* bad news. You really *do* look like him—and Marcus had a particularly shall we say *personal* involvement with this *vicious, abusive* man during the period he harassed our club. To his credit, after you had your . . . *disagreement*, Marcus said to me, "The moment I accused him of being that piece of shit, *I knew I was wrong.* But the words somehow had already come out."'

"'I understand,' said the formidable Mr. MacKlatchie. 'But I'm afraid his apology wasn't believable in the least! He never looked me in the eye nor did he offer to take me inside for a *proper* amends, i.e., to seek out his boss—*you*—"for the record," as they say. The only conclusion I could draw was that it was the end of his shift and I simply wasn't worth the trouble; that he sorely wanted to go home to whoever or whatever awaited him. It's as easy as that! I should tell you I've already spoken to my lawyers, who've assured me that a case for defamation is clear. They've advised that in such instances, the courts do not "consider" apologies. They are *after the fact*—the damage has been done.'

"It made no difference that the manager was profuse and proper in *his* apologies—all day long Franklin stewed in his suite at the Drake over his public shaming, a violation of ancient taboo that unexpectedly aroused a volcanic atavism in its target. He no longer felt he knew himself at all.

"Suffice to say that my teacher never returned to Minnesota, more or less abandoning his affairs of business. (The corporation's profitability was never at risk, thanks to an ingenious system of checks and balances implemented by its brilliant founder decades ago.) A bevy of close friends and colleagues made pilgrimages in an attempt to unravel the mystery and lure him to his senses, to no avail. His wife *did* finally come, after many months, begging an explanation of what had happened, or *was* happening (if he felt the latter might more easily be answered). "I'm suing a local club" was all she could get out of him. When the baffled woman pressed him on why the legalities couldn't be handled from elsewhere (meaning Duluth), he had no response. As a last resort, she begged him to come home, if only for the sake of their special-needs child, who cried out for him at night—he remained unmoved.

"If the fabled Frank MacKlatchie's billions were born of a series of

Big Ideas, he was suddenly struck by a thunderclap with the biggest of them all. As the Buddha's prior life had prepared him for his seat beneath the Bodhi Tree, so had my guru's secret yearnings and aspirations made him ripe for what he now planned—the death of all he'd come to represent, not just to the world but to himself. He knew that a life of wanton commerce and rampant lovelessness had tattooed his very soul, marking and defining him as surely as those insipid guidebook symbols did Mandry's Gastropub. Franklin MacKlatchie *saw* that he was already dead; and like a grandmaster, plotted his checkmate. If you'll allow, I'll recite the moves of the game as they were told to me . . .

"The case against Mandry's settled out before trial. (Victory had never remotely been in question; Mr. MacKlatchie's attorneys routinely scorched the earth to procure it.) The token figure agreed on by both sides, fifty-five thousand dollars, was given to a home for wayward children. When word of the legal resolution became known, executives at the highest company level sighed in relief with the presumption his 'aberrant' behavior had run its course. How little they understood of what Franklin MacKlatchie was becoming! But how could they have known? To have even had an *inkling* of his imminent sea change, one would need to have been cut from the same cloth.

"His stroke of genius was to purchase Mandry's outright—lock, stock, and wine barrel. He wanted the new ownership kept secret, so the transaction was carried out anonymously by three trusted successors. What he told those gentlemen next was shocking: he would be pleased to now vanish off the face of the earth! (Or at least wished to give the *appearance* of having done so.) For all intents and purposes, my Sir would henceforward be *dead to the world*, whereabouts unknown. Only the handpicked triumvirate would be privy to his new role as spectral CEO and ringmaster, running the whole circus from a cheap motel room. In order to effect such a plan, my Sir drew up an encyclopedic contract worthy of Borges—oh, I *loved* Borges, wrote three papers on him at Loyola!—that would make it virtually *impossible* for any person, entity, board member, or trustee to compromise Franklin MacKlatchie's status as *majority owner*, regardless of perceived quote-unquote absenteeism or, say, on the basis of perceived quote-unquote abandonment and dereliction of duties; nor could he be deposed or expelled by the assertion he was in breach due to mental incompetency. The contract was signed by the necessary parties forty-eight hours after the defamation case against Mandry's was resolved, which coincidentally happened to be the day his put-upon wife made her last stand, with a renowned psychiatrist in tow. (My guru indulged the missus, knowing he'd be vacating the Drake that evening and disappearing for good.) After a brief interview and some careful consideration, the learned man suggested a diagnosis of *idée fixe*, optimistically suggesting the condition would eventually 'clear' with the same mysterious abruptness with which it took hold—though naturally, it was impossible to say just *when*. Mrs. MacKlatchie was despondent.

"While spouse and handicapped child were generously provided for *in perpetuity*, those selfsame handpicked men thought it cruel, both to 'the widow' and to *them*—the triumvirate—to be forced into telling her lies of omission. The *ex cathedra* whims of their boss now seemed punishing and unsavory, but, alas, the contract tied their hands; if they dared reveal to *anyone* the peculiar actuality of the situation, well, the draconian provisions of the signed agreements would trigger immediate termination, along with financial penalties designed to be ruinous. My heart went out to Mrs. MacKlatchie when Sir told me of the numerous detectives she hired to find him—if he should ever leave *me*, I wondered what desperate measures *I* would resort to!—but their efforts came to naught. Though it's probably more accurate to say that whatever she paid them, her husband increased by multiples sufficient to allow the investigators to sidestep their professional ethics and report back to their client empty-handed. They even returned her fee.

"A final section of the covenant had a bewildering stipulation that you'll come to see as the acme of his achievement, the jewel in the crown, the bell tower of the cathedral. In simplest terms, it stated that the entire edifice would collapse—the contracts he'd so meticulously crafted be rendered null and void—*in the moment he chose to reveal, whether by deliberation or in error, to any person or persons, in writing or in speech, that he, Franklin Tannenbaum MacKlatchie, was the sole legal owner of Mandry's Gastropub LLC.* In the event of such a seemingly innocuous occurrence, all controlling interests in FM Industries would immediately cede to the triumvirate, and its founder be permanently ousted. By the time those trusted (if greatly discomposed) servants read that clause, they knew in their hearts that the man they once revered and loved, and who so brilliantly mentored them, was completely insane. Yet they had no choice but to follow his instructions to the letter. As said, the charter he drafted was insuperable—a castle keep of elegant logic whose divine proportions, akin to those of a late Beethoven string quartet, made it an exemplar and holy grail of Golden Ratio jurisprudence.

"But let's get back to Mandry's. When he took possession, not only did Mr. MacKlatchie insist on retaining the manager *and* the bouncer—the very men who'd spurred his momentous transfiguration—but lavished them both with substantial raises and benefits as an incentive against their finding other work. With that hedge in place, he was now ready to implement an unthinkably bold, unthinkably strange artifice. I'll sketch it for you now: he began to drink,

heavily, in his own place of business. In two weeks' time, my guru became a failed pickup artist, a lewd and lascivious nuisance to the lady
patrons—a tacky replica of the troublemaker Marcus initially mistook
him for. Now remember, the bouncer was unaware that Mr. Mac-
Klatchie was in fact his employer *and* benefactor, and only familiar
with him as the once outraged gentleman who in response to a
false accusation—*Marcus's*!—had sued the pub and *lost*, a falsehood, of
course, which had been artfully publicized. And by the way, the backstory concocted for the Sir's 'drunkard' persona was that after a pro-
tracted bankruptcy and divorce, the failed defamation suit had driven
him to the tipping point of sanity.

"What followed may seem hard to believe. You see, the bouncer felt
somewhat responsible for what had befallen him—so, instead of eject-
ing the poor soul, he opened his heart and gave gentle counsel, looking
out for Mr. MacKlatchie as he would a brother. And the manager did
the same! They even offered up their homes for sanctuary. After a
month of such ministrations, Frank MacKlatchie admitted to them
that his drinking had in fact become unmanageable and resolved to
go on the wagon, thanks to their great kindness and care. Soon after,
he arranged through intermediaries to fire them both—without malice, of course—he simply felt it was time to 'graduate' into the wide
world that awaited them outside Mandry's doors. He endowed each
with 'single-trigger parachutes' ('so-called in the *parlance*,' said my
Sir), settlements large enough to make at least *one* of the unwitting
pair burst into tears. The manager was said to have purchased a six-
floor apartment building with his severance . . .

"It was by the design, eventually, that not a single Mandry's
employee remained who knew 'Frank MacKlatchie,' either by face or
reputation. And for the next few years, my Sir revolved through
every hirable position: busboy, bartender, accountant, dishwasher,

server, chef. (Managers who balked at this eccentric-seeming game of musical chairs quickly found themselves jobless.) When those roles were exhausted, he came to embody the full array of customers too — cross-dressing, upstyling, and frumpy Fridaying his way through the bar as he took on Everyperson's passions and longings, celebratory moods and suicidal regrets. Only once did he reflect on the life he'd erased. It was the time Mrs. MacKlatchie drifted in for an Irish coffee, seeking warmth on a snowy, inhospitable night. She was on a final, solitary field trip, in futile search of her long-lost husband, and found herself loitering at ground zero. She came in like a ghost, as if hoping to find one more of her kind. He was 'playing' bouncer that night (things had almost come full circle) and she looked straight at him but failed to recognize. Her obliviousness may have been ascribed to a distracted state of mind or the camouflage of beard he'd grown or even the Union Army cap chosen as part of his 'look,' but *I* think she couldn't see him because Franklin MacKlatchie, simply, was no longer *there*. You see, by then he was nearly done and for all practical purposes (only purposes of *energy* remained) had excused himself from this world.

"My guru told me that was an exceptionally difficult night — seeing his wife that way—an encounter that became the 'period,' so to speak, on the last sentence of the book he once was. On awakening in his seedy room the next morning, he felt entirely refreshed. He was almost free . . .

"In his last 'turn,' he became one of the homeless men often adopted as charms and mascots by places such as Mandry's. The *original* gentleman with the job (who never missed a day) had only recently retired by succumbing to hypothermia (he'd been promoted, or 'kicked upstairs,' as my teacher put it), which left the much coveted position vacant—and so the soon-to-be-former Frank MacKlatchie eagerly submitted his application. His CV easily prevailed, landing him a corner office on the same square of frozen walkway as his forebear; he lowered himself onto that grimy cardboard with the endgame cocksureness of the lowliest piece in *king and pawn versus king*. The new hire was accorded privileges commensurate with his predecessor, in other words, punctiliously attended to by kitchen boys bringing soup and bread and fussed over by waitresses many generations removed from the servers who'd made Franklin's first acquaintance. He knew the moment had come to light the fuse of the clause that would initiate self-destruct. Presently, he began to share with employees, postmen, and passersby—not immodestly but as statement of fact—that 'I, Franklin T. MacKlatchie,' happened to be the exclusive owner—and *ipso facto* proprietor—of that cherished neighborly Gold Coast nugget known as Mandry's. Of course no one *believed* him, though his confession, viewed as nothing more than a wild hair in a wig of delusion, *did* have the effect of attracting even *more* soup (piping hot) from the minions—and entrées, desserts, blankets, and so forth. The refractory CEO didn't think it would take long for 'the principals' to be informed of the breach, for he was well aware of having been closely watched from the beginning by the designated three who awaited the day of the contract's sundering as a Christian awaits rapture.

"He had broken it with glee and abandon, because he heard the bells of Silence finally ring! So it was done and he tarried calmly to be routed out. It was during those last days, when Bella was in hospital and myself perambulating, that I befriended him. I did my share of fussing over him too—oh, but he was fussable! When I noticed a sore on his leg that was stubborn to heal I dressed it with ointments. I gave him money and books and sweets and vigorously massaged his legs to ward off the frostbite. (By now, he'd given up even his tiny motel room.) I shared with him my life and current situation—a real chatterbox! But *he* didn't seem to mind. Then one day he said, 'It's time for me to leave this place.' He couldn't have been clearer but I still wasn't sure what it *meant*. Taking my arm for an assist, he rose up. 'They won't come looking for me—I've broken the contract, you see, I've made *sure* of that. Broke it every day for the last month! Took 'em longer to find out than I thought . . . but now I am *certain* of it, I'm *certain* they know.' He said the men chosen to succeed him had detectives on retainer who did nothing but record and observe his doings round the clock, from close and afar—a constant surveillance whose goal was to catch out the offender as soon as he violated the agreement's terms. To that end, they had secured hidden audiovisual proof of my Sir's 'delusional' public declarations of ownership. It was of no interest that their quarry bore scant resemblance to the thin, close-shaven, conservatively dressed titan his colleagues once knew, nor did the private eyes (or FM Industries honchos, for that matter) care a whit about the motivations behind his sudden turnabout . . . they had a job to do and now it was done. The board was overjoyed and only too anxious to close this galling, perplexing, unsavory chapter of the conglomerate's storied history. But the ordeal had taken its toll. The three appointed wise men looked far older than their years, a consequence of being hamstrung and betrayed by that tragicomic figure, a mentor turned capricious madman who for no comprehensible reason had reveled in trampling upon their dignity, dampening their autonomy, and casting dark shadows over their futures and fortunes—a shadow that could now be removed at last.

"They were free now themselves. And that's what my guru wanted. For everyone to be free."

Jeremy looked into her eyes. They were cool, blue-green, limpid. So fucking weird and so beautiful she was, and he felt his heart stir. To his chagrin, *everything* stirred.

"That was seven years ago." She was smiling at him. "Seven years I've been at his side, seven years of wandering and of miracles—the miracle of being in his presence, of *listening* to him, of loving. I know you must be curious how we live—and the *way* we sometimes do." The wink no doubt referred to the house on Malibu Road. "In his worldly wisdom, my guru made certain we'd be amply provided for. 'Trust in God, but lock your front door.' Ever hear that saying? One of the codicils of the grand contract he designed created an account with enough monies to make not just a bouncer but a *centimillionaire* burst into tears!" For some reason, she made herself laugh. "It has been more than enough to take care of us, and will get us where we are going."

"And where is that?" asked Jeremy.

He almost didn't want to know. It had all become too heart-breaking.

"To a region known as Summerland. My Sir says we are close now."

She moved to a hotel.

Allegra had a few hundred thousand dollars in an account her wife set up for her years ago. Some of it was money she'd earned herself.

In residence now, at the Four Seasons: footloose, jangly, black-hearted.

Couldn't reach Jeremy—who else *was* there?

She felt like an asshole for calling Ginevra a second time—*again* the cunt didn't return the call. She *wouldn't*, right? Because Dusty *owned* her, right? *If I drop dead tomorrow, she'd help Bunny move on—at $475 an hour, seven-fifty for a house call.* Allegra was jolted by a surge of revulsion as she realized how involved the therapist must already be in their business; privy to every nook and cranny of her wife's revo-

lutionary new love . . . quarterbacking the breakup of their marriage. Their *life*—

She puked right there on the California King.

She kept getting texts from Dusty to please come home. Home!
Why would she even use that shitty word? (Only "love" was shittier.)
Maybe Ginevra told her to.

She deleted the messages.

And just lay there, letting all sorts of memories take her.

Allegra ached for her mother . . . but how? Why? It'd been years
since she'd had two thoughts about Willow (née Claudia Zabert)—
and now she was aching. She hadn't seen the woman since she was a
teenager, living together in that scummy flat. (*Hated* London but
anything was better than the phantasmagoric cesspool of India.)
She remembered the pouring rain. She was on her way home and
ducked into a gallery for free wine and cheese. The rich painter hit
on her—she was forty, Allegra pretended to be nineteen—and that
was that. The artist brought her to New York. They lived in a Chel-
sea loft for a few years and it was cool, it was superfun, it was all
good. But the lady was crazy possessive, and Allegra couldn't keep
her panties on.

After they broke up, she did deep-tissue massage—way deep—at
fancy hotels (did astrology and crystal readings too). Took solace in
her deep, cultish roots . . . Got into some heavy coke, sex, and yoga
scenes—dead-eyed pixie, an adventuress, an excitable girl who'd
seen too much. Hung with violent and hilarious hermaphrodites;
hung with Raëlian sex workers; stayed in Vermont a few months
with twins who happened to be lovers, becoming *their* lover too.
(Ironically, they were the daughters of a Twelve Tribes couple who
ripened into FREECOG kahunas bent on destroying her alma
mater, the Children of God . . . *sheesh!*) She finally got tired of all the
fascist third eye crystal *qijong* esoteric chakra bullshit and remade

herself as a serial au pair. More Upper Yeast Side sexual hijinks ensued. At twenty-three, she fled to California, back to the mountainous commune at Black Bear Ranch where she and Willow lived before that fucked-up kingpin spirited them away. (Some folks she knew as a kid were actually still there.) God, how she loved that land. Human beings always failed you but the land never did. For a few healing years she lived comfortably in her yurt and her skin, like a child again, not a slave-child of some insane erotomaniacal god, but a *free* child—of river and forest, of mountain, moon, and stars.

An innocent . . .

So many terrible things had been done to her body, especially in the Family when she was so, so young, and when it all got too heavy even for Willow, they escaped from that hell house in the Tenderloin and hid out in Black Bear, fugitives from the lie and the law. *Oh, halcyon days* . . . why couldn't they have just stayed? In the Siskiyous, with the good new people, she was safe. As if to expiate all the sins she had sponsored, Willow introduced her daughter to the river. It washed her clean. They skinny-dipped in a glorious Huck Finn swimming hole and she befriended the fishes, tadpoles, and tiny frogs—how they welcomed her! The men of the commune were kind and respectful and left them alone. (She couldn't even believe men like that existed.) Allegra recalled the path that snaked to the water and how she would run, her mom chasing after—in they'd go, and again she was cleansed. Willow washed her daughter's hair on the edge of the brook, lathering it to a beehive meringue. Then one day Gridley Wright arrived, the *Rasputin* of Shiva Lila—Mr. Right!— and wanted Allegra to lay on the bed while he fucked her mother, and Willow just let it happen, like she let everything. He made the girl join them, not that Allegra fought that, because by then she was up for any kind of parental guidance. And it seemed like when she blinked, they'd been stolen away to Bombay . . . Goa . . . Mysore, Kochi, and Kerala—where everything smelled like a gang rape of incense, shit, and death. The grown-ups were freaking and all her little friends were getting sick and disappearing and brand-new monkeymen kept saving and destroying them, saving and destroying, saving and destroying.

So: after she left her half-mad mother in Brixton, after she left her apoplectic painter in New York, after checkered careers as au pair and energyworker, and nostalgic Black Bear sabbatical with restorative old friends—mountains, river, yurt, night stars—she settled in L.A. with a droll, quirky psych nurse from Panorama City whom she met at a Sex and Love Addicts Anonymous meeting. They rented a bungalow off Sawtelle. Allegra worked at Trader Joe's and at a bonsai nursery on weekends. Five years of that—*five years*—such happiness, unalloyed! *Why* then the sudden, oh-so-bold, so *creative* transition to waitressing? She couldn't remember. *Prolly just bored.*

Then she saw Dusty Wilding at the Hotel Bel-Air and every cell in her body woke up, every hair stood on end. She went to the house in Point Dume and they laughed and cried for real, hours of it, stoned on hash, singing out SUFFERING *was the only thing made me feel I was alive thought that's just how much it cost to survive in this world—till you showed me how how to fill my heart with love how to open up and drink in all that white light* POURING DOWN FROM THE HEAVEN! as they roared up PCH to the movie star's secondary love shack (in Carpinteria) in the canary yellow Alfa that Dusty wound up giving as a birthday gift.

And now she was at the Four Seasons.

How fucked was that?

So fucked.

In three weeks, she'd be thirty-seven . . .

Allegra sent a quick text—im ok will write later—in response to another flurry from her wife. For the first time she allowed herself to think *Maybe I can get through this*. Then: Maybe *we* can get through this. Yet whenever she started fantasizing about reconciliation, the cold reality of the situation gave her whiplash. She tried to feel better by reminding herself that marriage had afforded certain legal and financial protections—then instantly recoiled, not only from the horror of her predicament (unthinkable only a few short weeks ago), but from the idea that she possibly wasn't protected at *all*. California being California, the law could be tricky. Plus, with the shit going down the way it had, it suddenly seemed plausible Dusty might not be the generous partner Allegra had always imagined, because she didn't even really know who the fuck Dusty *was* anymore. The woman who she'd taken for granted no longer existed, and maybe never had . . .

As if beginning a series of hellish aerobics, she visualized a future without her wife. Dusty Wilding would be in the news *forever*, on billboards and award shows, joyous and bulletproof, pictures in magazines, jumping off yachts with new loves, new lovers, new *friends*—time-lined and tweeted in millions of Internet pages, while she, Allegra, would be in the non-news forever, the hapless, humiliated ex, a loser thrown off a hit reality show, dredged up by the press and eternal loser links of the Web, to body-shame a depressive weight gain, or money-shame a ruinous investment, or slut-shame a calamitous post-marital hookup, or soul-shame for merely being born—chronicling DUIs, shoplifting arrests, and other rumored occasions of injury, death, and dishonor . . .

Her wife sent another text asking if they could just please meet. Allegra's heart quaked and she said yes but that she was going away for the weekend, what about Monday. (She didn't want it to be on Dusty's terms.) She wrote back of course and Allegra said you can come to 4 seasons. Her heart clenched again; maybe she shouldn't have even told her where she was. *I keep giving my power away.* Dusty texted ♥♥♥ and Allegra puzzled over whether the hearts were respectfully reserved, hopeful, positive—or contrived, thoughtlessly businesslike, and negative.

But she *did* feel a little better. Maybe she should book a rub at the spa? She grabbed her iPad instead and scrolled through the videos. She hadn't looked at the sextape in months. They drolly referred to it as their "performance piece" and it was the only one they'd ever done. Their faces were deliberately obscured; even Dusty's birthmark had been scrupulously shot around. Allegra watched it dispassionately, like an anthropologist puzzling over an artifact.

Her cell rang, throwing her into electrified chaos for the thousandth time that day—but instead of Dusty, it said

Jeremy
mobile

"Hey!" she said.

Nothing—nobody there.

"Hello? Hello? *Jeremy?*"

After some clicks, rattles, and throat-clearings, came a honking nose-blow and loud rustles.

"Hello?"

"Jesus, did you butt-call me?"

He started to moan, then wail—totally crazy-sounding.

"Jeremy, what the *fuck?*"

"Tristen died," he said, in scary deadpan basso. More phlegmy, aggressive throat-clearings followed.

"*What?*"

"He crashed his car."

"He died?" she said dumbly. "*When?*"

"Four days ago!" he blubbered. "He kind of *disappeared* and I was starting to worry—so I Facebooked *Larissa* . . . oh, Allegra! He crashed in his car! He crashed in the car I gave him!"

"Jeremy, I'm so sorry! Where are you?"

"Home."

"I'm coming over."

"You don't have to—"

"*I'm coming over.*"

"Okay."

He sounded like a three-year-old.

"Do you need anything?"

Long pause.

"Oh, Leggy . . . he's dead, my Tristen's dead, he crashed in the car I gave him . . . the Honda! He crashed in the Honda! He *loved* that car, he loved that *car!* It's my fault, it's my fault, it's my *fault*, he wouldn't have even had a *driver's license* if I hadn't paid for the lessons—"

He was off to the races and wailing again, ugly and high-pitched, then wandered away from the phone. After a few minutes, she hung up.

When she got to the house, Jeremy was a resplendent mess—on the phone with this one, laughing and weeping with that, rushing around doing his tragic Blanche DuBois hostess thing then collapsing on the couch, a drunken queen in her cockeyed crown, waving a broken fan. It moved Allegra to see how much he really cared for that boy. He went on about the night he died, how only hours before, Tristen had been sobbing in his arms about his dad, and how Larissa later said their son must have had a sixth sense that something was wrong because the tantrum of tears would probably have been right

around the time Derek was having trouble breathing—Derek's girlfriend called her and Larissa was on her way there herself—how
Jeremy was obviously rushing over there to help when he lost control of the car. "He was so full of love! He played it so *cool* and so
spiky, but *Leggy*! He was such a *love bug*! And he loved *me*, Lego, he
loved *me*. He really, really did, I *know* he did . . ."

With an actor's instinct to rein in the maudlin, he abruptly stepped
out of himself to ask, apropos of Allegra's general marital *meshugas*,
"And how are *you*?" She squinched a tight little smile, shorthanding,
"At the Four Seasons." When he said he *still* hadn't heard from Dusty,
Allegra was about to ask if he left word about what happened to
Tristen but friends were arriving with flowers and plates of comfort
food and Jeremy kept leaping up for hugs.

She hung a while longer then snuck up to kiss him and crept out.

On the way to the hotel she thought of phoning Larissa for
a condolence-*bla* but decided against it. Then, with a shock, she
wondered if Dusty was with Larissa this very *moment*, providing
solace, money, palliative sexual favors, whatever . . . the thought
sickened, her rage reigniting as she pictured the distraught stand-in
cradled in her wife's arms. Perversely, Allegra fantasized that when
they finally talked, Dusty would open with the conversational gam-
bit of "Jeremy's loss" in order to defuse/minimize her adultery by
implying that *in context*, their own troubles paled in comparison to
such an event. At the same time, Dusty's hands *were* sort of tied—she
couldn't really get into Tristen's death without dragging in Larissa,
one way or another, which she'd want to avoid, or put off, for as
long as she could. So actually, she'd probably know better than to
bring it up.

Though maybe not. Maybe Dusty so didn't give a shit anymore.

When she walked into the suite, Allegra noticed an envelope
propped against a vase on the living-room coffee table. Someone

from the hotel must have delivered it. She recognized the Smythson stationery she bought for Dusty a few years ago in London.

A calligraphic *A.* was written on the front. Trembling, she pulled out the thick square note inside:

> *Everything is going to be OK,*
> *Please please trust*
>
> xD

They found a pistol belonging to Derek in the trunk of the crumpled hybrid. (The editor used to go shooting with his geriatric director friends.) Larissa theorized their son came across the gun while at Derek's apartment and took quiet custody, out of worry that after the diagnosis his father had become so depressed he might harm himself.

Larissa was shocked when the E.R. nurse informed that Tristen was an organ donor. It seemed so out of character and made her question everything she thought she knew about her complicated, secretive boy. Later, Jeremy shed some light. He shared the scarifying backstory of the girl who crashed her dad's Porsche, and Tristen's mischievous contribution to that unsavory Internet legend; and how, when he took her son to the DMV to get his license, Tristen revealed he'd signed *Nikki Catsouras* on the donor form.

When she wondered why he would do such a thing, Jeremy said he had asked him the same thing. Tristen replied, "For the LULZ."

Jeremy told her what that meant too.

Derek saw an opportunity.

When he learned of Tristen's improbable donor status, he immediately brought to the doctors' (and Larissa's) attention a recent conversation with his son in which Tristen had expressed "his wishes" that Derek be given his heart "should anything ever happen." Overamped and high on painkillers, he gilded the lily by saying the boy had even written a letter to that effect.

After taking Derek's dictation by phone, Beth printed out the informal "instrument" and brought it to the CCU. (He made her do it over again because she spelled Tristen with an *a*, as in "I, Tristan Dunnick . . .") He told her to initial it but she had qualms so Derek hastily scrawled a *TD*. He kept telling her no one was going to bust him for forgery. Jumping the donor queue was a victimless crime (kind of), a noble white-lie fraud perpetrated to save a life. Nobody in their right mind would question the "document" except maybe Larissa and even *she* would see the pointlessness of crying foul. They were going to take everything else—lungs, liver, kidneys, and corneas—what difference would it make where the heart wound up?

He panicked on realizing that in his haste, he hadn't factored in whether Tristen was a donor match. Then Derek remembered what the doctor said weeks ago: "You're a universal recipient."

Anyone's blood would do.

Larissa saw an opportunity as well.

She told Jeremy they couldn't afford the thirty-five-hundred-dollar cremation fee—a lie, because the Neptune Society was taking care of it, but she knew he wouldn't probe. He was so tortured by guilt over the car and the driving lessons that he happily gave her ten thousand.

Larissa sat alone in the viewing room. He died on Tuesday and now it was Sunday. Tomorrow, the body would be burned at a facility in Van Nuys. Tessa, her only real friend, was in Cabo. Rafaela was full-on camping at the hospital with her dad. When she learned of her brother's death, the force of the girl's grief took Larissa by surprise.

In the cool stillness, her son on the other side of the room, she regretted not having asked Jeremy to come. It would have been nice to have had another human being there who loved him. Tristen had been so unloved in this life, or loved *improperly*, yes, that was it, been so poorly, wrongly, egregiously loved, unworthy of his roving, prickly, lionhearted, rebellious, brutally loyal and generous nature. *I should have left Derek when I was pregnant with him. Why didn't I leave? Or at least why couldn't I have just shut my effing mouth?* She'd confessed her affair in a moment of psychobabble fervor and Human Potentialist delirium, after having convinced herself that people—*family*—could forgive, that anything could be healed by the truth, and love only grew stronger when secrets couldn't thrive.

Here was the truth: telling Derek that Tristen wasn't *his* had killed her son as surely as that telephone pole. The police said he'd probably been reaching for a dropped cell phone when he crashed, and Larissa had done a little investigating of her own. Beth (who fled to Portland right after Derek's surgery, this time for good) had already shared with her that Derek was obsessing over health insurance that night, trying to reach his son. Derek later told Larissa that when the two finally spoke, "the kid was *insanely* pissed," he wasn't even sure about *what*, because Tristen "wasn't making *sense*. He just started *screaming* at the top of his lungs. He got so crazy he *hung up* on me— loaded, no doubt. *Toxicology will establish*." But the evidence showed that he hadn't hung up on Derek at all, merely fumbled his cell during the rage-out; when he tried to retrieve it, he lost control of the car. Larissa wondered what he could have been so mad about and kept pressing her ex. *What did you SAY? What did you TELL HIM,*

Derek, *that he got so* ANGRY *about* and Derek just said *Nothing! I said Nothing!* but she kept pressing until finally he said uh, well, maybe it was something about where he came from, you know, maybe I think it was something about where he might have come from and when she said *what are you talking about* Derek said uhm maybe it was something about who his father was and Larissa said *what the fuck do you mean what did you* SAY *what did you* TELL *him* and Derek finally blurted out that the kid maybe somehow learned the *"reality"*—ferociously snarling the word—learned what the *reality* was and she asked her ex point-blank *did you tell him* and Derek said *NO, I never told him*, he was super-emphatic about it, maybe *too* emphatic, he said *why the fuck would I tell him* then reiterated that he never told him EVER, and not while they were on the phone *either*, and besides, he wouldn't have been able to even if he wanted *anyway* because he couldn't get a fucking word in *edgewise*, not that he didn't *feel* like telling him, the thought always crossed his mind (though not on that fateful night), but even if he wanted to he would never have had a fucking *chance* because the kid was foaming at the mouth like a rabid dog. None of what he was saying made sense to Larissa, all this shit about wanting to tell him but *not* telling him, none of it added up, it was beyond passive-aggressive, it was just more bullshit and she didn't believe him, not for one second. So she just kept saying *Oh my God* while Derek did his usual number of *if you never wanted me to know then you should never have done what you did and he would never have fucking been born!* and of course both of them thought of the hacking thing right away, that Tristen might have hacked his way into finding out the *reality* of his bastardhood, Derek remembering the email he sent to Beth a while back, one would think he wouldn't have because of the state he was in during its composition . . . he'd never tried to retrieve or restore the damning note or whatever, hadn't looked at it since, not once, but knew the content was incriminating. *No way would he have hacked into my shit. The kid told me he'd never do that, my shit was sacrosanct, and I believe him.* Believed *him* . . . That stoned email moment with Beth was literally the first time he ever "talked" about it, the *reality* of Tristen, or even shared it with anyone—*anyone* (except Father Wayne)—but of course he wouldn't divulge that to Larissa. For a nanosecond he even thought maybe *Beth* told Tristen as some kind of payback but no, too improbable, Beth could be a bitch but she wasn't malicious. Had a good heart. Larissa wracked her brain some more about Tristen hacking his way into the truth but knew there wouldn't have been anything *to* hack into, not on *her* end anyway, knew she had never breathed a *word* on the topic, not a drunk-text, not a bare-her-heart email, not a single poignant, bitter journal entry that she hadn't burned long ago . . . and confident as well that it was one of those totally taboo things that Derek would never write or speak to *anyone* about, it was all too painful for him, too shameful for his fucking elephantine *ego*, not just that he'd been *cuckolded* but that he'd kept the boy in the *fold* and *family* after knowing what he knew: that Tristen was of another man's blood. Instead of giving him props for being nobly compassionate, his sick junkie editor friends would have called him out as the ultimate Ashley Madison'd *Blue Angel* pussy. Then suddenly she thought she knew . . . of *course*!— *Pastor Wayne*! It would *had* to have been him—the man Derek confided in during his/their darkest hours—and so she asked Derek if Tristen ever talked to Pastor Wayne or if he thought they'd have maybe been in touch but Derek got testy and said how the fuck would *I* know and she said *Oh my God* then rather bombastically announced that maybe she'd reach out to the man *herself* then immediately couldn't bear the thought of it, even the fantasy she couldn't bear, no, just now she couldn't bear the thought of anything—

When her son turned ten, she was already in a period of intense self-reflection. The Twin Towers had fallen the year before and Larissa took that as a sign. She was thirty-eight, deeply depressed, and pregnant with Rafaela—a mindblower because she had been so sure she'd never have another child. It occurred to Larissa that she would never be famous, which apparently had been obvious to everyone on the planet but her; the second child was the final nail in the career coffin. She'd been acting since her twenties, running the hideous L.A. 10K of doomed equity waiver runs, pay-to-play daytime improv "workshops" in rented comedy clubs, power-drunk pilot-season casting directors, and failed cartoon voiceover auditions (though she did get occasional loop-group work). In her golden years, the late eighties, she booked nonspeaking roles on *Murphy Brown*, *Alf*, and *Married with Children*, and got Taft-Hartleyed into SAG when a showrunner gave her a line (subsequently cut, but no matter) on *Knots Landing*. She thought she was on her way, but nothing happened. Nothing! Why was it so impossible? And why was it so possible for others? She was getting lapped by everyone she knew, they blew by her on the track, all her friends and acquaintances were getting rich and famous. She frequented the bars where actors hung out. She met Tony Danza and Bob Saget and Kelsey Grammer that way. As a conversation starter, Larissa invented a story about how she was the illegitimate daughter of Richard Harris, that he had a one-night stand with her mom in Cannes when he won an award there for *This Sporting Life*, and how her mother was a chambermaid (she actually used that word) at the Hotel du Cap. She tried to seduce Danza et alia but wound up sucking off the bartenders instead. Then she married a film editor . . . how losery of her! And nothing happened in her *fakakta* career until years later when she had *another* golden era, in the movies. She was a day player in *Kalifornia* (Female Officer), *Indecent*

Proposal (Dress Shop Saleslady), and *Ace Ventura: Pet Detective* (Reporter #5). She dipped her toe back into the television waters (it was all about being versatile), getting a gig as a *Law & Order* stand-in—fun! She was good at it and networked her way into camera doubling for Gillian Anderson and Fran Drescher. Then she hit it big and became a full-time stand-in for Katey Sagal (they really did look alike) on *8 Simple Rules* but when John Ritter died, her niche career got buried along with him. The Stand-In Years dissolved into the Switching Price Tags at Department Stores Years. She wasn't even sure why she did what she did because Derek was making more than okay money. The first time she was arrested it wasn't too huge a deal but the second time they had to pay a lawyer $23,000 to keep her out of the hoosegow. That was when she started going to Landmark Forum, looking at her deep dark secrets and the ones her family kept, trying to get to the root of all her shit. She really thrived there, she was a Forum *rock star*. Larissa even thought of becoming a Landmark personal coach or maybe a therapist, like an MFCC—all her struggling actress friends were aging out and hanging marriage- and family-counselor shingles . . . She started feeling so much better about herself, the whole empowerment cliché but for real, and after she gave birth to that second child something inside her said it was time to tell Derek about the affair and about Tristen. What happened was, she caught Derek in *his* affair three years into the marriage (he was an editor on *Lethal Weapon*, and she was his intern; so totally his M.O.) and he begged Larissa not to leave him. A few months after she took him back they had some argument and she slept with a stranger as a *fuck-you*. (Landmark allowed her to see that it was really just a fuck-you to her dad.) So because of her own personal evolution it was time to come clean and she confessed all and of course he was shaken but *seemed* to be okay. (As okay as he could be.) He asked for paternity tests on both kids, and when the results confirmed that Rafaela was his and the boy wasn't he broke both of Larissa's arms. She cabbed it to the hospital and said she got mugged. At the E.R. a lady cop pushed her to file charges on her husband but she stuck with the mugging alibi. Her mom flew out to help with the new baby while Larissa mended. Derek got his own place. She could never explain why she hoped he'd come back.

He was working on *Resident Evil*, making good bread. He never stopped taking care of her and the children. He sent regular checks; then sweet notes with the checks; then small thoughtful gifts in the in-between. He apologized for the beat-down and said he understood what led her to betray him. He even said he was in therapy! That he *agreed* with everything she'd told him about the devastation wrought by capital-S secrets, and was proud of her *moxie*. (Actually using that word.) He said he was deeply ashamed, and really seemed to mean it. By the end of the year he was living at home again, bedding down in the garage. Tristen was overjoyed; he had missed his father terribly, and been so confused. (Thank God he wasn't there the night Derek broke her arms.) On his return, Derek really did try his best. The miracle was that things went well, relatively, for a moment anyway, between father and make-believe son—that Derek *behaved*. His performance wasn't perfect but it was solid, like a good understudy's; he fell back on all the years he'd loved that boy as if he was his own. In time, even after becoming Tristen's tormentor, Derek never told him that he wasn't his real dad. Didn't that count for something, for anything? Didn't that count for some kind of love?

She stood beside the body now.

He wore the clothes he'd be burned in—that gorgeous grey Prada suit she bought for his graduation from Crossroads. Larissa touched the cold forehead. Just beneath the sternum rose the tip of the closed excision atop his heart; through the white shirt's thin cotton she could see the cowlicky infestation of black threads that sewed it up. Her finger reached out to trace the fabric covering the unruly tendrils' bristle; then drew back, like the twiggy phalange of a timorous witch.

Dusty had been in constant touch with Ginevra since that unfortunate row in the driveway, yet *again* she vacillated about telling Allegra—*Aurora*—the full truth and nothing but. Insofar as her daughter had filled in the blanks with an imaginary adultery (the therapist encouraged her to actively say "my daughter" and "Aurora" instead of Allegra), Dusty thought it would be easier to just capitalize on the misunderstanding and make it legitimate; confess to multiple affairs and break it off. The blow had already been struck, albeit for the wrong reason, and she saw no benefit in delivering the *alternate* coup de grâce. Of course, Ginevra didn't agree, urging her to be strong, bla.

On Monday, they met as agreed at the restaurant in the hotel. The actress had no plan. The primary thing was to get back on some sort of even keel, whatever *that* looked like, then see what she could see. So there they were, having a surreal and civil tea; she wouldn't have been surprised to be interrupted by a hatter and a dormouse— though Bunny, bereft, lacked the *oomph* just then to give any kind of March hare its marching orders.

The two looked as beautiful as an *arrondissement* between downpours. For the first time, Dusty sat across from the storybook creature who'd been transfigured by a single kiss (though one that lasted years) from defiled, warty frog-wife to daughter-princess, impossibly, luminously restored. It was breathtaking, and gutted her. They danced around their recent estrangement. When Allegra brought up

Jeremy's loss (in spite of herself), Dusty startled, claiming not to have known. Allegra was certain the actressy denials were for show but held her tongue. Anyway, it was a good distraction to be gossiping about travails other than their own.

Picking up on Allegra's skepticism about her reaction to the news of Tristen's death, she recalled her therapist's edict to take courage and take charge, and dove headlong into the whole Larissa business. (Allegra bridled but Dusty heroically pushed through.) She was *not* having an affair, she said, not with the camera double or anyone else. She left Allegra's driveway shout—"I've been fucking her too!"— well enough alone.

"Bullshit!" Allegra said, unable to maintain decorum. "You are *gaslighting* me!"

Mindful of their surroundings, Dusty took a breath and dialed it down.

"Look," she said, somewhat sternly. "I don't know *what* that woman has been telling you but she's unstable, okay? She's been sending *crazy emails*, not just to *me*, but to Marilyn and *Elise*, okay? And I haven't seen Larissa since we wrapped, okay? I don't do *yoga* with her and I don't do *anything else.*"

Allegra was about to mention the earring in the bed but stared at the table instead, making jailhouse crosshatchings in the linen with a butter knife. Her eyes got watery. "So what do you want to do? Are we getting divorced?"

"I just want . . . to talk about some things, Allegra. But not *here.*"

"I'll take that as a 'yes,'" she said, bitterly. "And why *shouldn't* we talk here? Because the *patio* of the *Four Seasons* is the wrong place to end our *marriage*? Like, you need it to be a better place for your *memoir*?"

"No one's writing a memoir, Allegra."

"Well, *I* might!" she snarled. "Is the Four Seasons too boring? Is

Point *Dume* a 'sexier' place for a breakup? The *name* sure as fuck is more accurate. Doom!"

This is your daughter. Be loving. Be calm. Be courageous . . .

"I have some serious things to . . . discuss—and I just don't feel comfortable doing that in a public place."

"You mean you'd rather talk somewhere with *lawyers*? Is that where you want to meet, Dusty? With your *lawyers*?—"

She sighed and said, "Can you just come home?"

"That isn't my home anymore," said Allegra. "It's *your* home." She made a few more slashes on the table cover and gulped her tea. "We can talk in my room."

In the tense silence on the way up Allegra said to herself *We are* NOT *going to fuck, no matter* WHAT. But as the elevator rose she couldn't help shuddering with the memory of all the cold-hot moon-shadow makeup sex they'd shared, that bosomy, timeless, syrupy pull of body and unruly blood that she had always had for *Her*, Dusty, her love and her life—she who had conquered, liberated, and given form, she who still conferred all meaning and security, sanctity and sanity—the four seasons themselves.

A minute after they sat on the couch it was done.

There were moments when Allegra felt doubly gaslit—as if, through a desperate, psychotically bold stratagem, her wife was attempting to erase betrayal by means of a ghastly, unspeakably preposterous invention. The young woman stood up a few times in angsty confusion but was led back to her seat by Dusty's command that she hear her out.

She told her everything, starting from when Ronny Swerdlow knocked her up—how she ran away when Reina took her to L.A. for the abortion—hitchhiking to Wickenburg then getting homesick for her dad and returning to Tustin with the certainty everything would be okay—how one apocalyptic morning, her baby was gone. How that *destroyed* her and how she'd punished herself her entire *life* for having *stayed* with that monstrous woman, stayed with her *after, after* she'd stolen her child away, for three tragic years before fleeing to New York. *I've asked myself why a thousand times.* (Though she wasn't going to get into the hornet's nest of why she never went looking for her baby, not unless Aurora specifically asked; it didn't feel like the right time.) She talked about "Snoop" Raskin and the email Ida Pinkert sent after Reina died, how the old woman said she saw Reina give her away, literally *hand her off* to Claudia Zabert, babysitter extraordinaire. (Just then, in an aside, Dusty, with a tearful smile, said, "Your birth name is Aurora," the cognitive dissonance of which Allegra of course already knew, so that its formal announcement was rendered as a balmy, poignant baptism) . . . and how she was in New York a few weeks ago for the Meryl party when out of nowhere Livia and the detective showed up to tell *all*—which was why she'd been out of touch. Because she needed time to digest, and think about what to do . . .

When she finished, Allegra sat there without saying a word, which Dusty thought was a good thing. Because anything was better than—what? High-decibel screams? Breaking a glass and using a shard to sever Dusty's tits? It wouldn't matter: she could take whatever dishes, words, or tantrums her daughter might throw. She could see now that anything was better than the anything of not telling her. If telling her didn't feel good, it felt *right*.

Allegra ceremoniously excused herself to the loo.

She came back around ten minutes later (Dusty had started to worry), returning to the couch like a remorseful prisoner. She asked a few questions, occasionally interrupting her mother's response with "This isn't a joke?" (Just as Dusty had said to Livia and Snoop, and with the same lilt.) She wanted to know about her father, as they'd never really discussed the details of Dusty's Provo pilgrimage. "Does he know?" Dusty said that he didn't nor was she planning to tell him, at least not for the moment. Who *are* you going to tell, asked Allegra—with a mixture of outrage, fear, and befuddlement. Only you, said Dusty. Unless you wish otherwise. Allegra snorted at that, not in a mean way, but to indicate how insane it was to be entertaining one's "wants" in the face of such a thing. Dusty hastened to add, *I guess that's premature*. "We'll find our way. We'll go slow and find our way." When Allegra asked about "Willow," Dusty said the detective apparently had visited her in Albuquerque, and that she wasn't *well*, emphasizing the word in such a way to denote grave psychiatric issues.

Dusty wanted to learn a few things herself. Did Claudia ever *inform* her of the *circumstances* by which she'd been *acquired*? Those were the stilted words she used; the woodenness made her cringe but she couldn't help expressing herself that way. Allegra said she hadn't. "She never mentioned you *or* your mother or ever even having seen one of your films." Dusty said that Claudia wouldn't necessarily have been able to put any of it together, as she had changed her name from Janine Whitmore when she started to act. "I always thought she was my biological mom," said Allegra. "I mean, I didn't have any reason to think otherwise. She may have even told me she was, directly. I don't know."

They sat awhile in silence.

"So, she *babysat* you?" said Allegra. Her mother nodded. "And this *isn't* a joke."

"Not a joke."

"Holy, holy *fuck*."

There were worlds upon worlds for both of them to suppress—a gargantuan history of body intimacies lay frozen beneath the tundra of the hellish new normal—and they shivered together like survivors awaiting improbable rescue.

"Do you want to come to the house?"

Allegra stared into space (they'd been doing a lot of that). "Okay."

As if talking to herself, Dusty added, "I know I didn't want to be alone—when I found out. But I kind of had to be. *You* don't."

Allegra winced and said, "Well . . . I guess the big decision is— Dr. Phil? Or Dr. Wrigley?"

"Diane Sawyer," said Dusty with a smile.

(The ice, and everything else, had broken.)

Allegra told her to go on ahead, she'd be up in a bit. She thought she might check out of her room, but didn't have the energy. Why should she, anyway? As if everything was just fine now! The only person who would fully appreciate the batshit bonkers-ness of it was Jeremy, but for now, telling him would have to be off-limits— who *could* she tell? She wondered if she should even tell herself, because it felt like she hadn't.

The supercosmic joke of it—and it *was* a cosmic joke, because how the fuck *else* could you describe it—slammed Allegra as she drove through the flats on the way to Trousdale. The overall miscarriage of her life dogged and assailed: the esteemed, numerous non-accomplishments of a parasitical, childfucked existence had led her like a flower girl to *this*, her greatest achievement, the jewel in her crown of thorns. The snakes in the road that Tiresias would be separating for eternity were none other than she and her mother. No wonder the myth had riveted so! At last, she understood her destiny: to be one of the women she'd read about, plucked from her library's bouquet—the daughters of Aphrodite that Herodotus wrote of, sacred whores who practiced in temples, consorts of divine marriage and tantric rape. Like defrocked priestesses, they were always out of their robes; just now, Allegra couldn't remember where she'd left hers.

The gate was open. It felt like she'd been away for months. Dusty waved nervously from an upstairs window then retreated. *Probably worried I wasn't going to show.* She imagined Willow up there too, waiting in the wings.

She entered the old house (she didn't recognize it) as in a dream, wanting to awaken—but where? In Big Sur, for the wedding? In Cuba, when Dusty (and "co-hostesses" Anderson Cooper and Nathan Lane) threw a surprise party for her thirtieth? On that amazing day when she learned she was pregnant for the first time? In what moment of the slipstream did she want to wake up, before the propellers broke off? Well, there *was* no moment, because she'd never taken flight. All these years, she was really just a cripple sporting 3D goggles.

Dusty called from the landing, "Down in a minute!"

Allegra went up anyway. It was still her house, wasn't it? More than ever now. *Maybe she's gonna surprise me with a nursery,* she thought mordantly. *With stuffed bunnies and a mobile dangling over a crib that I can be fucked in after a nice bedtime story.* Overcome, she plunked herself down on the carpeted steps. She heard the flush of a toilet. She didn't *want* Dusty to be her mother, she wanted Dusty to be her *wife*—for it to be like before and *stay* like that, when they were both so happy . . .

Dusty reappeared. "I know," she said of Aurora's little stair collapse, as if reading her thoughts. Like a mother would.

She roused herself and stood. When she reached the landing,

Dusty touched her arm and the young woman smiled as she walked slowly by. Entering their bedroom, she thought of that glorious, sun-dappled path to the swimming hole at Black Bear that her mom—AKA Willow, Claudia, babysitter and kidnapper, sex and death cultist, madwoman—loved to chase her down, Allegra squealing in ecstasy before seizing the rope that would carry her far over the water before she let go.

She ran to the terrace, hurdling the balustrade.

THEN

I see the sleeping babe, nestling the breast of its
mother;
The sleeping mother and babe—hush'd, I study them
long and long.

Leaves of Grass

heart sutra

"Today, we have an amazing guest—amazing *guests*—with an extraordinary story. Four months ago, Derek and Larissa Dunnick lost their twenty-three-year-old son Tristen in an automobile accident. Just three weeks before his son's tragic death, Derek was put on a waiting list . . . to receive a heart transplant for a condition doctors said might end his life at any moment, without warning. Now, it wasn't until an emergency-room nurse checked their son's driver's license that Derek and his wife Larissa learned their son had chosen to be an organ donor—even going so far as to leave behind a note instructing that should anything happen to him, if it were in any way *possible*, he wanted his dad to receive his heart. Within hours of

Tristen's death, that wish came true. And because of his sacrifice, his father is able to be with us here today. Please welcome . . . Derek and Larissa Dunnick."

The audience, who'd salted the host's pithy introduction with sighs and murmurs, broke into applause. Dad smiled as Mom's hand fell upon his. Rail-thin, Derek still looked healthier than he had in years. Larissa's blown-out hair was a vibrant, recolored red, with maroon-gold highlights. She was overdressed for the occasion in the Givenchy gown she bought at a high-end vintage store on Melrose with some of the additional $25,000 that Jeremy had given the couple in support of Derek's recovery.

Dr. Wrigley walked them through a gripping play-by-play of the events leading to his surgery, and Derek didn't disappoint.

"I understand," said the host, "that it was something . . . completely unexpected. I'm not talking about the *accident*, which of course was a terrible, terrible *shock*. But that your son had decided to be a *donor*— that took you both *completely by surprise*. Can you talk about that?"

"We'd had a conversation about it," said Derek. "When I first got diagnosed, and it became clear that I would need to go on the list, the transplant list. But the conversation was brief. To be honest, it was something I'd *totally forgotten*. I think at the time I thought it was a beautiful thing for him to express, for a son to express. Then that was the end of it. Because you know . . . I don't think there's a mom or dad out there who even wants to *consider* the idea of their child . . . passing away . . . while that parent or parents are still living. And *especially* in my case, if that even makes any sense, because I was so close to dying. I really—I really did have a death sentence—and I don't think—well, there just wasn't a *possibility* something like that would happen with one of my kids before it happened to *me*. It wasn't something I was even remotely capable of imagining."

"Tristen mentioned it just that once," said Larissa. She almost believed what she was saying. "Then dropped it. Which was a lot like him! Our son was, in many ways, a *very private person*. If he did a good turn—you know, a 'pay it forward,' which we now have an understanding that he did quite often—well, Tristen wasn't one to advertise it. He was very humble that way."

"That's very true," echoed Dad, in somber agreement.

"Were you surprised to find the note? That described his wishes?"

"Yes and no," said Derek. "*No*, because there was no indication. As I said, it never entered our minds. Mine and Larissa's. And *yes*, because that kind of gesture was . . . very much in keeping with *who he was*."

"*Always thinking of others,*" said Mom, emotionally. With a leavening smile, she added, "Something he definitely didn't get from his father!" The audience laughed warmly, politely, tragically.

"Do you think he had a premonition?" asked Dr. Wrigley.

Mom and Dad grew introspective.

"Boy," said Larissa. "That's a tough one." She looked toward Derek to pick up the thread.

"That thought has kept me up at night," he admitted.

"Were you close? Were you close to your son? What was your relationship like?"

Derek took a deep breath and mused. "We had our rough patches . . . like fathers and sons do. We're both pretty headstrong, and the road wasn't always smooth. But I'd have to say *yes*, we were close." He turned to Larissa and smiled; she smiled back, squeezing his hand. "And now"—a catch in his voice briefly interrupted him as Derek patted his heart with his free hand—"now we're closer than ever."

The audience melted.

Dr. Wrigley stared into the camera and said, "We'll be right back, with the amazing story of Derek and Larissa Dunnick—and their son Tristen—on this special edition of 'What They Did for Love.'"

He moved back to the house in Mar Vista.

Larissa had her trepidations but it made sense financially. Anyhow, the whole deal was especially good for Rafaela, whose life had been upended by divorce, and now by the trauma of her brother's death; what was good for her daughter was good for Larissa. Even with the smoking hole left by Tristen's amputation, it was starting to feel like old, better times.

She'd been worried that Tessa would take a shit on her for letting him come home, but nope, she was *down*. She'd been totally amazing— Larissa's hardcore cheerleader. Her BFF gushed for three weeks about how amazing she looked on *The Dr. Wrigley Show*.

After Jeremy cashed them out, he disappeared from their lives but it was all good. Larissa got busy turning up all kinds of funding— it was *crazy* what was available out there in the public and private sectors. Chasing health-care hardship monies was pretty much her new, full-time gig and she thought she could totally make a career out of it. To top things off, they even started getting random IATSE checks *sans* EOB (explanation of benefits), which she assumed had been generated by Tristen's hacking exploits.

Things were looking up for Derek as well. The response to his appearance on the "What They Did for Love" segment was overwhelming. He got cards, calls, and emails from people he worked with a hundred years ago and a lot from folks he'd never met. He took a bunch of meetings for potential jobs—one over at the C.W. for *iZombie*, one for *Mountain Men*, and one with an FX producer whose sister died three years after getting a heart-lung transplant, not from complications but from being run over in a crosswalk (the bus driver was texting). Equinox gave him a free two-year membership and he was working out with a trainer, an Iraq War vet with a prosthetic leg who was donating his services in exchange for Derek mentioning him in magazine profiles.

He even heard from Pastor Wayne. It was at least ten years since they'd spoken. Derek's new heart really got a workout when he took that call (apparently, everyone at the nursing home where the pastor lived was deep into *The Dr. Wrigley Show*) because for the first few minutes, while the nonagenarian offered his respective condolences and congratulations over Tristen and the "new ticker," Jeremy waited for the shoe to drop, the one that would prove his ex's random theory about Tristen and the pastor having been in touch. He kept steeling himself for *and by the way, son, part of the reason I'm calling is to let you know that I reached out to Tristen right before his accident and informed him of the Lie. For God told me that was what I must do because the end of my life is nigh; perhaps I should have told you and Larissa of His glorious plan, but* which wouldn't have bothered Derek, not at all, because he really didn't *give* a shit, no, the *real* reason he got spooked by the call—apart from bringing him back to that incredibly shitty time when Larissa's betrayal was fresh and he'd beaten her up and wanted to die—was on *his former wife's* behalf (of all people), lately he'd been feeling her pain, the whole encrusted *theme* was always such a sore spot for her, Derek's horrible behavior hadn't helped, had made everything so much worse, but right now he really *needed* her, needed Larissa in his corner, thought he might even be falling in love with her again *whoa* thus having little tolerance for *whatever* might carry them backward from the (very good) place they were currently in, anything smelling of *old shit* could do it, could carry them away, especially anything that picked at the Tristen scab (a phone call from the pastor to Larissa would do it, something Derek wasn't able to control), he just didn't want to see Larissa *hurt* anymore, that was an *authentic* feeling, yes, no, he couldn't *afford* to have her walking around *hurt*—now that the old once-marrieds were sort of getting married again, or at least engaged, they had to keep looking forward not backward, forward was where the money *and* the future were, and lately the money and the future looked fucking *bright*. Still, as the pastor mumbled on, Derek half resolved, for Larissa's (and OCD/closure's) sake, to put it to him point-blank—"Hey pastor, didja ever happen to talk to Tristen? I mean, did *he* reach out to *you* or did *you* reach out to *him*? In the months or days or even *hours* before he passed?" Which suddenly struck him as insane because how would Tristen have even known of the preacher's existence? *Larissa* never met the man, though of course knew of him through Derek's encomiums about the importance he'd played in "saving" their family . . . but right while they were on the phone it came to him with manifest clarity/incontrovertible authority that the whole Pastor Wayne/Tristen confab conspiracy theory was nothing but a bogus, guilt-trippy jerkoff fantasy, so he wound up skipping the due diligence. What surprised him most was that *Larissa* hadn't brought it up since she first mentioned the crackpot theory. Derek thought she'd have been seriously *on* it, you know, in a hurry to track down the old man and give him the third degree, but to his surprise, she let it ride. Another funny thing he noticed was that ever since the fatal phone call wherein Tristen apprised him that he had *proof* of the secret that had been kept from him all those years, Derek felt lighter, like a load had been lifted off his shoulders. The more he thought about it the more he regretted not having told Tristen the truth *years* ago (ironically, it was the pastor who urged him not to, who nearly *commanded* that he refrain) . . . though maybe in actuality he felt lighter because that piece of shit fag was finally, permanently out of the picture. Derek also noticed that he still didn't think of Tristen as "dead"—he'd been dead to him for so long as it was—he just thought of him as being *out there floating somewhere*, but floating with the *knowledge* that Derek *wasn't his father*, nor ever had been. No, if he was going to feel shitty or paranoid about anything, it wouldn't be *that*, not anything to do with the kid having found out *whatever* before offing himself: no. The major thing fucking with Derek at this time was an ever-present fear that with Tristen's demise the encrypted walls had come down and he was now more vulnerable than ever to an exposé of the IATSE fraud that had been perpetrated to maintain their health insurance. If *that* was uncovered, it would be a nightmare . . . *though maybe not*. In his head, he spun the revelation and subsequent criminal charges into gold—the Dunnicks would get a shitload of press, some bad, but most eventually good, probably *great*, maybe he'd wind up becoming the face of some kind of half-assed cultural flashpoint Obamacare kerfuffley bullshit, to wit, the desperate measures ordinary people in extraordinary circumstances must resort to in an era when one-percenters buy $125 million apartments they never even move into and rent yachts for $600,000 a week while regular folks are forced to commit felonies in order to get catastrophic care and literally keep their *lives* and *families* together, bla . . . That's right, he might become an Everyman hero, representing the *Hell yeah!* mentality. *Gotta do what ya gotta do, specially when it comes to your kids and your health. Fuckin' Derek Dunnick's a rock star! His son's the one who did it anyway, right? Hacked into the system? Hell yeah! That's how much he loved his dad. That heart should have come with a fucking gold medal.* Still, it'd be a huge hassle if it ever came to light, so even though they *thought* about it, Derek and Larissa made the decision not to poke around in whatever ginormous, larcenous, impenetrably cancerous folderol was hidden in Tristen's computer. Not that they'd have known how or where to even start or what the fucking point would have been viz whatever panicky, unformulated goal . . . so they just decided *out of sight, out of mind*, and when Jeremy returned Tristen's Mac they locked it up in a cabinet in the basement. Derek laughed about that to himself. It was a total sign of how old and useless you were when you thought you could keep a laptop's secrets by tucking it away somewhere like an old toolbox.

When he was growing up, the pastor led his parents' church in Sioux City and the family got very close. It was Pastor Wayne whom he turned to when Larissa told him that his "son" was a sham, a whore's con. The news made Derek suicidal; for a few weeks he was in the serious planning stage of a triple murder-suicide—he was going to take himself out and bring the bitch and her bastard runt with him. And it totally blew him out when the pastor dropped everything and showed up in L.A. to spend a long weekend, that was how righteous he was, how much the man cared, a man of God for real. He ministered to Derek about love knowing no birthright, that all God's creatures resided not beneath earthly roofs but in the humble tents of our Lord, and that to betray His will would be blasphemous. As a result of his compassionate hymns and panegyrics, his generosity of spirit and relentless sermonizing (it went on for months, by phone and letter), Derek slowly healed and became half human again. He found his way back to the marriage and his new daughter. Living in the same house with Larissa and the boy was a challenge, and Derek freely admitted to his confessor that his attempts at reunifying the family weren't perfect by a long shot, that he continued to be rough on the boy, but the pastor said he'd done the right thing and that his love for "this special son" would come in time, and both he and Tristen would reap not the whirlwind but the reward of kings.

Pastor Wayne said he was so proud of him, which meant a great deal. But Derek never made peace with himself about taking up again with his wife and her demon seed. Looking back, he saw that his heart really did break, so it made sense that all these years later he needed a new one. It was like the pastor had given him an artificial one yet it too had failed.

He was never sure why he returned. It wasn't from the guilt he carried from breaking her arms, nor could it have been solely from a Christian sense of duty instilled by the pastor. *Some* of the reason would of course have been Rafaela—he loved her more than life— and some, a kind of crawling back to his mom. Larissa had always reminded him of Mom.

Queen Jeremy's *annus horribilis*:

The Miscarriage.

The Death of the Boy . . .

—and now sweet Allegra, broken and brain-ravaged.

Yet in seven months—on July Fourth no less!—he would be a father.

How had any of it happened?

It astonished . . .

He was one of the chosen few allowed to visit her in the hospital, not just because he already had membership in their private club of sorrows, but because Dusty had always welcomed the comic danciness of his wounded heart and in these darkest of days needed the solace of it more than anything. She'd even thought of telling him— about *Aurora*—but something stopped her. Those doors would soon be closed to everyone, forever.

Tristen's death struck Jeremy with unexpected severity; a second blow, landed by Allegra's botched suicide, caused much suffering, but had the paradoxical effect of freeing him (like an antivenin creates immunity)—though from what he wasn't sure. Perhaps it had to do with their last conversation and the stickiness of Jeremy striking out on his own to have a child; now, all fell neatly under the Darwinian euphemism "It just wasn't meant to be," affording some relief. *Them that's got shall have, them that's not shall lose* . . . but the joy of locomotion was there too—the kinetic pleasure of *moving on*, a skill set he'd long been in possession of yet never fully implemented until the death of his mother and sister. (It was royal habit now.) The familiar elation evoked by the morning prayer of "Onward!"—and the attendant day's march through fields where friends, acquaintances, loved ones, and strangers lay dead and wounded—often *presented* as schadenfreude, and it was important for Jeremy to take note of that distinction; for it pained him to even briefly confuse the relentless rush of forward movement that was the nature of life itself with a reveling in others' misfortunes, an emotion which he wasn't remotely capable of.

He had truly absorbed the Wildings' horrific travails as his own.

Only days before Tristen and Allegra met their defeat on that foregoing field (now months ago), he received an unexpected call.

"It's Frank. I'd like to buy you lunch—just us boys."

Jeremy's brain glitched at the demotic, seductive proposal—his mind frantically searched for *Franks* in his ample database of old hookups—before confirming the mumbleboomy voice as none other than Franklin T. MacKlatchie's (Esq.). He wondered why he would use *that* name. To Jeremy's ear it sounded like, "When I con *that* one, I call misself 'Sir.' When I con *you*, I use 'Frank'!"

They met at a coffee shop in the shopping center by the Colony. The Minnesotan magus was in fine spirits. He kibitzed with a waiter about a football game and did a hail-fellow-well-met with all who crossed his path. After a while he sobered up, so to speak, and sunk deep within himself as he drew the invitee into his confidence game.

"I'm going to tell you some things that I've kept from the girl—which I have decided to share because I'm leaving soon. Devi doesn't *know* that yet, nor do I wish her to. So we agree this shall be strictly *entre nous*?" He clasped his hands together like a devout and humble man about to embark on a great voyage. "From everything the girl has told me, and all I've observed *misself*, I believe you to be a most sensitive, trustworthy soul. Am I correct?"

"Well, I *have* been called sensitive. 'Trustworthy'? That's something I aspire to. But I think it may be prudent to leave my soul out of the discussion."

MacKlatchie roared—the reply had the effect of a magical password, and he tucked into his monologue with the same gusto as those drumsticks on that Sub-Zero beach house night.

"Devi and I *did* meet in the manner—the *exact* manner she described. It is true that for many weeks I made my home on the walkway outside Mandry's, dependent on the goodwill of its employees and the civility of passersby—when at last we crossed paths, she *was* in the midst of one of those constitutionals wherein she strove so valiantly to distract herself from the cruel *eventualities* of that dear, tragic little angel's fate—her wilting flower, her Bella. You see, we were two *dislocated* creatures, destined to meet! And we've had an *extraordinary* time, oh just marvelous. We've had *adventures*. I could never repay her for the kindness she's shown, the *companionship* and trust. Well, I *could*, I *have*, in my own humble way. And I hope I've done no harm.

"Jeremy, at this juncture, there are two things *imperative* for you to know—though she likes to call you Jerome, doesn't she?—very well then, *Jerome*, here is the first (he leaned in to deliver what followed): *Everything she told you about my gastropub 'sojourn'—the bouncer's*

harassment, the lawsuit, the buying of the place, the role-playing—was a lie.
Nothing but legend and folk myth! All lies . . . well, not *everything*. I
did have a wife and son. And was—still *am*—a man of vast, *inherited*
wealth. (I was born into it but under my supervision it went forth
and multiplied.) But the rest is pure fiction! And lest you rush to
judgment, allow me to inform that *Devi* believes *all* of it to be true.
All of it, and *then* some! In other words, she knows *nothing* of my
subterfuge. She is faultless and pure, an *angel* just like her Bella."

Jeremy practically choked on his frittata. "But . . . *why?*"

"Because the truth would have been too much for her."

He thought he might die if he couldn't hear more; he thought he
might die if he heard one more word. He fought the urge to bolt.

"The *truth*, dear friend, was that I *had* a wife and son. An *autistic*
son, as our faithful Devi so delicately described." The giant hands
clasped together again. "And I murdered them both."

Jeremy's heart screeched and fluttered like a defenseless thing
set upon by a cat. He made lightning escape plan calculations and
rejected them with the same speed; to outrun this cunning *figment*
was a foolish, impossible enterprise. The man would hunt him down
for sport.

"And after that deplorable act, I felt a rush of freedom! Some
of that sense of *release*, no doubt, I attribute to complete *shock*—the
shock of *excitation* that I was able to go through with such a thing *at
all*, after having *thought* about it for so many years . . . you see, the
thrill wasn't in the *getting away with it*, but in the *doing*. There's no
point in speaking to the details that drove me to commit the act. Suffice to say that little Jim—'Jimbo,' my son—had become savagely,
incurably violent, and my Margot—well, he'd effectively *destroyed*
her, *enlisted* her, and now *both* were *actively* conspiring to destroy *me*."

For a long moment, his gaze turned inward. The heavy, hooded

lids blinked and flirted with his eyes, promising the opiated sanctuary of sleep—but were spurned.

He resurfaced and became present once more. "And when it was
finished, I wondered—not *What have I done?* but rather *What else am I
capable of?* Oh, *that* query *possessed* me! What *else* was I capable of that
was beyond my power to imagine? *Not* in the sense of the monster-
hunter becoming the monster, or the abyss staring back into *me . . .*
You see, I had always favored the 'mystical,' Jerome—in my teenage
years I was of the type who haunted the metaphysical section of
booksellers, those traders who were moribund even in pre-Internet
days . . . Well, an *answer* to that came (in the form of another question): *Am I capable of enlightenment?* And am I a *"candidate"*? It was a
thought that was actually in the back of my mind a long, long while.
Could murder—*might* murder—for *me*—might it be the *avenue* of that
first step of the journey to moksha, kaivalya, nirvana? I'd read certain *parables* that seemed to assert an 'enlightened murderer' was no
oxymoron, and the so-called liberated state may soon be attained
through the homicidal act itself. If that were true, imagine how one's odds
at being liberated would be increased by the killing of those whom
one loves and protects, one's very own blood! Isn't that what Krishna
counsels Arjuna? That *not* to kill those kings and fathers—in *my* case,
mothers and sons!—was to be impotent by sheer weakness of heart?
That *not* to kill would incur sin? Is it not written in the Gita? The
ingenious hypothesis was simple, and only in want of a 'test phase' to
prove or disprove its worth. And I'm no sociopath, lad, far from it!
Though I know the declaration encourages the rejoinder, *Thou doth
protest too much.*

"There's an old saying that if one is going to tell a lie—a *significant*
lie—one must plan it as carefully as a murder. In my case, I planned
the murder *first* and *then* the lie that I eventually told my Devi . . .

what's the lovely thing Twain said? He said so many funny, lovely things. Oh, here—'The truth is a fragile thing but a well-told lie can live forever.' *Haha*. You see, my plan was to make a getaway from far more than merely the *jejune* scene of the crime—it was to flee from all that I knew, and all I was *known* by. I chose the invisibility of home-lessness because I imagine it appealed to a romantic fantasy I'd car-ried throughout the years of *cutting anchor*, divesting myself of reputation, relationships, possessions. ["I suppose the *double murder* accomplished that!" he said, in a chilling, theatrical aside. "Though 'triple' would be more accurate, as it wouldn't be fair to leave myself out. I killed *misself* off as well."] This desire to *self-excommunicate*, you see, was an impulse I'd had since, well, adolescence. And if it weren't exactly spiritual enlightenment I was seeking at that time, it certainly would have been an illumination of Self—though I suppose in many quarters it's hard to draw a distinction between the two.

"Let me interject a little something about *solvency*, because I have the feeling you've been puzzling over it. I know Devi mentioned some business about my having made arrangements vis-à-vis access to funds—which is true. Before the murders, I'd spent months stash-ing money away in safe-deposit boxes around the country . . . which the prosecution would of course use against me as evidence of pre-meditation, *will* use against me. And I shan't argue. In fact, I shall rush to their defense! Isn't that what Lord Krishna urged? In *defense* of war? To urge that one *enlist* in the war against Self, through the supreme act of *violent surrender*?"

While unable to shake a queer, out-of-body feeling, Jeremy was pleased to have found himself comfortably settling in (or nearly so) to the sonorous rhythm of his companion's speech. In other words, he no longer feared ambush. While listening to MacKlatchie's words, he took in their surroundings with a preternatural attentiveness—the reactive expressions of fellow luncheoners engrossed in private conversations; the telltale gait of servers and their wry, conspiratorial whispers; the very temperature of the large, sunlit room, and its minute fluctuations therein. *What's all this?* Jeremy mused, then understood: "all this"—impressions, perceptions, and *feelings*—were nothing more (or less) than a heightened, holy, inordinate sense of being alive. And *now* he saw firsthand the very thing that *Devi* had: a man before him who belonged to energetic royalty, exemplar of a gang whose controversial greatness could be defined by the possession of two qualities, diametrically opposed—a convivial command of the commonplace and a proficiency in the untranslatables of the dark Unknown. It was the effortless personification of those extremes that made the guru.

He spoke of the months immediately after the crime when he lived as a fugitive in Mexico. For a while he kept abreast of the frenzied stateside search for the wealthy heir who'd slain his wife and troubled son, but interest soon ebbed; the public, in its haste to make room for fresh kills and faddish reality shows, moved on. He kept a small room for a while off the Zócalo, where he took flight in profound meditation, channeling the "assemblage points" and "lucid-dreaming bodies" of his Margot and little Jim—before *and* after death. During one of these *zazen*, he came to understand ("By a truth revealed through the act of 'reading' energy") that "they hadn't died at *all*, because they were never *born*. *None* of us were, don't you see, Jerome? It's *true*, my friend! I always thought it was balderdash, but it's true!" The fallacy of man, he said, was in believing anything else. "This puerile 'doctrine of Death'—so primitive!—is man's undoing. For I am *telling* you that it isn't the *thing* of Death, it's the wrongheaded *idea* of it that lays waste to man's joy, his Love, his *Freedom*."

His work in Mexico City done, he decided to return to Minnesota, where he'd broadcast his revelations in a court of law. "Because they have to *transcribe* it—isn't that marvelous? Anything I said would be permanently enshrined: *transcribed by law.*"

Sidelined along the way by a brutal beating in Monterrey; another one shortly after crossing the border at Laredo (with the same flawless counterfeit passport used in his original flight); and a small heart attack in Oklahoma City—he rode a Trailways bus through that wilderness of megachurches and porn emporiums on the banks of the I-35 ("'The Highway of Holiness,' they call it! Locals say the I-35 refers to Isaiah 35:8: 'A highway shall be there, and a road, and it shall be called the Highway of Holiness'") before finally arriving in Chicago, where, "a tad bit worse for wear," he at once felt himself again, *himself* being a hundred pounds heavier (his body's counterintuitive response to all manner of travails) than two years before, with a beard like a forest growth after a deluge.

"Well, I didn't *feel* on the lam. I *had* planned on returning for my 'just deserts' . . . but for the moment, was absolutely *glorying* in American cuisine—one could say I was eating just desserts!—and after the *grandes avenidas* of D.F. and the horrors of that most consecrated of Interstate highways, found the gemütlich chaos of Chicago streets to be thoroughly refined and amenable. And as I said, I *had* been crafting my return all along and was *meaning* to get on the road again—to Duluth and its courthouse—yet there I was, happy as a soft-shelled mollusk, making camp outside that venerable institution of Mandry's, and there I seemed, by fate and inertia, to remain. Until *she* came along. One day there *she* was, and I fell in love. I heard the sirens, Jerome, not the bells! It was a passionately romantic *and* carnal love—from *my* side—though the dear soul never knew it because I never let on. I was startled by her interest in me—at first anyway, till I *understood*—it seemed so unlikely, as I was an obese and *very* peculiar sort, of unidentifiable genius *and* genus of foul-smelling changeling (my normally fastidious toilet had suffered greatly by then), a transcendental *ogre*, and I wondered—as perhaps you have!— *why* she would have paid such attention. But you see *another* part of me was watching and *knew*. That I was *not* my former self. That I had *become* someone, some-*thing* else—a *thing* to be *reckoned with*. That *new thing*, you see, was a five-star *general*, who could lead men to freedom or lead them to death. From the moment of that realization, I never looked back, and let myself be taken . . . by Energy.

"And I love her to this *day*, Jerome, but no longer in that fashion. Oh, it's been years since I loved her that way. The *transformation* of my love was a by-product of my so-called enlightenment; I say 'so-called' because it's treacherous to crow about such a thing. Though perhaps I *am* a guru after all, have *become* one, or some *sort* of one! No, I never took advantage of her innocence and trust—though I know that may be arguable, from your point of vantage . . . *Friend Jerome*, that girl taught me as much as she claims I've taught her. She tutored me how to go *beyond* love, into that 'Silence' she speaks of unendingly: the realm of her precious, confounded bells. (The bells that confound because they live in the space between belief and nonbelief.) By concocting that story about Mandry's, born of those meditations wherein I got *under the skin* of my wife and son, *inhabiting* them (where *did* such a narrative come from, where *did* it, really? From that damned 'Source' of hers, from that 'Silence,' where else? *How* else?), by telling the story of Mandry's I was set free. It was theater—the theater of Infinity! And Devi became the witness of my *moksha*, my liberation. I told her a story of *becoming*, of embodying the personae of the workers and denizens of that bar—that burlesque magic lantern show that represents the world—told it so many times, I actually believed it did occur! And each anecdote, each *incarnation* was a step that led to Freedom . . .

"The MacKlatchie murders—of Margot and little Jimbo—you'll note that I always say *killed* or *murdered*, I never shirk from that declaration because I know the power of the mind, if I don't state the naked truth aloud, one day I'll come to believe I had nothing to do with it!—in recent weeks, the unsolved *double homicide* has gotten some attention in the media. Perhaps you're aware of it? [Jeremy shook his head.] I *do* manage to keep up a bit on what's happening in the world. It was featured on one of those cold-case shows . . . what's *funny* is that before I learned of this latest piece of information, I had resolved—once again!—to return to Minnesota, to confess and face charges. The timing is strange, no? Cosmic fairy dust is in the air. And of course it's nothing anymore for me to go from one dream into another . . . the other morning I was mulling the whole thing over when I awakened to Devi's damn *bells*. She'd washed the strop and hung them outside like a wind chime; the Santa Anas made them sing. 'The world is like the impression left by the telling of a story.' Have you heard that marvelous Hindu saying? Isn't that the most gorgeous thing? And so true! What it means to say is the world is a dream, that's all. And *I* am going back to a dream called 'Duluth,' a dream of justice and retribution—*society's* dream of settling accounts for crimes committed against the state, against its people. A dream called penitence . . . *penitence* is a *lovely* dream, isn't it, Jerome? I will go back to their dream in order to tell them of another, the dream of deathless death, the dream of liberation, *the dream that is a dream*, and the stenographer will memorialize my words, my *dreaming words*, for the public record. (There shall even be courtroom artists to sketch me, in mid-dream oratory.) And when I awakened to the ringing of Devi's bells I *knew*, as surely as I did that day on the sidewalk in front of Mandry's, that it was time to move on from *this* dream. I heard the sound of the bells and knew it was time to leave the dream of wandering this precious land with that beloved being I call Devi—she who'd become *my* teacher, *my* guru, *my Ma'm*! Perhaps she is right, after all. Perhaps the bells speak to us all the time, if only we would listen."

Just then, Jeremy heard the hard clank of a bell, and thought he was dreaming himself. MacKlatchie smiled, outstretching his leg to show off Devi's bells—a déjà vu of when she'd done the same that night at the restaurant on Chautauqua. They looked much smaller on their new owner's edematous ankle.

"When I made the decision that it was time to leave, I *snatched* 'em from her. Took 'em back, 'cause they're mine. You see, I had 'em on when Devi and I first met (she was 'Cathy' then) and gave 'em to her as a gift. This morning I said, 'You've worn 'em long enough—time to be free!' She was upset at first, then understood. *She understands all*. She *pretends* she doesn't, 'cause she's so decorous."

He paused to devour an entire club sandwich. It was like watching a feeding at the zoo; the action took a minute or so but seemed to proceed at a most leisurely pace. He washed it all down with a vanilla shake then with great finesse, used a handkerchief to wipe his mouth before resuming.

"There's a wonderful Sufi tale of a young man who went to Calcutta to earn his fortune and make his parents proud. Is it Rumi? He was a stranger in a strange land and had a hard time of it. They stole his money and he found neither work nor shelter. After just a month of begging, he'd had enough and resolved to go home. On the eve of departing, he was so beaten down, so broken, that he thought he might lose his mind before morning—and with it, his will to return to the place he was born. Truly, he feared being trapped in that foul and terrible city forever! So he came up with a strategy. He found a little patch of sidewalk to make his lodging, just as *I* did outside Mandry's, I suppose. On that last night, when he knew he'd be most vulnerable to 'the demons,' a fellow traveler occupied the space next to him. (A gentleman who, while down on his luck, was more seasoned than our hapless friend.) The young man shared his hard-luck story, and that he was leaving Calcutta in a matter of hours. 'But why are you wearing those bells?' asked the more seasoned fellow. The young man said, 'The city is too vast. In my final hours here, I fear falling asleep! The *demons* might cast a spell and entice me to stay. So I've tied these bells around my ankle so I'll awaken to their sound. And if they *make* no sound, I'll at least *see* them and remember their *reason*—to ward off the demons who might interfere with my homecoming. When I see the bells, I won't be confused. I'll know exactly where and who I am.' His new acquaintance pretended to enthusiastically agree with the logic of such nonsense. When our friend fell asleep, the mischievous vagabond carefully untied the bells and fastened them to his own ankle, partly as a little joke and partly because he coveted them. Soon after, they plunged side by side into that special sleep only poverty, hunger, and hopelessness confer. At the break of dawn, the young man awakened—and panicked, just as he knew he would. But at that very moment, he heard the ringing of bells (his impish neighbor had rolled over in his sleep) and reflexively looked down; his own ankle was bare! Was it a dream he recalled about affixing them there? He rubbed his eyes and looked around—that was when he saw them attached to his fellow traveler's foot. He grabbed the man by the shoulders and shook him. 'Are you me?' he cried, thinking he might still be dreaming. 'Answer me! Answer! *Are you me?*' The vagabond startled and grew fearful, and rightly so, for our friend was in a state! While he didn't confess to stealing the bells, he was compelled to be as truthful as he could. 'No,' he said. 'I am not you.' When the young man heard that, his worst (and best) fears were realized. He stood up and stared blindly at the rising sun. 'If you are *not* me . . . then who *am* I? And *where* am I?'"

A chill raised the hair on Jeremy's arms. MacKlatchie smiled at him with warmth and sorrow. Like the perplexed man in the story, Jeremy found no comfort in the bells, real or metaphorical, and fretted, not knowing what to believe—whether his lunch companion had actually killed his wife and son; whether Devi had a daughter who died, or even had a daughter at all . . . he hardly believed the stories he told himself about his own life anymore.

"'Now I am alone—all alone,'" said the guru. (Like the bells inhabiting that "space between belief and nonbelief," it seemed to Jeremy that the man across from him now lived in the space between guru and murderer.) "'In all India there is no one so alone as I! If I die today, who shall bring the news—and to whom?' That's Kipling," he said. "Isn't it marvelous? Isn't it glorious? Here's a little more: 'Few white people, but many Asiatics, can throw themselves into amazement by repeating their own names over and over to themselves, letting the mind go free upon speculation as to what is called *personal identity*. When one grows older, the power usually departs, but while it lasts, it may descend upon a man *any moment*.'"

His face became grave, before a smile flitted across, as if softening a stone.

"The *second* piece of information I wanted to tell you—well, this *second piece* has far more significance, at least, for *you*. I should add that I've already discussed it with Devi and believe you must go ahead, without delay."

"'Go ahead'? With what?"

"Why, having the child! No need to use Cathy's egg though, if it's genetics you're concerned with—I mean, because of the disease that beset her child. Though it's my studied opinion that as a breeder, our Devi's *top-notch*, irregardless of poor little Bell's fate; the little one's cancer was a rare and anomalous event, I can assure. But *if* you still have your doubts, why not use one of the eggs you've already paid for? Devi'll carry it. She told me your surrogate reneged, true?"

She had. The gal was a military wife with three children of her own. When one became deathly ill, she told Jeremy that the strain of care was too much and remorsefully bowed out.

"Don't hesitate—it's what the girl *wants*, with all her heart. D'ya think you two met for any *other* reason? That baby will save you *both*."

She blamed Ginevra for pushing her to tell—

She blamed herself—

She blamed God . . .

The irony was that she no longer blamed her mother.

For a while, there just wasn't time for guilt. In those first weeks, Aurora was touch and go. So many broken bones, so much trauma . . . They had a little birthday celebration in her room—Dusty took a cuddling selfie with her still-sleeping princess, who wore a rhinestone "37" tiara—and the very next day the doctors discovered something called compartment syndrome in a shattered leg. For an entire month there were whispers of amputation but the actress said no fucking way, *I don't want to even hear that again.*

A miniature palm broke the fall but she struck her head on a giant terra-cotta pot. Her brain swelled and she didn't emerge from the induced coma until the end of Month Two. Even then, it was impossible to assess the degree of neurological damage. An eye—that beautiful blue eye!—went fetus-milky. Thank God for Elise. She took on the "new challenge" like some Mafia shot-caller.

The usual website suspects insinuated that it was a suicide attempt over a "looming breakup"—they said Allegra was "living" at the Four Seasons, and claimed "she had returned to the Trousdale residence to pick up a few personal items" when she *fell*—and the usual wingnuts claimed divine retribution for sins committed against our Lord. Thanks to the stewardship of Elise and a handpicked P.R. team, perceptions began to slowly shift from self-harm to misadventure. *Yes*, the Wildings were checked into the hotel because of recent home renovations. *Yes*, Allegra had been drinking (a small, pre-birthday celebration) and was innocently dancing/carousing when the freak accident occurred. The doomed cover girls launched a thousand magazines, each newsflashy, retrospective-style feature adorned by photomontages of inner-circle A-list BFFs, wedding festivities, and sundry happier-days domestic horseplay—all the articles predictably ending with twenty-four-hour bedside vigils and the implied certainty of brain damage. (A chart of available B-list bis and dykes were on Perez Hilton's site, with the caption *Who will she be with next?*) But the haters were swept away by the floodwaters of public sympathy; until now, Dusty had been unscathed by tragedy, and the horrible event had all the aspects of a tribal initiation. Elise kept assuring her it would "blow over." One of the publicity gals tried to be supportive by telling the star it was a tempest in a teapot, coolly comparing the eventual outcome to the Shatner case in '99. The actor came home late one night to find his estranged wife at the bottom of the pool "but now, no one even remembers!" Dusty wasn't thrilled with the analogy.

Mostly, she was oblivious. A mother's instinct kicked in—the only thing that mattered was seeing Aurora through and getting to the other side, whatever that would look like. In eight months, she was supposed to be in England for the *Bloodthrone* sequel. Every time she said there was no way that was going to happen, Elise told her not to think about it, that no decisions needed to be made "just now." One time, breezy and can-do, Elise said, "Bring Allegra with! By then, a change of scenery might be *just* what the doctor orders—for both of you." As if Aurora was detoxing in some fancy rehab . . . It was crazy-surreal but Dusty understood what her manager was doing. She was keeping hope alive.

When she emerged from the coma, Dusty was up on Carla Ridge, gathering clothes for her daughter. By the time she got to the hospital, Aurora was in the middle of a sponge bath, a big goofy smile on her face. Dusty tearfully kissed her forehead but Aurora pulled away, shouting "No! No! No!" *"Awwww,"* said Dusty. "Are you cold? Are you cold, little one? Baby girl? Are ya cold?" Aurora kept saying *No!* while an R.N. dried her legs with a towel. Aurora squirmed and cried NONONONONO and Dusty asked them if maybe she was itching or hurting underneath her leg cast. "She's just fussy," said the nurse. "She's been *asleep* for a while." Then she turned to her patient. *"Haven't* you. Oh *yes,* you've had a *very long nap.* Did you know that, Allegra? Did you know you've been napping? But we're *so happy* you woke up! Look who's here! Your *wife's* here, *Dusty's* here, and she's so, so happy to *see* you!" Aurora was crying and her mother enfolded her, kissing the pasty white, sweat-laden brow. "It's okay, baby!" she told her. "It's okay, I'm *here.* I'm here and you're going to come *home* soon. Bet you want to go home, huh. Don't you? Poor thing! I've got your room ready, and all your favorite stuffies . . ."

"Mama! Mama! Mama!" she cried, to no one in particular.

Dusty swallowed her tears, and the nurses did too. It was always super-emotional when patients woke up from comas.

While Aurora was in the hospital, Dusty knocked out a wall between the upstairs guest rooms, creating an "open plan" suite. She wanted caregivers to be able to sleep in the same space as her daughter, without barriers. She outfitted the gym with special equipment recommended by the physical therapy team; they said the pool would play a key role in Allegra's recovery as well. The medical team thought it too soon for her to return home, and that transitioning to a rehab center might be better. They were overruled. Dusty said she could create the exact same environment on Carla Ridge. When Aurora was discharged, the actress invited the doctors and some of the staff to the house for a thank-you dinner. Everyone was genuinely impressed by the renovations.

She'd been gone almost five months. Having her back—*this* version—was unbearable on so many levels. The kink and the anguish, the *madness* of it, were mitigated by the whirlwind of professionals who came and went, prosecuting Aurora's hurlyburly schedule with military precision. Half of the activities focused on repetitive movement and relearning the basics—grasping and holding silverware, drinking from cups, brushing teeth, toilet training—while the other half was taken up by the honing of cognitive skills: word recognition and pronunciation and the expression of wants and needs. She was prone to random outbursts of laughter and tears (the doctors called it PBA, for Pseudobulbar Affect). She took medication for seizures but had them anyway, frightening Dusty, who made certain her daughter would never be alone. Progress was impossible to gauge, though once or twice a week there was a much ballyhooed "miracle," e.g., she'd appear to *get* the obscure humor in a subtle remark of Jeremy's or be caught on a nanny cam, dancing to Michael

Jackson with a carefree elegance reminiscent of her old self. Yet such moments were always countered by discouraging setbacks. The caregivers said it was a marathon, not a sprint, and their clichés comforted. They insisted that Aurora was doing incredibly well but Dusty didn't know what to believe. "It's a process," they told her. "You're in recovery too, you know."

Elise hadn't brought up *Bloodthrone 2* again but Dusty started thinking it might be good to go back to work. She was conflicted, though, about the selfishness of that impulse, torn between the notion of what she did and didn't deserve. (Ginevra, whom she'd resumed Skyping, encouraged her to "dip your toe.") But how could she? How could she indulge in something as frivolous as *acting*, that gave her so much pleasure? What right did she have to experience those movie-set feelings of camaraderie, jubilance, fulfillment? Those *erotic* feelings . . . how *could* she, while Aurora convulsed or cried out in physical, psychic, and spiritual pain? Dusty fantasized about leasing that cottage in the Cotswolds . . . *why not?* Maybe Aurora *would* be well enough to make the journey. And if she weren't, she'd bring her *anyway*, because what the fuck difference would it make? What difference did it make *what* part of the world they were in, as long as her baby was doing all the things she needed, to heal? It's not like there aren't doctors, speech therapists, and P.T. folks in the U.K. They're probably even better at it in Europe . . . what if Aurora *thrived* over there, if she straight-up bloomed?

As the house settled into a routine, the actress felt a tenuous balance return. Jeremy half joked, "I think your sense of humor might be coming back—in a *minimal* way." The trick was never to have a chink in the support system. If a practitioner wasn't pulling their weight, they were immediately fired and replaced. It was like running a small corporation; she'd always excelled at overseeing the practical minutiae that governed the ease and necessities of everyday life. They spent weekends at the Carpinteria love shack because the beach there was private (though security still kept a watchful eye for drones and seaworthy paparazzi) and she believed it essential that Aurora experience the ocean. When she nervously waded in for the first time, squealing and running from the waves with primal delight, Dusty bawled. They built sandcastles and threw mud pies at each other and barbecued on the sand.

Fireworks and tiki torches . . .

The couple was swamped by well-wishers. Dusty hired a service to sort the thousands of letters that arrived through agency, law firm, and management—vowing to answer them all. She got the most amazing orchids "from your Bartok Family," with a heartfelt note signed by the chairman, Dominic, the Gertrude, and the Missoni. George and Amal sent boxes of the chocolate truffles Leggy fell in love with when they spent part of their honeymoon in Lake Como. Tom Ford and his husband, Richard, had a huge assortment of Legos delivered from London (the therapists said they were an excellent tool for hand-eye coordination)—*so* thoughtful . . . she got the most touching call from Liam. She had dinner with Natasha a week before her death, and while he didn't speak of her directly, Liam's former wife wove through his words of consolation like a golden thread.

Dusty made the decision not to look at emails or listen to phone messages for a while. (If anything was urgent, her assistant would let her know.) Friends wanted to visit Allegra but she wouldn't allow it. Not even Patrice the hairdresser, whom her daughter adored. Dusty wondered if she was doing the right thing; there were so many people that loved Allegra, and who she loved back. It might have been beneficial for her to interact, but in the end, Dusty went with her gut. Only Jeremy, Elise, and Livia had backstage passes—though she *did* enjoy inviting the kids and grandkids of caregivers over for picnics and beach days. Aurora was great around children but somewhere along the line had grown fearful of dogs. (*Allegra* was a total dog person.) Angie Dickinson was one of the few exceptions to the visitor rule. She'd known Angie for years. Her daughter had been challenged from birth in ways now reminding Dusty of her own; watching them, back in the nineties, was something she'd never forgotten. She had been honored to bear witness to the fierce grace of Angie's patience and devotion, her unconditional mother love.

Aurora called *everyone* "Mama." One of the aides said, "But she knows *you're* the only 'Mama.' When you're not here, she likes to call us that." Other helpers said the same, and while Dusty knew they meant well, the little campaign being waged on behalf of her primacy embarrassed her. Though in time, when her daughter cried out in fear, it was Dusty who soothed her and no one else. That was an observable fact.

They watched movies in the plush home theater. When they saw one of Dusty's, Aurora laughed in delight, pointing to the image on the screen and then to her mother. They saw *Frozen* and Aurora knew the song perfectly, singing along like they used to—

> *Let it go, let it go*
> *I am one with the wind and sky!*
> *Let it go, let it go*
> *You'll never see me cry!*

Sometimes, overcome by medication and mangled circuitry, Aurora fell asleep without warning, say, smack in the middle of the noisiest, most outrageous scene of her favorite, *Mad Max: Fury Road*. She'd lean her head on Dusty's shoulder, and begin to snore; her mother would lower the volume and stare at her baby while the projector threw images onto Aurora's features, to create a living metaphor of the actress's colliding worlds—a pietà of film, fame, and blood, of fractured family regained.

It was a good day. More IATSE checks arrived and someone who saw a late-night rerun of *Dr. Wrigley* offered to anonymously pay the debt on one of their credit cards—$27,000.

Derek had been staying in Tristen's room but crawled into Larissa's bed around midnight and fell right to sleep. She woke up.

It'd been a few weeks since she thought of her—her son had been dead only a few days when she heard that Allegra tried to kill herself. Larissa was already out of her mind with grief and her imagination ran wild; she became convinced she was responsible for the botched suicide. She knew Allegra had "broken up" with her out of guilt, and assumed she must have finally told her wife of their dalliance. Dusty was probably so pissed that she threatened divorce, or even *insisted* on it, which was why Allegra did what she did.

Still, she was thankful her obsession had run its course. She was no longer "in love" with either Mrs. Wilding. She turned on her side, away from Derek, and drifted off . . .

In the dream, Tristen was in the passenger seat. They were driving to Whole Foods on a sweetly boring day. Everything was uneventful, sunlit and divine. It felt good to have him with her again, even though she had an awareness in the dream that he was dead. He spoke boyishly; she couldn't make out his words. He wore jeans and was shirtless. It didn't bother her that his chest was gutted— the inside-outs were slick and clean, painted a deep maroon, hard-rubbery, like the anatomical model in science class when she was a girl. Larissa began getting uncomfortable in her body as she strained to understand what he was saying. She couldn't breathe. She felt pressure now, and winced in pain behind the wheel—when she awakened, Derek was heavy on top of her. She startled, then let him keep fucking her.

She felt her son's heart pound against her own.

She bathed her little girl, something that calmed them both. Aurora loved a bath more than she loved the pool, and Dusty thought that was because the tub was *fun* but the pool was *work*—all that resistance-training the therapists demanded (with peace and love). She thrilled when Mama drew the giant sea sponge over her skin, squeezing out the warm, soapy water.

She examined Aurora's body closely, noting its small and larger transformations. The leg was healing well; the white scar from the incision over once-infected bone looked like the bleached, toothy nose of a sawfish. Coarse black hairs had begun to sprout topside between ankle and knee, like blades of grass after a fire. The other breaks were healing remarkably well. The shoulders were lopsided from the awful dislocation (it would never be totally right) and a foot arched cartoonishly, causing a slight limp. Her midsection had thickened as an effect of the meds, and also because she'd been eating like a draft horse since she was home. The weight gain hadn't distributed evenly—her legs remained spindly from the weeks spent in coma and her rear end suffered accordingly, grown wasted and slabby—steroids had provided a classic moonface. The staph-infected bedsore that threatened her life when in hospital had completely closed and all that was left was the pinkish crater of a dead volcano. Dusty washed her privates like a mother would her babe's, making Aurora giggle and squirm, and Dusty laughingly chide. Sometimes when they lay in bed and she sang the girl a lullaby, Aurora reverted to the self-calming frottage she once practiced as a girl, and Dusty would stop her, gentle yet firm, flashing for a moment on the pride and care Allegra used to lavish on the waxing and manicuring of those nether parts, now overgrown and homogeneous. And the face: that gorgeous face! So different now, always changing yet somehow still the same, still her love, her lunar child—still her wife, in a way, forever and always—avid in its familiarity and otherness, the disorganized, perfect features like a valentine from Eternity. They'd capped the teeth that broke against the pot; thank God Aurora had been unconscious when so much knitting and rebuilding had to be done. There'd been sieges of cystic acne in the last few months, worsened by Allegra's compulsive, scratchy explorations—her nails had to be clipped way back. But the cosmetician who came each week doted over and nourished the lovely skin, and just now, as she bathed her, it had sloughed pristine. The hair on the head had grown out. It was vibrant and gorgeously cut, and grew wilder than ever, as if willfully asserting its independence of all that was ravaged.

And how Dusty adored that milky eye!

Like the rarest of marbly gems, rolling from the recesses of an Egyptian tomb to land eerily at the foot of a humbled explorer.

Δ

The cottage—Dusty referred to it by that architectural misnomer—was in Somerset, just outside Bruton, which is to say not a far soak from Bath, nor farther still from Glastonbury, as the starling flies; though the birds *did* tend toward a more vertical migration, ascending in helices so dense and perfect one could easily imagine the hand of God tugging them home.

"The humble abode," as she called it in dry-wit emails to Jeremy, was actually a seventeenth-century Grade II–listed manor along with outbuildings for staff and guests, though in the nearly three years they'd lived there, guests had been few and far between. Shetland sheep, Old Spots, and Gloucester cattle were more common, having run of the property, which gave Aurora (who had no memory of ever being called anything else) and the *other* mistress of the house great, giddy pleasure. The carriage entrance of the two-story, slate-roofed stable block of paneled stalls and mangers was grazed by an unexpectedly elegant frieze and cornice; adjacent was a heaven-sent paddock; venturing beyond, one found oneself in the dream of a Grade II–listed garden with a weather-worn Grade II–listed gazebo, graffitied by Aurora herself with fancied words and phrases of the hour. The whole affair—all twenty-five acres of it—was enclosed by a crinkle-crankle wall, whose bricks often wore a necklace of soft, hanging fruit, and wove a charming cuff of talismanic protection around the property's borders.

With its stone abbey, stone bridges, and stone streets, its medieval chapels and graveyards older and stonier still, its endless succession of weddings between rolling hill and sky (officiated by that which pulls the starlings)—marriages that weathered all manner of domestic ecstasies and abuse—with the glittering river that stood in for the cathedral train of all those bridal gowns, and its towering dovecote famously presiding over all, the Paleolithic county's *genius loci* resounded like the celestial pieces of a lost, cherished reverie the actress had finally gotten to match.

It was more than a new life—it was home, and always had been.

Apart from the generous staff required to manage the farm and its environs, the mistresses employed a Badminton-born cook and Pucklechurch pastry chef, nannies from Axminster and Temple Cloud, a Dean hamlet swim trainer, an equine therapist from the

Vale of Evesham (Aurora was never more her old self when being led along on a horse), and all manner of visiting tradespeople, from masons and apiarists to artisans of stained glass. Yogis were entrusted to soothe Aurora's finickiness, while other practitioners, schooled in massage, Pilates, and the Alexander Technique, did their best to fill the potholes of recovery, pouring in enough holistic gravel to keep the fair semblance of a navigable road. Dusty's bimonthly Saturday night musicales—Aurora gleefully dubbed them *hootenannies*— were a major hit with the villagers (who couldn't have given two shits about her celebrity nor anyone else's) and already felt like ancient rural tradition. On Sundays, mums rallied the broods for arts and crafts. Dusty built a small amphitheater where mimes, jugglers, and *marionettistes* held court; fanciful theater productions tapped a rich local vein of natural (and unnatural) talent, booking thespians of all ages, from squalling newborns to village wallflowers who'd managed to locate, and passionately liberate, their inner Judi Dench.

Dusty stayed away from America and had no yearning to go back. The gossipy national Sturm und Drang recycled into a new mythology: the iconic star breaking ground yet again in her latest role as the selfless caregiver who, in defiance of the prevailing rules of throwaway culture, refused to abandon her spouse, her mate, her ladylove. The macabre fairy tale had all the elements of a pop passion play and served as a kind of there-but-for-the-grace-of-God *telenovela* for the masses, a confessional and general bloodletting with built-in dispensation; the actress, crucified and in exile (in the name of love!), became a dashboard saint touched for luck while navigating one's own dark night of the unrequited, lovelorn soul. It gave sacrificial solace. Dusty didn't *feel* like a martyr, not remotely, but the world's ghoulish, sentimental spin on her tragedy, uncomplicated by the even more tragic truth, allowed her to hide in plain sight. For the most part the press respectfully let her be. She hadn't acted since *Blood-throne 2* (they *did* rent that place in the Cotswolds, and her daughter did just fine; Elise was right, as usual), a heroic absence that garnered more praise than controversy. She'd been talking with her manager about the idea of producing, maybe even directing. When Angelina visited a few months earlier, her enthusiasm about the experience of *Unbroken* was inspiring.

Helen Mirren visited as well. It was nice to return the favor, as Dusty and Allegra had had such wonderful times at Helen and Taylor's house in New Orleans. (They'd never worked together and had a running joke about the fates being against it.) "Popper" was a hoot— she claimed to have zero maternal instincts, and said the thought of childbirth "disgusted" her—the mordant stories she told about her bitch mother always reminded Dusty of Reina. But she was *so* tender with Aurora when she came to Bruton, like the most perfect fairy godmother, putting Dusty in mind of that mushroom story Marilyn told about the "battalion of women who'd never had children," and how it really *was* impossible for a woman to be childless.

Everything was abuzz with plans for Aurora's fortieth.

In her head, Dusty had been planning a "Renaissance Faire" extravaganza, replete with jousting knights, jugglers, falconers, and commedia dell'arte, but when she let Helen in on her brilliance, the dame replied (with acutely English sangfroid), "I'm afraid that *will not do.*" She suggested *A Midsummer Night's Dream* motif, which felt instantly right, and Dusty set about making preparations.

She invited Jeremy, who was in London working on a film. He was traveling with his son and it would be the first time she met the boy. They'd kept in touch but seen each other only once since she left

L.A.—in Rome a few years ago when she took her daughter there to see a specialist. Still, they managed to Skype every few weeks or so and Aurora thoroughly enjoyed raucous screen time with "Uncle Jar Jar," who refreshingly remained his usual, uncensored self. Each time after they spoke, the household was forced to endure days of Aurora parroting every inappropriate thing that came out of his mouth—and even *more* sampled horrors from the hip-hop mixes he emailed, that she maddeningly rapped along to. Dusty discouraged him, with a wink, because she really did feel it important for Aurora to have that outlet. Someone who wasn't so careful with her and acted more like a peer, who could be silly and disrespectful and let it all hang out.

But Dusty was still nervous about his coming.

With the care of a scientist, she'd created a hermetic world, and the experiment had been a resounding success; and so it would remain, as long as the pleasure dome was intact. Yet as the visit drew nearer, her life as a recluse and de facto "fugitive" struck hard. This citizen and former ambassador of the world, now living in Shangri-la under country house arrest, suddenly worried the intrusion of a key player from the past might introduce a virus that would be the death of the organism. Some of those concerns had to do with the fear that such a homecoming could blur the line she'd so firmly drawn (for Aurora) between mother and daughter/lover and wife, bringing with it certain *associations* that would sow confusion and trigger a host of anxieties whose abeyance had been hard-fought and half-won. The irksome daydream of their old friend (and donor) strolling the hallowed grounds of "Mind Your Manor" (*his* name for the cottage; he called the village *Et Tu, Bruton*) like Rochester to Dusty's Jane, with the locked-away madwoman Aurora planning fire and mass murder, filled her with shame— and the sleaze of that old, familiar feeling too, the one so familiar when

Reina was alive: the recognition of an ever-present low-frequency hum signaling something was amiss. That she was living a lie.

And she'd been doing so well! *Swimmingly* so, considering the hand she'd been dealt. There was more candor, honesty, and joy in her life than ever. Still, the nagging sensation descended like a flu.

It was wonderful to see him again. He looked lean; he'd never been more *present.* Wyatt was almost two and a half, one of those towheads who look alarmingly like their dads. He'd brought the au pair along.

Aurora hugged him and wouldn't let go. (Allegra's new name had been easily explained when they ran into him that time on the Spanish Steps: the actress said that from the minute they arrived in Somerset, she'd *insisted* on being called Aurora, like the princess in *Sleeping Beauty.* To which Jeremy said, "Does that make you Maleficent?") He was startled by her physical transformation. Her nose was pierced, a recent concession of Dusty's that restored peace to the house after months of pleading and occasional outright horror movie screams that ended in safe-room quiet time. (So far, so good—Aurora took great pride and care, and it hadn't got infected. Yet.) Her hair was dyed in streaks of magenta and silvery blue. Acne brazenly snow-capped her cheeks, ill-concealed by a clownish frosting of foundation and Clearasil. She was forty pounds heavier; Jeremy had of course noticed the gain when they Skyped, but in person it was jarring and too real. *Everything* was too real. She had on an "I'm a Belieber" T-shirt, and Dusty jokingly apologized. "I tried to get her to wear the Kanye you sent. What can I say?" When Aurora heard the reference, she sang-shouted, "How long you niggas ball? All day, nigga! How much time you spent at the mall? All day, nigga!"

Wyatt thought she was hilarious.

(The au pair didn't know what to think.)

After dinner, Aurora begged to watch *Frozen*, which she'd only seen about seven thousand times. Halfway through, she wanted to play games, so they did for a while, some kind of gonzo variation of charades (the look on Wyatt's face vacillating between utter fear and utter delight). Then she wanted to go to the karaoke club that her mother built on the far end of the paddock. (Whenever she called Dusty "Mama," no explanations were needed; neurological damage conveniently covered all bases and regressions.) At first Dusty said no, because Jeremy and Wyatt were tired from their trip, but Jeremy said it was fine and off they went. Dusty sang a Taylor Swift and Jeremy the Sinatra freak did a more than serviceable "One for My Baby," then Dusty said *all righty that's enough,* time for bed, and Aurora started yelling and Jeremy told the au pair to take Wyatt back to the guesthouse and Dusty wouldn't back down on bedtime so Aurora gave her a *shove* and that's when Dusty got in her *face,* barking *That is not okay! Not okay!* Aurora backed down a little and started to cry. Jeremy knew to stay out of it, Dusty *poor thing* had full control of the situation, probably happened all the time *Jesus!* and Aurora calmed down *totally* when Dusty threatened, "Should I call Edwina? Do you want me to call Edwina?"—Edwina being the one charged with enforcing safe-room quiet time. Dusty sniffed Aurora's mouth and said she smelled chocolate. She told her to open wide and the girl shamefacedly submitted while Dusty did some deep sniffing. She insisted Aurora tell her where the Kit Kats were hidden— turning to Jeremy to let him know it was a house rule that sweets were a no-no after four p.m., which was why Aurora was so hyper (plus excited of course to see him and Wyatt)—and Aurora cried some more, but in drib-drabs, and Dusty intercom'd one of the night nurses (*not* Edwina) to come take her to bed. When the woman arrived, Dusty informed her of the Kit Kats caper and also to make sure Aurora took double the melatonin on top of her usual bedtime pharmacopoeia. She said *Now say goodnight to Jeremy* and Aurora sulkily hugged him again, and was embarrassed too, and wouldn't look at him when he kissed her cheeks. In the quiet that descended after her leave-taking, Jeremy said, "Wow," and Dusty said, "I know. I need a drink."

They sat by the fire in the living room of the main house and caught up. She asked about his London film; he asked when she planned on working again. "I don't really have anything on the *slate*." She said she'd actually been thinking about producing. He loved that and said they should be partners. They got excited about it for a little before he circled back to Aurora and said (with love), "I don't know how you do it." "Well, it has to be done!" Her smile came out brittle, not at all how she'd meant it to. Jeremy didn't want her to get the wrong idea, i.e., that he thought it a thankless task, so he backpedaled, complimenting her on the new and nurturing life she'd built for them and how happy Allegra seemed. She turned the focus to Wyatt and asked what fatherhood was like. "Amazing. If I talk about it, I'll just sound corny." "Better corny than horny. You *have* changed." (She was drunk.) She asked him to describe a typical day with the boy and he started with Wyatt clambering into bed in the morning, making him pancakes and bacon, bla, and how much fun it was to take the boy to Trader Joe's or wherever because "he's a total twink magnet." Dusty laughed and he was glad because she didn't seem to be doing enough of that. There was a moment, there were a few, really, during his stay, when she'd flirted with telling him the truth about her daughter-wife, just *unloading*, for the fuck of it. She wondered how that would make her feel—if there'd be any kind of relief. But an invisible hand took her by the scruff of the neck and told her not to, because Shangri-la, *and* Thornfield Hall, would burn.

"We never really talked about Wyatt's mom. Is she still in the picture?"

"Nope."

"But he—Wyatt's her biological son, right?"

"Righto."

"What happened?"

"She just . . . couldn't stay," he said.

Because of the bittersweet vibe, Dusty didn't want to press. At least not till she had another glass of *vino*. "Did you—was it IVF?"

"Nope. Did it old-school."

"Are you *serious*?"

She was shocked and oddly delighted. She knew he was bisexual but for some reason had always scoffed at his being anything other than a full-time queer.

"Yup."

"Whoa! What's up with *that*?"

"Shit happens."

"Babies too, I guess."

"Babyshit *definitely* happens."

"How would *you* know?" she said dismissively. "Your au pair takes care of *that*. So where'd you meet Wyatt's mom? On Tinder?"

"In a park."

"Bull-*shit*."

He told her what he told everyone—that they'd met when she came to his office to pitch an idea. The bare-bones anecdote ended in Devi returning home to her husband, somewhere north of Juneau. Dusty commiserated, saying all she cared about was his happiness.

"And you *are*, aren't you, Jeremy? Happy?"

"Bunny, it's beyond. Beyond my wildest dreams."

They snuggled up, in weariness, kinship, and a love that abided. He wrapped his arms around her and she said it felt good to be held. It'd been a while.

"So—gettin' any?" he said.

"Ha! I wish."

"Oh *come on*, you *can't* be celibate. What about Edwina? Kinda hot, right?"

"Goiters don't really do it for me. I mean, not so much."

"Was that a goiter? I thought she was just happy to see you."

"Guess I kinda haven't been feeling . . . *in my body*," she said, with sardonic Californiaspeak emphasis.

"I *know* that you're having it on with your *mucker* or your *valette*. I'm sure it's all very Miss Julie."

"That's *Mister* Julie to you, Uncle Jar Jar."

"And that's *another* reason you should start working, Bunny: *location hookup*."

"Yeah, well. Not really feelin' it."

Her mood toggled from jokey to irritated.

"Use it or *lose* it, baby girl—I am *serious*. I mean, isn't it kind of, like, *time? Look*. Everything you're doing is *totally amazing* and *totally beautiful*. It's not like one of those things where I'm saying 'Move on!'—because I would *never*. Obviously. And you *can't*—you *wouldn't*, you wouldn't *want* to. We *know* that. Can I ask you something?"

"Sure." She hated the whole topic but it was just easier to let him talk.

"Are you guys still . . . *active?*"

"*No.*"

He could see that she was annoyed and dispirited. "Okay. I just needed—*wanted* to ask. Don't hate me, Dusterella."

"I don't hate you, Jar Jar. I don't *like* you, but I don't hate you."

She smiled at him and he gave her little kisses. "You know, if the shoe were on the other foot, what would *you* want . . . for *Allegra?*"

"Aurora."

"Would you want her to stop being *human*? To stop doing the things that would ultimately make her a stronger, happier person? Who could love you *more*, take care of you *more*?"

"I may have to call Edwina. You *might* be in need of some quiet time yourself."

"But you have to have some *fun* in your life, right?"

"I *do*—I *do* have fun. And I'm going to have fun *tomorrow*. We're going to have *fabulous fun* on Aurora's birthday."

"You *know* what I mean, Dusty."

She grew serious. "To introduce someone . . . to bring someone *into my life*—my life is so *crazy*, Jeremy. I mean, this is what I *do*. This is who I *am*. This *is* my life. And it's *not* very sexy."

"But *you* are."

"Aw, you're sweet."

"You know that I'm *not*. Okay—just tell me this. What's the harm in testing the waters? You don't *know* who you'll meet until you're *out* there. And you *might* just find that incredibly *brilliant*, incredibly *hot lady* who's *okay* with your 'crazy' life. Which, by the way, *isn't* crazy, it's actually *amazing* and *spiritual* and *beyond*. And *filled* with love and devotion. You might just find that *certain someone* who's completely *blown away* by that, blown away by *you*, and who wants to be *with* you not just for your amazing jacked and rock-hard body but because she *loves* you and does not *give* a shit because she loves *all* of you. Someone who's great with *Allegra*—"

"Aurora."

"—great with Aurora. And the whole nine fucking yards."

"Tell me more about how sexy my body is, you . . . silver-tongued faggot. You child-bearing, woman-fucking queen."

He'd forgotten how funny she was when she was high. She'd say anything.

"You *can't* just . . . cut that part of your life *out*. I mean, you're totally in your prime—"

"What about *you*? Have *you* found this perfect person? This perfect man, boy, woman, whatever?"

"I'm *looking*. But at least I'm *out* there."

"Oh you're *out* there, all right."

"*You're* out there—outta your frickin' *mind*. Well, I gave you my two cents—"

"And I gave you *mine*."

"—go join the world again. Renew your membership. If all else fails, get the village idiot to go down on you."

"My life *ain't sexy* and it *ain't gonna change*. So put that in your cock and smoke it. Or wank it. Or stick it in some *broad* you met in a *park*. Or whatever other nasty things you do with it."

He lay in bed, enshrouded in the ghostliness of that old, shared L.A. life. Its recentness astonished. How long had it been since he and Allegra rapturously visited the midwife? Four years? Not even. And Tristen, dead and buried! And *Wyatt* . . . The march of time passed through cities of rubble, cities of gold, cities on fire. Cities gone mad from the light of the heavens.

Dusty's innocent query led him back to Devi. His mood grew elegiac. Jeremy missed the mother of his child and wondered if she might have come to a bad end. (At least her guru wouldn't be able to murder her, though it really did seem like he already had.) It was a shock when he learned that MacKlatchie died not two days after his coffee-shop confessions—but inestimably more so when, shortly after their son's birth, Devi announced she'd be leaving him and Wyatt for good. They had been living together in Nichols Canyon, and while Jeremy hadn't given much thought to future scenarios, he had been wrong to presume the baby to be an unconditional hedge against her going—a guarantee that she'd always somehow be in their lives.

He asked himself if he was in love with her but the question bewildered, which alone made Jeremy feel it was true. She was the wiliest, weirdest, most willful, barbarously charming, dangerously sane and erotic creature he had ever met, and proved herself much looser, warmer, and goofier than she came across in those historic, soliloquizing first encounters. More important was the added, irresistible detail of their *fatedness*, the sense that a supreme destiny, random and divine, was mysteriously at play in their having found one another—a rare and fragile thing, a *privilege* he'd never remotely experienced with another human being. (Except maybe for Tristen, but they were never going to have a *baby* together, they could never have created *life*.) A further complication was that he had grown to love her body. Throughout his life, Jeremy had had more encounters with women than he let on—turbulent, sexual, deeply emotional attachments. They were atypical but no less intense than male-to-male combat.

He understood that by advising Dusty it was time to explore, he was being hypocritical . . . because just like she, Jeremy wasn't feelin' it. He took the arrival of his son as an evolutionary marker—emblem of the commutation of a life sentence of perversion and promiscuity, a symbol of escape from the prison of bodies and enslavement of flesh. The age-old question watered his musings like a soft rain: *What does it all mean?* The cock goes here, the mouth there, the proprietary heart and obsessive thoughts follow with the predictability of blind donkeys descending into the recesses of a spectacular, spectacularly meaning-less canyon. In his twenties, he was in love with a hermaphrodite (they called them "intersex" now) who had a vagina with a swarthy nub of cock dangling above it like a boutonniere. How perfect that shemale was for him, how he loved that being! What a cruel, lusciously asinine farce was the game of love, desire, and need! With no escape other than the false exit of celibacy . . . and what was celibacy but a smug entr'acte in a dead-end, compulsory burlesque?

Summoning Devi again, he could smell that meadow of spring flowers that seemed to live on her nape (inexplicably on one side only). Their time of domesticity, measured in months, was surreal. He never said a word about her to friends or colleagues, which only served to heighten the phantasmal aspect. When he came home at the end of a workday there she was, sometimes barefoot, always preg-nant, in the kitchen, cooking, like the beatific, soon-to-be-slain wife in a film noir. She'd been curiously dispassionate in telling him she had found her guru dead on the bathroom floor of the beach house, as if all was prefigured. After that last lunch with MacKlatchie, Jer-emy Googled *Killer, Longtime Fugitive, Dead in Malibu*, but there was nothing . . . though he *had* found a rather obscure article which may or may not have been the spur that goaded Frank to return to Min-nesota for his second-attempt helping of "just desserts." The homi-cides occurred in the winter of '83 . . . Yet even after Devi told him Sir had died—"gone ahead" was how she put it—Jeremy never brought it up. He doubted if she knew her teacher had murdered his family but decided it unlikely, as *Franklin* would have shielded the woman he had loved from the beginning against a thing so unsavory; Jeremy didn't feel it was his place to disabuse her. Another caveat of Mac-Klatchie's might have been that such knowledge on Devi's part may not only have challenged the "energetically incontestable" beliefs he had so carefully imposed and inspired but made her criminally complicit in harboring him. In the same vein, there had been a few moments, before *and* after MacKlatchie's passing, when Jeremy pondered reaching out to the police to report what he knew.

But he let that go.

As sleep overtook, he drifted back to the Buddhist dinner party, recalling Michael Imperioli's story. The actor said that after the retreat in Ukiah, he never saw his friend again, yet got postcards, in which the man wrote that he was on his way to a place called Summerland to meet his dead wife. The strange thing was, Devi had more or less said the same thing—she and her beloved teacher were on *their* way to that very place, when destiny had interrupted, in the form of "Jerome" himself. The article in the small-town Minnesota paper that Jeremy found online, *The Summerland Sentinel*, recounted the notorious unsolved murders of Margot and "Little Jim" MacKlatchie more than three decades before, in the hamlet of the same name.

What did it all mean?

The soft rain fell . . .

When Devi summarily announced—again, with odd dispassion—that it was her turn to "go on ahead," she said it was by dint of finding "my Sir, who waits for me." By then the lightness had gone out of her, and the light from her eyes too, replaced by something indescribably different. She was no longer his, nor was she Wyatt's.

On the morning that she left, she told one last story in the "old" style.

"After my Bella died, my guru said we must go. That he had heard the bells and they beckoned us to take to the road—to the 'Highway of Holiness,' he said, that would deliver us to freedom. To *Silence*. I gathered what few possession I had (I threw everything away when

Bella went ahead) and spent my last hours in Chicago with pounding heart, blushing like a bride. My Sir bought me a beautiful suit at Marshall Field and told me to have my hair and nails done because 'one must begin such a great adventure with understated elegance and easy formality.' So I did. And as I was rushing to meet him at the train station, I bumped into a boy I knew from middle school. We'd gone to college together too, and while we didn't see each other much because of our schedule of classes, I knew he had always been in love with me. He was shy and held back, but I knew. When he saw me he was shocked at how I looked because I was usually so plain! I never cared about makeup or how I did my hair or what I wore. When he saw it was *me*, it made him crazy. I'll never forget the look on his face. 'Cathy!' he said—I wasn't Devi yet, I was still Cathy to the world, and to *that* world I suppose shall always be—'Cathy, my God, I didn't recognize you!' We chatted, though he could see I was anxious, and in a hurry. And finally—finally!—he asked me out. I was polite, but said that I was on my way to the station and was going away on a long journey. His face got sad and he said, 'Did you meet someone?' I just looked down at my shoes. How could I tell him the truth of who—of *what*—I had met? How does one say one 'met' Silence? I could scarcely say it to *myself*. And how paltry the question was, how *human*, yet how poignant, how beautiful! So I stammered *yes*, kissed his cheek, and ran off."

Jeremy remembered her final kiss to *him*, and the one she bestowed on their son.

Then, those last words:

"I'll see Bella soon—and my precious Sir . . . his *wife* and *son*—and my . . . why, I'll see *Mother* and *Father*—and Tristen too! Then *you*, Jerome, and then *Wyatt*—

"And all whom I ever loved."

The flirty, dark-clouded skies snubbed the storm, and the birthday party was a marvel. Nature was in an uproar—as if thrilled to have been invited, she changed costumes like a teenager who couldn't make up its mind. (Her room was a glorious mess.) Thankfully, she *had* decided not to bother the event with any petulant, hormonal displays, at least none that a light umbrella couldn't handle.

Cell phones were confiscated on entry, the unpopular chore carried out with panache by an affable stable mucker, size Extra Large, who'd dopily squeezed himself (and been well squozen by others) into the chrysalis of a grungy old Quiksilver wetsuit, festively adorned in leaves, twigs, Post-its, and glitter. The donkey ears that his smaller, even more puckish counterpart would soon attach to a snoring Bottom were taped to his battered cycling helmet like a HELLO sticker at a jackass convention. In regard to the banning of electronic devices, the invitees already knew it to be a policy of the manor. When she first took up residency, Dusty threw a housewarming whereby she welcomed the new neighbors with a heartfelt speech expressing her hopes that one day she might be deemed a worthy addition to their community. She also spoke of her partner's "accident" and its effect on their lives, before congenially segueing to enlighten her guests as to the obscene bounty placed upon post-trauma images/videos of Aurora (there had been none as yet) "should they become available." Such an eventuality, she said, was doubtless an intrusion she wished to postpone for as long as she could. The actress took great care not to tar the villagers with that brush, making sure they understood that even friendly group shots, taken by the innocents now gathered, and *photobombed*, as they say, by the sometimes scampish Aurora (the guests tittered but warmly understood where Dusty was going with this), had the potential to be hacked by professionals with all the stealth, speed, and brutality of wolves slaughtering sheep. Their embarrassed but resolute hostess couldn't apologize enough, as she felt the whole business to be *unneighborly*, but really had no need, because the good and honorable Brutonnières, won over by her sensitivity, humility, and earnestness, not to mention the touching heroism of her predicament, heartfully assured those wishes would be respected. And besides, their sons' and daughters' smartphone umbilicuses were ones they looked forward to cutting, be it only for a few hours. The prospect made them right jolly.

The amphitheater was graced with revolving sets of forest and castle hall, but the former, with its breeze-twitched bramble, carpet of leaves, and overhang of painted stars, was what captivated Aurora most. The excitable girl, more of a girl at forty than ever, sat in the audience beside her mother, thrilled to teeth and bone by the tin-rattled tempest—courtesy of the forearms of Sir Extra Large—that accompanied the drama. (The scudding drafts of the *real* storm kicked up their heels in delight at the tin-eared impersonation.) Her manic gaiety was such that Aurora temporarily forgot she had a part to play in the night's ensemble; Dusty feared she'd spent a greater part of the week preoccupied more by habiliments than the learning of lines. But the resultant outfit, a sensational catchpenny mash-up of punk-royale fairydom, had well been worth it: a tiara of safety pins, waggles of black and bloodred tulle and chiffon, a vintage Belstaff biker jacket, tatty ermine stole, and enormous rhinestone-spangled butterfly wings. She spent hours scuffing her new Capezios, meticulously spattering them with paint, and carried a skull-knobbed scepter with a rocker's hauteur—half Siouxsie Sioux, half Queen Cersei. Dusty had already emailed pictures to Vivienne Westwood, due in July as a houseguest.

So as not to try the patience of its audience nor the elements,

Shakespeare's romp had been condensed enough to be rendered more conceit than dream. As in the play, actors took on multiple roles, though more multiple in *this* show than likely meant by the author. The cast comprised manor employees, among them a shepherd (who made all the daughters swoon, as shepherds tend), a gardener's apprentice (a close swoony second), and the son of a caretaker (not even in the running). A flock of Aurora's carebirds—minders, P.T.s, and the like—rounded out the company, with hawk-like Edwina divebombing the coveted role of Titania. She proved herself far freer in expression and lighter on her feet than one would have guessed from her strict day-shift demeanor and fighting weight.

A crowd of around forty gathered to watch. When he wasn't making sly asides to Dusty about how he should liked to have been cast—being a "natural Bottom" and all—Jeremy fought to keep hold of the lap-dancing Wyatt, while the au pair remained ever vigilant of a hand-off. About halfway through, a minder pulled Aurora backstage. When it came time, the shepherd (as Quince, whose beauty prompted Jeremy to remark on all kinds of jellies), addressed the Duke of Athens—though he made his speech directly to the movie star—begging permission to put on the storied playlet of the star-crossed lovers. The wall and the lion soon made their entrance to much applause, then the birthday girl made hers, to an acclamation so raucous it gave pause, even to the trees, who respectfully stopped their thrashing. Aurora blushed and curtsied, and the child's play, with subtle accompaniment of strings, began. She acquitted herself of cherry-lipped lines whispered to Pyramus through the chink in the wall traditionally represented by scissored fingers—in this case, those of the apprentice gardener who got lost enough in his role to be paralyzed (pruned?) by an unexpected fit of stage fright, made infinitely worse by the traitorous sniggering of those fickle girls who not long before had hung on his every word (and eyelash), so much so that one of Aurora's posse was forced to stand behind the lad and go unto the breach, dear friends, *more* than once more, by speaking his lines directly from the text held in the prompter's hands. In summary, Pyramus saw Aurora-Thisbe's voice, heard her face, and so forth; the catatonic hole in the wall was kissed by both parties, to an eruption of squeals from the iPhoneless lassies; the lion appeared (assuring the spectators he wasn't a *real* lion—not to be alarmed); and at last, a pony Moon clomped dutifully forward, an LED lantern strung from its neck by a lanyard. The king of the forest, no longer defensive about his so-called lionhood and mindful of furthering the narrative, lurched at Aurora, who, in fleeing haste, dropped her scepter, which was promptly retrieved and handed back by the timorous wall itself. Jeremy perspicaciously shouted to Aurora not to forget to let the big cat have her scarf (one of the carebirds was about to address that very issue). The leonine *poseur* set to bloodying it with a mouthful of tomatoes—causing a hemorrhage of *ewwwws!* from the younger set—then both lion and girl ran off. The man on the moon, or in its saddle anyway, was left to pronounce his only words: "The lantern is the moon; I, the man in the moon; and this pony, my pony." (There was, oddly, a shortage of wags, not of ponies.) Much hilarity was thrown at the players, which the banjo, violin, and zither caught, fluffed, and threw jauntily back. An ebullient Pyramus arrived on the scene but upon seeing the bloody scarf buffoonishly took his own life—though not without a gasp from a confused child toward the rear, which set off the car alarms of *other* baffled toddlers, which triggered a few five-alarm sirens in the form of bawling infants, etcetera, etcetera. When Aurora returned from the wings with a wing of her own inexplicably intact—she was no monarch after all—she saw her hapless love and said, "Asleep my love? What, dead my dove?" and proceeded to unpack the death speech in an effing, ineffably *moving* way, with a tragicomic flair that no one saw coming. She covered the dead man's eyes, lips, nose, and cheeks in regret, and then, with that bloodied shroud; by the time she farewell'd her friends and bid the fabled three *adieus*, Dusty and Jeremy felt stabbed along with her.

A not too distant crack of thunder pretty much said it all.

Any prudish notion of shelter was abandoned as the audience jumped to its feet, roaring and stomping in approval. Onstage, everyone began to dance; the spectators ran up to join them. Through a path between the litter of tumbled folding chairs, Dusty, in pell-mell procession, was ushered to Aurora, and as her daughter led them in a rocky, rocked-out Dionysian jig, the mother's heart nearly burst at the berserk and joyful travesty of this life. The au pair danced with the Wall, and Edwina with the carebirds; the oldest of the old, with the youngest of the young, and the XXXL, with the Extra Small; the pony moon tangoed amidst a tangle of squealing piglets; and Wyatt bounced on his daddy's neck with pure, fierce pleasure as the skies emptied themselves, and Nature set about blasting all of Sussex in exaltation, determined to make more than some corner of a foreign field forever England.

Nine o'clock—

Aurora's fast asleep, spent from the day. Her mother can't remember the house ever being so peaceful at that hour . . .

Jeremy is off to London in the morning and Dusty needs to be up early to see him off. She *loved* that he came; it meant so much to Aurora as well. And having him here *wasn't* like old times—they were making *new* times. *New old times.* Nostalgia could go fuck itself.

She felt hopeful, expansive, resilient.

Every few weeks, her assistant sent a pouch from the States with fan notes and whatnot. She had slacked off on writing people back—burned out. Jeremy said she should just post a video on her website ("Like Ringo did") saying she was busy living her life and would no longer be responding to letters. "Fans need tough love too. But be sure you add 'with peace and love'!" In the pouch this time was a folder with a faded *Whitmore* written on it, in Dusty's hand. Her assistant found it tucked in a box in the Trousdale garage right before the house was sold. Inside were the letters her father had written from his final place of residence, a flophouse on South San Pedro in downtown L.A. She pulled them out but didn't really have the energy for a comprehensive look. She plucked one at random.

> I hope ONE DAY you will FORGIVE, if not FORGET. I could not STAND UP to your mother because I was a DISHONEST MAN about SO MANY THINGS—things YOU have been so HONEST about in YOUR life for which I am SO PROUD, Janine! If only I had your COURAGE and STRENGTHS I would have LEFT YOUR MOTHER LONG AGO but more importantly I would have STOOD UP FOR YOU AND THE LITTLE ONE and NEVER LET HER GO. Never let go EITHER of you. Please please please FORGIVE,
>
> > your loving Dad

Poor, poor man . . .

She meditated on Arnold Whitmore as she fell asleep.

That's what she was born of: cowardly blood and tender bones. She thought she might dream of him tonight, but her sleep was haunted by Aurora instead—Allegra really, because the *ambience* was from that time. There they were on a lazy Sunday, downwind from Santa Bar-bara (not far from where Reina died), chillin' at the Love Shack. Nothing bizarre ever happened in this recurring fantasia, it was always prosaic. They just hung out together, without secrets, without history. Without drama.

Then she woke up.

Only 12:40—ugh. It was going to be one of those nights.

She felt crushingly alone.

She was so angry with Ginevra. In a Skype session last week, the therapist asked if she was still planning on filing for divorce—that maybe it was time. *Really, Ginevra?* Dusty was mad at herself for roll-ing over and saying nothing. What she *wanted* to say was, *Are you fucking serious? Do you* know *what kind of field day the media would have when people found that out? I mean, what is your fucking* problem, Ginevra, *do you have fucking* Asperger's? *Honestly, sometimes it's so shocking to me, and* disappointing, *how far your* head *is up your fucking* ass. She would have to schedule an appointment soon because she didn't want to sit on those toxic feelings for too long.

She turned on the TV then shut it off; thought about going to the kitchen to forage; grabbed her iPad and watched videos of the party—Aurora onstage, Aurora dancing. Jeremy and Aurora doing karaoke.

Smiling, she scrolled through the archives and selected another, without thought.

The wedding in Big Sur . . .

. . . high on a cliff whose ancient redwoods made it impervious to paparazzi helicopters. (Private photographs of ceremony and celebrations sold to *People* and *Hello!* for $8 million, benefiting Hyacinth House.) There was Sting, serenading them with Allegra's favorite:

I'll send an SOS to the world
I hope that someone gets my
I hope that someone gets my
I hope that someone gets my
Message in a bottle

They were smashing wedding cake into each other's mouths in slow-motion when Aurora burst into the room crying. The iPad tumbled from Dusty's hands to the floor.

"Sweetheart! What's the matter?"

"Bad dream, bad dream, bad dream!"

She climbed in beside her mother and held her tight.

"Aw! Tell me about it? Tell Mama about the bad dream."

"I don't want to! It was a lion!"

"A lion?"

"It was going to fucking eat me!"

"Watch the *language*. Was it the lion from the play? Because *he* was a *cowardly* lion. Like the one in *The Wizard of Oz*."

"It *wasn't* a lion."

"You *said* it was!" She laughed, and Aurora squeezed her harder. *"Ouch."*

"It *wasn't* a lion, it was a *wall*."

"A wall?"

"It was the wall, the wall, the wall! The wall was going to *eat* me!"

"The wall from the play?" Aurora nodded furiously, cheeks glazed with tears. "Now, that's just *silly*, billy goat. *Walls* can't eat anyone."

"They *can*, they *can*!" she said, unconvinced. "It was a *big wall*—"

"Was it Edwina?"

"No! I said it was a *big wall*, not *Edwina*, and I don't want to *talk* about it anymore!"

"Okay, we won't talk about it." She combed Aurora's hair with her fingers. "Wasn't it an amazing party?"

"There was a storm."

"There *was* a storm, but not till the end. You ready to go back to bed?"

"No! Staying *here*. With you."

"Oh no you're not! But you're safe now, billy goat."

"Don't call me that."

"Well, aren't *you* in a mood. Come on, buttercup, you're safe—"

"I am *not* a buttercup."

"—you're in the castle now, and there's sharks in the moat to protect you."

"Sharks?" she said, a little gleeful.

"Yup, *sharks*. And *sharks* are even worse than lions or *walls*; sharks *eat* walls."

That touched her funny bone and Aurora began to laugh. Dusty laughed too and soon they were in paroxysms.

"Think you can go to sleep?" She nodded. "In your *own* bed? Because we need to get up early so we can say good-bye to Wyatt and Jeremy."

"Where are they going?"

"Back to London."

"I don't *want* them to go."

"I know, honey, but they have to."

"Why?"

"'Cause Jeremy's working on a film. They'll come visit again."

"On my birthday?"

"Well, I don't think we'll have to wait a whole *year*! Now, go to sleep. You can stay a bit with Mommy. 'Kay?"

"'Kay."

Dusty held her close. After a minute or so, the girl said, "Nightie-night."

"Nightie-night. And what else? Isn't there something else?"

"Don't let the hot dogs bite!"

Dusty tickled and Aurora squealed.

"I know *someone* who had *lots* of hot dogs today." Aurora cracked up, scrunching her face and burrowing it into her mother's bosom. "Do *you* know who that person is? The person who ate all the hot dogs? Who *is* dat. Who *is* dat, d'ya *know*?" More tickling as she said, *"Do ya do ya do ya?"*

"I don't, I don't, I don't!" she chortled.

"Well, if y'find *out*, you better *tell* me. You better! 'Cause *they* are in *big, big trouble.*"

She almost said *Might have to send a wall after 'em* but thought better of it—when, just like that, Aurora was out like a light. Dusty watched her fluttering eyes a while before both were dead to the world.

CHANGE

"This year she has changed greatly"—meaning you —
My sanguine friends agree,
And hope thereby to reassure me.

No, child, you never change; neither do I.
Indeed all our lives long
We are still fated to do wrong,

Too fast caught by care of humankind,
Easily vexed and grieved,
Foolishly flattered and deceived;

And yet each knows that the changeless other
Must love and pardon still,
Be the new error what it will:

Assured by that same glint of deathlessness
Which neither can surprise
In any other pair of eyes.

—Robert Graves

The author wishes to express his devotion to Deborah Drooz and James Truman, for their courage, their loyalty, their unflagging great care. I give you my heart.

BRUCE WAGNER was born in Madison, Wisconsin. He dropped out of Beverly Hills High School and worked as an ambulance driver and chauffeur before making his living as a screenwriter. In 1988, he privately published *Force Majeure: The Bud Wiggins Stories*, which he expanded into his first novel, *Force Majeure*. In 1993, he wrote a graphic novel, *Wild Palms* (illustrated by Julian Allen), that became a television miniseries. His second novel, *I'm Losing You*, appeared in 1996. He went on to publish *I'll Let You Go, Still Holding, The Chrysanthemum Palace* (a PEN/Faulkner fiction award finalist), *Memorial, Dead Stars,* and *The Empty Chair: Questions and Answers*. He wrote *Maps to the Stars,* a film directed by David Cronenberg, for which Julianne Moore won Best Actress at Cannes in 2014.